Seizing an opportunity of revenge ... he fastened the inward doors of the castle and took the only son and heir of the governor of the castle to the summit of a high tower, from whence he was seen with the utmost concern by the people beneath. The father of the boy hastened thither, and, struck with terror, attempted by every possible means to procure the ransom of his son, but received for answer, that this could not be effected, but by the same mutilation of those lower parts, which he had likewise inflicted on him. The father, having in vain entreated mercy, at length assented, and caused a violent blow to be struck on his body; and the people around him cried out lamentably, as if he had suffered mutilation. The blind man asked him where he felt the greatest pain? When he replied in his reins, he declared it was false and prepared to precipitate the boy. A second blow was given, and the lord of the castle asserting that the greatest pain was at his heart, the blind man expressing his disbelief, again carried the boy to the summit of the tower. The third time, however, the father, to save his son, really mutilated himself; and when he exclaimed that the greatest pain was in his teeth; 'It is true,' said he, 'as a man who has had experience should be believed, and thou hast in part revenged my injuries. I shall meet death with more satisfaction, and thou shalt neither beget any other son, nor receive comfort from this.' Then, precipitating himself and the boy from the summit of the tower, their limbs were broken, and both instantly expired. The knight ordered a monastery built on the spot for the soul of the boy, which is still extant, and called De Doloribus.

GIRALDUS CAMBRENSIS

Also by Michael Baldwin

EXIT WOUNDS
HOLOFERNES

RATGAME

Michael Baldwin

Macdonald

A Macdonald Book

First published in Great Britain in 1991 by
Macdonald & Co (Publishers) Ltd,
London & Sydney

Typeset by Leaper & Gard Ltd, Bristol
Printed and bound in Great Britain by
BPCC Hazell Books
Aylesbury, Bucks, England
Member of BPCC Ltd.

British Library Cataloguing in Publication Data
Baldwin, Michael *1930–*
Ratgame.
I. Title
823.914 [F]

ISBN 0-356-19193-1

Macdonald & Co (Publishers) Ltd
Orbit House
1 New Fetter Lane
London EC4A 1AR

A member of Maxwell Macmillan Pergamon Publishing Corporation *for Liz and Barrie Glibbery*

. . . someone else be the pincer
Someone else the nail

The others are workmen.

VASCO POPA

ONE

1

Not the Danube proper. Some gutsy mountain tributary of the Gail or Drau, rupturing into mile-wide lakes. He slowed the car at the beginning of the seventh lake.

Number seven was like the other six – a thousand acres of rain-rattled water, then crag cut by cloud. Falls this end and a dam at the other. Number seven was the one, just the same.

Storm lights shone ahead, then disappeared in the weather. This would be the *gasthaus*, right where London said it was. The rest was on the map. Gated roads everywhere. Private mountains, privileged cliffs. Just one barrier open. The trackway that led from it did as God said it should. It drowned itself.

He eased the car ahead until he could see between the row of chalets. He confirmed the stilted platform no bigger than a landing-stage, which someone of greed and enterprise had turned into a tiny caravan park. Good: the camping wagon was still in place.

There was a boat on the lake. The man in it was either dead or fishing. He looked dead enough to be fishing. The watcher knew it would be Lippiat. Only an Englishman would stay out in a downpour like this. He rested his tired eyes by letting them move over the distant rock face. When he could pick stone from stone, he unlocked his binoculars from the glove-compartment. Twenty-fifties were fine for stationary targets, but their image bobbed all over the rain-pecked waves before he found the boat in them. It was a thousand yards off-shore. The lens equation gave it to him at fifty, and at fifty he had Lippiat, alive and intent on his rod. He didn't look as if he had the least idea of what was about to hit him.

Gerald Lippiat, 'Lolly' Lippiat, seemed unsurprised. He tied his little boat too carefully, even so, knotting its painter round a stub in the jetty as if he were finishing a parcel. 'Matson! What the hell are you doing, Paddy? Hunting or shee-ing?' The old-fashioned pronunciation was half joke, half insult. 'There's damn all snow up there. Good to see you, anyway. Come in and have a drink.'

It was a motor caravan, not a tow; and certainly not an immobilized mobile home. Mr Gerald Lippiat believed in travelling light.

Matson got himself up the half step at its rear and said to the back in front of him, ''Tain't a pleasure trip I'm on, Gerry.'

Lippiat unracked a bottle from above the wardrobe and turned with exaggerated caution towards a drawer on the other side of the van. 'I didn't know you did this sort of work, Paddy.' He got the drawer open. 'If you've come to do it, you'd better get on with it.'

'Don't go daft on me. I take it you've got a gun in there somewhere?'

'Just rummaging for the bottle-opener, dear boy.'

'Well, don't be too quick with the cork.'

Only a bottle opener as promised, but Matson had seen someone killed with one of those once. He eased his hands from his mackintosh pockets and said, 'The message is don't come home. They know all about you.'

Lippiat was facing him, pulling at the cork but watching Matson. 'Who's "they"?'

'Ralph Dixon is one. Then your own funny lot. But it was Dixon who found you out.'

'Why you?'

'They're embarrassed.'

'They *knew*, Paddy. They knew about it. I only did what they asked me.'

'They don't want you back, they say. They don't want a mess.'

'Suppose I insist on one?'

'If you go quietly and keep mum, then they *may* – I only

say may – continue to keep your family in clean laundry.'

Lippiat poured and sniffed at his wine. He set the bottle down among a litter of books in new jackets, and waved his hand over them as if they explained everything. Some wore the round Magyar art-type favoured by the northern Slavs; some were in Cyrillic.

Matson refused to be distracted by them. Lippiat was old, but no one supposed he was tame.

'So this isn't official?'

'It can't be, can it? I was on leave. On holiday, as it happens. They asked Fossit. Or Dixon asked Fossit. All Fossit's done officially is send me a decent car.' He backed away. He wanted to be out, but the rain smacked the shoulders of his coat, keeping him half inside the door. 'Look, I'm whacked up. I'm staying at that *gasthaus*, if they'll have me. If there's anything else you want to know, don't ask. And certainly don't bother to call London is my advice. I've been all day on the road. They've had plenty of time to change their minds.'

Lippiat dripped wine over his waxed boots, and looked annoyed with himself. 'Their news could hardly be worse than yours.'

'Bollocks. Any second thoughts they have are bound to be a sight crueller. Especially if they tell Washington or Virginia. You'll be up everybody's spout then.'

Lippiat was tired of offering him drink. He was holding out a book instead.

'You idiot, Lolly. Hawking departmental lists to the Slavs.' He tossed him his book back on the table. He was beyond being educated in causes. 'They're the bloody Balkans, for Christ's sake.'

'I was fighting for them – *and* with old man Tito – while you were just a rumour in your grandad's winkle. Balkans, he says!'

'I've got friends in Yugoslavia, too.'

'What I feel goes far beyond friendship.'

'Evidently.'

'You're one of the new professionals, Paddy. I'm one of the old amateurs. I wouldn't expect you to understand.'

The weather drummed on the metal roof and the ventilators, making the silence inside the vehicle sound even worse.

Tonight would be quite enough of Austria. London only wanted his straightforward nod that Lolly had packed his bags and got the hell out.

3

The storm lights shone through frets in the shutters. The *gasthaus* itself was built from limewashed stone, its eaves and upper floor from oiled pine. Matson had been to the country before, if not here. He hated it.

Inside was like outside: polish instead of oil, people rather than fresh air.

He sat at a table near the bar and ordered schnitzel, chips and a half bottle of wine. Normally he didn't drink half bottles – 'splits' as he immodestly called them – but he needed his faculties for the next hour or so.

The girl who served him was like the rest of the place, a footnote to an essay on the Causes of the Second World War. He studied her red cheeks, check blouse and leather miniskirt under crackle-starched apron. Or was she plastic? She wore white knee-length folded-down socks as well. She was the whole bloody *Anschluss* in aspic.

Normally he kept his mind away from politics, especially politics disguised as history; but he was frayed by his long drive through the mountains. Talking to Lippiat had done him no good either.

The explosion cracked the place hard, then gusted against it for several hot seconds while noise smacked across the water and came back from the hills.

Matson had just poured an inch of something red. The table jumped up under his elbows, and a boiling huff of air kicked the reinforced windows and made their oiled frames rattle. It was like a petrol tank igniting, or a gas bottle, and it came long and slow. It wasn't a bomb, but it sounded from among the tiny huddle of caravans or somewhere close by on the lake.

A back draught, or second explosion, lifted the lids off

4

drinking pots on their shelf behind the bar. By this time, which was only a fraction of a second, Matson was standing up, his teeth numb, the nerves gone in his elbows.

He stood because he couldn't help it, because it was the natural thing to do. By the time he checked to make sure he was behaving like everybody else, they were running to the cut-outs in the window – his fancy waitress and her clone, then the proprietor and the rest of the men in the place. Lederhosen swished like a bad case of damp knickers. If his ears could digest such nonsense, then it had been an explosion not a detonation. Matson followed over, and looked down across wet grass, wet tables, wet benches. He had his glass in his hand. It was empty. It was an afterthought.

Not much smoke. A shimmering space between two caravans. The shimmer suggested there might be smoke in a moment or two, when the birds got back from the lake. There was. Black billowing hydrocarbon, petrol or diesel, soot with a red centre, soot full of flame.

The gap, then the plume of fire, was where Lippiat's caravan had been. The gap was the caravan. Matson thought he could permit himself such an Irishism. His brain was in shock as well as instant syllogism.

He needed to get there fast. He tugged at the innkeeper's sleeve.

First he must be cautious. He tugged the sleeve again and said in his phrase-book German: '*Bitte. Ist das Herr Lippiats Auto*? Mr Lippiat's –?'

'The friend you came to see?' Exemplary English.

'*Oui*,' agreed Matson, tired and in France as recently as last night.

The man undid a door kept locked against the weather. Back steps led down into a beer garden. A hedge kept it separate from the track down from the road.

They all clattered down. Matson left his glass on a water-logged table.

4

The van was a collapsed, burning box of charcoal on an intact chassis with ominously ballooning tyres. A pair of legs in uncharred boots poked heels-up from the back, like kebabs from their nest of embers. Lippiat had slipped into English country gentleman's apple green wellingtons, presumably in disgust at the winestains on his other footwear. The rest of his body lay on top of the heat, but invisible inside the smoke. The flame was up front.

The innkeeper and Matson took a booted foot each and pulled.

What they pulled was partly tangled in the wreckage of the van, partly caught up in itself. They got some of it out and left some of it behind. The legs grew lighter. Things fell apart.

Matson's life had been full of nasties. Even so, he allowed himself to be very nearly sick.

While he was retching, a wheel exploded, showering the waitresses' blouses with black. Drinkers were noisy and wished they hadn't been.

A plump woman and assorted children came down from the *gasthaus*. The children were sent away, but did not go.

Only one person from the other caravans was on the scene. The chalets stayed bolted and unconcerned.

The fat woman explained: 'They all climb in the daytime.'
'In the rain?'

'They take the cable up into sunshine. It's not raining up there.'

It was down here. It was raining in a way that threatened to dissolve the charred demi-corpse at their feet on the planking.

The corpse steamed. The planking caught fire beneath it.

5

Two policemen ghosted up, booted and white-helmeted traffic policemen on muffled motorbikes. Austrian traffic cops were nicknamed 'white mice', he believed. This pair of rodents took a long cold look, then became as busy as water-logged rats trying to bite their way out of a flooded sewer.

One of them covered the worst of the mess with a strip of blue plastic, taken folded from his pannier. The rain pinned it to the corpse. The wind gusted it up again.

He shook water from his nose and had another try. He fixed Lippiat top and bottom with a brace of yellow and white traffic cones. He added another pair, cruciform, left and right. The first two were there to weight the plastic, the second two to warn the weather that steps were being taken.

The other man fed his radio a brief account of the disaster and a long description of Matson. Or that's how it seemed. Perhaps he found a breathing Matson easier to look at than a smouldering Lippiat. Then he made a list of names on wet paper, and waved everybody back towards the *gasthaus*. They were to be detained there until the arrival of the investigating team.

A few sightseers arrived under umbrellas. These were sent to the *gasthaus* as well. Some protested. Everyone who protested had his name taken twice, the second time with lowered umbrella.

Matson noticed a black hole forming in the strip. The plastic was melting where it was most humped up in the middle. Canvas would have been better. It would still have charred, but it wouldn't have given off those sickly gusts of hydrocyanic acid.

Lolly Lippiat gave off a gust or two as well, but nothing as prussic as the plastic.

The corpse's green boots emerged once more. The boots did not burn. They were unalterable symbols of English gentility.

The belly burned, and what was above the belly, short of the head. There was still no head. The head had come off in the cinderbox of the wagon, though there was no immediate sign of it in the wreckage. A pity. Lippiat had a good head.

Matson continued to pry among the flames.

The policemen swore at him. The rain fell on the lake, the jetty, the parking platform. It fell on what was hot, it fell on what was cold. The rain fell on everything. Mostly it fell on Lippiat and the patrolman who stood guard in stolid misery among the traffic cones. The list-making policeman at last managed to get everyone away, including Matson. The list-maker was in no more of a hurry to depart than his colleague was to stay. The two felt sorry for one another, though not, perhaps, as sorry as Matson felt for Lippiat. There is no *schadenfreude* in the rain. *Schadenfreude* is for the boozy interiors of *gasthauses*.

6

The restaurant had been stripped of its tablecloths and face linen. Naked it was no more than a bar, and a lot more comfortable as a result.

The drier policeman stood guard in that strange, chin-up, official way that makes Austrian officialdom even more Germanic than the German.

Matson sogged up to the fat *hausfrau* and asked for his wine bottle back.

She blushed. Her face was already red, but she blushed further out. Someone had removed his bottle and dare she say drunk it, or even emptied it in the sink behind the bar, done something irredeemably unthinkable to the gentleman's drink in the midst of these catastrophic circumstances which were always so bad for trade.

She paused to tell her husband and an assistant potman to be brisk and take everyone's order, then presented Matson with another bottle, a better bottle, a full-size bottle. He did not complain. Lolly Lippiat, headless or not, raw or cooked, the late Mr Lippiat would occasion a lot of wine, in these juicy circumstances.

People were looking rather oddly at Matson. The policeman was looking very oddly. It was time for him to face a few facts. The circumstances were too bloody juicy by half. That was one such fact. They were dripping with bloody juice. Matson was the marrow bone – or at least the Oxo cube – in the Lippiat gravy.

The *hausfrau* had to remove Matson's cork with her own elbow. The young women who were presumably her daughters were hunting for clean blouses upstairs, after that unfortunate explosion of crackling down at the burning motor caravan.

He waited patiently until the Danube was set free, then took it, with an extra glass, and sat at the table closest to the policeman.

The policeman moved a fraction, disapproving of Matson's informality, scared he might be offered a drink.

Matson ignored the official fidget. He poured himself a full one, and raised it to Lippiat.

The glass was halfway to his lips when the door opened and the real fuzz walked in.

TWO

1

A uniformed Federal cop in a green jacket with enough chevrons to spell importance; and a pair of gentlemen in civilian clothes, brown hats and incongruous blue raincoats. The raincoats were obviously uniform. The bad weather had taken them by surprise, or having to get out of a car to inspect the mess down by the lake had. They both threw their macs off with a curse, and ditched their hats to resume their invisible look again. Neither had cropped hair. One had curls. They either came from a sharp department or were senior enough to go their own way in a more conventional one.

The uniformed cop ordered coffee, coffee with something Matson couldn't translate – a local cognac he guessed. Then he called the motorcycle cop over and the four of them stood there, checking his list, listening to whatever he had to say, darting their eyes about the room with that blank look you see only in detectives in real life and contract killers in the films. Once, and once only, they turned and gazed at Matson, hard. Then they waited for the *frau* to put up their coffee and lace them with a little happiness from a tall yellow bottle.

The uniformed mastercop downed his at once, and gave instructions to the motorcycle lad, who hadn't been allowed a drink. The latter called everyone over to the far side of the room by name, reading from his soggy list; everyone except Matson.

The other two waited until this manoeuvre was complete, then came over to Matson's table with their coffee. They brought him the yellow bottle and an empty cup. They sat

10

themselves down, and offered Matson some of the firewater in the cup.

He took it as if it was a gesture of commiseration, and raised it sadly before saying, 'The funny boys were here bloody fast.'

'We do English,' the curly one reproved.

'*Kein Deutsch*,' Matson said cautiously. 'Well, only a little.' He had let the wine run away with his tongue.

'This man Lippiat – he was your friend?'

'If it is him, yes. I mean I'd been speaking to him a minute or two before, so it must be Lippiat.'

'You were the last person to see him alive?'

'I assume so, yes. I'd only just got back here to book a room.'

'You didn't book in advance?'

'No. He only phoned me last night.'

'He didn't book for you?'

'I said I'd come and see what the fishing looked like.'

'And?'

'In a rainstorm, I must say it looked bloody awful; but I told him I'd book for the night and we'd discuss it tomorrow.'

'Discuss what?'

'Whether I stayed and, if so, how long.'

'He phoned you where?'

'At the *Hôtel des Princes*, in Mulhouse, in France.'

'And from where?'

'From here, I suppose. He didn't say.'

'You know him how well, this friend of yours?'

'As a very genial fishing companion. Fishing makes its own friendships. We'd meet at fishing hotels, in the Orkneys, say, or in Devon.'

'We get the picture. Did you meet apart from this?'

'For lunch sometimes, in London. Twice or three times a year, to plan fishing trips.'

'So you weren't very close?'

'You share a boat with a man, you get to know him. You separate on a riverbank, it's true. But then there's the hotel bar at night. As I say, he's a genial companion.'

'He's dead, Mr Matson.'

11

'Yes, I suppose he must be. It's only half an hour ago that I was talking to him.'

'How long for?'

'Five minutes, perhaps.'

'Only five minutes? He's a friend you've just travelled half way across Europe to see.'

'I was tired. I'd motored from France. I wanted an early night.'

'What was he doing when you left? Lighting the gas cooker or preparing a meal?'

'He was opening a bottle of wine.'

'He finished opening it, surely?'

'I said I couldn't drink with him. As I said, I was tired.'

'Not tired now?'

'A bit shocked, I suppose.' Matson reached for his cup, treating them both to some more Stanislavsky on Gratitude. 'He'd been fishing all day. He was on the lake when I arrived. I moved the car into shelter, got a bit more sleepy while I waited for him ... what I mean is, I assume he would have wanted to eat something after a day in the boat. I didn't exactly make an arrangement with him. He knew I'd be off to bed pretty soon but I'd sort of assumed he'd be coming up here later on, not staying down there.'

Matson shuddered. First he pretended to shudder. Now he shuddered properly. One thing leads so easily to another.

The fair one smiled at him and said, 'Yes, we did get here quickly, Herr Matson. We were expecting you. Or someone like you.'

'You were *expecting* Mr Lippiat to –'

'*We*'ll ask the questions, Matson. You are under interrogatory arrest.'

2

'My name is Albin Leodolter,' Curlyhair said.

'I am Willibald Kammel,' the fair one added, this time without smiling. 'That's a joke in English, I think?'

'The English like animals. I'm Irish.'

'Willibald, I think, is the joke.'

'You're going a bit too fast for me,' Matson persisted. 'It's agreeable to meet so many policemen who are proficient in one's own language; but when they claim this is because they were expecting one to turn up, one can only –'

'We're not policemen.' Leodolter sounded impatient. 'And well you know it.'

'What work do you do, Mr Matson?' Kammel, too, was finished with the pleasantries.

'I am a civil servant. I work in a government office. It's a sort of passport office.'

'A sort of passport office? Show me your passport, please.' Matson found it in his side pocket.

'It says here – I thought so – yes, it says here "Issued by the Foreign Office".'

'That's correct.'

'You work in the Foreign Office, then?'

'The Home Office, actually. My department is responsible for foreign trade missions, parties on educational visits, that sort of thing.'

'Embassies?'

'Not really. If an embassy wanted to invite in some contractors from its own country – well, it might then be down to someone in my department. Someone senior.' He smiled deprecatingly.

'And this friend of yours, Lippiat. What did he do?'

'A bit difficult to judge. He used to run a series of small service firms. He thought I was a bit of a bore workwise, bloody civil servant and all that, so I didn't always get to share his latest thing, but for a long time he ran a specialist vehicle hire outfit. I believe he went into the private ambulance business, but burnt his fingers – didn't have the necessary background. Then he sold up and invested in security.'

'You mean he was a member of MI5?'

'I mean he ran a firm which used to supply security guards to factories and office complexes.' Matson hoped he'd said that without blushing.

'Ex-policeman?'

'I hardly think so.'

'Ex-Special Branch?' The curly-haired Leodolter joined the interrogation for the first time. 'Ex-Secret Intelligence?'

13

'Even more unlikely.'

'You seem to know quite a lot about his professional shortcomings.'

'I made it my business to find out. He asked me to manage things for him once.'

'Why would he did that?'

'Perhaps because I was a police cadet for six months. More likely because I was in the army for eight years.'

'And then this passport office.' Leodolter's irony was heavy. 'Wouldn't it have been a – how do you say – a come down, playing manager to a gang of security officers?'

'A promotion, believe me – in money terms, at least.'

'Then why didn't you take it?'

'I'd fished with him long enough to know that his little schemes had a habit of not lasting. *He* was always well enough off at the end of them, but I'm not so sure about his employees. Anyway, I didn't feel sufficiently confident to become one of them.'

Leodolter smiled and went to the bar. He came back and said, 'Your friend Lippiat didn't use the phone last night.'

'Then he phoned from somewhere else.' Matson felt in his pocket. 'Look, here's my last night's bill, with the French phone number. Check the hotel. They'll be able to confirm I had a call from Austria. They had to page me.'

3

The bar was empty again. The uniformed officer had super-vised the making of a second, more exhaustive list, then let everyone go.

Leodolter pulled a lugubrious face and said, 'That is Inspector Kaub. He has already reached an opinion. He doesn't think a bomb killed the man in the caravan.'

Matson did not comment.

'He thinks you hit the fellow on the head or perhaps twisted his neck.'

'Herr Lippiat is a friend of mine.'

'Then you lit a candle or simply left the interior lights burning or the engine running and turned on the gas.'

14

'Then walked up here and ordered a schnitzel and waited for someone like Kaub to come and arrest me for it? Suppose the man in the caravan had been my enemy, and I had killed him exactly as you say – or any other way, come to that? I'd have got back into my car and driven off. Why come to this *gasthaus*? I could be in Yugoslavia in fifteen minutes. Or down to the *autobahn* and back the other side of Innsbruck in an hour. I could have hired a different car by then.' Matson paused to sip wine, followed by some more of Kaub's yellow bottle. 'If I had been a murderer, in weather like this, I shouldn't have arranged any accidents to cover my tracks. I'd have left that caravan bolted and driven off and be damned to it.'

'You've given the problem a lot of thought.'

'I've given it as much thought as your Inspector Kaub has, and – with respect to the gentleman – that's clearly not very much. If I'd wanted an accident, or a delay while the police decided what they were dealing with, why not simply dump Lolly's body in the lake? If it was a body. Your Herr Kaub doesn't yet know whether Mr Lippiat was alive or dead when his vehicle blew up, whether he had a heart attack as he went to light the gas stove or whether he was simply grilling himself a piece of toast when he was killed by some fault in the tubing. Camping-gas explosions don't happen in England very often, but they're commonplace in some places, I believe. I wouldn't know about here.'

'You speak too much.'

'You appal me, that's why.'

Kammel held out his hand. 'Your car keys, please.'

4

Matson watched him go.

'I suppose he's allowed to search my car? He wouldn't be in England.'

Leodolter didn't answer.

'It's the green Range Rover,' Matson called, as Kammel muttered his way into a wet mac.

'He's got good eyes. He can recognise an English car.

15

What was your rank in the army, by the way?'

'Captain.'

'Captain Matson, then.'

'I prefer Mister.'

'Captain Matson in what unit?'

'The Parachute Regiment.'

'And the SAS, I wonder?'

'Not likely. I'd have given my right arm to serve with that lot.'

'Captain Matson, you're pissing us about. Is that colloquial enough for you? Now *we* know, my department knows, that Mr Lippiat is some kind of spy.'

'Surely not!'

'"Spy" is not the professional's term, I believe. Not in English. But it will do here. It's the word that gets men imprisoned and, in some countries, hanged.'

'I believe so, yes.'

'Which brings us to you. We know what happens in the British Intelligence and Security Services. We know what sort of people they recruit.'

'I didn't go to Cambridge or a minor public school.'

'And we know your background fits the template. It's our guess you're a spook, if not a spy. We know Lippiat was both.'

Kammel came back in. His raincoat took even longer to get off than to put on. His albino hair was reduced to a few dark strands amid much invisibility. 'Willibald' was a joke Matson was in no mood to make. Especially when he leant forward and hissed, 'Binoculars and a Pentax camera, and some Polaroid spectacles, Mr Matson.'

'*Captain* Matson,' Leodolter said, as if it was the final secret of the universe.

'Polaroids as for fishing,' Matson explained.

'But no fishing rod.'

'I was going to hire when I got here. And borrow some of his kit, as necessary. Did you look in the hatch? If you did you'll have noticed the oilcloth bundle, about two feet long.'

'I checked it in case it was a firearm. It is full of little sticks.'

'My folding fish rod,' Matson triumphed. 'There are floats,

16

hooks, a reel and a tin of flies in the first-aid box. Shouldn't he have checked my first-aid box?' he asked Leodolter.

'I don't know. He's senior to me.'

'Just what department are you two gentlemen in?'

'Let's say it's a kind of passport department. An Austrian version of your own passport department. How did Lippiat know where to contact you?'

'He didn't, not absolutely. It was a question of whether I could get some leave. I didn't know if I'd manage, so that's why I didn't know quite where he was likely to be. We had a tentative arrangement that if I wangled some time, I'd be at that particular place in France.'

'You've been there before?'

Matson watched the other motorcycle cop come in, now positively manufacturing water, and speak to Kaub. Kaub was approaching their table before Matson said, 'No, but he had. It was his idea of a possible rendezvous.'

'He didn't keep it.'

'I'd scarcely got there before they were paging me. What more can you ask of a friend?'

Kaub's words were slow and plumped out with self-satisfaction, but they were in German and too fast for Matson.

Kammel looked at Matson hard before saying, 'There was a gun in that camping van, or the remains of one. Inspector Kaub assumed you used it.'

'Much more like me,' Matson agreed. 'I never could stand strangling people.'

5

'Inspector Kaub wants to lock you up.'

'You know I didn't kill Lippiat. Why not simply impound my passport and leave me here?'

'Too near the frontier. A fit man can always find his way through the mountains, with or without a passport.'

Matson knew these mountains and did not altogether agree. 'Lock me up where?'

'Klagenfurt.'

'Klagenfurt's miles.'

'That's why we're taking you to Graz.' It was Willibald's first real joke, and he savoured it. 'Graz is one hundred and fifteen kilometres beyond Klagenfurt.'

'What's up with Klagenfurt?'

'We don't think this is a police matter. No, Captain Matson. You belong to us.'

Leodolter stood up and said, 'A word of advice, one professional to another –'

'I'll get my kit.'

'We've already had your case transferred to our vehicle, and explained to them that your car will be staying here. A word of advice, as I said. This isn't NATO. It isn't even the Market. No one is going to sweep this one under the carpet for you. A man such as yourself, present and probably active in the last moments of a scoundrel like Lippiat! On Austrian soil, here in Karnten!' Albin Leodolter allowed himself a hint of anger, a touch of awe. 'It has the makings of quite an incident.'

'I'm not a diplomat. I'm not an ambassador. I'm a civil servant on holiday.'

'Perhaps you'd prefer to be left here with Kaub?'

'He only wants you for murder,' Willibald added.

Matson watched Kammel weigh up their last exchange. Had they gone too far, or not far enough?

Willi decided to stoke the neurosis that Matson was already fuelling for himself. 'Your people have been shipping too much of their dirty linen over here, Captain Matson. This time someone's been foolish enough to get himself caught in the laundry basket. You can see *we're* not best pleased with you. How happy do you suppose London is going to be?'

'I'll have to sleep on it. I never can stay awake on a car journey.'

THREE

1

Klagenfurt was in Karnten. Graz would be hours away in Steiermark. They fed him place names like dog biscuits, and he chewed them obediently.

'Carinthia then Styria,' Leodolter explained. 'Just as with Shakespeare.'

Matson might have been on a guided tour.

Except for the two police motorcyclists up front, the communications van close behind. One of those ripple-sided Mercedes Benz pantechnicons, like a bus without windows, its roof ugly with aerial grids and broadcasting antennae. It had been out there in the rain, checking up on him big fib by little fib all the time he'd been swapping misinformation and laced coffee with the two chums. Willibald hadn't gone outside to search his car. All he did was ask what his rummage team had found under hub-cap and swab, then peep to see how much of Matson's spicy past was unrolling from their radio-fax.

Now the thing came bumbling after them, like some sort of space wasp, with its own brace of federal motorcyclists as outriders adding to the menace.

His two interrogators were too sophisticated to remark on this. We know exactly who you are, Patrick Matson, their manner proclaimed. We know when, where and what. As to the why, we'll continue to ask politely, but don't waste our time with another slice of shit.

He couldn't see Karnten. They told him it was mountainous, in case he hadn't noticed. He couldn't pick out much of Steiermark, either. They explained it was hilly, supposing he didn't know.

What he did know was that another Mercedes had joined the convoy. A big limousine this one. Its front grille was unmistakable, even in a rainstorm. So too the civilian glimmer of its paintwork: light blue, grey, or silver – something like that. It slushed up behind the communications wagon, kept nudging out as if pressing to overtake, but never came past. Matson wondered why, but not for long. He was having his first thoughts about doing a bunk.

He had to think them in braille. Night had settled on everything, and the storm glued it down like diesel on soot.

2

Leodolter drove. Kammel sat with Matson in the back. He was a thin man, Kammel, with plump knees. The journey was long enough to notice such things.

Matson located the man's two guns as a matter of habit. One under the left armpit where Matson could get it. One behind the right hip where Kammel couldn't. If things grew over-tedious, Matson could take the guns and the car, just for the fun of it. He was, as he insisted, on holiday; so fun was in order. But he knew, even as he made such a customary inventory of the available firepower, that no one in London would thank him for that. Lippiat was unfinished business. London would want to close the file with as much detail as possible. London would expect him to be extremely polite.

Leodolter opened the account the way chauffeurs do, from the side of his mouth. 'Have a nice drive from London, Patrick?'

'It rained.'

'So the sun didn't shine. And you didn't drive from London, either. You drove from Mulhouse.'

'I told you I drove from Mulhouse.'

'The car came from London, true.'

'True.'

'You flew to Mulhouse.'

'Untrue.'

'You flew to Habsheim, Captain Matson. Habsheim is

even nearer to Mulhouse than Mulhouse is. You must know that!'

'I know everything. I'm very old.'

'Who dropped the car for you?'

'I didn't see him.'

'Her.'

'I didn't see. It parked itself in the garage.'

'Then the driver parked herself in your bed.'

'I thought the mattress was lumpy.'

'Do you mean to say you didn't turn the light on? We are old as well, Willi and me.'

'You're certainly not old enough to ask me questions like that.'

'So you drove from Mulhouse almost to Klagenfurt – how far is that? Five hundred kilometres? – to go fishing with this old friend. What was he fishing for, Captain Matson? A new passport?'

'Still your little jokes about my passport office. I've already explained –'

'No, Herr Matson. *You* make the jokes. Not us.' Willibald had listened to more than enough. 'You waste our time with evasions.' He treated himself to a tiny frisson of the buttocks to disguise his irritation. Then he unglued his plump thigh from Matson's bony sprawl and asked, 'What was the message, Paddy?'

'Paddy is for intimates.'

'What was the message?'

'I didn't ask him.'

'What message were you told to deliver to Lippiat?'

'I'll let you call me Paddy if you really want to.'

Leodolter picked it up again. He didn't sound annoyed. He was a professional. 'Beside the lake, you spill us everything, Patrick. Now you give back nothing.'

'Don't count on it lasting. I get carsick when I'm not driving.'

'You still say you were fishing?'

'You saw the tackle. Willi did, anyway.'

'Whoever packed your car for you gave the contents a lot of thought,' Kammel said. He was through with irritation. 'I had a friend in London call a couple of friends of yours.

21

Intimate friends. Friends who call you Paddy. They've never in their lives seen you fish, or heard you talk about fishing or fishing-tackle.'

'You've phoned the wrong friends.' It would take ages to catch him out in this fib, days rather than hours, days of in-depth research. Willibald was bluffing. 'All Irishmen fish. If we don't admit to fishing, we brag about poaching instead. Now I'm a civil servant I can't afford to do either.' As if anybody could.

Willibald wasn't done with it. 'One of our London infor-mants –'

'Tut – canvassing on the telephone.'

'– said you only have the one hobby, and the evidence of it is in your council flat in Camden. In the kitchen, Paddy. You maintain a gunsmith's workshop, apparently, to service your collection of firearms. You can see we know who to ask about you! Guns are Patrick Matson's hobby, we're told. Not fishing rods.'

'Sure. I keep a lot of guns. I use them to shoot fish.'

Leodolter came back into the act. 'Any competent pistol armourer could make an explosive device, Patrick.'

'True, dear thing. But you know I didn't bring such a device with me, and you know I didn't plant one. Because my world is like your world, Albin, and your world, Willi. It doesn't work like that.'

The road ghosted with spray. Leodolter flashed his lights. He wanted the motorcycle outriders away from in front. They dropped back and fell into position behind the com-munications wagon. This put them in front of the Mercedes limousine. Its driver didn't mind their spray in the least. He seemed to thrive on it. He made no attempt to overtake the convoy.

Kammel fell silent for a moment, pondering where next to begin.

Matson did what the bumps in his bed had inhibited last night. He took a nap.

Matson used to think darkness lent an inviting glow even to a fish shop. Not to Graz, it didn't. Graz was the fish shop that proved the rule.

They drove through a suburb built like a barracks. Uniform five-storey blocks. Roads made of asphalt on balding cobbles. The rain had stopped, but it was up there above the streetlamps, waiting. The motorcyclists were still with them; so was the van. The big Mercedes had disappeared. Perhaps it knew the town well enough to guess where he was being taken.

Leodolter parked the car in front of the only stucco building in a street of brownstone.

'Graffiti,' Kammel explained. 'The place's history invites a certain amount of anonymous comment. This way it's easier to clean.'

'Does it invite stone throwers, too?' Matson indicated its rows of barred windows, their frames of wire mesh set between double thicknesses of glass. Most forces keep a place like this, where people can disappear until softened up. He let himself yawn in anticipation, feigning boredom with as much conviction as the schoolgirl who's just beginning to realise she's let herself be led a step too far up the back alley.

'This area was developed during the war to house *das Ersatzbataillon*, the Replacement Battalion,' Kammel said. 'These were the officers' lines.'

'And this was the officers' *Bordell*.'

They had him inside the place now, and into an open lift. No police, just Albin and Willi and two stout lads from the van, whose engine was left running.

'It is rumoured that even Weiss treated himself to a visit or two here,' Leodolter smirked. 'When he was in temporary command of this place, recovering from that wound in the arse. Gruppenführer Hendrik Reinhard Weiss, Patrick. Later Obergruppenführer Weiss.'

Kammel breathed impressively. The two stout lads left breathing to those who were paid to do it.

The lift stopped at four. Before touching the button, Willie added, 'The *Ersatzbataillon* of SS Division Seven, Captain

Matson. Seventh SS *Freiwilligen Gebirgs Division Prinz Eugen*. Also commanded by Weiss in his time.'

'Before mine, I'm afraid.' The two chums weren't making small talk. He couldn't suppose so for a moment. He wished he knew what talk they *were* making.

4

The fourth floor of a five-storey building. No roof to break through above. Vertigo and a sixty-foot dive onto concrete below.

The stout lads didn't kick him out of the lift. They didn't kick him along the corridor either. Still holding their breath they sank into the night. This left him alone with Willi and Albin and a big bunch of keys.

Kammel paused before a door built largely of keyholes and said, 'This needn't take long.'

Leodolter got the door open, and they went inside an apartment that was furnished on the lavish side for a cell or a persuasion suite. Any woman would have felt at home here, once she'd changed the curtains and the carpets and bought some new furniture. Any woman from the *Ersatzbataillon Bordell*, anyway. Someone had been badly frightened inside these four walls, and recently. The place smelled of disinfectant.

'We need some fast answers, Patrick, that's all.'

Kammel helped Matson to sit on a low easy chair, pushing him backwards as if he hadn't learned to fold his own legs properly.

Leodolter was still wearing his driving gloves. It struck Matson that these and golf grips are two of the most menacing objects a man can wear. One of Leodolter's hands came shooting out at Matson as if he were aiming a punch at his face. The hand held a slug of cognac. Some of it spilled in Matson's lap. Some stayed in the glass.

'Top him up,' Kammel said. They had played this charade with suspects before.

Matson watched Leodolter do something with a bottle of Martell. When it was finished, he refused the glass.

24

The coffee did not materialize. He found himself looking at a news cutting instead.

5

Matson could cope with phrase-book German. Newspapers were another matter, especially when they were printed in that Gothic gumbo.

He pretended to study the text.

Kammel left him no time to gather himself. 'You have pretended to us, Herr Patrick, that the late Gerald Lippiat had a substantial pedigree as a freshwater fisherman. We, in our turn, have acquainted you with the certainty that he pursued a lengthy career in espionage. We were scarcely interested in your lies. You already knew our nasty little truth. Now why don't we cut out the evasions and turn to something more relevant to us both?'

'Indeed.'

'Why don't we pool what we know about Herr Lippiat's senior preoccupation?'

'Money, you mean?'

'He was a Nazi-hater, Herr Paddy. A Nazi-hater and a Nazi-hunter.'

'So are a lot of people of his generation.'

'You knew this?'

'No. If it was one of his preoccupations, it was one Lolly and I did not talk about.'

'Read your newspaper and tell us what it suggests to you.'

There had been no background briefing at home. He had no more than three or four sentences from Lolly's own mouth. He did as he was told. He read his newspaper.

The chums had given him an edition, not a photocopy. His hands were black with printer's ink from sweating over it. When an interrogator gives you an actual text instead of a copy, you can bet he's got a filing cabinet full of both back in his office. A lot of identical pieces have lain on a lot of people's desks, all hot from the press, waiting for evaluation. Not police work. Intelligence. Someone putting a couple of

25

names together. His own, perhaps. Lippiat's certainly. Now this.

They knew he was a cobbins. They had squared round the item in one of those red markers that soak through a dozen pages of newsprint. He didn't take the sog as a further chance to play games with them, though. He saw which was the marked item. He read it, and didn't understand it.

He fought his tiredness for a minute, then decided to mask his dullness in a schoolboy excuse. 'I don't really read German.'

'Judging by your bar talk you can understand enough to take in the main headline.'

' "Lenz Abducted" – is that what it says?' Abductions were hardly his concern. He struggled to be interested. 'Lenz. Gunter Lenz. General Lenz the panzer leader? I thought he was dead long since. He must be a hundred.'

'Born in nineteen hundred and three. He's eighty-seven. Yes, he's missing all right. The report is ten days old. Missing and confirmed missing. Our question to you, Herr Patrick, is: do you suppose he is still alive?'

'How the hell am I supposed to know that?'

'See if you can find his address in the main text.'

'Techendorf. What's Techendorf supposed to mean to me?'

'We are about to find out. There are maps in your car.'

'And in yours, I daresay. Sorry, I'm trying to be cooperative within the limits of experimental error. I just don't begin to see why you're showing me this.'

'Techendorf is on the Weibensee. Weibensee is the name of a lake – a place frequented by fishermen like yourself, Herr Patrick, and people who merely pretend to fish. Men like the late Gerald Lippiat, Herr Paddy. Ten days ago, a certain motor caravan was parked on the edge of the Weibensee, at Naggl, across the lake from General Lenz's house. You follow that much?'

'I came to meet Lippiat today, not ten days ago. Not at the Weibensee. You know I came to meet Lippiat today.'

'I wonder what Lippiat came for.'

'To arrange for Lenz to be kidnapped – is that what you're suggesting?'

26

'No,' Leodolter said. He had been silent for so long that Matson thought he was asleep. 'To arrange something much more simple. To fix it so Gunter Lenz got dead.'

6

Leodolter stood up and refilled glasses. He continued to wear his motoring mittens. They were a nice touch, like the sergeant's pace stick that can be brandished as a club, the blackboard pointer that so easily becomes a cane.

'Now you can see what a certain honourable ex-soldier and mouselike civil servant from an alleged passport office has got himself mixed up in. Or does my vocabulary offend you?'

'"Honourable" is a bit steep,' Matson said. 'How do we know the General has not been abducted? Or eloped?'

'No one wants Lenz.' Leodolter was ever-patient. 'Not now. The worst anyone can say about him is that he once commanded a formation that included a unit which was alleged to have burned a barn stuffed full of villagers. It happened in Poland. A sergeant major served twenty years in Cracow, the unit commander was shot. Several NCOs were sentenced to death *in absentia*. The Poles don't want the old man for that.'

'Don't want or aren't allowed to want,' Kammel put in.

'There were no Jewish people involved, as far as we can gather from the files. Certainly the Jewish Bureau have not listed him. The Israelis have not asked for him.'

'If they had and if they did?'

Willi spat. It wasn't a pretty gesture. It didn't please Leodolter and it did not improve the carpet. 'Lenz said he regretted the barn. He is on record somewhere as deploring his subordinate's actions. Don't look at me like that. We are pigs in the middle here in Austria, Matson. Pigs in the middle.'

'Just pigs, Willi. The view is not my own – though I will, of course, grant you an exemption from the sty – but the view has been expressed that when it comes to war criminals the Austrians are pretty porkerish.'

'That was certainly the line taken by this Lippiat of yours,' Leodolter said smoothly. 'We know, because Austria was his hunting ground.'

Willi Kammel was also a hard man to annoy. 'He seemed to specialize in Nazis the Jews did not want,' he observed mildly. 'And that places him outside every law there is. We do hope you are not standing with him, Patrick Matson.'

Matson saw no need to answer that. 'What you tell me is very odd.'

'Why odd, Herr Paddy?'

'Lippiat's a Jew himself.'

'I see.' Kammel looked at Leodolter, who pretended to make a note. 'I sympathize with this continuing disorient-ation of your grief, of course, Herr Patrick. English *is* your first language, isn't it?'

'Almost my only language.'

They were being so very clever with him. Soft then hard. Deeply probing then childishly trivial.

'In which case I shall return later to this curious dislocation of your tenses.'

7

Matson knew where this must be leading, though he cursed himself and London for all he had not been allowed to know.

He decided to move things forward a little. 'So, they all live by lakes, do they, your Austrian Nazis?'

'You find me a lake and I'll find you a Nazi beside it,' Leodolter agreed.

'To each puddle its toad?'

'Every European country has its peculiarity, Captain Paddy. Austria has Nazis, lots and lots of Nazis. Hitler was an Austrian. Now let us have an end to history and morality and proceed with what we have to.'

'I salute the new curriculum.'

'What we have is this. A prominent Nazi, a *German* Nazi not an Austrian Nazi, on a lake beside which your Mr Lippiat lodged and on which he fished. Prominent Nazi is killed. Your Lippiat changes his lake, and arranges to meet you.'

'This paper only says your prominent Nazi disappeared.'

'Into the lake,' Kammel said. 'Police divers have been looking for days. They won't find him, not if he was dropped from a fishing boat with some stones in his pockets. Mountain lakes are as deep as the mountains – is that a possible expression in English?'

'Only in English poetry, Willi. You speak the purest poetry.'

'Or he could have been dumped in the river. The police pull about two dozen bodies a year from the entire system. God knows how many stay undiscovered. They've already fished out a chap of about the size, weight and age of the missing man, give or take the usual additions and subtractions. Those corpses are never much help to us. It's a mountain river, the Drau. It strips them. It sandpapers them. Some it traps in an underground pot while the fish go and buy potatoes. Some it sieves into gobbets.'

'Then we come to the burning caravan.' Leodolter was tiring of hyperbole. 'The burning caravan and the dead man. We told you we were watching that man. Now let us remind you why.

'The caravan site is near Bogenfeld. Bogenfeld and your little *gasthaus* are on the Matschacher Stausee. Even *your* car map will have told you that much, Captain Paddy.'

'One *stausee* is much like another on my map. But let me guess. No, don't tell me. Our conversation got there several minutes ago. This particular pond has its general as well.'

'A general SS this time.'

'And which SS general is this one?'

'He lives at Rosental. His name is Weiss. General – more properly Gruppenführer – Hendrick Reinhard Weiss.'

'Oh, him.'

8

'So you know about General Weiss?'

'I was reminded by your charade in the lift. I am

acquainted with Prinz Eugen, too, and Handschar which you neglected to mention, simply from boyhood reading.'

'Ah, war-games?'

'War is never a game, Willi. Even Austria had an army once.'

'It has one now.'

'An army with soldiers in it, Willibald. So you keep that fellow in lettuce, here in Shakespeare's Austria; and you wonder if a man with Lippiat's background might have wanted to stick a poisoned carrot or two in his fodder, just to indicate some decent human disgust? Or even plant one right up his arse. Well, it's a theory, given Lolly's war service.'

'So you *do* know?'

'I *fished* with the man, Willi. I don't need to read a file to be aware that he was in Yugoslavia in his teens as a wireless operator, and fought alongside Crn, Djilas, Tito and the rest of them. A young man has his heroes, and compared with most heroes those fellas were gods. Even a cynic like me'll grant you that.'

Kammel grew hearty at the thought of it. His left hand planted itself in Matson's hair. He stepped round the seat and tugged his head back hard. 'Our problem, Albin's and mine, is to determine whether you're enough of a professional to act on orders to stop a man like Lippiat *once you realized who his target was.*'

'It's a genuine teaser, Willi. Quite a moral conundrum.' Matson's scalp flared as Kammel increased the pressure. 'We'll all have to ponder that one into our old age, won't we? Me with my devious brain, you with your dirty mitts.'

Leodolter had been watching impassively. Now he leant forward and spread his finger and thumb against the nerve points of Matson's jaw. 'Austria has had a statute of limitations in place for a quarter of a century now.' He began to dig in. 'For most of my adult years and all of yours, dare I guess.' His voice remained calm. 'Weiss did his dirty work across the frontier in Yugoslavia, as you and Herr Lippiat well know. He killed a lot of Serbs, a few partisans and the usual assortment of Jews and gypsies. He didn't kill Austrians or –'

'People?' Matson's head was still wrenched back, his chin

distorted, but he forced himself to mouth, 'I'm impressed by your vocabulary, Albin.'

'I'm a Austrian, Matson. In everything I say you can detect the current flavour of local opinion.' Leodolter patted Matson's face, as if it was a bit of fun and games in the locker room.

Several hours of pressure had been aimed at making him feel under-informed, over-exposed, badly briefed and probably set up by his own side. The physical reinforcement had been totally unexpected, and timed to the second.

Willi spoke again, still from behind. 'We would have hanged him, this Gruppenführer, believe me. He surrendered here in Austria, did he not? He surrendered Handschar and those few orts and remnants of Prinz Eugen that the other fool hadn't surrendered to the partisans in Istria. But he surrendered to the British, and you – from the lofty viewpoint of your superior morality – you decided you had a use for him. Odd, isn't it?'

Matson couldn't answer. He was beginning to understand his alleged fishing companion rather better.

Kammel let go at last. 'You used him after the war. Your Control Commission deployed him in the Trieste Strip, for example, exactly where he had learned his little tricks in the first place. You used him against – guess who? The Yugoslav partisans. Once again the partisans won. But I believe he was useful to you.' It gnawed, did the Willibald voice. It chewed its way in. 'He's a rottweiler, Matson. He knows how to bark at a wolf.' He smoothed Matson's hair, still from behind. 'Then the Americans took him over. They were more interested in bears, if you catch my meaning.'

'Dear thing,' Matson watched Kammel move in front of him once more, and sit down.

'So nobody stretched his neck, or stood him against a wall. I daresay the possibility was always there, especially with the Americans. But every time the Jewish Bureau, for example, grew noisy here in Vienna where we did our best to protect it – and do you remember any *other* noises? – every time the Zionist lobby became active, the Anglo-American Gruppenführer would stick his snout among the trees and catch them another communist. He was good that way in Berlin, in the early days of the Four Power agreement. He was productive throughout the entire American Zone. A mad dog, Captain Matson, but with a keen nose for a communist crotch, and fangs to follow, I daresay.'

'What was it like for his fellow Nazis, this sniffer of his?'

'I don't recollect seeing it on his file. You tell me.'

'How the hell should I know?'

'Because Herr Lippiat knew. And what Herr Lippiat knew you would need to know also.'

'Not true.'

'You were sent here to make Herr Lippiat do something in connection with General Weiss. Perhaps to deflect him from Weiss, perhaps to set him on further. I think you were empowered to kill Lippiat, if need be.'

'My life isn't constructed that way.'

'Empowered to kill him or to offer him the moon in return for some common sense and restraint.'

'I know Weiss as a name, period. A Sunday newspaper name. A *Scourge of the Swastika* name. I don't know a damn thing else.'

Leodolter looked at Matson's head as if his brain was a painted balloon he could either blow away or burst. 'A child,' he said at last. 'Am I to believe that, Captain Matson?'

'I see we're being formal again, Albin.'

'Willi has his contacts in London. They say you're limited but lucky. A bull that finds his own china shops.'

'I make a bit of noise sometimes.'

'Stamping passports? I distrust coincidence. Lippiat there, the General dead. Lippiat here, the other General. Lippiat again, Lippiat dead. You here. *You* just a messenger? A very noisy messenger, if that's all you are. A bull, perhaps, but not one to trample porcelain.'

'I'm a Catholic, Albin. I don't understand parables. I think they're magic and therefore beyond me.'

'What I'm saying is, you could not have got where you are if you've got maggots in your head.'

'Is that what you're saying? It's true, Albin. I don't have maggots.' He fingered the pain in his skull. 'I've got a lot of dandruff, though.'

Matson hadn't learnt his lesson so Kammel and Leodolter

32

rose to their feet again. There comes a time when interrogations need a fiercer nudge, and this was one of them.

Both sides understood what they were after now. They knew where they stood, and they knew Matson's feet weren't very well planted.

He watched Albin glance at Willi for orders, and Willi search Albin's face for inspiration. Albin adjusted his driving mittens.

Albin, whom he quite liked, was going to work him over. And Willi, whom he could not entirely dislike, was going to let Albin do it. They knew he couldn't complain: he was too deeply implicated in the business of the exploding caravan. He was a professional. He had denied it and they had let him deny it, but it takes one to know one. They knew him for what he was. Their communications truck had spoken.

Albin smacked a fist into a palm. Willi looked sick, all the way round the edges of his smile.

'Lads,' Matson said. 'Lads.' He had only been doing a departmental favour for a friend, and he saw no need to take a bashing for it. He had been hurt enough already. He got to his feet, too. He was bigger than Albin and in better training than Willi. It was time to surrender. 'Lads,' he said. 'Let us not be hasty.'

9

Leodolter took a frustrated grab at the air, and Kammel sank his gone-away ghost of a voice even further, 'Let me ask you a hypothetical question, Patrick.'

'No. Let me instead offer you a few pointers *gratis*. Nothing hypothetical. I don't know much, because these titbits you have on offer concerning poor old Lolly are not in my line of country. However –' He paused, wondering just how much bait to sprinkle on the stream. A fair pinch of low-grade chatter would be in order, surely? 'I really was on holiday, going off on leave to Italy. I was intending to fly there. Instead, my department asked me to fly-drive and make the detour you know about. I was – as you surmise – asked to deliver a word-of-mouth package to your dead fisherman, and then to continue with my holiday. What that verbal consisted of hacksaws will not remove from my gullet. I am, after all, a civil servant in privileged employment. However, let me assure you of this much: German generals formed no part of my message. Nor did anything else to do with Austria's security. Karnten was simply an area where Lippiat was to be found with his fishing-rod. If he had been in Italy or the Pyrenees I could have gone there. Not, of course, to kill him. My department' – he gulped some reconditioned air – 'my department is not into that sort of thing.'

'Ah yes,' Albin Leodolter murmured, 'the passports.' He glanced at Kammel inquiringly.

Kammel didn't speak. He looked at Matson at length and with a new interest, almost as if something had been peeled away from his attention, then he rose to his feet and went out through one of the doors off the main room.

Matson could hear him talking to someone there. Their whole conversation had been eavesdropped, monitored. Matson felt briefly alarmed, wondering if he had given too much away; but he knew why he had spoken.

He needed them to slacken the pressure on him, and leave him some time to think. He needed it even more than he needed sanity and sleep. It was no longer a matter of what questions London would ask him. There were the even more urgent answers he needed from London.

The door opened and Kammel returned with a plastic tray.

'Coffee,' he said, leaving it on a low table to Matson's right. 'Come along, Albin.' He led Leodolter back towards the monitoring cupboard. 'Enjoy your coffee,' Willi smirked. 'Albin and I are going to listen back through the tapes.' At the door he turned and added, 'Oh, and sleep if you like. Take a little nap. Not a big nap. A little one. On the couch there. There's a bed through that door, but you've no time for that.'

He had no time to reach the couch, either. His third mouthful of coffee saw to that. It was gentle enough to sip, but it made him retch dizzily all the way to his boots. There was nothing down there to bring up, except the bloody floor, which rose in a giddy spiral and smashed him straight in the teeth.

34

10

Someone was pounding steak with a kitchen mallet inches away from his ear.

Matson woke to the deliberate thunk thunk of his face being slapped. Leodolter wasn't wearing his driving mittens any longer, and the moment Matson opened his eyes and stared up at him he stopped his exercise and appeared apologetic. 'Sorry old chap, but you'd dropped right off.'

Matson's watch told him he had freefallen through sleep or narcosis for eight hours, though there was no light outside the window to confirm this.

'Only curtains, I'm afraid,' Leodolter said. 'We bricked the openings up on this floor. Some odd types come up here, and we'd hate anyone to chuck a bomb or anything.'

Matson was on the bed, not the couch, with his shoes and jacket off. Whoever had lifted him and partially undressed him could equally well have tampered with his watch; but he doubted if Albin and Willi were into such obvious games.

'You must have drunk a bit too much,' Leodolter said. His face oozed moral advantage.

'The Teutonic conscience abhors a drunkard, I know.' Matson swivelled off the bed and scratched around for his shoes.

Evidently they had slipped him some sort of hypnotic in the Martell last night. Then the twin-tub in the coffee. First the rinse, then the spins. He wondered what they'd got him to say. He remembered splashing out a huge tubful of carefully considered hogwash, but the rest of his brain refused to recall how many piglets the two chums had actually driven through the dip. Then there was the problem of what they had induced him to say in his sleep.

In the bathroom he felt better about the narcosis idea. They hadn't used any of the lycergics – his brain would still be rocky. His arms, his legs and his bum were free of pinpricks and bruising – unless they'd fed him a subcutaneous needle round the chubs – so they hadn't used an intravenous drip or anything which needed to go deep. They'd probably done no more than lace his drink with cocaine or even neat alcohol, and what would that have got them? A limited

35

timeshare of the lumber in his cranial loft.

He patted his brains into place, pulled up his zip, and rejoined Albin with renewed confidence, though no great hope.

11

Doughnuts and coffee. Doughnuts on a plate, coffee in a jug.

Albin drank coffee himself and said, 'Doesn't your statement of last evening leave you in a difficult position?'

'Yes. I'm still here with you.'

'I mean back home.' Ledolter tried to stay patient while struggling not to yawn.

'I was always in a difficult position, wasn't I? Whoever came out on an off-the-record number like this was risking his back. It would have been worse still if everything went according to plan, and Lippiat merely did as instructed.'

'You think this wasn't according to plan?'

'One question at a time.'

'Let's stay with you risking your back, then.'

'It's a question of need-to-know, isn't it? I took care that enough people knew.'

'You leaked an operational order?'

'Pass.'

'"Pass."? There's no bloody pass in this interrogation, Captain Matson.'

'Then show me some intelligence.'

'Who briefed you?'

'That's an intelligent question. I don't propose to answer it.'

'So. Either the right person was at the briefing, or the right combination of persons?'

'Yes.'

'Which was it?'

'Take your pick.'

'Well, I know how you stand in your own office.'

'I wish I did.'

'So perhaps your own Head of Bureau was there – that's still Leonard Fossit, I take it? – and someone trustworthy from the Foreign Office.'

'No one at the Foreign Office is trustworthy.'

'Always the little interdepartmental joke.' Leodolter broke off to look at his notes. 'You felt your back was protected because there were witnesses at the briefing. Leonard Fossit was there and Marcus Pomeroy was there. It would have to be somebody like Mr Pomeroy, wouldn't it?'

'Not to ask a favour.'

'Pomeroy has the rank.'

'But not the desk.'

'I don't follow you.'

'You've got the dead man's records. You've told me what you know of him. Marcus's sphere of influence is pretty well advertised and so is the way he works. I see no reason for their two paths to have crossed, do you?'

Leodolter made another note. 'At least two others at the briefing then, one from your own department, one not. Leonard Fossit probably. Marcus Pomeroy probably not. How's that?'

'Try another one.'

'Do you think the explosion was according to plan?'

'Somebody's plan, clearly.'

'But not yours?'

'Definitely not mine.'

'I mean not an English plan?'

'Why send me *and* a bomb?'

'Would you have killed him if the right person had asked you?'

Matson saw no reason to answer that. 'What I'm saying is they'd have sent someone who would.'

'To Austria?'

'Try not to sound outraged, Albin. We'll be wasting time if either of us plays the diplomat. Somebody killed him in Austria. I know nothing about it. I'm working on it.'

'Will your people be cross that Herr Lippiat is dead? Or that you seem to have killed him?'

It was a question that bristled with traps.

'I merely ask because a Mr Pilkington from your embassy wants to see you. Mr Pilkington is not on the embassy staff. He's flying out tonight. I wonder if he's bringing you a medal or a very big stick.'

The last time Matson heard the name Pilkington it belonged to the Home Office head of internal security. If it was the same Pilkington, it could only be because something to do with Lippiat's death had landed him in trouble back home.

He helped himself to a doughnut. The two chums had clearly read the same significance into the visit. It was the only way to account for Albin Leodolter's pretended concern for his status.

The doughnut had just squeezed itself out between his fingers and spread sugar round his face when the outer door swung open and Kammel stepped in. Willi was wearing the self-satisfied expression of a man who knows he is bringing unpleasant tidings. Whatever it was, it was printed on a piece of fax paper he waved in his hand.

'What's up, Willi? Heavy news?' This was a Freudian slip. The occasion was so weighty that Kammel had brought his two stout lads along to help him usher it in.

12

Matson massaged his smile into place with a paper napkin and wiped the sugar from his hands.

The big fellows stepped behind his chair, and were silent. He had thought his chair was too close to the wall for anyone to pull this sort of manoeuvre.

'You told us Herr Lippiat was a sort of private security expert – oh, a bit of this, a bit of that – but the implication being that if he ever worked for government, as we all know he did, then nowadays he was no more than a freelance?'

'*If* he worked for government, right.'

'And that story still stands?'

'As immutable as Gog and Magog at my elbow here.'

'Gerald Lippiat was an accredited member of your embassy staff in Berne. *Accredited.* A *diplomat*! He has served continuously in the Foreign Service since he was demobilized from the British army. He has served in Ankara, in Athens, and – as one would expect – in Yugoslavia, both at the embassy in Belgrade and the consulate in Split. So where does that leave our trade-off last night?'

'We didn't have a trade-off. I merely cleared a little lumber by admitting I had come to deliver a message.' Matson's laugh was at best nervous. 'I told you the other stuff right at the beginning, back at the *gasthaus* when I thought you were cops. Cops have simple minds and prefer uncomplicated answers. The moment you told me you had Lippiat under surveillance and for what, I assumed you had taken the trouble to find out some basic truths about him.'

Kammel watched Matson patiently, like a man whose hands are regrettably full and who is forced to wait while a toilet roll unwinds itself endlessly from the wall. When Matson finished speaking he said, 'And just what did Her Majesty's government suppose their accredited diplomat was doing in Austria these last weeks? We *know* what he *was* doing. Tell us what he was *supposed* to be doing.'

'He was on leave.'

Kammel sighed. Leodolter sighed. The two big fellows said nothing, and hid in the wall.

'Agents are always on leave,' Kammel said. 'First they're not agents at all – no one ever admits they are anything so naughty. They're always "perfectly respectable businessmen" or "innocent holiday-makers". But if they're caught with their hands in the pickle jar and a foreign power is proved to have provided them with the key to the food cupboard, then they've always stolen the key and they're on leave. Sometimes they've even been dismissed from the service. You didn't come here to tell him he'd been dismissed from Her Majesty's service, did you, Captain Matson? If you did, and you were to tell us you did, I'm afraid you would confirm our worst fears.'

'That's what I'm telling you.'

'Well, well, well. And before that you were telling us you were on leave, too.'

'Tenses, Willi. Tenses are your preoccupation, you say. "Are" not "were". I *am* on leave.'

'You, of course, are not accredited, Captain Matson. That is unfortunate for you.' He smiled. Matson's little print-out of lies had finished unrolling itself on the floor.

Something fastened on his shoulder, crushed a nerve end

or two and gathered him from his chair. One of the big boys picked him into space like a bale of loft insulation on the arm of a gantry crane.

The first thwack sealed him off above the third thoracic vertebra. His jaw locked, his neck spasmed, his nose flooded with blood.

No time to enjoy the pith of it. The next blow went in over the pelvis between spine and left kidney. White pain first, going immediately darker. Jaundice perhaps, then a red stutter of traffic lights.

Willi murmuring conversationally, 'Albin has been waiting to do it to you for hours now. You must keep an idea or two somewhere, he thinks.'

Only it wasn't Albin, was it?

Matson sicked up black coffee, doughnut and a lacy archipelago of bile over Kammel's shirt and necktie. Good old peristalsis. It never lets you down.

Then he was fully airborne. He flew across the room and through the couch, bones first. The couch pulled itself together and held him.

He hadn't been hit in the face, but he'd certainly landed on it.

'Tut!' Willi said.

'Ask yourself if you still think he wasn't working to Pomeroy,' Albin advised. 'Bloody ask.'

13

He needed to. In the circumstances, some modest reflection would be best.

Matson had many reasons for lying, but none so compelling as the one Kammel had just hit him with. He had lied, and would lie again through his vomit-soured teeth, to disguise the fact that he was totally ignorant of the truth. One truth, his own truth, would have been shockingly simple to tell. It would have been, 'Sorry, Willi. Apologies, Albin. I'm as rocked by this latest bit of news as you are. I knew he was a member of the Foreign Service *once*; but that was twenty years ago. Moreover my own common sense and the basis of my message to him persuades me he had access to more than his pension. That being said, he's too old by the same twenty years to be any member of a legation except chef or ambassador; and we can take it he was neither of those, in such an important station as Berne in Switzerland.'

If Lolly was accredited *anywhere*, it was for some extraordinary reason. To supervise the annihilation of geriatric Nazis? Hardly, but it was bound to be for something pretty bizarre, something Matson hadn't been told about.

And if Lolly had been caught leaking secrets – as he *had* been told, and the man had scarcely disputed it yesterday – then the ambassador would have been required, through official channels, to ship him back to London, in a packing-case if necessary.

His own expedition was no longer an unorthodox manoeuvre, but a major impropriety. Heads would be sure to roll, his own only the first and least exalted among them.

Mr Pilkington, whoever he was, would be one of a long procession of axemen.

He wondered if he was being sick again or merely bleeding. It was a soporific problem.

If Albin woke him with a slap this time, he couldn't feel it.

'Crawl into the bathroom and squeeze your pimples. Willi has some words for you.'

FOUR

1

Willibald Kammel massaged his scalp as if encouraging his hair to thicken. He scratched his temples, his chin, his widow's peak. He managed this without embarrassment and without soiling his fingers.

He smiled. 'We've been instructed to kick you downstairs to Kaub.' Willi's smile was not one of his better disguises.

Albin's grin was more expansive, but it left room for his ears. 'Kaub will have you looking at the inside of a block of concrete until halfway through the next century. One thing about our prisons, they're air-conditioned. You'll be protected from the greenhouse effect.'

Lack of sleep inducing hyperbole?

'You may even miss the next ice-age too,' Willi smirked. 'There's blood on your lips. I should hate it to stop you tasting things as they are.'

Matson ran his tongue round the inside of his face. It no longer felt like a mouth.

'All we want,' Willi's eyebrows explained, 'is an excuse not to hand you over. Nothing excessive, you understand. When you meet this man Pilkington, for example, we shan't expect you to wear a wire.'

That was almost a joke, coming from Willi.

'Embassies, we know, are not co-operatives. Intelligence is a free-market commodity. But our external services have an *excellent* relationship with your people.'

News to Matson. 'Excellent,' he mumbled. There had to be a straight ball somewhere among the wides.

'What we want to know, Captain Paddy, what we *insist* on knowing' – Leodolter giving him the full frontal manly look, so this had to be it – 'is why do you think Herr Lippiat was not the corpse in that caravan?'

'What makes you suppose that?'

'Tenses,' Willi triumphed. 'I said I would come back to your tenses, Patrick. You keep on speaking of the dead man in the present tense.'

'So does many a widow when she talks of her husband.'

'Fishermen daren't have wives.' Was it Willi's eyebrows semaphored that one, or Albin's? The chums *were* being bright this morning.

'Where would this get me?'

'Share your thinking, and we'll look after Kaub for you.'

2

They brought him a change of clothes, and his razor. It gave them a chance to go through his luggage, of course; but they would have done that anyway.

'Tell me why Kaub thinks the corpse isn't Lolly's. I take it he's suspicious of something?'

Leodolter offered him a fresh cup of coffee, coffee with steam you could see because it was poured in a room that had sunlight. Matson's face was too sore for coffee and sunlight.

'The corpse was cooked,' Leodolter volunteered at last. 'You can't detect too much from a cadaver in that state.'

'The feet were still medium rare,' Matson coaxed. 'They'll doubtless tell a pathologist something.'

The feet bothered Albin. Matson decided to come back to them later. 'Dental records?'

'No head.'

'Can I take a peep at what Kaub's got in the laboratory?'

'No.'

'I may be able to identify him.'

'For you, perhaps. Not necessarily for us. Why should we believe you?'

'So I'm to share my thought processes, but my conclusions aren't to be trusted.'

Time began to bother Leodolter. Matson was happy for it

43

to accumulate. 'Come on, Albin,' he said. 'Talk to me about the corpse's tootsies, and I'll tell you what I know.'

'Cold feet,' Albin muttered. 'And they look like a young man's feet.'

'Old men's feet often do.'

'A wild man's. Dirty, with uncut nails. Very badly kept.'

'Lolly was a bit of a primitive. The lab will do a bone section, and then you'll be certain.'

'If they are a young man's feet, then we'll know they are not Herr Lippiat's. But they may be an old man's feet, and the doubt will remain. Besides, how certain is certain? Even a tooth transparency is only accurate to within a ten-year bracket, and we have no teeth to look at. We need more.'

'You're basing your whole neurosis on a dirty toe-nail. He'd just climbed out of a sopping wet fishing boat, you know. Feet callous very quickly when the skin's damp.'

'Cold feet. You missed my point the first time. The corpse had cold feet.'

'So did everyone else.'

'Think about the body. It had its head in the fire. Its torso – is that the word? – in the ashes, and only its feet out in the sunshine.'

'Rain, actually.'

'Didn't you notice anything else about the feet?'

'I noticed they wore green English wellingtons, and the legs were in Lolly's trousers.'

'They were frozen, frozen stiff. That body had been refrigerated, or at least kept up in the snow somewhere.'

Matson was intrigued.

'A sore-footed rag-arse.'

'Ragged arse.'

'What do cooks call ice inside fire? Isn't there a culinary term?'

'*Une bombe surprise*,' Matson said. It was a sick joke, but it was the truth. 'It's an ice cream. That pressurized camping gas is pretty cold, and when it evaporates quickly it must refrigerate.'

'Not when there are flames around. Are you trying to make out that the corpse *is* Lippiat, Matson?'

'I'm asking you to be rather more sure than simply saying

it can't be because it's got a frozen toe.'

'I'll get the lab to run some tests. They won't like playing with that pressurized butane, though. And why should they? It's the corpse itself that's the clue: a frozen stick chars differently from one that's thawed out on the hearth.'

'Perhaps. And perhaps, when the flames are out and there are no embers – remember the rain – camping gas squirts from one of those ten-litre jars as a pressurized liquid spray at about minus twenty centigrade – damn it, *I* don't know the liquefying point – then evaporates off on his leg, sucking out even more heat.'

'I'll ask a refrigeration company.'

'You do that. Liquid oxygen turns a cube of meat to an ice block very quickly.'

'Yes, but oxygen and how big a cube? I've said the body was an outdoor type, Matson. A mendicant, say. A gypsy.'

'Perhaps Lippiat didn't wash his toes or cut his nails. He was a bit of an ape. I'm merely pointing out that the frost is making you jump to conclusions.'

'Our lab isn't like that.'

'Not much science ever goes into disproving the obvious. It's against a scientist's training and inclinations. You know that. There's a live man with warm blood in his body. Suddenly his wagon's on fire and his body's in the fire. You assume it's him, until it turns out the legs are frozen and he had uncivilized feet. Then you believe the reverse. I suggest your evidence isn't conclusive, either way.'

'So what have you got that's any better?'

'A couple of questions.'

Willi came storming in from some cupboard or other. 'Answers, Patrick Matson. Not questions. Not –' He daren't let himself repeat such an unfortunate word. Eavesdropping had given him claustrophobia.

'I don't know how much forensic you'll have on a case like this.'

'Forensic? I don't understand.'

'Sorry. It's an English misuse of the word. I want to know how scientific your investigation will be. Scientific as in the availability of laboratory techniques. I'm not questioning your investigative methods, your actual policing. I've seen

45

enough of that to know it is admirable.'

Leodolter beamed. 'Kaub is giving this our best lab work. Our laboratories at Innsbruck are equal to anything in Germany, say.'

'Questions, then. I'd like a list of as many of the titles of the books he kept in that caravan as it is possible to deduce from the cinders.'

Willie looked puzzled, and swallowed. 'And?'

'I'd like to know how much of his lovely Austrian climbing boots survived the flames. When I saw him, he was wearing those boots. Ten minutes later his corpse was wearing wellingtons. The trousers looked all right, but a man often buys several pairs at a time.'

'And the boots?'

'The boots are like the books. Precious. I saw not a fragment of either, not a single charred piece. Also, the boots were laced up in that old-fashioned over-and-under way. It would take him ages to unlace. It would take a killer a bit of time even to cut them off.'

Leodolter looked thoughtful.

'Then I've a third question. Did he rent his fishing boat from the *gasthaus* – or camping site owner, if they're different entities – or did he bring it with him?'

'I can deal with that by making one telephone call. You intrigue me, at last.'

Willi went out. At last intrigued.

3

The call took him in an hour. Or the anger it generated in him did. 'He brought a plastic boat,' he said when he came back. 'Orange with wooden skids.'

'That's the one. Fibre glass with wooden thwarts.'

'He brought it with him on the top of his wagon.'

'So what does it tell your laboratory? Has anyone examined it for signs of the surrogate corpse?'

'It isn't there. It never came to our attention because it never was there.'

'I saw it,' Matson said.

46

'When he rowed in, yes.'

'And after the explosion. It was there when your police motorcycle patrol arrived. They wouldn't have thought it significant, or even connected it with that particular caravan. Someone must have removed it overnight.'

'I assure you –'

'That that kind of thieving is extremely rare. Perhaps it's what I dislike most about Austria. You are able to say it with such conviction.'

'So you think his murderers or abductors took it.'

The chums were going too fast for Matson. Increasingly his mind dwelt on Lippiat's books and Lippiat's climbing boots. Lolly's smile also. At sometime during the night, Lippiat's boots and books had climbed into the boat and stolen away in it. The problem for him was: had Lolly's smile gone with them?

4

Matson had given Willi and Albin things to do and thoughts to think.

As they went to do their things and think their thoughts, Willi said spitefully, 'We'll send a girl in to put some ice on your face.'

'Someone nice from the *Ersatzbataillonbordell*?'

'Someone to mend your bruises and give your features a clean start. Then we'll be able to see what this Pilkington fellow does to you. Don't try to run now, will you, Matson? There's nowhere to hide in an airport. You'll only make Kaub's people angry.'

'Why not have my Mr Pilkington come here?'

'Here belongs to us.'

The girl they sent in was at least fifty. She had a ginger body and hair the colour of carrot rust, and she was large. Most of her was on the outside of her uniform, and consequently camouflaged it. Matson couldn't tell whether she was a policewoman, a nurse or a hod-carrier. She was bigger than most heavyweight wrestlers he'd seen, more the size of the female attendant in one of those closely guarded German

47

lavatories for men, the ones who ration the toiletpaper and make sure you do no more or less than you're meant to.

She did as she had been told. She took hold of Matson with half a hand and put some ice on his face. 'Poor Tommy!' she crooned. 'Poor poor Tommy!' She stroked his head with her flat-iron fingers and began to frighten the lumps away.

Albin came back and poked his voice in. 'Sorry to interrupt.' He spoke as if to an orgy. 'We don't need to run those refrigeration tests. Our corpse had been dead for at least twenty-four hours, so it wasn't Herr Lippiat's.'

Matson got his head out from between a couple of amazonian freckles and said, 'I still want to know how the corpse got frozen, don't you? And when. Whether it was chilled in some gas spray before or after the bomb.'

'No bomb. Something else we now have for certain.'

'When your victim carries gas bottles you don't need Semtex. Kaub will certainly want to know what froze that piece of meat. It will help tell him where it came from. One of you said something about it being kept up in the snow. That's only one theory. Where's the nearest school of anatomy? The nearest refrigeration unit? How big is the icebox at the *gasthaus*? Do you know the dimensions of the fridge in Lippiat's wagon? Is there a drinks facility on the caravan site?'

'You're letting your imagination run wild.'

'It's paid to. I didn't see *all* of a body. How much did Kaub's people find? Half a body stores relatively easily. Medical students divide corpses in half. North and south for dissection, east and west for the skeleton sale. Heads fetch a special price, so the study bones are often topped off in plastic. You didn't, for example, come up with a head, yet? Heads tend to disappear.'

Matson tended to disappear. Leodolter gave a signal, and the big girl kept him from surfacing. While he was under, she woke up a few more nerve-bundles with her ginger hands. They're like that, the Teutons. They do everything the painful way, even cleaning their teeth.

Leodolter got her to let him up. 'We found the boat, however.'

48

'On the General's side of the lake?'

'Nowhere so obvious. About six hundred metres along the shore in the general direction of Klagenfurt.'

'Downstream? Towards the spill?'

'Yes, but tied up. People do pull other men's boats inshore in Austria, and tie them up. But I doubt if that is the explanation. The road is only a few steps from the water there. So he had an accomplice.'

'Or a bicycle.'

Rusty Thumb took him in hand again.

FIVE

1

Graz is a walk-in airport. Walk in, walk on, walk off. There are no moving footways, and certainly no boarding gantries. No one, not even a Mr Pilkington, could step into the VIP lounge straight from a hole in the sky.

Willi and Albin weren't prepared to let Matson meet his nemesis in Vienna, just the same. Vienna was a long way from Graz, and once he got there someone might bundle him into a fast car and whisk him off to perpetual asylum in Reisnerstrasse Number Forty, where the British keep their embassy and a variety of other wonders.

Someone such as Mr Pilkington.

Mr Pilkington disapproved of Matson's appearance. He looked upon his bruises and the stumble of his walk with the disdain that people who despise poverty reserve for tramps.

'Why did you top him, Paddy? Did he try to come it over you with a geriatric karate chop? He certainly beat the hell out of you.'

Mr Pilkington was not who Matson feared he might be. This one would be a little better or a lot worse.

2

Matson led Leonard Fossit into the airport coffee bar and seated him in front of a jug of black stuff and some awful sticky strudel before saying, 'I was the only one of you to really like old Lolly, for Christ's sake, so why would I do that?' He managed Fossit's pot of cream for him as if Fossit were his aunt, as in a sense he was.

50

Fossit was his Head of Department and he wasn't yet started. 'Marcus Pomeroy is cross. Ralph Dixon is very cross. Shortly the Minister will have have to hear – officially, I mean – and he'll be extremely cross.'

'What, exactly, are you, Leonard?'

'Cross.'

'I'm on leave,' Matson said.

Fossit picked up a coffee spoon, balanced it between thumb and finger, and found he had bent it. He said, 'You'll file as soon as possible, of course.'

'Will I?'

The spoon bent even more acutely. Leonard Fossit frowned, turned Matson's question around as if searching insolence for a redeeming tinge of levity. In the end he said, 'Facts will oblige us.' The spoon was now grotesque.

'The Austrians are pretty certain Lolly isn't dead. Fact.'

'Fact he isn't dead?'

'Fact they're pretty certain he isn't.'

Fossit stopped spoon-bending for at least half a second. This was news to him, Matson could swear it. Lippiat was either intended to be dead, or presumed to be dead as far as London was concerned. Or as far as Fossit knew.

The silence grew so long that Matson was forced to say, 'How do you want me to play it?'

'Write the truth. No, not that. Simply put down the facts.'

'Facts so often reach their own conclusions, don't you find? I can write down facts that prove Lippiat's a half cinder.'

'You can't have half a cinder any more than you can have half a hole.'

'In my reports you can, Leonard.'

'There *was* a corpse.' Leonard was uneasy. 'There are also those who want me to suggest you don't come home in consequence.' The spoon was knotted like a water snake.

'He had cold feet, Leonard. Very odd for a demi-cinder. Also he burned. Niffed a bit, too. Not of mortality, but of immortality. About seventy per cent proof, I'd say.'

'Lolly was a boozer.'

'He liked wine. He was drinking a glass of wine.'

The spoon snapped, and lost its head in Fossit's coffee. He dropped the twisted bit in his pocket.

'There are two ways to preserve a body, Leonard. You can freeze it. You can pickle it. If a body with ice instead of blood in its feet were to burn like a primus stove, I'd tend to feel it had been subjected to a bit of both, wouldn't you? Who exactly will be wanting my report?'

'You think we're surrounded by tricksters. I don't.'

'Not tricksters, Leonard. Tricky dickies. Pomeroy is such a one. Men who are undoubtedly honest but frequently perturbed to find themselves so. So what can you tell me?'

'I think we should talk somewhere more private.'

3

Matson didn't move. If Willi and Albin had ways of listening, then they were listening. Electronic surveillance could target almost anything, including talk in washrooms with the taps full on. The clever moment could wait. He said, 'The Austrians are pretty certain – unless they have unguessable reasons for lying to me – that Lolly killed a certain German General Lenz just up the road from here.'

'I don't know what's in this for me.'

'They think he was planning to assassinate another ex-Nazi as well, a general in the SS this time. I'd like you to have someone in the office – young Jacintha Hyem'll do – sniff around press-cutting libraries and find out why Lippiat was attracted to him. His name is Weiss. Gruppenführer or Obergruppenführer Hendrick Reinhard Weiss.'

'Oberst. Oberstgruppenführer according to *The Times*. Young Mrs Hyem will do no such thing for you, now or at any other time. At your request, I let her deliver the firm's Range Rover to Mulhouse the other day, and she's been broody ever since.'

'Come on, Leonard.'

'Weiss is about to sally into Lolly's old killing grounds in Yugoslavia. There's your motivation. He has title to some property there and he intends to claim it. Quite a story. I daresay Lolly might want to haunt the beggar for going there, if his ghost can remember the way. I was having a chin with Popovic at their embassy, and it seems the Yugoslavs no longer want this Weiss for war crimes.'

'Can that be so?'

'It can be, and according to Popo it is. A lot of German money is going into their industrial programme, and they don't want to scare it off. That's the Party line, anyway. A chap like Lolly might well see it differently. And so might a lot of Serbians, Montenegrins and ex-partisans generally. Could this provide a motive for our lad's shenanigans?'

'Is property the sole reason for Weiss's trip?'

'Generals in wartime are a bit like pirates.' Fossit reached for Matson's spoon and stirred loudly. 'Pirates on the run sometimes bury trinkets.'

'What about this general?'

'I'm told –' the stirring battered an empty cup, the voice sank to a sibilant whisper. 'I'm told that Weiss's formation – the Seventh Division SS – refreshed the parts that other invaders couldn't reach. Not even the Turks got into Montenegro, or found the Serbian Orthodox monasteries. As for the Catholic Church in Croatia and Slovenia, it made the mistake of thinking Hitler was a friend.'

Matson retrieved his spoon. A sane man can't persist *ad infinitum* with silly noises.

'In consequence, there's an enormous catalogue of loot: altar furniture, icons, religious artefacts of all sorts. In the normal course of wickedness, some of it should have turned up by now, at least via private collections. So the inference must be it's tucked away in the original hidy-hole.'

'Or destroyed.'

'After being stripped of intrinsics, such as stones and gold overlay? Surely something would have come to light in the ashes around the bonfire.'

'What an encyclopedia you are, Leonard.'

'I got that bit from Marcus Pomeroy.'

'There must be some more to it, then. I'm not as good at history as Marcus, but I'll be willing to bet it's been a long time since the British Foreign Office last sent anyone on a treasure hunt. Sir Walter Raleigh is the most recent bloke that comes to mind.'

'Lolly wasn't briefed about any of this.'

'So who told Mr Bloody Pomeroy, then?'

Graz might be no more than a second-line airport, but security was a whole lot better than Matson had counted on. He had been waiting for jet turbines to open up and provide some cover for the really important chat. He watched through the coffee shop window while a dark haze of vibration built up around the BAC One-Eleven that Fossit had arrived in, then tried to get the pair of them outside on the apron.

One-way doors.

They opened for someone coming in, and Matson barged through. An airport security guard turned him back.

Leonard tutted, and then tut-tutted. He never did approve of going out through doors marked 'In.' Or not at times like this.

Matson's untidiness of mind needed no further rebuke. A dozen of Kaub's Feds lined the tarmac outside the window, and the big man himself pressed his face against the glass, breathing words they couldn't hear. Leonard preferred to hear, even when he knew he wouldn't understand. He looked pained at Matson's maladroitness. As Mr Pilkingtons go, Leonard Fossit was proving to be a disappointment. Matson grinned at Kaub, or perhaps only grunted. He turned and led Leonard upstairs.

He found a small open-air observation terrace, crowded but noisy with the One-Eleven. He could see Leonard hated the smell of kerosene, so gave his boss one of his more encouraging smiles before hissing, 'No one told me Lolly was currently accredited. On roll, yes. Serving officer, no. My briefing suggested he was a freelance who had delivered some of the firm's paperwork into the wrong hands and might do it again.' He bent Leonard's arm, like a tea spoon. 'Why didn't I get *told* he was a bona fide ring-kisser on the Foreigners' Swiss quota?'

The kerosene had made Leonard look yellow. Now he became properly poorly.

'Chummies who help crooked diplomats to abscond have lousy career prospects, Leonard. Not to say life expectancy. I've just been encouraged to join a distinguished group that includes Burgess, Maclean and Philby. If I think there's any *funny* business –'

Fossit winced because of his bent arm, then again to deplore an incomplete sentence.

'– I'll sodding well resign.' Matson completed it for him.

Leonard didn't like 'funny business' either. 'Don't be childish, Paddy. You have a way of life to support.'

'No, Leonard. You have the way of life. I live in Higher Rented in Camden. It costs me damn all.'

'Show some respect.'

'I'm on a ticket of leave from an Austrian nick.'

'For the language, if not your position.' Leonard got his arm free, then his ego. 'I thank you for bringing me out here,' he said at length.

Both men looked around carefully, but the people on the observation platform seemed curiously indifferent to a pair of foreigners engaging in a lovers' tiff. Electronic surveillance would be difficult here. It would take time to situate and target. Doubtless, their low-grade chatter in the coffee shop would be on tape. Here they could feel free, at least for a minute or two longer.

Even so, Leonard kept his voice down. 'The accreditation *could* be awkward, not least for myself. I wasn't told. If I whinge to anyone they'll say it was an oversight he was left on the diplomatic list. That'll be a lie. The host country scrutinizes anomalies like that. It's what you and I do for a living, for God's sake, Matty.

'What they told me was this: Lolly was running the main Balkan network from Berne. Berne and London. There's a cosmetic thing conducted by one of the attachés in Belgrade – Lolly used to be that attaché when he was military bloke there – but that's just to keep the Yugoslavs feeling content that they've got our operation covered.

'The real show, Yugoslavia, Albania – not Greece but with odd strands into Bulgaria and, I suppose, Hungary, and Slavonic Austria – is down to Lolly.

'So what did he do? He parted with some agents' names – the identities of three key controls – to Yugoslav intelligence, more or less as I told you before you came out here. Lolly had them by the balls, two up in the Riyeka area because they were Croats he personally could identify as Ustaza with some bad killings against them, one his sub-head of Bosnia because he was second-in-command of that Handschar lot who did the Mostar rape and massacre.'

'It figures. It would tie in with what the Austrians claim to know about him.'

'But *controls*, Matty. The Bosnian bloke is already dead. They would have been bound to have revealed agents' names before going.'

'This is Balkan politics, Leonard. Lolly's no George Blake. He would have assumed the Ustaza pair were using ex-Ustaza, and that the ex-Handschar was running a bunch of thugs similar to himself. Lolly was merely closing some books – books he had opened himself – not damaging Western Intelligence.'

'But why did he do it?'

'As a *quid pro quo*. Weiss is going over the border. Lolly wanted to be free to roam about Montenegro and Serbia when his old arch-target goes there in a day or two's time. I'd say he was paying Yugoslav security the price of being let in with a gun, wouldn't you?'

'I'd call that paying twice, since he's proposing to do their dirty work for them.'

There were two pairs of Federal policemen on the balcony. Leonard turned away. If Matson were to be re-arrested, he wanted no part of it.

Matson grabbed his elbow. The policemen didn't move in, not for the moment.

'Suppose I get out of here, Leonard? I don't think they're intending to charge me. They let me meet you.'

'You're due for a lot of leave, aren't you? Last year's and earlier.' It sounded like an invitation to get lost. 'Take it and dig this thing out. Take everything you're due. I'll see your confidential doesn't carry any black marks. Or not on that account.'

The two big lads from the van were here now. The power handlers from Graz.

'We need to know who set us up. *I* need to know. Before I have to explain to a committee of enquiry, and perhaps a select committee, our intimate connection with the murdered head of Balkan operations. Bad. Or our no less intimate connection with his defection. Very much worse.'

The big lads didn't hang about any longer. They emptied people from the observation platform. They shifted Leonard one way and lifted Matson another, but gently this time.

Leonard's last word was, 'I'd hate to think someone was trying to embarrass us out of existence.'

5

Willi was jubilant. '*Leonard* Pilkington. A Mr *Leonard* Pilkington. We have a new name to dump, Albin.'

'Computer talk.' Leodolter beamed at Matson. 'And a new photograph for our album. This Leonard Pilkington was obviously about to dispatch you across the border.'

'In pursuit of the *late* Herr Lippiat,' Willi said.

The irony was heavier than the known facts permitted. The two chums felt unable to contain their good news any longer.

'Kaub has found your friend Lippiat,' Albin revealed. 'Not ten metres from where someone had tied up his rowing boat.'

'New Austrian climbing boots, Serbo-Croat literature in his pocket,' Willi continued, 'And his lungs full of pondweed and water. So you won't need to go to Yugoslavia, after all.'

Matson wanted to ask them how long they'd known this. Instead, he said, 'You'll let our embassy inspect the corpse?'

'He's quite dead. Even we could tell that,' Albin purred. 'And absolutely –'

'Unrecognizable. Not a pretty sight. There's an especially voracious freshwater shrimp in the stausee shallows.'

'Not *crangon vulgaris*, of course.'

'Of course not.'

'Nor *gammarus pulex.*'

'I wouldn't suspect it.'

'The body isn't here, I'm afraid.'

'It's up the chimney. We have our embarrassment about this one, too.'

What a pair they made. They shared and exchanged each other's parts, like the mythical sisters.

'Believe us, there was a body. Exactly as you described it to us.'

'With green boots and books.'

'The books were not green, Willi. Nor were this pair of boots.'

'The truth is what counts. The details are only facts.'

Someone had helped Lippiat disappear. Then that self-same someone had nobbled him. Was that their scenario?

'Kaub is a very bright fellow,' Kammel said. 'A most intelligent man as police inspectors go. He knows you didn't kill *this* Gerald Lippiat.'

'Because you were with us. And since there's more to work on –'

'He sees no reason to present you to his superiors –'

'As the murderer of the first Gerald Lippiat,' Willi said. 'Call it innocence by attraction.'

'The word is "association",' Matson said, more sour than sweet.

'In your case, it's attraction,' Albin Leodolter smirked.

SIX

1

A face in a beard of shrimps. Or tiny freshwater worms. The left trouser leg skeined in weed, climbing boots still laced tight in Lolly's old-fashioned diagonal crossover. Two more close-ups of the head, one of them minus the hairy feeders. Result – face regrettably absent. All three in double-postcard-size Kodacolor slicks, made even glossier by flash-light. Stuff for a police file, not for a grieving relative. Nor for a friend with a hangover. Three shots in all, presented with three lookalikes.

Albin Leodolter thrust them under his nose, exactly at six a.m., then turned away while Matson dressed, giving him time to fold one of each inside a face towel and stuff it into his suitcase. Lolly was past objecting to a damp environment. Matson hoped Mr Kodak was equally impervious.

He returned the rest of the nasties and mumbled his thanks.

Leodolter pretended to count them, then said. 'The height's right, according to his passport. Also the eye colour. There's an eye intact somewhere, if you care to check it out. No teeth. Any observations?'

'No knowledge on that one. He was old enough, and vitamin-deprived enough during the war to need grinders.'

Leodolter grunted, and Kammel came in to signal that the exchange so far had been unofficial. 'Nothing remains but to reunite you with your vehicle. Albin will take you, I daresay.' He let go of Matson's hand almost as soon as he took hold of it. 'I'll have someone put the newspapers in Albin's car. We did what we could with the press. But for some of them, no news is always the best news, I'm afraid. They've made connections.'

59

So Leodolter drove, in a decent black Mercedes this time, the sort that takes families to funerals. It was daylight and the sky was a steep blue, like a lake, and full of the vapours of spring.

There was snow on the distant mountains. Matson watched the heights come closer: grey rock, blue ice, a thin blue this one, like a bruise drying out or the memory of a headache. There's always a way for a fit man, Willibald Kammel had said. But how fit is fit? Icy hills have a way of making fitness redundant.

'Willi meant what he said about the press. We'd like to be sorry, Patrick, but we're not. The reporting is divided, as you'll see. Some papers describe you as a probable murderer – no harm there, of course.'

'If you say so.'

'Others – the ones who are interested in Lippiat's pedigree and have done some work on his background – well, they tend to portray you as the dead man's friend.'

'I don't follow.'

'Nazis are tolerated here, as you insist on reminding us. Nazi-hunters are regarded as big trouble, not just by the Nazis themselves. Watch your back. We can't be everywhere.'

Matson had been watching his back all the way from Graz. Albin's preoccupation with the driving mirror had prompted him to take off his jacket and throw it onto the rear seat. Later he needed a packet of tissues from his pocket. He took them a tissue at a time.

They had another Mercedes in tow, hardly a sibling. It was certainly no funeral car. This one was silver grey with a blacked-out screen. It was one of those stretched jobs that take heads of state to airports. A similar vehicle had trailed them to Graz. Now he was being followed back. Not tailed: trailed. Not shadowed: followed. Everything arrogant and open.

It drew alongside. Surprisingly, it had clear side windows. Only its photosensitive screen was dark.

It was driven by a uniformed chauffeur. His dress jarred

Matson's memory oddly, but he let the thought go. He wan't interested in the chauffeur. He wanted to know who else was in the car, but in that brief moment he saw it was empty.

Then it dropped behind again, to crowd Albin's mirror.

'Someone wants to race,' Matson said.

The big Mercedes was everywhere. The road took a half-kilometre curve, while Leodolter's thoughts were in straight lines. He paused long enough to sort everything out, then said, 'Somebody wants to look you over, I suspect.'

The silver grey Mercedes followed them onto the side-road, then to the *gasthaus* at Bogenfeld. Once it had turned off the autobahn, there weren't too many other places for it to go.

When they pulled up in front of the *gasthaus*, it swooped past, only to brake sharply and swing into the lane that led to the caravan site. It reversed out and sped back towards the autobahn.

Unless it intended to stop at one of the other houses on the lake.

3

The large man in lederhosen, the proprietor, did his best to keep his face from squeaking. The red-faced *hausfrau*'s blush was now so big they could use it to paint the shutters. The girls were, well, girls. If Matson were a murderer, he was better here in the hand than out there in the bush after dark. They had washed Lolly's bits from their blouses, or not-Lolly's bits as the case might be. The Carinthian peaks were clean. Now they stood gawping at Matson, perhaps because he was thinking aloud.

They didn't gawp for long. His car was in the parking lot, some of his luggage was in a room upstairs, and his firm was paying the rent, so daddy sent them to fold table-napkins.

Leodolter bought a drink at the bar to show the world that Matson's freedom was official. He ordered Mazagran, which Matson had always thought of as a whore's drink, but perhaps it was meant that way.

When he had left, Matson went to the car park and found

the Range Rover. It started first time. The Austrian papers had been tossed on to the front seat.

Very decent of Albin. Matson took them for a drive along the lake. He wanted a closer look at the habitat of the so-called General Weiss. He needed to find out if the silver grey Mercedes came from there.

4

The newspaper could have taken him all day. Fortunately his German could not match his notoriety. There were too many column inches about Lippiat, the caravan, himself, the missing General Gunter Lenz, another missing Nazi called Ertl, with more than a passing glance at the career of Ober-gruppenführer Hendrick Reinhard Weiss who did, after all, reside just a ripple and a splash away from the exploding camping wagon.

There was even an article about the latter's intended journey to take possession of his property in Yugoslavia. Matson left that sort of reading to wait until he was reunited with his luggage and his pocket dictionary back at the *gasthaus*.

He unlocked the glove compartment and took out his binoculars, but there was no time to focus upon Weiss's house, or any of the other buildings that surrounded it. That's the trouble with twenty-fifties: they're always full of distraction.

A streaker was coming towards him along the lakeshore footpath, a streaker with a difference. He was on roller skates. Brown and bristly-boyo naked he might be, but he had a transistor radio in his hand and a listening extension plugged into his ear. The transistor was mute. The rollers made no sound on the sticky asphalt; nor did the genial flip-flop of his penis against his unanxious scrotum.

Matson was not terribly interested in male nudes. Nor, at this moment, in female ones. If a mermaid had risen tail-less from the depths for him, he would have pushed her gently back again. His mind was on other matters.

Until the lad stopped and said, 'English?' His own English

was round-vowelled and uncertain. 'The English fisherman?'

Matson's expression must have offered some sort of linguistic encouragement, because he added, 'We thought you was dead.'

He tugged his transistor aerial and spoke into it. Matson would have been prepared to bet it was only a fun radio, or Walkman cassette player, but a woman's voice answered from it, squeaking in excited German. Then there was silence, the insect-like buzz of a radio that is receiving the pulse of an uncluttered carrier wave. Then a male voice, loud, bossy, unflustered. The voice of a man used to giving orders, and to soothing excitable underlings.

The streaker allowed himself to be soothed. 'He wants to know,' he said to Matson. Then his English jammed. 'He wants to know,' he insisted with lame aggression.

'So do we all,' Matson agreed. 'The quest for enlightenment is one of the cornerstones of our common humanity.'

'He wants to know are you the Englisher who is dead or the Englisher who killed him?'

'That is a very pertinent question,' Matson complimented. 'Perhaps if I could meet –'

'Because he wants you to know this is private property. All private property, Herr General says. Why do you think we have this path under here if this is not private property? Why do you think I have the nothings on, if this is not private property? Why do you think? Do you not see I have the nothings on?'

'You're wearing roller-skates,' Matson corrected. 'And a two-way radio. Also I don't like your aftershave.' He said the last bit in German. He knew how to order aftershave in German.

The lad was no conversationalist. He slipped out of his skates in a very matter-of-fact way and was now unhooking his headset like a matron taking off her hairnet, doubtless according to instructions from the crisp voice on the radio.

Matson began to appreciate, much too late, what every well-brought-up woman knows by instinct – that a naked man is not necessarily as harmless as he seems. The lad might be on the pretty side, in a blond bomber kind of way. He was also dressed up in a newly scrubbed and powdered one hundred and sixty pounds of bone and muscle.

You can recognise hostile intention by referring to a chap's balls if you can't see the whites of his eyes, Matson's unarmed combat instructor used to tell him. The Bible has something on the subject too.

Without the least tightening of the scrotum, the young cruiserweight caught him a double blow across cheekbone and temple with his strap-swung roller-skates.

Matson's outrage was total and intact. His face bled, his lips snarled, but his legs had meanwhile betrayed the excellence of his reason and given way beneath him.

The lad caught him up in solicitous arms and ran with him into the lake.

5

Drowning is a gentle death, the Romantics say.

Matson had a headache when he began to die, a headache, a face-ache and most probably a hangover; and between them they diminished what might otherwise have been a pleasingly analgesic experience.

He was about to become another corpse for Inspector Kaub to dredge out of the system, after the fish had chased him through the sluices of the Gail and the Drau.

His blond executioner had stuck his head in the lake some six or seven hundred yards from the nearest lip of rapid – or was it of weir? – but he seemed to have drifted alarmingly close to the white water in no time, such was the piled up rushing in his ears. His transit was being eased by the very expert pressure of fingers on his throat, including a thumb-end as relentless as a tungsten-coated jack ramming into the caratoid pressure point.

It was a self-defeating refinement. Oxygen might be in short supply, but a man cannot be strangled and swallow water at the same time.

As Matson's brain began to enter the whirlpool, its past had no time to flash before it. It remembered just one word: *cranjuls.*

His instructor had insisted that an assailant attempting

manual strangulation left you with both hands free to devote
to his cranjuls. Matson's de-oxygenated brain had always
understood the meaning of cranjuls, but not its derivation.
Some men say bollocks and some men say knackers, just as
some prefer toilet to lavatory. His instructor said cranjuls, a
twee word inferior to either, a word rather like loo, an
instructor's word.

A sudden insight into the obviousness of its derivation
exploded inside his head and came close to killing him. A
naked man is but a wee forked thing, especially underwater.
Matson seized the reminder gratefully. The grip on his neck
exploded, like a tyre coming off a rim. His face came out of
the water and into the dangerous air. 'Crown Jewels,' he
rejoiced. Fancy being educated in Camberwell and failing to
perceive that. 'Crown fucking Jewels!' And he struggled to
prise the pair of them from their setting until he felt poor
Queen Victoria squirm in her grave in protest.

Only for a moment. Only until the return of oxyhaemo-
globin, reason and compassion. Then he released the agony
in his right hand and straight-edged the pretty face below its
bloodshot eyeballs or highballs, as the cocktail makers of
Camberwell also have it, straight-edged it from a great
height, himself standing waist-deep, itself gulping and
thrashing about over then under the water, sometimes with
limbs attached, sometimes alone in its wet blond hair,
collapsing its nose in the accepted fashion.

Then, with his still fastened-on left, he sent the lad
bollusing ashore, remembering just in time to release his grip
on the Star of India.

Flesh seemed to hit the asphalt in several stages. Being
drowned had overheated Matson's imagination. He walked
the water and reached dry land.

6

Dry land was extremely wet, what with the pair of them. Wet
and increasingly red. A terrible mess kept falling from the
young man's nose, several buckets of precious stones, and a
bubble as big as a testicle.

The broken meat was too messy for the firm's Range Rover. Matson gathered up what he could of it, blood against wetness, and set off for the Weiss house via the asphalt shore.

This was a mistake.

He estimated the carry at eight hundred yards. After a few dozen steps, he thought again. Waterline distances are hard to judge: he stretched his guess to a thousand. In the event, it was probably a full kilometre.

By the time he was halfway there, his shoes had stopped squelching and water no longer fell in an embarrassing drip from his crotch. The casualty's crotch did not bear thinking about. Not by his crutch.

The house was bigger than he'd calculated. So were the buildings in the hamlet behind it. Most of them were scaled-down versions of his own *gasthaus*, overblown dolls' houses for fretwood egos. Not Weiss's. His was gaunt and square-built and without usual domestic feature. If it had ground-floor windows they were boxed behind the high stone wall which surrounded it like the outer bailey of a Norman keep. The upper-storey windows were merely slots beneath the eaves.

No one was going to get the Obergruppenführer with a sniper's rifle from a boat or heave him from his bath with a rod and line. Lolly must have been intrigued.

The injured man stopped blubbing and wheezing, and began to moan. He groaned on every breath, and he breathed with each step Matson took. Matson's steps were becoming awkward and short.

When Matson didn't take a step, when he paused to adjust what he was carrying, the blond boy stopped breathing and howled.

Matson knew about anaesthesia. He dropped the lad on the asphalt path, levered him on to his side and kicked him in the guts with a wet shoe.

No more complaints, but it took an age to hoist him across his shoulder again.

The visible reapplication of violence had its reward. A gate opened in the landward angle of the wall, and three figures stood at the top of high steps, looking down at him.

66

One of them was feminine. Like Blondie, she had been sunbathing. Unlike Blondie, she hid a small piece of herself in beach shorts, but only so she could wear a belt, and holster a gun.

All three of them were tall. She was the big one. She weighed at least two hundred and twenty pounds, of which some two stone was tit. Her mammaries were enormous and naked and nippleless. They jutted, they did not hang. As Matson drew nearer, they enlarged like the rest of her into an expanding jigsaw of detail: tattoos, acid-burns, surgery, warts. Lipstick, eyeshadow and nail varnish were not for her.

Just as well. At thirty paces, Matson realised she was a man – one of those pieces of superlard more usual in bath houses and wrestling rings, places where there are supposed to be rules. Out here Weiss made the rules. Matson began to regret bringing Blondie home.

The other two men were much as he expected, and highly sinister in consequence.

Both were in their mid-twenties. They were tall and rangy, and – as with the lad Matson wore draped across his shoulders – they didn't look as if any of their weight was wasted. Like him, they had blue eyes, hard facial bone, and neck hair cropped so short it looked as if the clippers had gone in under their skin.

One of them was wearing a silver-piped black cap with glossy peak, black tunic with silver buttons, black breeches and calf-tight black knee boots polished to match the glitter of his headpiece. There were no eagle badges, no death's heads, no zigzag collar flashes, and certainly no formation patches or marks of rank on the epaulettes. Otherwise it was an exact replica of an SS officer's dress uniform. Matson had been looking at it, and not recognising it, an hour or so before. He'd been looking at its wearer, too, while studying the interior of a big silver grey Mercedes.

Weiss's chauffeur from Weiss's car.

The other man was modest in field grey fatigues. He was probably the handyman gardener, and less likely to accompany his employer on journeys outside the house. His boots and his belt were black even so, and he wore a black and white forage cap folded beneath his left epaulette.

Neither of them moved forward to help. Nor did Auntie Goliath, who seemed to be in charge.

Matson reached the bottom of the steps, shifting his load in case of trouble.

Now at last the two uniformed men came down.

8

The one in fatigues looked the nastier of the two. He and the wounded streaker were a matching pair of burgers, probably minced from the same ox.

Matson waited while the man descended to stand toe to toe and eye to eye, then draped him with his unconscious friend. 'This whacker tried to drown me,' he accused. 'I told him I was dead against it.' He spoke in English, but so what? The English are arrogant, insular and stupid. English would be expected of him.

The man caught hold of his friend and examined him carefully, top to bottom, so to speak.

The chauffeur still barred the way.

'*Polizei*,' Matson insisted. 'I'll need to phone the fuzz from up there.'

The chauffeur belonged to an orderly tribe. He stole a glance at his friend, then stepped aside.

Auntie Goliath stood himself in the wall instead of a gate, and closed it off.

Matson climbed wearily upward, put his hand against the big man's chest and pushed.

Goliath didn't open. Auntie stayed shut. Matson pressed harder. It was certainly no muscle-transplant he leant against, or silicone. The flab was all powerhouse, and it chuckled – not the most pleasing of seismic sensations.

Matson had no time to grade the tremor on the Richter scale; because, still chuckling, the big fellow took hold of him by the jaw and the small of the back, and began to turn him as a prelude to breaking something, presumably his neck and lower spine.

Matson slid the welt of his left shoe down the nearest bare shinbone, unpeeling its sunburn from knee to the exposed tendon on his foot. He finished with a textbook stomp and grind.

Why should a man always wear hard shoes? his instructor had asked. *Because, without them, no man is man enough.*

A shin scrape reroutes even the deepest voice into the upper sob-pipe. The giant produced a puberphonic wail, then went from tremolo to juddering grunt. The stamp had broken something, and the grind had spread it about.

At the beginning, the end, or in the middle of this, Matson felt the threatening fingers unfasten.

'Aarh!' the big man said and tried to hold Matson once more, but as a crutch this time. 'Aarh! Aarh!'

Matson knew the words but to a different tune. He dropped his hand to feel for Auntie's gun.

It was a Walther P38, the old shoot-yourself-in-the-buttock pistol, but in reliable hands an excellent weapon. Presumably anyone working for an SS general would have reliable hands. Matson lifted the pistol from its holster and dropped the eight-bullet clip into his hand. Luger ammunition, not the more usual Parabellum. They had been milled into flat-ended wad-cutters. This way they wouldn't have much of a range. Nor would you once they'd hit you.

He kept the clip as a knuckle liner, tucked the pistol back among the indelicacies of Auntie's briefs and took a step or two forward.

9

A courtyard, not a garden. Cemented crazy-paving close to the house, noisy granite chips nearest to the wall. A few tubs of freshly forked soil placed either at random or according to some arcane geometry. None of them held plants.

No dog visible or audible. No geese. Muscle everywhere. Two bone-faced middle-aged men, also in fatigues, stood halfway up ladders. They pretended to repoint the stone frieze of the building, but the mortar looked good enough already. They worked over-carefully, scraping much too quietly with their trowels as if listening for the least incentive to drop in on things.

Five men plus Auntie Goliath who, when fit, would make another five. The Obergruppenführer was being cautious. Not for the first time in his life, Matson had stuck his head into a rat box. This time he was alone and unarmed.

The General had ordered him killed, and Blondie had done his best to oblige. If the old man wanted him back in the mere, this four had enough clout to put him there, even if Auntie Goliath didn't recover.

He glanced around. Auntie was sitting up and shaking his head. The chauffeur had gone inside to report. The odd-job man came up the steps behind him with Blondie's wreckage in his arms. Auntie stood himself painfully upright. Matson began to wish he'd done him some terminal hurt.

Ladders juddered. He heard the uprights vibrate against the wall. The brickies were stepping down, with their pointing-knives in their hands.

Damp hair. Dry mouth. A tongue sad with lake water.

He licked his lips and called out loud, 'Herr Weiss! Herr General Hendrik Weiss!' The voice of a man who breaks down doors to disconnect gas.

Silence, which is what such voices deserve.

The chauffeur reappeared from inside the house. Matson clenched hard on the pistol clip. He could punch through ribs with that weight of bullets in his hand.

A man laughed. The sound came from a long way behind the chauffeur, from an inner room. It was strong, very sure of itself, yet much too deliberate. Matson had heard goats cough with more conviction.

'Herr Weiss!'

Again the gesture of laughter. This time overlaid with young women's laughter – several young women, one of them with an undercurrent of hysteria, one chilly as flint.

Footsteps on interior flagstones, quick feminine footsteps. A voice coming closer, answering someone in German. He couldn't unravel the German from the laughter.

A young woman stood in front of him. She wasn't laughing now. She was in mourning. She didn't look as if she

70

knew what laughter was. 'An old man,' she said. 'Why do you want to harm him?'

'I don't,' he answered. 'I've never hurt anyone in my life.' How soon he needed to lie. 'I don't even know who you're talking about.'

'My father-in-law.'

The ladder men moved closer. They all moved closer. Matson liked closer. He might need to place daughter-in-law between himself and father-in-law's masonry trowels.

'So,' she said. 'Never?'

Blondie wouldn't go away. Matson thought someone would have bandaged him or buried him by now. The handyman grew fed up with holding his sibling, and stepped forward to drop the evidence at the feet of authority.

He lay there leaking blood, like a Spartan warrior without the decency of his shield.

She eyed the bruised plums with brutal fascination.

A child appeared. A boy, Matson thought. An irrelevance, whatever it was. It tried to put its hand into the woman's, but she wouldn't take it.

It walked towards Matson.

'Idiot,' called the voice in the house. 'Idiot, come here.'

It was a boy. It toddled on.

A finger-and-thumb made a snap of command, and the child stopped in terror.

'Idiot, come here,' the voice insisted.

The child hurried back inside.

Idiot was not horsewhipped or hanged, though perhaps he wished he had been. Matson could hear him being kissed and fondled. Still protesting, the child was carried closer. An upright figure moved to the door without coming outside. The child was in its arms.

'Well, Hauptmann Matson, we shall know you again.' The English was good enough, the 'Hauptmann' a mark of contempt. Matson didn't know if the 'we' was royal or inclusive.

Matson stepped forward, but was stopped by the chauffeur, with a hand against his chest. 'I wonder if I might come inside and towel off?'

No answer, just the child being kissed aloud.

'This isn't a *gasthaus*,' the woman said. 'There's one across the lake.' She had strange, haunted eyes. Perhaps she hated to hear the child being kissed like this.

10

Matson heard police sirens. Weiss had decided to play it by the book. Matson had asked for the police. He had insisted on police. The chauffeur had consulted his master, and Weiss had instructed him to phone for them. He was almost ashamed to feel relieved.

He got the same two motorcycle patrolmen as for Lolly's first demise. They gazed upon him coldly, like a pair of old strangers. Again they looked like simple traffic reinforcers. Again he concluded they were nothing more, in spite of what he knew of Willi and Albin's surveillance operation. They were competent enough. They had dealt with a murder. This was a much more straightforward case of unlawful parking, trespass, rude roller-skating, attempted drowning, unsuccessful manual strangulation, stamping on a wrestler's foot, and fondling by the balls. It was all in a day's work to them.

They took his particulars for the second time in seventy-two hours and grunted nastily. Leodolter had told him no one in Karnten liked Nazi-hunters, or their friends. He wasn't even an old stranger to them, alas. He was an old enemy, and this time the weather was dry enough for them to look into the matter.

They began by examining Blondie, and didn't like what they could see. Then Blondie was taken away by ambulance to Klagenfurt for a gonad transplant, and that left Matson.

Matson, Auntie Goliath, the woman and a set of hostile witnesses. Auntie Goliath by now smiling nastily, and exhibiting his leg.

'There's the damage to my cheekbone and scalp,' Matson offered.

The old man translated this into German for them, still inside the kitchen or wherever he was, before adding, 'Superficial,' in English. 'He says my fellow did it with a pair of roller-skates.'

72

Roller-skates did not surprise them. Traffic policemen see people being brained by roller-skates every day of the week. What surprised them was that Matson could not produce these roller-skates, had abandoned them to the silence and the waterbirds out there, and thus suppressed evidence.

'I was carrying the injured man,' he protested. 'Some things I could not bring.'

'Roller-skates are deeply material to the case,' the General said, again from the doorway, again in English. He wasn't skulking, Matson realised, merely enjoying himself in private. He seemed to have got rid of the child in some way, got rid of it or kissed it to death.

Roller skates appeared to be the crux of the matter. Either Matson could walk a kilometre to find them and another kilometre to fetch them, and thus demonstrate their existence. Or he could fail to do this and be held guilty of causing them to disappear, which was a theft, or a tampering with a police investigation, or some other foreign act like blowing up motor caravans that would get him into deep trouble.

He sighed, like a Virgilian warrior, cold in his wounds. Inevitable it should be this pair of Austrian cops, he supposed. This was in their same map square, and identical area of mind.

The woman decided to intervene. 'The boy was wearing roller-skates,' she said. 'That I can tell you. There was a difference of opinion, and this Englisher fell into the lake. It is very slippery out there.' She translated for Matson, and said, 'Do you agree this? Do you agree Carl jumped in and saved your life?'

'I certainly wouldn't be here if I hadn't managed to grab his balls – you'll have to supply the word,' he prompted. 'And they were slippery, yes.'

Her expression didn't soften as she translated this.

The General's hoot of derision did nothing to change her mad, stiff-eyed look.

11

The police conferred with the General. Or the General instructed the police. They let him leave. Auntie Goliath hobbled after him to the gate, dragging an angry foot; but even he was under orders to let Matson go. Matson returned his pistol clip, and walked away fast.

As he did so, he tried to assess the morning, but his thoughts came back to the woman. She filled his mind. He didn't know who she was, or what. Or how she fitted into that fortress household. She had spoken of the General as 'father-in-law'. Was the little boy her child, and thus a branch of the Weiss blood-line, and perhaps also marked for trouble?

It would account for her tragic, locked-away expression. Her face had the glow that comes to dark women who stay away from the sun, or give themselves to too much grief.

A pale face, with a shadowy smudge to it. 'A touch of the tarbrush' was no longer possible, even to Matson's Granny, who would have called her 'jet white.' Fancy a Weiss marrying such a woman. He wondered what the General had thought about it. Perhaps all things are white to those who are named so.

He didn't think of her for long. A man was waiting by the Range Rover.

12

Matson approached him carefully. He was even more cautious once he recognised him. The fellow was jarringly out of context. Popo Popovic from the Yugoslav embassy in London.

'What are you doing here, Popo?'

'Watching the underwater wrestling, my dear. Stand me a meal in that inn you're staying at, and perhaps I'll tell you the rest of it. I've brought my own car.'

Matson manoeuvred the Range Rover on to the lane that led towards the *gasthaus* at Bogenfeld.

Leonard had spoken of Lolly running the Balkans from

Berne and London. Popovic must have been keeping an eye on his comings and goings at the London end. Leonard had been told the Yugoslavs didn't know. Clearly he had been told wrong. Popo knew it, or he knew enough. He wanted to be absolutely sure the old wizard was dead. Lunch promised to be interesting.

SEVEN

1

The necessary ingredients for the perfect meal: good food, ample wine, witty talk and two people who didn't trust each other.

Matson came from an oral culture, but his Old Mum had seen to it he used his mouth for listening, so he wasn't as practised as Popo. The latter had spent a dozen years on the embassy cocktail list, laughing at fools in English then lying to pretty women in any language they could listen to.

'Patrick, my dear, you were about to ask me what I am doing here. Let me answer you straight away. I am here to see no harm comes to that Obergruppenführer Weiss when the shitbag crosses my frontier.'

'You're embassy, Popo. How can that be?'

'I'm a soldier, my dear. If I said I wasn't Military Intelligence you'd know it was a fib, but I'm a soldier nonetheless. I can be given a new job whenever the mood takes them back in Belgrade.'

'Why protect a Nazi?'

Popovic had become a whisky snob while he was in England. There are plenty of those in Austria, too, so he was able to indulge in a lengthy tasting session behind the bar before remembering to answer.

'They're everywhere. Even thirty years ago you could point to a hundred breeding pairs. Not just in Croatia and Slovenia. Even in Serbia. They shat on us during the war, then in peacetime they came back to rub it in with their boot.'

He gave Matson a lesser island malt that tasted like cat's widdle.

'Our economy depends on them. The young have no memories, anyway. Especially young communists. It's the young who go to Germany to work.'

'So your old men should teach them better.'

'I'll tell you an odd thing about Weiss, Patrick. Wherever he went there aren't that many old men left around. Not with tongues in their head and their reason intact. What we have among the Southern Slavs is a younger generation without ancestors. That's what we owe to Weiss and the people like him.'

Popo stalked the red-faced *hausfrau* along the bar and demanded food. For Matson, he had a throwaway question he could not quite make casual: 'Do they believe your Gerald Lippiat is dead?'

'The hour is too late for lunch, too early for dinner,' the woman interrupted flatly.

'Then we shall content ourselves with a meal that is neither lunch nor dinner.' He turned back to Matson with a deprecating laugh. 'Do they really think he is dead, my dear?'

The *hausfrau* went grumbling into her kitchen, while her husband laid a table. It was Matson's table of a few days earlier, and its choice was meant to indicate the precariousness of his position.

'You see,' Popo said, sitting noisily, 'they're from the same breed of shitbag as the Obergruppenführer. You still do not answer me, Patrick. What do the Rikers think about Mr Lippiat's death?'

'They believe I killed him, Popo.'

'So he really is dead?'

'I saw his corpse. About half of it. Head blown away. Entrails on fire. Legs detached.' Matson enjoyed the drama of a long swig of wine. It tasted bad after whisky, and even worse after the ice-cold water of the *stausee*. 'I really can't talk about it further. I'm a squeamish man, especially when it comes to the death of friends.'

'Of course, Patrick.'

'I got bloody overcome, let me tell you. So much so, I thought I might slip into Yugoslavia for a week or two. For the rest of my leave. To take my mind off things.'

'You'll be very welcome.' Popovic needed a swig on that

one. 'Very welcome.' A fifteen-second swig. 'I'll let one or two people know you're coming. With your permission. So you'll be spared any embarrassment at the frontier. You won't be getting yourself anywhere near the Obershitbag, will you, my dear?'

'As a matter of fact, I thought I might stay obsessively close to the old villain.'

'And why would you need to do that?'

'He's surrounded by beautiful women – one in particular.'

'Ah, the ice maiden. Ice widow, actually.' Popovic pretended to sound relieved. 'She wears iron petticoats, that one. And her blood is battery acid.'

'I don't intend to drink any.'

'Frau Vincenz Weiss. His daughter-in-law. She calls him "Henk", the monster!'

'Isn't Hendrik a Dutch name?'

'Is it? You're the cosmopolitan, Matson. I'm the Serb. Even Austria is too far north for me.'

Some meat arrived, to sit with the wine, veal in basil and breadcrumbs. Popovic was overcome by the opulence of it. He put his napkin to his mouth and made for the cloakroom.

Matson watched a plate of veal grow cool, then curl like the tongue of an old boot. He'd long since eaten his own.

2

'Constipated?'

'Conscientious. I thought I ought to use a telephone somewhere private.' Popo chewed a little privacy, then said, 'I am happy to tell you your rating with Belgrade is such that you can look forward to a very happy holiday.' His veal was too dry for eating, so he grunted unhappily and went to the bar to pay for their meal. 'So long as poor Gerald is dead,' he reflected.

'Blown to bits, Popo.'

'I'd be unhappy if I thought the least part of him might still be trailing the General. His trigger finger, for instance.'

'Absolutely annihilated, as I say.'

'We had him on fiche, you know. I went through his file.

78

Apparently he was a noted shot. Way above Alpha. Could shoot the eyelashes off a fly at a quarter of a mile. Circumcize spiders. That sort of thing, my dear.'

'Flies don't have eyelashes.'

'Not since God gave that man a rifle.' Popovic buttoned his wallet. 'While you are here, you should try some of their Carinthian savouries.' He drooled his enthusiasm. 'Delicious. There's a cross between a paste and a pâté. You eat it at the end of the meal, on rye bread, to encourage drinking.'

'What's its name?'

'Tell them it's freshwater shrimp. It's a flavoursome beast.'

Freshwater shrimp was cheeky. Popovic had been ignorant enough of Lolly's fate to stand Matson lunch and pump him, then he had made a phone call and learned about the second corpse. Either from the murderer, or from Willi and Albin. Presumably not the former. If he had dealings that way, he wouldn't need to treat with Matson. It had to be Willi and Albin.

So what tidbit had he been able to give them on the telephone, to make it worth their while bringing him up to date?

3

Matson waited until Popo was clear, and then made his dispositions. He idled up to the husband and began to haggle for a more strategically placed bedroom.

'Herr Matson already has the best room in the house,' Frau Red Face chipped in. She scolded so softly she seemed only to whisper. A fat woman with a quiet voice. Her mouth was over-expressive, as if God had fitted her with teeth too small for her face. She put a lot of lip-work into 'best room' and 'already'. She did not expect to be contradicted.

'I need to overlook the lake,' Matson insisted. He beamed at them both in turn, wagging his head like a chicken or a Labour politician. Then he was inspired to excuse himself. 'I am, after all, a fisherman.'

He was given a new room. A suspect in a murder case is treated with respect.

4

Matson's new bedroom overlooked caravan park and lake. Three kilometres away he could glimpse the *stausee*'s narrow shore margin. On it stood the little hamlet of Rosental, and the Nazi's house. He could see these without moving from his seat on the bed. Lippiat had chosen his place well.

Each night, Matson put his glasses on it. It stayed shuttered, like a castle under siege. He watched until dark and ate dinner only when the evening was pitch black, late for the hotel, but that's when he ate it.

'There's the staff to consider,' Red Face and husband said.

'You have a beautiful pair of daughters,' Matson congratulated. His German was up to such asinine poetry. 'But do not think to disturb them. I can grill a schnitzel myself, especially in such a splendid microwave. Chopping a lettuce is second nature to me. And who needs chips?'

Red Face cooked for him. Her husband would have done so if she'd let him, but she didn't. Mein Herr merely served him.

Trade at the *gasthaus* didn't get any brisker because of the notorious guest. There were the usual takers for *steins* of beer, bottles of wine, and – long before Matson ate – baskets of salad and chips. There was no one extra, no one selective. Matson heard no clamour of protest outside, no torchlight procession of masked vigilantes hungry to dip his bottom in a bucket of boiling tar. Protest lives in towns. Carinthia might have a suburban soul, but it lacked houses. 'Watch your back,' Albin had said. It was good advice. It wasn't the place for anything brutal and face-to-face. It reeked of middle-class villainy, orderly, soft-spoken and sly.

Once again, Matson had the feeling he had the whole of twentieth-century European history in this wayside inn. They were mountain people, waterside folk, an old race. They were the heirs of Mozart, of Strauss, of music itself. They were all that was left of the Austro-Hungarian Empire, even though their last princess was dead. They were also the first nation of Europe to let in Nazism as an honoured guest.

Matson drank a bottle of wine each night and stood his host a liqueur as an act of reconciliation. He never alluded to the General across the lake. The innkeeper did not mention Lippiat. The guilty have no history.

Then Matson slept, his alarm always set for four in the morning.

5

On the third morning a packet was waiting for him. The postmark was Klagenfurt, the handwriting unfamiliar.

He carried it to his room and examined it carefully. It felt like a book, one edge concave under pressure, the facing edge convex. He knew no one to send him chocolates, no one to send him socks.

A girlfriend of his had been killed by a parcel bomb intended for him.

He pressured the parcel while he knifed it open.

A harmless picture-book, the illustrations mostly gummed together. Arty jacket. Magyar design, published in Lubliana. He had seen one exactly like it on the table of Lippiat's camping wagon.

The print was not up to the standard of spine and title-page. Nor was the proof-reading. It was in English, but cheaply translated, occasioning errors of the sort encountered all over Europe in select-your-own-language guide-books.

No signature of ownership on the flyleaf, but liberal annotations in pencil throughout the text. The scrawl was markedly different from the writing on the wrapping.

He went downstairs and looked at the visitors' book. Nothing to help him.

'Do you own the caravan park?' he asked the husband.

The husband said he did, and let him look at the register.

Gerald Lippiat had signed for fourteen days in ballpoint pen. The signature looked similar to the fist that had scribbled the annotations, if signatures ever look similar to anything.

The pages weren't water-soiled. Then a man intending to ferry his library in a row-boat could be expected to render it damp-proof. Some of the books must have been found in the

81

boat itself, rather than the corpse's pocket. Willi and Albin had been extremely coy about this.

Matson went back to the room to puzzle over *SS Commanders Against the Southern Slavs*. An authoritative book, however execrable the English translation.

Why had Lolly prepared it, and for whom? It couldn't be his own copy, surely. He was proficient in Serbo-Croat.

There were vertical pencil lines beside the sections that dealt with Weiss and a handwritten note at the top of the first such page: '*This gentlemanliness is the worst thing about the bastard. How can a decent man exist in such a context? He deserves to be –*' The pen dug itself into the page, needing no words.

As Matson leafed on, he decided this badly printed English edition must have been all Lolly could lay his hands on. The book clearly wasn't intended for anyone else's eyes. Lippiat was a man consumed with rage, screaming to himself. An obsessive, in other words.

Fortunate for Weiss that someone had stopped him dead.

6

'Bring them down here,' Weiss commanded. 'They are not cattle. I can't talk to men in a truck.'

He was being inconvenient. He was often inconvenient. He liked to show even the best of his soldiers who was boss.

There were twenty-four men and youths in the big canvas-sided TCV: partisans, townspeople who did not cheer, a boy who had thrown a stone in the vain hope of damaging the track-feed of a tank. It took at least five minutes to unshackle them, and kick, prod, curse them down. Seven were so badly injured they had to be lowered or thrown.

Weiss waited patiently until they were grouped about him, then examined their faces one by one. Some were sullen, one or two strangely exultant. All of them were defiant. Several of them could not even be bothered to open their eyes and return his gaze. One man was held up between two of his friends, clearly dying. This three were in some kind of uniform, part cetnik, *part Yugoslav Royal Army.*

Weiss straightened a tunic, indicated an unfastened collar clip, and stood back while an SS trooper hurried forward to fasten it.

The dying man bled from a wound below his left collar-bone. Weiss, otherwise immaculate, was wearing a long white scarf as befitted a panzer leader. He took it off and padded the man's dressing with it.

The man opened his eyes and nodded to him.

'Tell them I respect them,' Weiss insisted. 'Respect them and salute their bravery, if not their sense of military propriety.'

The Croatian interpreter fumbled 'military propriety'. He lost it among positive and negatives.

'Tell them I am sorry to have to hang them. Tell them further I regret that the only instruments at my disposal are the back of this lorry and the municipal lamp-posts. Consequently I cannot drop them far enough to be certain of breaking their necks. A German officer is expected to be resourceful, but the equation in this case is rendered even more difficult by the necessity to suspend them with their heels well above head height, lest their relatives or other interested parties try to steal them, occasioning yet more public hangings.'

The Croatian took some time with this, finishing by saying, 'Your bodies are the property of the Third Reich.'

'Everything belongs to the Reich.' Weiss corrected. 'Your bodies are the immediate property of the SS. Because we have only the one lorry at the disposal of this detail, we shall be forced to hang you one at the time, twelve as we go up this side of the road, twelve as we return. I congratulate the Serbian townsfolk of Belgrade, and in particular the city architects, for their foresighted provision of double-headed lamp standards.'

One of the soldiers spat.

'That's most unmilitary behaviour,' Weiss said. 'Hang him last. I was going to hang the priest last, but this lout's behaviour has forfeited him even the most minimal benefit of clergy.' He beckoned towards a Serbian Orthodox

priest, in chains like the rest of them. 'I'll hang the boy first,' he explained, 'then the dying soldier. You'll need to comfort the boy, father.'

When the Croatian had finished speaking he said, 'I'm going to give the priest a lot of licence, up and down here with the crowds at his back. When he escapes, I want him followed. Pass the word to some of your people to kill whoever he reports himself to.'

'How can you be sure he'll make off? He's a priest.'

'He's the only free man in a nightmare. Sooner or later he'll wake up and realize the dream need not be his own.'

This was the first series of public executions in the Terazija in Belgrade. Soon afterwards, Weiss was injured and relinquished command of his battalion in the Second Division SS. He recuperated in Graz, then went to Romania to train a brigade of the recently constituted Freiwilligen Gebirgs Division Prinz Eugen. *It was in this capacity that he returned with renewed vigour to the war against the partisans.*

7

The day passed. Matson read about Weiss in the thick book he had been sent. Once or twice he nodded off to sleep, sickened by the sheer bloody nastiness of the Balkan campaign. Gerald Lippiat's graffiti started calmly enough. *All in God's time* was the comment at the end of the Belgrade chapter. Later this progressed to *Bullets are too gentle* followed by quotations from the Serbian: *Hang his feet in hot wire* and *May crows eat his face.*

The book's tone had obviously upset Lolly. Was this because its authors sought to mark Weiss out from the common order of butcher? His atrocities were plain for all to see, they implied. Yet he was also a hard-hitting four-square soldier. He treated the condemned with respect. He had a special way with women. He deplored the excesses of the Ustaza, and of his own people even more – especially the *Freiwilligen Division Handschar der SS.*

What really got up Lolly's nose was this assumption that

gentility could reside in a man who lacked gentleness.

At the end of the book there was a chapter which haunted Matson's dreams. Inside the back cover, Lolly had written *'There is a ritual in such a case. The Ustaza use it. First you rape the woman. Then you kill the child. Then you blind the man to lock him in with his memories. Then you burst his eardrums so he can hear no word of comfort, nor his woman's voice ever again.'*

None of this read any better for coming from the pen of a murdered colleague. Nor for not knowing who had sent it to him.

Albin, Willi and Kaub had some of the missing reading material, but why forward it incognito? Difficult to envisage Kaub parting with evidence of identity so soon after a murder.

This left Matson with the killers themselves, and a distinctly chilly feeling.

8

He always woke heavy in the *gasthaus* at Bogenfeld. The night presses oddly on water, and these nights were mountain nights, full of dampness and Lolly Lippiat. There was no frost, no moon, no stars, no clarity.

This morning it was fog and bad breath. He swigged bottled water and poked his binoculars into the twilight. He sat knees up in bed, shivering with the window raised and the shutters open.

His glasses weren't night optics. There's no such thing as a mist optic, unless you count radar and infra-red. But fifty square centimetres of object lens collects a lot more light than the human eye. There's always a chance.

Don't look into mire, his training said. *Your brain isn't up to it. Focus it away.* He focused.

Germans start early. They are the sleep-breakers in every European hotel, on every continental camp site. They invented 'tank light'.

He could see the top of a grey car in the courtyard, the apex of high garage doors shuttered behind it. It looked like the Mercedes. Whatever it was, it had been fitted with a roof box, itself made taller by matching grey cases. The greyness was his brain colour. Matson remembered silver grey, but everything was grey, grey without silver, then greyer again as the cases piled up and the mist welled in.

He got out of bed and phoned downstairs.

No answer.

He dressed in the clammy darkness, and threw his few unpacked belongings into a bag.

Then he tried again with his binoculars. The *gasthaus* was high, but so was the Weiss outer wall. Luckily, the mist rolled to one side, carried beyond the hamlet of Rosental and over the *stausee*'s lip of tumbling water.

At three kilometres the extra five minutes didn't get much light enhancement. But the magnification brought him fog at one hundred and fifty yards. He could spot the heads of two men, and two women. One of the men and one of the women were unknown to him. The General and his daughter-in-law were to be guessed at rather than recognised.

Who were the others? The chauffeur and a governess for the child? Matson couldn't see the child. He was probably asleep in the back of the car. A young man and a young woman. She moved like a young woman. A governess for the child? A nurse for the General? A mistress, sometimes called a companion?

The husband met him on the stairs, but it was the wife's voice that barred his way. 'Won't Herr Kammel –?'

'Yes,' he agreed. 'Willibald will probably get the hump.' He threw money, too much of it, on the bar. 'Keep my room for three weeks.' The firm would have to pay.

He ran outside, tossed his kit into the Range Rover and started up.

He drove fast. Unless he was very much mistaken, the Mercedes had the legs of him. The General had a five or six kilometre advantage of him by road, and the German who can drive slowly has not been invented.

EIGHT

1

To rush towards Rosental was daft. He would lose the Mercedes in the maze of roads at the back of the lake. He had to assume Weiss would make directly for the frontier, and position himself accordingly.

East of Klagenfurt there were some half dozen crossing-points. Some of them were on minor roads that would certainly be closed by snow this early in the year. The nearer ones were mountainous and unlikely to be clear, and it seemed unreasonable that Weiss would want to detour too far.

South of Klagenfurt was the Loibl. Matson had walked his bicycle over the pass when he was a teenager, and it had been steep and badly worn at the top – closed by ice between November and early summer, he remembered. His maps didn't date it, but there was now a tunnel. In theory it should be open.

Matson could get on to Loibl easily, firstly by main road and then by autobahn as far as Klagenfurt. Somehow, he doubted if Weiss was the kind of man to double back on himself just to get a better road. He knew from his home-work that there was a back road of sorts via Rosegg, St Jakob and Ferlach. The Range Rover had a better chance than the Mercedes of staying on it. He ignored Rosental and drove directly for Rosegg.

This was a mistake. The road was misty, hump-backed and slippery. The Mercedes had not come by this route. No other car had been ahead of him to leave wheel marks in the moisture.

At St Jakob things were better. He joined the properly

metalled lane for Ferlach, running west to east. It was higher and white with frost. There were tyre marks. He couldn't tell if they belonged to Weiss. He wasn't Sherlock Holmes. The mist rolled away, or perhaps it was cloud. He was climbing steeply. Dawn broke properly, but there was still no sun. There were high mountains over the road, and he could feel the chill of them even with the heater on full.

Before Ferlach he hit the main road running south from Klagenfurt to Ljubljana in Yugoslavia. Light snow began to fall from a clear blue sky. Perhaps it was ice-dust blowing in from the frosty altitude of Triglav. Perhaps his brain was freezing.

He passed Deutscher Peter and the road sign that says 15%. One in seven. He put the Range Rover into four-wheel drive. Between the tiny hamlets of Loibital and Raidenwirt the signs averaged seventeen per cent, and he came to a double hairpin bend that looked more like twenty five. The world was glazed with ice or built from mirrors. He stopped to put chains on the tyres and wondered just why he was doing this.

In four-wheel drive and with his snow chains chiming like a medieval belfry, he roared up to the Loibltunnel.

Slowing for the last bend, he was forced to hit the brakes hard. A jack-booted ghost was in the centre of the carriageway and striding straight towards him.

Bad weather frayed the road. He lost the outside wheels in a camber of snow and was drawn down a rut of chippings. As he went, he saw the belt, the peaked hat, the sleek SS walking-out uniform, and heard the clang of fists on metal. Weiss's chauffeur lurched in front of him, then punched himself away from the sliding Range Rover with gloved hands. The bonnet thumped against road-works or piled snow, then slewed back on to the road in a dead stop.

Matson spun round in his seat. The young man had been walking blind, his face clotted with shock or some other dazing emotion. Now he swore at Matson, swore or shouted something, and went stumbling away downhill.

Matson got out and inspected the vehicle for damage. The English racing green was scabbed around the grill, and pitted with lumps of frost he thought it prudent to leave in place.

No flat tyres, no blood. He kicked his shoes free of snow, and restarted.

Beyond the near hump of road was a frieze of crags and ice, pierced by the black hole of the tunnel. The tunnel mouth was dark. No time to reflect on unlit mountain tunnels. The silver grey Mercedes was parked here. A lowered frontier gate barred its way through the Loibl.

The car was an odd sight, unbalanced and snail-like under its huge stack of roof luggage. The rear suspension was depressed, and looked lopsided, hardly the best preparation for rough or slippery roads.

A man, two women, and a child were standing by it. Matson drove forward slowly, and wound down his window. The child was as before expressionless, the two women bone-faced with fear. The man sipped reflectively at a pocket flask, but not as if in need of Dutch courage.

Matson came properly face to face with Weiss for the first time. He didn't look like a man who would skulk in a back kitchen. 'Ah, Hauptmann,' he said. 'I have had to get rid of my chauffeur. As you can see, the tunnel is closed.' He ushered the two women into the back of the Mercedes, then sat himself beside the little boy on the front seat. 'You won't be following any further, I think.'

He started the engine and snaked up an almost invisible track towards the top of the mountain.

2

Matson found himself unable to follow. Weiss's two adult passengers were terrified out of their wits at the thought of going over the Loibl summit. His chauffeur had refused to drive him. The chauffeur and the two women had the saner instinct. Weiss was obviously quite mad. As Popo had said, 'The shitbag has the death wish on him.'

Matson had met it before. Young leaders in the Thugs who wanted to redeem themselves by pushing other people's lives a long way too far. It was unforgivable enough in the young. In the old, it was obscene.

Matson watched the Mercedes race for the first hump of

ice, become briefly airborne, slew sideways, then disappear in a plume of snow flakes. He heard over-revved engine, tyres sliding, the wail of brakes or of wind, then just wind. He listened to the mountain wind until it became its own form of silence. Once he heard gears in it. Frozen water continued to fall.

He climbed back into the Range Rover, to think. Folly strikes hard on a frosty mountainside at five in the morning.

He had tried to follow Weiss to satisfy a whim. Leonard had asked him to, but it was a request of even less credibility than the one that had brought him out here in the first place. It was based on outdated information. If he'd wired home about the second corpse, Leonard would almost certainly have told him to continue with his holiday.

Weiss was interesting to the department only while Lolly was alive. If Lolly put a bullet through him, that was mintable information. If anyone else killed him, it was news and then history.

Strictly speaking, Lolly was nothing to do with the department either. Leonard was watching his own back, curious to know what games were being played. As with most intelligence work, he could discover more by sitting with the newspapers in his club than by sending an operative out into the hills.

Matson wasn't an operative, an agent. He was a desk officer. He didn't like his desk, true. What he liked was holiday. He let the Range Rover roll backwards on to the road, then turned it in a half-circle towards Klagenfurt.

3

Only as a prelude to being entirely stupid. He needed to take the upward ice on the burst. He completed his circle, revved the engine, looked at the sealed-off tunnel, then the track that rose over and beyond it like a piece of frozen water sculpture. He looked and nearly shat himself, then lined the bonnet square on the first bank.

The map suggested a tiny settlement up there – whether of

90

restaurant, rest huts or hospice he couldn't tell. Probably a cemetery for trolls.

Still no sun. The moon in a daylight sky. It was round and full and mad. It either shone through the mountains or was reflected in the latticework of ice.

Crags this side, said the hachures on the map. Crag beyond, said the cartographer's sketchy crinkle of track. The track wasn't drawn: it was suggested. Broad enough, perhaps, for a skeleton on horseback, or a fair-weather girl and a hot-blooded man in a size nine boot.

Weiss had gone that way, Weiss and the child and the two petrified women. But Weiss was one of the living dead, and the rest were probably dead dead by now.

The moon was on the frozen waterfall of track. He checked the four-wheel drive, took the handbrake off, and belted towards lunacy.

4

Beyond the bank came a bend. He took damage on that bend, stuck on the next one, took more damage sheering free. Then it was left and right, one wheel always in air, sometimes nothing touching anything, then piling straight into space into rock, the engine howling like a brain storm. He clenched his backside and kicked the bugger onwards.

The map showed a zigzag, a ladder of hairpins. Matson spun and continued to spin, turning right. Steering went witless. He hit his head, shedding bits of brain, or bits of the Range Rover. It guided itself, then what was left of itself, choosing mostly upwards. He flew it by the bones of his arse.

A flat world of nothing. If this was the top, where were the buildings? He saw a petrified face in a frosted wall. The car went blind. It hit the plume of vapour at the head of the pass, sheeting its screen and offside windows with ice. The nearside stayed clear.

He came off the accelerator on to the brakes, and spun sideways over the far lip of crag in uncheckable slow motion: the edge came slowly, the way accidents do when you get the chance to enjoy them.

91

As he hung on the top of the Loibl with Yugoslavia before him and Slovenia a thousand metres beneath, he saw the Mercedes way down below him through a slivered chink of window. Not so much the car as its roof, with its rack slewed awry.

If Obergruppenführer Weiss had crashed there, its occupants would obviously be dead.

Matson had missed the track, but he tumbled ten feet on to it, sidewinding through a cornice of snow that slowed him just enough.

He felt no relief, not even thankfulness. He was too numb in the gut. In a while he would inspect the Range Rover, then try to make his way down to the mess in the Mercedes, God being willing.

The windows were granulated with frozen water drops. Obviously he was resting on the wrong side of the weather, but rest he must. He came off the brakes, engaged bottom gear, applied the handbrake, turned off the engine.

The Range Rover didn't notice. The Range Rover had an identity crisis. The Range Rover thought it was a toboggan. Its four wheels just wouldn't bite. It slid down the steepening track over bumpy ripples of ice. No good Matson trying to prevent it, his master was calling him down.

5

Gravity, as they say, always comes out on top. Matson was a parachutist and knew such things. If he didn't want to go the same brainless way as Newton's apple, he must exercise choice. Fast. Before he slid off an edge.

He punched at the screen. The glass wouldn't break. His fist was in awe of his employers. Zebrazone was too good for it.

He triggered down the windows. The electrics flourished, even inside an icicle. He flicked into second gear, made peace with the ignition, then jammed his hands on the wheel. He daren't ever let go again.

Now the Range Rover rolled free, he could steer it. He peered both ways of the screen in hopes he might steer it enough. He needed elastic eyes and a rubber neck.

Still on the track. The Range Rover was attracted to tracks. What there was of this one was too narrow for it, too crooked, and much too slippery, but the Range Rover was on it.

Matson kept his bum on the uphill side, at each twist in direction making a change of seat. The uphill wheels were mostly on ice, the downhill wheels were often on space. Mountains are like that – plenty of ice, even more space, the former abysmal but infinitely preferable to the latter.

The first two hundred metres were the worst. The first two hundred metres down, that is. He didn't know whether he moved two hundred metres forward while he went two hundred metres down, or no metres forward at all. He might even have been on a negative graph. All he knew was the curve was down. Down was what he knew. Down was slabs of rock, scree, stone fingers, ice-sentinels, razor-sharp jags of injury, vehicle wreck, death. Newton chose to be kind to him. Newton already had his apple.

At some point, with the engine overheating, the demister roasting upwards, the screen moulted and unfogged. He could see straight ahead.

Life became easy. He rejoined the metalled road beyond the tunnel. He was in Yugoslavia, and only God had stamped his passport.

Here was the steep side. Up had been easy. The metalled road had taken a bashing from the weather – perhaps it was weather that closed the tunnel. Even here, on the decent metalling, he came to a gradient board that said 20%.

He saw the Mercedes. Weiss, poor sod, had been in a car ill-equipped for this sort of thing.

A split-second glimpse is like a photograph. When he had seen Weiss's car from above it had been the right way up, battered, on its belly, but undoubtedly bent. It appeared to have fallen from a great height. Great height being the only visual certainty, great height being in abundance.

Bent or not, it was now on the move. Lower down the hill, it was true, but on the decent road and moving fast.

Whatever the state of his roof and roof-box, the Obergruppenführer was alive and confident enough of leaf-spring, shock-absorber, geometry and half-shaft to have his hoof down hard.

6

Ten kilometres along the main road south towards Ljubljana there was a garage. There had been other garages, but this one was open.

Matson didn't need petrol. He needed comfort. There was a kind of roadhouse hard by, part bar, part restaurant, built in the same girder and cinder-block architecture as the garage, this in a valley of green slopes and sunken fields, a landscape where men could dig stone.

The Mercedes was parked on the garage forecourt. It had been positioned to gain the best shade and cause the maximum inconvenience once the sun was high.

Matson could see the General, and the General could see him. He was prominent at the road-house window, keeping an eye on his car and sipping from a red plastic beaker.

Matson parked between the Mercedes and the window, right in the General's line of sight. He liked to think of himself as an honest man, open and direct. Such a man can permit himself any number of tiny acts of sheer cussedness.

His watch said seven a.m.

He inspected the Mercedes. The roof box had been re-fastened. The rest looked relatively unscathed – nothing that a couple of hours with a good panel-beater couldn't sort out. His Range Rover was in worse shape. It would need a long weekend of mechanical attention from a lot of rugged equipment.

Inside, the General was the only customer. The ladies were somewhere else, comforting the child or powdering their morale.

Weiss greeted him exuberantly. 'Mine was the greater feat, I think.'

'You frightened more people than I did, General, I grant you that.' Matson went to the bar and ordered a glass of tea and a tumbler of slivovitz. He sipped moodily at both until his blood felt alert enough to catch up with some of his heart-

94

beats, then added, 'I was mad to follow you.'

'Then you mustn't think of doing so any longer. Let me tell you where I am going.'

A door opened at the window end of the wall behind him. The child was pushed out first. The two women followed. They sat together at the table while the General stood above them, watching them drink what he had ordered for them. It looked like cold coffee.

Matson burrowed his nose into slivovitz and tried not to breathe.

'I shall be stopping here,' said the General's voice at his elbow, 'at Kocevje Gora. For one night only.'

Matson turned to find Weiss thumbnailing a cloth-backed Halweg road-map.

'The place has memories for me.'

'It's off the main road.' Matson tried to keep his voice neutral, but his disbelief was obvious. 'Way off.'

'My memories mostly are. I engraved them before the roads in these parts were even thought of. Were you a proper soldier, Hauptmann, you would know that battles very rarely confine themselves to the autobahn.' Weiss folded his map. 'I tell you this, because I intend to motor fast.' He clicked his fingers. Matson had heard him call the boy like this a day or two earlier.

The two women left their coffee and followed him through the door. The Loibl summit had scared the fight out of them.

Matson watched what he could of them. They were both of an age, a year or two either side of thirty, the daughter-in-law aloof but with a kind of amber glitter, as skinny as a sergeant major's pace-stick; the other woman fuller, pinker, more obviously sexy. They trailed an after-breeze of alcohol. At least one of them had been drinking out there in the cloakroom.

Who was he to censure such a thing? He downed the rest of his slivovitz, paid over-generously with Austrian money, and hurried outside.

The Mercedes was no longer there, but he doubted if it would double back on itself.

Two minutes later, say two miles later, Matson saw the man in the tree.

No, not quite that. Perception is never so simple. What he saw was a kind of giant stare's nest made of broken branches and a green and white travelling rug. The man was in the nest. The imaginary bird had flown. The man was broken because the tree was broken. They had done awful things to each other. The tree was all of thirty yards from the road.

The man's car was unrecognisable, except to men familiar with undersides. It lay deep in the roadside ditch, all those yards from the tree and its back wheels were spinning fiercely. Its engine went boring on. Its exhaust gusted happily. There would be petrol spilling in there, and a lot of trapped vapour. Sooner or later it would burn.

Matson stopped to digest this. Where, for example, were the other occupants of the car?

'A figure of eight slide,' the voice boomed. 'A full figure of eight slide followed by a double somersault.'

Matson had heard Weiss mouthing from dark places before, but it came as a shock to see him emerge from beneath the broken branches, skirt a bush or two and join Matson on the roadside. Was this the Mercedes upside down in the ditch? Surely not.

'I correct myself.' Weiss gazed on the sunlit underbelly. 'One and a half somersaults.' He spoke with total enthusiasm, like a man who's seen miracles.

'Anyone in the car?'

'A broken neck or a broken back. He agrees he's lucky to be alive. I had the boy go up and put a rug on him. An American, the lad thinks. Sense of humour, too. A man needs a sense of humour to try and force me from the road. Or from anything else, once I'm committed.' He gazed about him, as if checking the sunshine for honesty. 'I thought he was trying to kill me, but nothing else followed. We are quite alone here.'

The old man's conversation was best for its silences. In the first silence, Matson heard the daughter-in-law's voice. She spoke in her sharp English, comforting the injured man in the tree. Battery acid? No. Then she spoke in German, in a voice softer than consolation.

The child sat among the branches, huddled like a tiny bird taking love from its mother.

'She's your son's wife?'

'My son's, yes.' Weiss smiled. 'Women have to belong to someone.'

'And the boy is –'

'Her son, yes.'

'You must be very proud.'

'More than you can possibly know or I can possibly express.'

Another silence fell, broken only when Matson said, 'Your English is exceptionally fluent.'

'So is yours.'

'I'm Irish,' Matson said. 'As a race we do well with foreign languages.'

'I learned my English among Irishmen – the Irish Guards to be exact.'

'Were you on a liaison posting?'

'No.'

'A secondment, then?' Matson was determined to pull some of his arrogance down.

'A secondment from life. I was their prisoner.'

'I had thought perhaps your contact with them was the result of some NATO –'

'I am not a member of NATO. Germany is: I am not. I do not choose to serve with people whose arses I have kicked.'

'We kicked yours.'

'In the end, yes. After we'd spent four years teaching you how to soldier, and we'd run out of boots.'

'How did you come to be captured by the Irish Guards?'

'Because I chose them. The Americans had lost their military manners by then. The Russians would have hanged me. The Russians have good military manners, contrary to general opinion, but they would have hanged me. The Irish Guards were an anomaly with which I could be comfortable.'

'Will your son be joining us?'

'Not unless he can obtain an extraordinary leave of absence.'

'He's on special service?'

'He's dead. He was killed out here – assassinated – in Serbia seven years ago. I was with him. So was my daughter-in-law.'

'I'm sorry.'

'Sorry for what? Sorry they don't like us? It's our destiny not to be liked.'

'Sorry your son should have been with you and that he should have been killed.'

'If it hadn't been him it would have been me. The bullet was meant for me. He served his purpose. I brought him here to show him what I had done and let him see some of the places I had done it in. He was a NATO apparatchik. I brought him here to brace him up. He was on his honeymoon.'

'You brought them here on their honeymoon?'

'He had things to learn. His honeymoon fell on an important anniversary of mine.'

'Poor girl.'

'She had less to learn. Or perhaps women learn more quickly.'

'Now there's the boy to consider.'

'He has been considered, believe me, Captain Matson.'

'Not Captain. I've left the Army.'

'So have I. I have my sources of information, just the same. I know, therefore, that you are a British Intelligence officer. What I need to know is why you were ordered to attach yourself to me.'

Matson cleared his throat. The capsized car answered for him. The air above it shivered, brittle with heat. A blue spark of flame danced briefly above the sump, then sparked along the driving shaft.

Matson collared the General, and dumped him on the seat of his trousers. The ditch flooded with fire, then extinguished itself in a great huff of deafness as the tank below out. He heard a woman scream, but a long way off. The flames nibbled back again and everything burned properly, sump, spillage, tyres. One wheel still spun, and its half-shaft kept time with it.

Weiss found his feet sooner than Matson. 'There's nobody

98

in the car,' he said. He was dazed into remembering an earlier question. 'I would never, not even in those bad days, fry a man's wife because her husband was a fool.'

The vegetation took fire.

'Lucky the wind is this way,' Weiss said.

'Lucky for the injured man.'

'I was thinking of my travelling rug.' He spoke of those bad days as if they were none of his doing. He left the women and the boy to make their own way over to him.

8

The black plume of burning brought a police patrol, who radioed for an ambulance.

Weiss's car was several hundred metres ahead, and he made it clear he intended to return to it at once.

Again the snap of fingers, the hurrying in of family like so many well-trained dogs. The General's treatment of his household was too calculated to impress Matson. He was too much the studied stereotype of the populist cliché. Most of the Nazi bully-boys had been uxorious, woman-dominated indecisives. They were mummy's darlings.

Not Weiss. Or not now. Perhaps like many another old man he was attempting to live up to a past he never had.

Matson wished he hadn't let his wits lose themselves.

'My name is Obergruppenführer Weiss.'

A patrolman had tried to detain the General for questioning.

'You will doubtless have heard of me. If you haven't, ask your grandmother. If you hinder me in any way, it will be contrary to the wish of your central government.' He spoke in German, insistent that policemen in Slovenia should know the language.

Later, he produced a card and said in English, 'Give this to the fellow in the tree.' He was speaking for the injured man, and perhaps for Matson. 'His thanks can be sent on to me at either of those two addresses. The one here in Yugoslavia is likely to find me for some time. I wish him good luck.'

The patrolman looked at the card and at the man in the tree. He hadn't understood a word, but others had heard for him.

The General now indicated Matson. 'This man has entered your country illegally. You must proceed with him as you think fit. That concludes my advice to you.'

The patrolman understood enough German to look extremely earnest at this.

Weiss switched languages again: 'Only my little joke, Hauptmann. I've told you where to find me tonight. If they ever let you go.'

NINE

1

'You poor bugger. "Bugger", from me, is a term of affection. I'll call you "shitbag" when you start getting up my nose.'

'Three hours, Popo.'

'That's how long it took me. You can't expect the police to allow a dangerous fellow off the hook in a place like this. You might steal a tree.' He whistled, but not in admiration of Matson. 'So he came by Loibl summit. He must have a death-wish on him, as I say. Yourself is merely mad.'

'The new route was closed.'

'I ordered it closed. The partisans were partial to tunnels, and some of the old gang might think Loibltunnel particularly appropriate. Blast him out of Yugoslavia entire.'

'He's returned before.'

'Yes, and been shot at before.'

'You didn't tell me his son was killed down here.'

'I can't think to mention everything, my dear. Besides, you're the expert on the Obershitbag now. He refused to meet me in Rosental – something else I didn't pass on.' Popo tugged at his tunic. 'Now he's on my side of the fence. He'll meet me whenever I require him to.' He coughed. The soil seeped smoke. The car chassis – still in the ditch – was stripped and twisted. The tiny roadside plantation was reduced to half an acre of char. 'Like a tank action,' he sputtered. He included the dents in the Range Rover. 'You can have your vehicle back. It's a mess. You should buy a Yugo.'

'Ta.'

'My fellows have searched it, of course. Three toothbrushes. No guns. No condoms.'

'I'm Catholic, Popo.'

'You're Irish, too. No fucking teeth. Well, you had best be on your way before I change my mind.'

'Cold trail now. Three hours cold, you old sod.'

'He sleeps at Kocevje Gora tonight. By arrangement. Or didn't he confide his travel plans?'

'He did, but why Kocevje Gora?'

'He killed a couple of villages near there.'

'Villagers?'

'Villages.'

'There are no villages near there, not on my map.'

'That's because your map understands Balkan history, my dear.'

2

Yugoslavia has roads meant for tourists, and roads meant for people. Twenty kilometres beyond Ljubljana, Matson's route branched along one of the latter. It confirmed what he'd long suspected about inland Yugoslavia: people don't use roads.

There were bad bits and worse bits.

The bad bits were the ones the engineers hadn't needed to touch: soft, dry dirt, or a decent streambed patched with rubble. The worse bits were macadamised. Sometimes the amalgam was fissured with cracks wide enough to screw a wheel. Often it was cratered with holes that could swallow a tractor or minibus.

Worse became worst.

The tarmac had been poured straight onto the landscape, and the landscape was rocky. All along the gulched-out valley bottoms it was. In places the surface had shrunk like a geriatric's gums. The teeth that poked through were as tall as tank traps.

Matson spent half the journey out front, carrying his own red flag. He would race ahead at five miles an hour for twenty or thirty seconds, then spend an age of anxiety levering with branch and crowbar at boulders as bloody-minded as his Mum's gas-cooker.

On one he used the winch. It lay there like a legless grand piano, blocking and dividing the road. When he set the gear, the thing didn't budge. The Range Rover slithered towards it instead. Then the rock moved a little, and he unhooked and inched past.

Weiss hadn't come this way. Not with a sagging axle and a dromedary on his roof. Either the General had lied to Matson, and to Popo as well, or his memory had suggested a better route in.

Night was a long way off. Up there in the bright sunshine above the deepening hills it was. Down here the shade was turning to twilight; and, as he drove even more slowly because of this, he came into a place of desolation. The vegetation dried, and the knuckled hills stood high and spare. They were built from that make of karst that looks like a natty pin-stripe in the sunshine and glimmers a romantic silver by the light of a lovers' moon. With the shadow on it, it was invisible as glass, edging into the road.

He switched his headlights on. To be lost was unthinkable. Mountains might move, maps be in error, but Matson was never lost.

The road blundered into flatter country, the sun only halfway set, its rays dusty with flies.

He heard voices above the slow turn and crackle of the tyres. Beside the sun, nearer and momentarily bigger, flame leapt and died back in a gust of sparks. A fire burned inside a tumbledown building. Flesh, aromatics, berries were roasting or burning.

To hell with poetry. The Mercedes was parked there, neat under an unladen roof-box. It had come from the opposite direction. This ruin must be what was left of the road-house at Kocevje Gora. Of the town or village itself, he could see no sign.

Balkan geography was like Balkan history, subject to alteration.

3

Matson's was only the second car. How come there were so many voices?

He stretched his legs for a minute or two, then pushed on

an iron courtyard gate and went inside. As he did so, a third vehicle arrived and someone slammed out of it in a hurry.

Matson saw war-damaged masonry shored up with rubble from the surrounding karst. The masonry was ancient, probably Roman; but Hitler's war, the General's war, was the one that had damaged it. The result was a flagged court-yard with holes in the enclosing walls – holes with inadequate doors. One of the holes had a fire in it, a furnace in a cavern. He smelled woodsmoke and dripping meat. A youth in an apron stirred the fire with a ten-foot fork of iron. That was why it gouted so hugely just now.

A man came though the gateway, pushing past Matson and among empty tables. He shouted for a room. The youth shook his head. The holes were full. The man pointed at an empty table. The youth leant a chair against it. The empty tables were taken.

The man stormed out, elegant in his town suit. His car started with a great revving of anger, sped towards the valley Matson had come from, then braked dramatically. It went grinding into the outer darkness in bottom gear and spent an eternity crawling away.

Matson asked for a tumbler of wine and stood drinking it by the kitchen corner.

Weiss and the boy came out from one of the courtyard rooms. They spent a long time choosing a table. The old man wanted the fresh air. The child wanted the fire. The fire won, and the General began to cough. Then he saw Matson. 'We got the last beds, I'm afraid.'

'It's the time of year,' Matson agreed. He kept his scep-ticism ajar.

The daughter-in-law appeared, moving across paving and straw as if this was the most natural place in the world for her to be. She wore a white halter-neck dress. It was already flecked with soot, and she found the soot acceptable too. She accepted everything with the calmness of the truly mad.

The other young woman joined them. She was in sensible black, and did not seem at ease in this place. That made her normal.

The General approved of both his women equally.

The rest of the tables filled up. They filled up table by

104

table in fours, and the men that filled them came in from outside, entering like the chorus in an opera. They did not acknowledge one another and they did not acknowledge the General, but Weiss was the reason they were here. They needed him so much that they could not bear to watch him. They averted their gaze, like a hanging jury, and they sat silent.

Behind Matson, the kitchen bulged with voices. This was the sound he had heard from the car.

He watched an older man, he thought the innkeeper, serve the General with cheese and sausage, and the two women help themselves to salad by way of hors d'oeuvres. The boy ate nothing. He twisted bread into little cylinders, then rolled them off the table.

The General cursed roundly in German. He was not rebuking his grandson, he was demanding a clean table cloth.

The owner served him, in German.

His daughter-in-law sat looking ahead, her mind elsewhere. The boy called for more bread. The other woman noticed Matson watching, and went on noticing him. She said something to the General. He favoured Matson with a look. Always the daughter sat still, seeing nothing. She sat like a beautiful madwoman, like a heroine who has experienced one catastrophe and expects another.

The General spoke aloud, not loudly, but aloud, again in German, and everyone in the courtyard stood up. It was only when they stood that Matson realized what was odd about the gathering. There were no women among them. The General had the only women, and his daughter-in-law had been quite enough woman to take all of Matson's attention.

So the General and his two women sat, and the men stood around him and waited. They waited, it seemed to Matson, like men who were expecting to leave. But they didn't leave.

The daughter-in-law waited for her catastrophe.

The General made a gesture, of right hand to heart, or to the opening of his shirt. Matson couldn't see exactly what he did, because the child's head was in the way. Weiss moved without fuss, and a gun lay on the table in front of him.

The child rolled bread towards it, and the General

105

reproved the boy's hand by striking it with the back of his fork.

A Luger Parabellum. Surely Weiss could do better for himself than an ancient Wehrmacht pistol?

Matson sipped his wine and enjoyed the crassness of the evening. The inn was well off the touring routes, true; but this was still holiday Europe. A man does not usually equip himself with a hand-gun before sitting down to sausage and salad.

Unless he is a former SS officer from Seventh Division Prinz Eugen in a place that has memories for him.

As if to emphasize this, the standing men scraped their chairs on the flagstones.

Matson sensed a rehearsed timetable going awry. The men did not leave, nor did they do whatever they had planned to do – strangle the General or burst into folk song.

He had been a spectator for too long. He took his tumbler of wine and pushed among them to sit at one of the tables they no longer occupied. They fidgeted against him, angrily.

A woman came out from the kitchen to turn his cloth. She reclipped it to the edges of the table and laid a clean place mat. No woman had served at the General's table, nor – until now – at the men's.

As Matson tried to order, the General called her over. He called in German, then in Serbo-Croat when she refused to understand. When she at last approached him, he reverted to German. He reached out and gathered her close to the table by pushing the flat of his hand to the small of her back.

She was a plumpish woman, handsome, perhaps forty years old. She might well be related to one of the standing men, and almost certainly to someone in the kitchen. The General was sitting with the women of his own family, and with his little grandson; yet he mocked her, flirtingly, in his slow, condescending German, and let his left hand slide lower to take hold of her backside. He squeezed the flesh between finger and thumb, as if he were testing a heifer or greyhound for firmness of the skin. Still the caressing German. In case the point was too subtle to be taken, he reached up with his right hand and felt the front of her blouse, then pushed her away and told her sharply to fetch

106

her man. Matson's German was up to that, if not the rest, however slowly spoken.

She turned away, her cheeks red with anger. He had not groped her breast; he had not dignified her sex by perpetrating any kind of assault. He had simply involved her in his idleness, and found her wanting.

In the charged circumstances it showed an arrogance that went beyond the foolhardy. Weiss was being what he was, he was enjoying it and daring anyone to stop him.

Then the rat appeared. He appeared in the kitchen doorway and savoured his moment by brushing his front paws on his whiskers.

He did not like what he smelled, who he ate with, where he was. He crept anxiously forward to sniff at the ground where Matson had stood, and Matson saw why the kitchen had been so glad to have him out of the way. Someone had been waiting for this moment, and the rat had been kept waiting in his turn.

The men had been waiting too. Matson realized the tables had been placed to focus on the rat and the doorway from which the rat would make his entrance. The rat was to be important, not the fire.

The rat wasn't well. The kitchen had delayed him too long, and prepared him too harshly. There was a blood-drop on his nose, and it glistened with a separate cunning. The rat licked it back, pulled a strained face, and kept on coming forward.

He needed a drink. Matson had seen plenty of rats poisoned with anticoagulants – plenty in Camberwell, plenty on his aunts' farm in Ireland. They need to drink, and they kill themselves by drinking.

He took a sip himself, and watched the rat totter towards the dried-up guttering that was laid beneath the gates.

An old man spoke. He indicated the rat. He did not look at the General or anyone at his table. If he spoke to anyone, it was to Matson. He spoke for some time, and before he finished the rat reached the edge of the courtyard and died. A youngster stopped and picked it up by the tail, flipping it through the front gate and across the road.

'You do not, I think, understand the Slovenian dialect?'

The General was speaking to Matson. 'I thought not. The Slovenians are an interesting bunch, so are the Croatians – but nothing except expedience would ever make me learn any Slavonic tongue.' He raised his glass to the old man. 'But of course, I speak them all. Some languages are made for the world, and some are just syllables. This is one of those. It is all whores' grunts and thieves' whispers and children sniffing after dark.'

The old Slovene stood up straighter to hear the General's voice, but did not understand him.

Matson wondered why he had been singled out, then realized that he was the only spectator, the only true witness. Whatever happened was a play acted by a cast of thirty-odd men for an audience of one. A cast of thirty and a grey rat.

'What the man said is that honourable men do not dine with a rat. When the rat comes in for a feed, the true man leaves.'

Matson nodded, a fine neutral nod he shared with the old man.

'It's an allegory, of course. An allegory that took them a long time to set up. A rat game. And now the rat is dead.'

The General stood and addressed the men for the first and last time. '*Dobra vecchi,*' he said, and waited for them to leave.

Even Matson understood that.

The men stood looking at the General for a few moments more, and then filed out.

The old man spat once, on the floor, and followed them.

The General sat down and put his gun away. 'Yes,' he said, 'the rat is dead. I wonder if that is what they really intended. More to the point I wonder who the rat is.' He gazed sadly at Matson, as if concerned for his health, then went back to talking German. The two women spoke too, even the daughter-in-law. The child chattered. Their voices filled the evening until Matson rose to leave.

4

'You could sleep in the courtyard,' the innkeeper said. He indicated the fire. He feared escalation and needed someone to stay.

'I'll use my car.' Matson was touched by the fellow's anxiety. If the rat was merely the curtain-raiser, he preferred to watch the rest from the wings.

He drove a couple of hundred yards in the direction the Range Rover was already facing. The surface was easier this way, the flat landscape sharp under the headlights.

There were rules against camping, and if Popovic had spread any police around he knew they'd feel obliged to enforce them. He turned off along a cart-track and stopped beside a large rock skeined with snail slime and ferrous oxide. The land behind the rock was enclosed by lines of uneven drystone. Towards the inn, a layer of limestone karst lay over everything.

There was a tent in the back somewhere, if the spare can of oil had left it alone. He always pitched a tent. It helped people think they knew where he was.

The tent was a mistake. He heard cars high in the valley. Three of them stopped at the inn, found it locked, came on and caught him in their lights. They backed up and whooped down to join him. If they'd travelled that road in the dark, a tent must have looked like civilization after the wilderness.

Three Czechoslovakian families. The youngest man had some English. 'It's best we stick together. Cut-throats. Bandits.'

'Bad people?' Matson pretended to be affable with drink. 'Or pan-Slavonic rumour?'

They agreed in turn. There were ten of them, so there was a lot of agreement. They stood with their smiles held high like a colony of penguins, until someone remembered to switch off headlights.

Several half-bottles of Courvoisier had nested in his suit-case all the way from Mulhouse. It seemed a bit grand to open one, but there were young women in the party. They produced picnic mugs of tin or plastic, much more quickly than they'd dowsed their lights.

If they felt welcome, they wouldn't be watchful. Matson kissed them good night and crawled into his tent.

5

After due interval he crawled out again, and carried his bedroll several hundred yards further from the road.

He felt uneasy, as if he was being followed. Perhaps he had indigestion. He had drunk enough one way or another. So had the rat.

Once he'd followed Weiss over the Loibl, he'd declared his hand. Anyone concerned to protect the Obergruppen- führer would have marked him down.

Now there was the business at the inn. He couldn't have made Weiss' enemies too happy by intruding himself there. He decided to bed down very carefully indeed.

A wise man always sleeps in two places. Matson believed in abundance.

He dropped his lightweight bag, walked twenty paces more and unfolded his bedroll under the rustling stars.

He luxuriated on his bedroll for a moment or two, then ghosted back towards the lightweight bag, which lay in deepest shadow.

He listened. Nothing. He moved his mind over the scene, going back towards his bedroll then beyond, sweeping in a slow arc across the limestone then round to the Czecho- slovak camp and his own tent. Nothing.

He opened his eyes and repeated the process. He heard women chatting, laughing. He had thought the visitors were asleep.

Those young women had made eyes at him. One of them was unattached. Why wasn't he doing something about her?

Was it a part of ageing, or simply that he didn't wish to share his sleeping bag? He wanted to lie alone with his memories of other women, women who were dead or unavailable.

Or was it the threat of danger? Danger was bound to cling to those who fastened on to the General.

If the Czechs weren't what they said they were, then he didn't want one of them getting close to him. And if the danger were from elsewhere, then a sleeping partner would be an encumbrance.

Perhaps it was the General's daughter-in-law kept them at bay. She went on moving her mad eyes and stony body in and out of his sleep.

He was concentrating on not thinking about her when someone took a shot at him.

A handclap in the air, that violencing of the adjacent atoms you can never capture on celluloid. His dreams of the Weiss woman were all celluloid. He left them and sensed rather than saw the second bullet huff up his bedroll and bounce off the stones beneath it.

He didn't hear it come. He heard it go. As it went away, he heard it arrive. There was no sound of gunfire, merely its explosive passage through the night.

So the bullet was supersonic. So it had been fired at a range not greater than three hundred yards. So it was a rifle-bullet and not from a pistol. Not a carbine, either, or any of the modern assault-guns – an armalite, for example, would be subsonic after four or five hundred feet, and he was certain the sniper was further off than that. The ricochets had gone away downwind. The rifle was upwind. If it were that close he'd be smelling cordite. He breathed in, detecting young women, petrol, the inn's rack of charcoal, farm animals behind stone.

A rifle with a silencer, or it would have awakened the campers.

It would need a night-sight, a trilux at least. If the sniper had an optic he could still be watching through it.

Matson lay and listened.

6

He heard water trickle, deep water, somewhere inside the limestone at his back between himself and the inn.

His watch had a luminous dial. He unfastened it and left it in his sleeping bag. He darkened his face and hands with soil, and gave himself five minutes, counting slowly five times to sixty, then once more for luck.

He knew limestone's habits. Therefore he knew karst. The stream would lie beneath a stream. The galleries would have deepened over the centuries, but on top there would be some kind of gully to give him cover.

He rolled on to his stomach. The limestone lay in slabs, with lateral divisions running between himself and the supposed watercourse.

These weren't hollows, certainly not deep enough to shade his backside from a bullet, but they offered great webs of darkness. They promised invisibility.

Unless someone was watching intently through a night glass, *now,* as he made his first move.

He made his move, and was invisible. He was night.

He thought: there's a man out there. He tried to kill me. He knew enough, or was trained enough, to know I wouldn't stay in my tent. He used his night-sight to track me to fresh cover, and he shot at me once I was still.

Or did he see me leave my bedroll as well and therefore not shoot at me?

He stopped at the dried-up watercourse, and followed it towards the road. In about a hundred paces he would be the three hundred yards from his sleeping place he regarded as the maximum range.

The shot must have come from the watercourse, not from on top of the karst. He hoped the rifleman had stayed around.

Matson didn't fear any death that could come from close to, not from a single man. Knife, sandbag, garrotte – he could deal with these. If he was wrong about this, wrong or too old, there'd be no time for fear, just the second of surprise.

The gully narrowed until it was a deep cut, nearly man-deep and scarcely wider than a potman's belly. The perfect slit trench.

Two brass cartridge jackets were available to his fingertips, knocking together, niffy and sweet with fresh cordite, still warm. Impossible to crawl this way and not find them.

Centre-fire, with an extended rim. They had the size and

slope of .303 ball, older than Weiss's Luger, but still a good sniping weapon for a poor man. A lot of short and long Lee Enfields had been parachuted in to the partisans during the war, and to Colonel Mihajlovic before them.

He tried to be absolutely certain, but his fingers couldn't read in the dark.

He dropped the cartridges into his pocket, and went on down the gully, hoping not to be offered bullet number three over open sights.

Someone was determined to take him off Weiss's back, not to say life's back in general. The General had dismissed his chauffeur at the Loibl. He mustn't assume that members of the entourage hadn't followed on from Rosental by a safer route.

Anyone coming from the inn would need to go back there. He continued until the gully reached the road, midway between the track and the iron gate to the courtyard.

He waited until an hour before dawn, but no one returned to base, if base it was.

No need to elude the Czechs. They were already stirring. Late to bed and early to rise, like the Germans.

He wandered up and down, collecting his kit, then put himself briefly to bed. He was dressed in a fine growth of stubble and a headache.

7

The sun was up, and then away under moist cloud. He was aware of this without waking. There was nothing to frighten his hour of sleep.

Four of them were watching him from close to. So much for psychic certainty.

A grizzle-haired man, an elderly woman, a young woman, a boy. They looked like gypsies. The boy threw little stones into the air and caught them on the back of his hand. He did this by feel and by guesswork. His eyes, like the adults', never left Matson's face.

Not only his face. They registered Matson's emergence from his lightweight bag, his white singlet and navy boxer-shorts, his pale skin and disgusting gingerness of hue. They saw that his underclothes and legs were soiled from last night's crawling about.

They watched the half-naked Matson crush his bag into its holdall, and walk across to his bedroll and pull on his shirt, trousers and socks, then fasten his shoes. He took down the tent and stowed it in the Range Rover. They admired the dexterity with which he folded his bedroll round his light-weight bag and tucked away a dirty sock or so. He did not halt this process to examine the two bullet holes in the lower half of the roll. He did not need to. He had seen bullet holes in waterproofed canvas before. He knew what bullet holes looked like. They looked like a circular absence of cloth. He knew what bullet holes meant. They meant the waterproofed canvas would leak in the next shower. He knew what calibre rifle had made them. He had the evidence in his pocket.

When he stood up, he had a toothbrush in his mouth and some dry toothpaste.

The quartet stood close behind him, holding out their hands. He turned and gestured them to wait. He wondered what they were begging for. There had been a loaf of bread inside the bedroll with the dirty socks. He had cheese and *wurst* and his several half bottles of cognac. They had stolen nothing. They had waited for him to wake up. Their manner implied how very decent they had been.

The younger woman wished him a safe journey. Perhaps she was being ironic. He thought not. Every beggar wishes you a safe journey. So does every petrol placard. *Sretan put* are the two words of Serbo-Croat every foreign motorist knows.

He pulled out a couple of banknotes, perhaps a pound's-worth. His watch said after five. He was in a hurry to be gone. Five a.m. was a late reveille for a motoring German.

The woman took the money unhurriedly and said something to the boy who went away among the scabs of Karst. He came back almost at once with a tortoise and three figs. They were spring fruit, tiny, bright green and hard as bullets. Matson couldn't see any fig trees, but he remembered there had been some near the gateway to the Inn.

He received the presents graciously. These people weren't

114

beggars, their mouthings implied. They were merely sales-persons afflicted by prolepsis.

The younger woman was wearing a shawl or a knotted overshirt. It was hard to tell which because it was the same off-black colour as her blouse. Peeping above the knot, square-edged and muckily bound in green buckram, she bore a second gift. The book was buckled and hot from her breastbone, moist from her young skin. It cost Matson the equivalent of an English fiver. A fiver would scarcely have bought him a coffee and bun in Austria, but here it was worth castles in the sky. He had to have her second offering, that was for sure.

He cradled the book between the handles of his bedroll, gathered in his figs and his tortoise and wished them goodbye. They didn't smile. They didn't follow him. He didn't have enough Serbo-Croat to ask who had sent them to him with the book.

Halfway to the car he set down the tortoise. It had dribbled some leaf-chewings on his sleeve. Otherwise it didn't thank him. He dropped the figs beneath a trackside culvert and did what he could for his sleeve.

The book was what he thought it was. He had seen it in the caravan: *Atrocity on Black Mountain.*

On the flyleaf there was a set of pencilled initials: G.L.

It was another one of Lolly's, in Serbian and Cyrillic this time, with some very atrocious pictures. Weiss was prominent in several of them. He was easy to recognise because, although the photographs were crowded, he was always the only man in uniform and the only one who was alive. Whatever Matson was meant to deduce from the book's reappearance, he couldn't accept the circumstances of its delivery.

Willi and Albin weren't involved. Geography said so. Geography favoured someone in Weiss's party.

That someone would have to be Lolly's murderer – a location of guilt that didn't offend Matson's sense of things in the least. What did was the thought of a professional thug daft enough to hoard and then advertize his victim's possessions. Kaub could work wonders with the first gift: there was the packaging, the postmark and the handwriting. Popovic or the local police could do even more with this one, simply by bending a gypsy's ear.

Matson was being relied on to stay sly and extra-legal, even by his enemies.

8

The Mercedes had been parked behind the iron gates of the courtyard. A small child was playing between the bars of the gateway and the car's bonnet.

Not the General's grandchild. This one was scarcely more than a toddler.

Matson spoke to it, diffidently, in Anglo-Irish. The child wasn't an it, but a tiny boy with all the emergent skills. He pissed beside the Mercedes to prove it. He did not direct himself against the car or against the wall. He was an inn-keeper's son. He had been taught about such matters.

The gate was no longer locked, so the Mercedes wasn't locked in. Matson entered the courtyard and tried a *dobra* or two in a voice too loud for his headache. He stooped towards the child. The lad promptly swung on his hair, dragging his headache out by the roots.

It was then that the daughter-in-law came outside, fragile as a dream. 'Oh,' she said, disappointed. 'You slept here.'

'I slept,' he agreed.

She slipped back into one of the rooms like a genie into its bottle.

Matson put his nose through the largest doorway. Did Yugoslav inns have a register? If they did, it was not where he could see it.

He beckoned the child. He made imprecise gestures. He found money. The child brought him toilet paper. He swore. The child found him writing paper. He made more gestures. He discovered more money and pointed to the Mercedes. The child did not bring the register. He brought the passports.

Only three of them. No chauffeur. No hired help. Hendrik Reinhard Weiss and Lotte Weiss. He recoiled from 'Lotte'. She was twenty-nine. That was news.

116

The third passport was Italian. Signora Constanz Ehrenberg-Zanetti, *professione giornalista.* Thirty-two.

He thought she was the child's minder. A journalist? Was it likely? A German relation married to Italian money? He went back to the notion that she was the General's playmate, not that Herr Weiss would want to foodle with any kind of publicity.

Romance surnames of the Zanetti variety were not unknown in Germany, any more than in England. In the ancient provinces of the Austro-Hungarian Empire they were even more common.

He had the passports in his hand when Weiss arrived in the yard and began to do his morning exercises.

9

'You're up early, Hauptmann.'

'I was given an early call.'

'Noises in the night?'

'A silenced rifle.'

'Imagination. Or you suffer from wind.'

'Two shots, General. An old campaigner like yourself will enjoy the bullet holes.' As he went outside to the Range Rover, he hoped the toddler would do something sly with the passports.

When he came back he found the boy had given them to the General.

Weiss was more interested in the bedroll. 'I'd say point seven six. The ubiquitous calibre.'

Matson had a cartridge in his pocket. He did not contradict him.

'It seems there's more than one of us the locals don't like. War makes strange allies, Captain Matson, and this is the strangest war of all, believe me.' He moved to one side, like a commander composing himself for an orders group. 'As it happens, you might be in a position to do me a favour.'

Matson felt reluctant to grant him anything.

'I am over-womaned on this journey. That American thing gives me the jitters. I wonder –'

'American?'

'The Ehrenberg-Zanetti. I wonder if you would let her ride in your vehicle for a few kilometres? One lunatic we can stand. Two neurotics together are bad for the child. Also she smells of tobacco. I think she doesn't wash her armpits.'

10

Mrs Ehrenberg-Zanetti seemed clean enough to Matson. On the Loibl she probably stank of fear, as he himself had. Fear was an odour the General did not allow himself to recognize.

She did not transfer her kit to the Range Rover, and he found that fact interesting. As for the rest of her, *giornalista* seemed as silly a misnomer as 'point seven six'.

'You travel on an Italian passport,' he said.

'I had an Italian husband.'

'Had?'

'Your tone of voice and my nerves are not going to get along.'

He wished she hadn't volunteered her nerves quite so soon. His suspicions were given another sprinkle of salt when the daughter-in-law came through the gate, approached the waiting Range Rover and held out her hand, obviously by order.

'Lotte Weiss,' she said.

Her hand felt comfortable, as hands go.

'Since I marry, some people prefer to call me Lili.'

Was Lili 'lily' in German? Matson didn't know. He disliked 'Lotte' and 'Lily' about equally. 'You speak very good English,' he said. He had heard it before, but this time it was pretending to be friendly. Lily White indeed.

'I speak English.'

The General was surrounded with widows, but genocides grow used to that sort of thing.

The Mercedes hooted inside the yard, and she hurried back to her child. At least the old man hadn't snapped his fingers.

118

11

The Mercedes left Kocevje Gora with only the toddler to watch it. No more men. No more rats. The innkeeper stayed in hiding. So did his wife.

Weiss drew up beside the Range Rover and wound down his window. 'Don't lose me, Hauptmann. I'm going to take in a bit of scenery. Prinz Eugen was surrendered near here.'

'You didn't surrender in these parts.'

'No one who surrendered in Yugoslavia lived to tell the tale.'

The General drove and Matson tried to follow him. The road was better this way, but he couldn't hope to stay on it at the General's kind of speed and give Mrs Ehrenberg-Zanetti the attention she deserved.

'What are you?' he asked. 'A staff reporter? A correspondent?'

'A stringer.'

'A stringer?'

'Yes, a stringer. You make it sound like "hooker".'

'Got any of your stuff with you? I'd like to read some.'

'I'm a working journalist, not some fucking author of books.'

'What's your by-line?'

'Constanz Zanetti. Small zee, big zee.'

She'd learned that well.

'Not Connie?'

'I work for *Newsweek*, not the *New York Mirror*.'

'I enjoy the *New York Mirror*. It's got pictures.'

'*Newsweek* has words as well. On the grown-up side for a soldier.'

'You work out of Rome or Naples?'

'Athens. I'm travelling back there now.'

'With Obergruppenführer Weiss!'

'With dear old Henk, yes. Not to forget Lili. He prefers "General" to all those SS ranks, by the by.'

'Only in public, I bet.'

'Understand this, Matson. This trip is big for me. The General going back to that place of his is astronomic.'

'There are Serbs and Montenegrins who'll see him dead before he reaches it.'

119

'If they get lucky, the story'll be even better.'

'In the USA?'

'*Newsweek*'s international. But yes, in the USA. We're very sensitive about all these senior Nazis that we, and the Russians, and you dear old Brits seem to have let through the net. Especially the Jews among us.'

'Does Weiss know you're a Hebrew?'

'He doesn't even care that I'm a journalist. He's not quite your stereotype, you know.'

'What is he?'

'He thinks he's God.'

'So what is he?'

'A fucking old murderer who likes young women.'

TEN

1

They motored for fifteen minutes – fifteen minutes free of armpit but full of bad-tempered clack. They left the tight valleys of the Northern Dinarids. They left them at eighty miles an hour on a thirty-mile-an-hour road that hovered above sunken circular fields.

Matson braked hard. He was fifty yards behind Weiss and the distance was stretching, but he saw that the road ahead of the Mercedes was cluttered with grey-pink lumps of karst limestone as blushful in the early morning sun as tits on a nudist beach.

He did not know they were pigs until the Mercedes hit one.

Weiss might brake for tits or rocks. For pigs he did not brake.

The Mercedes hit four more with a multiple judder that Matson felt in his belly and Connie Zanetti smack up her by-line. Five little rocks lay dead on the road, and the rest became squeals with curly tails.

Matson skidded to a halt among butcher's lumps, while a sixth rock-pig took total revenge. It lay in Weiss's track like a cathedral doorstep and stopped him.

Lotte Weiss fell from the car on one outflung foot and one bent knee. Her mouth was smudged and bleeding, her cheek iodined by an instant bruise. She was stunned or shocked or pretending a deep faint.

Matson stepped out to help her, and stooped his nose straight into the barrel of a single-tubed shotgun. There were three other shotguns with double barrels. These too gazed exclusively at Matson.

121

One old man and three men of middle years. A father, perhaps, and his sons.

The General emerged from behind the wheel. His chest heaved, his breath caught, but his eyes were steady. He thrust himself between Matson and the other four, and turned his back on the guns. He prodded his daughter-in-law with his boot. 'The lad will be all right,' he told her.

She opened her eyes, looked at a slab of pig, then a bloodied marble of bacon. She saw the guns.

She attempted to scream, or at least cry out. His foot restrained her. His foot in its boot and its friendly sock. It touched her not untenderly but with total disapproval. 'Pull yourself together. Pick yourself up and go and kiss your son.'

She climbed to her feet, using bits of Matson to help her.

'Don't let the boy see your face,' the General advised. 'It's a bloody mess.' He was a man who would issue instructions to the last, even impossible ones.

'Jesus Christ!' So far Mrs Ehrenberg-Zanetti had kept her English inside the Range Rover. Now she let it do its work.

The General turned to face his executioners, glancing up and down the road as he did so. He spoke briefly in Serbo-Croat to the old man, then said to Matson, 'I've told him they've got time on their side.' He looked at the carnage strewn around the Mercedes. 'Yesterday it was a rat game. Today the stakes are higher. They are spending pigs. Always the insult, you see. They can't bring themselves to shoot a man without first of all soiling themselves with insult.'

The oldest Slav glanced at the Range Rover. He had heard its passenger's language. He acknowledged the neutrality of its English registration by making a small sideways jerk with his gun-muzzle to encourage Matson to step aside and out of his line of fire.

'Stand back, Matson. The old coot'll brown you if you don't.' The Ehrenberg-Zanetti sounded abnormally cool and collected for a woman so recently *in extremis.*

'If he does one of us, a little mature reflection will lead them to tidy us all up.'

The General merely grunted.

One of the younger men glanced down at his gun and

122

discovered something that made him feel foolish. He cocked it, first the left hammer then the right. Cocked it, eased the hammers forward against his thumb, re-cocked it again and again.

'If I have to be shot, so be it,' the General said. 'But I don't intend to be shot by accident. Especially by an idiot with bad teeth.' He began to scold in passionate Serbo-Croat. The younger men were about fifteen or twenty years older than Matson, and they didn't have bad teeth. They were toothless. Pig-breeding men, they must have been pork-eaters, too, so they'd need to have dentures. A man removes his teeth for a parachute jump, so he probably does the same for a murder, teeth being there to choke him or drop out and be a clue.

You think these thoughts while foreigners with faces as empty as gun-barrels chew over the will-we-won't-we of your life, and the Ehrenberg-Zanetti is going into her shoulder bag in the corner of your eye as if for a handkerchief or lipstick but complicating the issue by coming out with a neat enough pistol which is nonetheless half-a-dozen inches too long for discretion.

A woman with mad eyes and lips dripping blood makes a disturbing picture. The General must have seen any number of them in his time and so, perhaps, had the other old man. He was probably here to avenge one.

His sons were more fortunate and therefore less prepared. They had the shock to come. There was a knocking on the rear window of the Mercedes, and they half-turned towards it in turn. They took their eyes off Weiss and Matson one at a time, but when they did so they were distracted by blood smearing the glass, the bruise whitened with pressure, the mouth howling, the eyes as unfocussed as marbles, not to mention the pistol she was knocking with. Weiss's Luger Parabellum was cocked and pointing in the general direction of their father's kidneys.

'Snap!' said the Ehrenberg-Zanetti from behind her very decent-looking Smith. She held it two-handed straight out, with the action thumbed back. 'Snap!' It was such a good word to say that she tried it again. It had a terrifying effect because practically no one understood it.

123

'Pigs,' the General said in English. 'These imbeciles let their pigs stray on the road and I inadvertently killed them.' He told the father off in Serbo-Croat for a good two minutes, ignoring the sons and their shotguns entirely. In English he said, 'I shall now be entirely conciliatory. After all, they were only trying to kill me.'

He produced some banknotes. He pushed past the levelled rifles and examined each carcass with his boot. He used his thinking boot, the one he had used on his daughter-in-law, and he held his head to one side and riffled his money as coyly as any battalion catering officer buying in black market goodies for Christmas.

Then he came back and made as if to hold out the money to the old man. 'I am buying his dead pigs, and presenting him with them back again,' he explained to Matson. 'He will have double profit. It is how such things are arranged.'

The Slav's dignity was unmoved by the money. The women's guns were the decisive factor – the Ehrenberg-Zanetti cool and steady for one good shot, Lotte Weiss stuttering like a machine-gun and liable to brass off the entire clip in a single defensive spasm.

The old fellow's lot had the edge in firepower and would undoubtedly prevail, but his tribe would take casualties, himself among them.

Revenge is a labyrinth. A father needs his wits to guide his sons. He is far from at his best with a hole in a kidney and another in his head.

One of his sons forgot himself far enough to cradle his gun and begin peeling and sucking an orange. His father hissed him forward to collect the blood-money.

He didn't get it. The General saw his daughter-in-law as if for the first time, and his voice grew stern with rage. He demanded reparation for her damaged face. He showed the Slav the money he had. He made as if to give it to the son with the orange, then pushed him away empty-handed.

He selected three banknotes of minuscule value, and pushed one into each of the sons' gun muzzles. He pointed a finger towards Lotte Weiss, and climbed back into the car.

Shotguns are not car stoppers. They damaged the General's paintwork. They damaged Matson's. They did more damage to the Range Rover, because it was nearer and last.

Matson built up the revs. For a moment, he and the Mercedes were side by side.

2

'A steady gun-hand, Mrs Ehrenberg-Zanetti.'

'Only when sober.' She went into her shoulder bag and came out with a half bottle of Austrian brandy. 'Want some?'

'Not now. Somebody taught you well.'

'I watch TV. It was you who poked your nose in and saved the old sniff's hide.' She spoke distantly, deflecting his curiosity. If she had been English, Matson's mum would have called hers a lettuce-chewing voice. It wasn't the voice of someone who chewed lettuce very delicately. It thickened at the first sip of liquor in anticipation of slush to come. 'Christ,' she said. ' I nearly crapped myself back there.'

He objected to that and to her opening the bottle again. He concentrated on keeping up with Weiss.

The Mercedes bounced a herd of goats from behind, white with a black buck to lead them. A long ridge of karst was eating into the green pastureland. On karst only goats and snipers can live. No goats died. Even the buck jumped aside. It turned to face them, but it jumped.

The Mercedes did not stop to give the snipers a chance. Weiss leant out and yelled at the goatherd. She was a woman with a white beard. Wrong again, Matson. A man in caftan and sandals. The beard looked better on a man. Shades of battleground trauma.

Weiss leant from the right-hand window. The battered Lili must be driving him – had been driving this last two minutes.

'My Serbian friend tells me he killed two villages back there.'

'He was there when they died.' Talking about it hurt her, so she talked too much. 'Two villages is a misnomer. Twin villages, on either side of the valley by last night's stop-over.'

Matson remembered the chill before the sunlight, his place of desolation.

'Constituting a small town. It was Slovene, just, and affluent. It served a big rural community. There was a boarding school for girls of high school age, an annexe for smaller boys.'

He knew what was coming, but for a second she couldn't continue with it. The landscape had interrupted itself with cooling towers and chimneys – always a shock in wild places. There was a mile-long road of hard concrete leading past a bauxite mine: overhead skips and closed conveyors on stilts. Rows of concrete prefabs, then new tower blocks as cheerless as the karst pinnacles overhead.

The Obergruppenführer had Lili slow down. There was a crossing with lights, and a policeman in a traffic tower. The Obergruppenführer was obedient to police with white gloves and whistles. Policemen keep history in order. History, not time.

'Weiss was there when they rounded up the men from the community, and the little boys, and shot them in the gully where the road runs. It was a reprisal, they said, for an ambushed patrol. A hundred for one, the so-called legal Aryan ratio.' She took a sip of brandy with that. 'The women were variously butchered, allegedly by Ustaza. The high school girls were systematically raped and then bayoneted to death.'

'The story keeps cropping up,' he said. It was a dim attempt to console her.

She didn't scream. 'It crops up in the places it happened,' she agreed. 'It happened on the Naretva, true. And here in the Dinarids. It happened at Kocevje Gora.'

They drove slowly then more slowly still as the sidewalks became granite pavements with shop-fronts, and there were people who thronged into the street.

A band was playing. There was lots of oompa-oompa on fine Viennese brass. A marching band. They came face to face with a procession and had to stop. Even the Mercedes gave way to the big bass drum.

Matson detected no menace, not even curiosity. The march was full of young faces, Popo's 'youth without history'.

Constanz Zanetti translated a banner and leant out for a

126

leaflet. 'They want Slovenian autonomy,' she explained. 'Urban Yugoslavia is not concerned with yesterday's monsters, not even the ones called Henk Weiss. They are too busy promoting themselves against the rest.'

Matson sat watching the marchers. The looked too affluent for people of student age. Their skins were palely dark – Lili Weiss dark: was *she* of Slavonic origin? – they were elegant, well-fed, with mod haircuts, more Western European than the Western Europeans. The boys were more like American college kids: as cleanly dressed, but with a touch of designer *chic*, and in richer colours. The girls were wearing regional costume, making them look as bright as court cards in the Magyar pack.

This was what the Nazis had taken it upon themselves to obliterate. Here, in Slovenia, less often. Among the Croatians always wherever they found ethnic Serbs. And, as at Kocevje Gora, they used Croatian puppets to kill for them, seven hundred thousand Serbs in one place alone, according to Lolly's book, seven hundred thousand in a single year.

Early in 1942, Josip Brod (Marshal Tito) persuaded the Politburo to set up a commission to look into allegations of atrocity. The commission required evidence to be collected by command region, taken on oath in open Court or Enquiry before at least one partisan officer of field rank or higher, himself aided where possible by a legal assessor or someone else in the movement used to weighing depositions.

The partisan officer in this case was Edvard Kardelj himself, formation commander of the Slovene brigades.

Examination of the boy Petr (surname lost)

'No,' the boy said, 'they were Ustaza. They wore forage caps.'

'Did not the Germans (i.e. SS Handschar, who were Bosnians) wear forage caps?'

'Not these Germans.'

'This Brigadeführer Weiss – was he there?'

'Yes. He shot my sister.'

'Tell us.'

'There were two Ustaza with my sister. One of them had thrown her clothes up round her waist, one was throttling her, or holding her chin in his hands, perhaps to break her neck. I could not see. This SS man in the peaked cap —'

'Weiss?'

'He came up and kicked the Ustaza away. He shouted at them in Croat. He said they were obscene. Then he told my sister to stop bawling and straighten her clothes. Then he pulled her apron over her head and shot her with his pistol.'

'Where were you?'

'I was with Ivo Zvrinska, and Piotr and Vasco Kranj, three other boys who watched this. We were hiding. I saw my sister's legs twitch and then they stopped moving, and that was the end of her. The Ustaza did not kill her. This SS man did.'

Another of those accounts in Lolly's book which were ambiguous in their treatment of Weiss and enraged the late Mr Lippiat. Especially when its authors had noted, with the chilly disinterest of professional historians: *'Obergruppenführer (then Brigadeführer) Weiss is scarcely implicated by this testimony, given as it is by so young a child. In evaluating the evidence of identification against this German commander one should remember that most of the allegations were laid after the Fourth and Fifth German offensive against Tito's partisans, codenamed operation "Weiss" and operation "Schwarz" respectively. There are a deal of atrocities laid at the door of this eponymous "Weiss" in consequence.'*

Lolly had scrawled one of his Serbian proverbs at the end of the boy's account:

'I have been pierced, I have been slashed, I have been skinned, but I did not die of it.'

3

The procession of young people rekindled Matson's dislike of Weiss. So did Constanz's story. He had stood beside the man, he had shielded him from a bursting petrol tank and the threat of buckshot. He had taken the wrong side and felt cheated as a result.

'So why did he come back here?' he asked.

'People always return to where they were happy.' She was a mite drunk to see anything wrong with that statement. 'They want to see if the reality will disappoint the memory.'

'Here. After that?'

'He's a German. They think that peace forgets war. They think thirty years of peace obliterates everything. You should try being a Jew or a Slav.'

'I'm Irish. We're another race that's corrupted its intelligence with too much memory.'

She began to drone on at him. She's like my aunts, he thought. They talk so much there's no listening to them. They certainly don't give themselves time to listen to me.

'So that's what eats you about Weiss,' he said, 'even though you'll break bread at his table. The everlasting hate, and the unconfirmed atrocities. Is that what you've got against him?'

'It's what God's got against him. I don't think I've got a say in the matter.' She took another swig and screwed the cap on the bottle. 'I'm in love with him, Matson. That's what I've got against Herr Whatsitführer Weiss.'

He didn't know what to add to that. He thought the crowd was clearing enough for them to get out of town, he and the General. When they reached the open road he would be more than glad to motor really fast for once. Lili Weiss was beginning to let the clutch out and Matson was fiddling with the ignition when a hand reached in through his window and snaffled his keys.

'I told you to buy a Yugo, my dear. The driver is harder to nobble. The Obergruppenbag is already under arrest.' Popo beamed at Constanz. 'Gruppenbag is wrong, I think. But a Serb never says "shit" in earshot of a lady.'

'Pig-killing is one charge. Speeding on the public highway makes another. Also, no one with my sort of authority has ticked him off about his traffic accident. It's a pity the victim was an American citizen and so well insured, or I could scold Herr General Weiss for much longer. Nevertheless he has been in Yugoslavia for twenty-four hours, and it is high time I have my minute in his ear.'

Uniformed policemen surrounded both cars, and carried on arriving. Uniformed policemen with pistols in stirrup holsters, with carbines and sub-machine-guns. Matson counted two hundred of them, and then couldn't see policemen for policemen. Popovic waited until they were in place, then rapped on the window of the Mercedes.

'Who, *exactly*, is that?' Constanz Ehrenberg-Zanetti was sozzled with self-pity, sozzled with two zees, but she still spoke nicely. 'And what the fuck are those?'

'Those are a camera crew. That is a Colonel Popovic, late of the Yugoslav Embassy in London. Colonel Popovic is here to supervise your lover's safety. The camera crew are here to film him protecting the Gruppenführer from a riot.'

'There isn't a riot.' She gazed wildly about her, eyes bulging with booze and alarm. 'Henk isn't my lover, either.'

'I think you told me he is. Or told me he was. I think you think he wants rid of you.'

'I've just saved his life.'

'So did his daughter-in-law.'

'*That* bitch. I should have let one of those pig farmers brown the pair of them. And that spitless kid. Let's have the bloody riot and be done with them.'

Matson started to say something about fools who climb the volcano to pray for an eruption. He thought better of it. She was too piddled for anything except pity. Besides, the advice applied to him as much as to her. He said, 'With so many policemen, who wants a riot? Certainly not Popo. This will be for television news. The camera will pan over millions of stalwart cops, shouting and sweating and milling around, and we'll hear crowd noises over.'

'Yugoslavia needs to feel outraged.' Popovic was back

again. 'And it needs to *see* itself being outraged. Those kids on the march need it more than anyone. They're walking in line to give away something their grandparents bought with blood.' He gazed in at the suddenly sleeping Ehrenberg-Zanetti. 'I wouldn't mind sacrificing one murdering Nazi if it would give us back a second's sense of nationhood. Except, of course, I'd be out of a job. I *will* be out of a job, when the inevitable happens.'

Women who feign sleep are the same as women who feign drunkenness. They're women. Matson stepped down from the Range Rover and hid his voice among a muffle of hot policemen. 'What, exactly, are you doing to ensure you stay in work, Popo?'

'People from my office have been on this for weeks. I'm the rolling head, the fall guy. You must see that. They've picked up everyone along the route who might want to take an organized pot at him. It's easy up here —'

'What about those pig farmers?'

'I said organized, my dear. Easy to protect him up here, as I say. Impossible in the south. Wherever he is, there would be an outcry if I were to provide him with a visible escort. Not least from His Greatness himself. You saw how slippery he was in crossing by the Loibl? Was that to deflect the arrow or avoid the shield?'

'The latter, Popo. I get the feeling he thinks he's invincible.'

'It's not such a costly mistake for a man of his age.'

Popovic grew brisk. Tapped Matson's chest. Gesticulated at nothing. Waved and shouted at the assembled police force, first like a farmer at a cattle auction, then like a madman in a storm. They were on camera. He said, again tapping painfully, 'I have a communications truck a mile behind you. I have a helicopter.'

'So what's so good about that?'

'I bugged your vehicle, my dear. I planted a little lozenge as it sat beside the lake. Now I have buggered the General. You will please allow me so small an indiscretion when your life is at stake. What you say or do to your young lady hitch-hiker does not even bristle my moustache.'

He led Matson back to the Range Rover, and leant in to

blow Constanz Ehrenberg a kiss. The lady was dry-eyed and awake, as Matson suspected.

He blazed round on Popovic and took a grab at his lapel. Now was as good a time as any to get under his guard. 'There's just one reason Belgrade sent for you to hold the bedpan. Lippiat. Lippiat was your specialism, and Lippiat was after your man. I take it you arranged his demise?'

Popovic was saddened by Matson crumpling his uniform. He prised his fingers free. 'Perhaps I only killed him the once, my dear.' He gestured his men away. 'Now ask yourself which time was that.'

5

Constanz took a Pentax from that capacious shoulder bag of hers, and began to snap the ambience as they drove out of town.

Some of her frames included him, were mostly him. He decided there would have to be an accident with her camera.

Her voice was full of well-mannered alcohol. She wasn't cool enough or secret enough for a professional, however tough she might be. She was probably paid a retainer to feed intelligence titbits to a control, like several other journalists he could name. His photograph might be one such morsel.

She leant across him. Perhaps she wanted to find a better camera angle. They were among sharp crags of karst again. Perhaps she just wanted to lean across him. He sensed cool flesh, remarkably cool for such a hot day, and the drink brought a rewarding whiff of armpit after all – crushed grass rather than last year's hay.

They had run out on to the coast road. This must be, or be about to be, the Adriatic Highway. It was beautifully engineered – what surface wouldn't seem that way, after the last twenty-four hours? – but there was no dividing barrier and it twisted between cliff and water, aeroplane high. There were carts and cars, pedestrians with only the road to walk in, men on donkeys, big lorries two abreast, and imbeciles selling biscuits. A minute ago they had been lonely as astronauts on the moon. Now the landscape changed from bone-white desolation to seaside postcard. A truck had actually stopped, and on a bend, to peddle cola in paper cups.

He elbowed her away with a delicate nudge so he could see the steering wheel, the windscreen and some of the pink road surface beyond.

She came back and clung. She clung long enough to grin, 'Play hard to get, then, Matson. I'll have you later. Then she unplugged her bottom from the wheel and gave him a glimpse of sunlit nipple before at last, at long last, the Rover emblem on the hub of the column.

He saw the Mercedes miss the cola truck. He missed the cola truck himself. The Mercedes accelerated. Her act had been for the benefit of its rear-view mirror.

The emblem steamed up. So did Matson. The emblem unfogged, then shattered. It sprayed bits of itself through his window.

He hit the accelerator and the window finished falling seawards. She screamed as the next shot went through behind her, not breaking the window, not smashing anything on the way, so making a nice offside exit.

'What the fuck was that?'

'My jockstrap exploding.'

'You don't wear one.'

'From now on I do.'

She saw the two holes in the glass. She did not have hysterics.

Matson tried to catch the Mercedes. Weiss didn't want to be caught. There had been bullets for him, too. His nearside window was starred. Matson saw their scars as he slewed into the next bend.

6

'I nearly got killed,' Constanz Ehrenberg-Zanetti said. 'Who do you suppose it was? I mean, why us?'

'Some jealous woman. You were sitting too close to me.'

'Be sensible.'

'I don't know.'

'People like you are paid to know.'

'So are stringers and people like you. The same person who shot up my bedroll last night. All I know now that I didn't know then is it's not you. What I want to discover is whether anyone's been hurt in the Mercedes.'

Finding out was not going to be easy. Whoever was driving behind the tinted glass – Weiss with his damaged chest, Lotte with her bruised face and closing eye – was going suicidally fast. The road serpentined about the crenellations in the cliff against a relentless swarm of traffic the other way. Someone chose to ignore this and push the battered Mercedes nose down on first left and then right front suspension as it decelerated into the apex of each hairpin, wincing and flattening the tyres until the back wheels slid away in a spurt of chippings. There were sparks from under the car. Either the exhaust had shaken down or the car was being braked hard enough to belly it on the sump. Unbelievable, but the driving was witless enough for anything.

Weiss overtook the world. He even overtook time. There are moments on fast journeys when you pass so many vehicles that there is nothing left ahead of you and nothing behind. They drove on a suddenly open road, an empty road with hairpins.

The old woman was in black clothes that had been in sunshine so long that they were as colourless as shadows. Her skin was weathered to look like her clothes. She probably had white hair, but it was covered in her shawl. She stood out in the road a hundred metres ahead of the Mercedes and waved green hands. She was holding out spring figs for sale, as she had done day after day since figs were discovered. Figs were all she was. She didn't have eyes. She was made of cloth.

Matson only saw figs. Weiss – and it must have been Weiss – saw nothing. She was halfway up a straight on the south-bound side of the road when the Mercedes hit her. She disappeared into less blood than a hedgehog and a small rolling basket. The sea was nine hundred feet below, shimmering with madness.

It was Matson who braked, not the General. Matson who spun in consequence, with Constanz's scream drying out in his skull and the thought evolving and revolving there that he would go helicoptering seaward just like the old woman.

He hit the northside wall, the cliff face wall instead – before hitting it, he dropped his near wheels into the guttering with a snap like a broken elbow and slid backwards to dismember the rest of the suspension in a culvert.

'Fart!' she said.

'You're lovely now you're sober.'

7

'Sorry, General.'

The Mercedes had come back, or backed up somehow. Its driver had need of him, perhaps as a witness.

Lotte Weiss was having hysterics. The child was in waxwork sleep.

'Save your apologies for your employers. And transfer the pair of you in double-time. I don't want any more madmen with rifles.'

Matson wondered if a shot-out tyre had caused him to spin. He dismissed the thought. The same idea got into Weiss and continued to grow. 'Hurry, hurry, hurry, Hauptmann.'

Matson joined the Ehrenberg-Zanetti on the back seat of the Mercedes. 'I was saying sorry because of the mush you'll have collected in your fan-belt, General.'

They were already moving at speed.

'That poor woman. You didn't swerve, Henk.'

'At one hundred and twenty kilometres an hour there was no way to stop. Swerve? I am not an aeroplane. I could only have flown us into the sea. There was traffic coming the other way.' He took another bend with all four tyres squealing. 'I considered the matter calmly, in the second or so available, and I thought: if I do not kill you, old imbecile, we will have a bad accident here.'

'Jesus!' Mouths open in spite of themselves.

'Make sure he doesn't punish you, Hauptmann. When a man has gods, he can be held guilty of blasphemy. She tried to sell me figs. I mean me, in a moving car, and the speed I move. Still, the car's safe. The figs look safe.'

'The old woman?' Constanz sounded short on love.

'It's at least three hundred metres down to the sea. These

135

people displayed many strange abilities in the war, Mrs Ehrenberg-Zanetti. Flying was not one of them.'

Lotte held her face, which had ripened, and went back to sobbing quietly.

'I had to keep on.' His English became moody, his driving even more shrill. 'Suppose I had slowed to miss her. Worse, suppose I had stopped once I hit her. What do you suppose would have happened? Someone would have shot me in the head. They start with a rat game, then it is pigs. Now they throw women at me.'

'You don't seriously believe that, General.'

Weiss brooded some more. 'In war, truth is not what a man believes, it is what he acts on. Now you ask me where the war is?'

Matson was more interested in the dangers of peace, but he was given no time to say so.

'It is here.' Weiss touched his chest. 'It has been with me since the Anschluss.'

'Then it's lasted you a damned long time.' Constanz again, but he spoke only to Matson.

'All wars are the same war, Hauptmann, and that war never ends.'

When such a man has a faith, it is an article of his faith that you do not contradict him about it.

8

Lotte was dabbing her face with wheatgerm, or some other form of liquid Vitamin E. She had a jar full of capsules meant for swallowing rather than for any cosmetic purpose. She pierced them with her teeth, and squirted the stuff over her bruised cheeks.

'Your car won't get out of that ditch back there,' Weiss stated. 'Not even if you ask a garage to bribe it with flowers. You should continue with us, Captain Matson. We'll give you a lift as far as Belgrade.'

'We'll be safer,' Lotte said. Then, seeing Weiss was offended, 'No one will try to harm Henk while you two civilians are here.'

Constanz squeezed his knee, and said, 'He's not a civilian. He's a British Intelligence officer, a gaolbird, and quite probably a murderer.'

'He was locked up because they thought he had killed a man who came to kill you,' Lotte Weiss said. She began to swallow capsules in confusion, as if she had been caught out at something. Telling him what he already knew was one such something.

Matson decided it had been rehearsed.

'Is he dead, this man?'

'There was a corpse, burnt beyond recognition.'

'And who was he?'

'A friend of mine.'

His eyes found Matson's in the mirror. 'So will you kill me, Hauptmann? Will you continue with the good work on behalf of this friend of yours?'

'He was an old man, General. Not as old as yourself, but old nonetheless. He had an old man's preoccupations. I'm much too young to kill anyone.'

Weiss laughed. It wasn't a good laugh. 'I did my best killing when I was a much younger man than you.'

The road continued to gyrate and the tyres howled.

Two police motorcyclists came past. They bucked alongside and examined the General's starred windows. They were even more interested in the Mercedes' radiator grille. They didn't flag him down. They thought about it, and while they thought he accelerated away from them.

The Ehrenberg-Zanetti was doing serious things on the back seat, scrawling hieroglyphics into one of those pop-over notebooks that no decent stringer is ever without. 'Why did you want to go back to Kocevje Gora?'

'It's one of a number of places where I did what I could for them in a damnable situation. I always treated them better than they treated themselves.' He made sure his grandson was asleep before adding, 'I was speaking of those Ustaza. They were animals. They mutilated. They tortured. They killed their fellow Slavs with clubs and drag ropes and axes, with hacksaws – even when we made the very best modern weapons available to them.'

'Why did we go there, Henk?' Lotte's bruised face

implored him through its mask of oil.

'I was looking for someone to thank me.'

Constanz-Zanetti forgot her by-line. She made a gesture in her shoulder bag behind the old man's back. It was only a gesture, but it wasn't her bottle she reached for, it was the hammer of her handy little Smith and Wesson.

'And why are we going on?' Lotte Weiss whimpered through blanched lips, more like a lily than ever.

9

Hard to drive fast and think. Now he was a passenger Matson could put his brain to better use.

He slipped his hand into his pocket and felt last night's cartridge cases as if they were some kind of totem. Too many things had happened to him since he'd come into Yugoslavia yesterday morning, and they'd all given off a distinctive whiff of the improbable.

The temptation would be to lump them together as part of the same messy intention.

Fact. Someone had put two bullets through his bedroll. The shots had been meant to kill him. The shots into the Range Rover were also intended to kill. Constanz had clung to him in the front of the vehicle, and the sniper had aligned his foresight on the ample outline of their two bodies and pulled the trigger. A hit on either one of them would have sent them off the road and down the cliff. No other way about it. Shooting the hub of the steering wheel was a divine accident, not a stunt. Nobody, but nobody, could trick-shoot like that on a moving target, particularly with Constanz's bum in the way.

Whoever had shot at him last night had taken another look through his Trilux and realised the target was somewhere else. He'd come on down the coast road for a second try.

The bullets through the Mercedes were another matter. The passengers were up front. Easy to fire through the back.

Perhaps that was why the General had suggested Constanz ride with Matson. He'd set the whole thing up, last night and

138

now today, and didn't want to present an accomplice with a choice of silhouettes.

Perhaps. It was the idea that made most sense, and Matson was a great believer in logic. Somehow, though, the explanation didn't feel right and he was an even greater disciple of intuition.

If he was in danger from Weiss, and he probably was, he felt sure it was all to come.

ELEVEN

1

'When I came here before, there was no coast road. Just a series of metaphysical propositions laid end to end.'

Men with no sense of humour always make the best jokes.

Rain fell. The sky was half clear, but clouds edged in from the sea, each of them as black as Lotte Weiss' cheekbone. The raindrops were separate and huge, and brought down insects to glue on the windscreen.

For a minute the road was only damp. Then the Adriatic wind took charge and the weather sheeted. The storm began falling in panes. Brightness gusted whole across the car and shattered against the mountain cliffs the Mercedes beetled against.

Then it was dark, green dark like a seafloor, and the lightning came. Weiss held the pedal down hard and went sliding through water that bounced hub high. 'It clears the windows,' he said, as if he manufactured the weather by pressing a button on the instrument display. 'I hate a smeared windscreen.'

He didn't drive like an old man. There was no bravado about his progress either. He went into each spray-concealed bend like a novice who's never skidded a car before. He survived because he was innocent.

Matson couldn't bear to think about it. Lotte Weiss was on the seat ahead of him, her face turned against the head-rest as she pretended to relax. He leant forward to watch her. Constanz had her bottle. He and Lotte Weiss had nothing.

Her bruise was turning brown, the colour of an apple when it rots. Odd that he wanted, briefly, to kiss her. At plague times the mating instinct is strong. Before the fear of

140

death or a parachute jump. Afterwards he always needed to drink.

He looked at her physical hurt, then at the boy. The child slept, his lips crushed below her bruised cheek the way children doze in summer lofts on farms. The child slept in his midsummer trance of apples.

It might be hot, even inside an Adriatic rainstorm; but it wasn't summer yet. Weiss wouldn't last till summer.

Hailstones now. They weren't big, but they fell thickly. Weiss came off the accelerator. They slowed by a whole kilometre an hour.

The General did not slow because the road was slippery. He slowed because he wanted to exult.

'Someone, somewhere, will be plotting my path on a map.'

'Two someones, General. The man who hopes to protect you, the man who intends to kill you.'

'Perhaps it's a woman.' Lotte Weiss's voice was as emotionless as the chorus in a Greek tragedy. She did not open her eyes to speak.

'What they will see is two flashes of lightning. Can you picture it, Matson?'

He was trying not to involve himself in any further flights of paranoia. He willed the General to stay on the road.

'My route conforms exactly to the double zed of the SS collar flash.'

'Bits of tin,' Constanz scoffed. She used her bottle the way street girls use lipstick – to give her something to do with her face. 'With a bit more imagination you could have scrawled SS all over their fucking country.'

'I wrote that story once. Don't use strong language. I don't mind that it's unfeminine. It blunts a person's force.' He added something in German. Matson realised he was repeating the same pronouncement. The General was more than happy to quote himself.

'Lotte's right for once,' Constanz growled. 'It could be a woman.' She took a further drink to show how reflective she was being. 'It could even be a fucking woman. *That* feminine enough for you, old fella?'

Weiss could be appalled, probably by a horse or a dog. Matson guessed that cats were animals he refused to tolerate.

141

2

The road came off the hills, and became a jigsaw of tarred cobbles, the unfenced waterfront of a one-street town. The Mercedes halted by an open-air bar of tin tables. At its back was a tiny hotel. A few dozen houses faced across the road to the sea.

'Here we stop,' Weiss said. He was a general. He stopped without consultation. He switched off engine and wipers. This put paid to the hail and rain.

Outside the wind was steady. It came straight off the sea.

'These storms never last,' the General said. 'They are love not war.'

'Breathless,' Matson agreed.

'I am never out of breath. Nor should you be.'

Lotte Weiss woke the child and led him from the car. He followed her unsteadily over the road and among the tin tables, which were red. Matson had not asked the boy's name. He was an irrelevance among too many possibilities of danger. Matson watched mother and son disappear into the interior gloom behind the bar.

'She's arranging for our rooms,' Weiss said. 'I stopped here to hang a man once. They didn't mind. He wasn't a local.'

'I'd better phone about the Range Rover.'

'She'll see to that in her time. I do not keep a dog. I've a daughter-in-law,' the General explained. He busied himself with her cases, just the same.

Matson took hold of Constanz's cases.

'Leave them, Matson,' she said.

'I need a drink.'

'It'll rot your teeth. Have some of mine.' Her bottle was empty. She stood waiting for Weiss to return, hating him to go away, miserable at the domestic trivialities of her ex-lover's life.

They stepped carefully towards the bar. There was wetness everywhere, sheets of rainwater never quite wide enough to tuck themselves into a drain. The place would look beautiful in fine weather. Today it wore badly fitting puddles.

3

When Weiss returned from the car for the third time, he was running. He ordered something at the bar, something which evidently surprised them. When they'd found it for him, somewhere out back, he did not wait to be served. He trotted over to fetch it. It was a carafe of water. He drank from it without a glass.

'You're very fit, General. Remarkably so for a man of seventy.'

'I'm fit, yes.' He spoke as though his fitness was absolute. 'You'd beat me over a mile, perhaps. Over ten, I wonder? Over twenty, certainly not. I can keep going. I don't talk of running, but in a big country like this, with a Bergen pack, I don't need to stop. Most men stop. Not me.'

'I believe you, General.'

'Stopping, staying – is "staying" right?'

'Do you mean "keeping going"?'

'Perhaps I do.' He sighed at the ugliness of English, Matson's English anyway. 'Stopping, staying – they are both in the mind. I keep my mind young, and I do not stop. It's all in the mind.'

'And the feet, General. Corns can take mileage from a man. Blisters even more so.'

'I do not think this turn in the talk is worthy.' The General had thin skin, pink nostrils, red earlobes. He breathed like a man who was totally in charge of his air.

'Sex is what keeps me fit, Captain Matson.' He glanced briefly towards the Ehrenberg-Zanetti, as if she were some kind of rubber inflatable. 'As a young man I used to fornicate often, many times a day if possible. I still do. Nowadays, I do it for its own sake. Then there were other concerns as well.'

Matson kept a straight face. The man wasn't joking. His life was on the short side for jokes. 'What were they, General?'

'Politics.' Again not a joke. 'I used sex a lot for its politics.' He watched a fishing-boat off-shore as if it was there to help him think. 'I did it a lot for politics, but always savouring the woman as well.'

143

'Doubtless.'

'I did the little *fräuleins* round here, and their mothers, to show them and their men who was boss.' He drank more water thirstily. What was disgusting about him was that he did everything at the same speed. 'For almost two years, I don't think I took a woman without it being to show some man who was boss. The women didn't seem to mind. It was like those communities where the girl has to be with the priest the night before the wedding.'

'To show them he's boss?'

'To show her God is boss. Here they did it with me and learned that the Third Reich was boss.'

'Let's hope they've forgotten,' Constanz said.

'It's a Croatian coast.' He spoke to Matson, not her. He answered Matson as if the man was the ventriloquist and the woman the doll. 'The Croats have very little reason to dislike us.'

He licked his lip thoughtfully. He was about to have something important to say. Something even more important.

4

'You stood beside me earlier today, Captain Matson. Let me buy you a drink.'

'You should buy one for Mrs Ehrenberg-Zanetti. She's the one who saved you.'

Constanz began to move in, but Weiss waved her away. 'She smells, doesn't she?'

'Not to me, General Weiss.'

'You'd better have her, then. The nostrils are important in such matters.' The General clapped his hands, and called to the bar.

Matson was handed a tumbler of sour wine in a sour glass. The General tasted his and grimaced. 'Ah, they serve us that woman's armpit. They like us but they do not love us.' He set his glass on a table. The drink was done.

Matson followed him across the road to the town's edge. Constanz was through with following.

The Adriatic looked clean enough, or the water at Matson's feet did. Clear as diluted ink.

'The sea is supposed to be full of mythology, Hauptmann. The Greek sea, anyway. I must have a Roman imagination. I notice only vehicles tipped from jetties. Burning boats and drowned men.'

'And women, General. And children.'

'*Impedimenta.* That's what Caesar called them. *Impedimenta* when alive. *Detrita* when dead. If men place their hands on their swords, women should avoid the edge.'

'You admire Caesar, General?'

Weiss didn't answer. Matson still had his glass, but the occasion was over. The General turned and went inside, leaving him with Contanz. She tried to stay buoyant, but at best she was perky, then very soon forlorn.

'Can I order us something to eat?'

'What do you want in return?' She pretended to smile, then shrugged to acknowledge the thought wasn't for real. She was one of those truly awful people who are totally likeable. And she knew it.

The General came back outside and said to Matson. 'We can eat in two hours. Lili has ordered us a meal.' He did not include the Ehrenberg-Zanetti, but Matson intended to see she wasn't ostracized.

'"Lily"!' Constanz scoffed. 'She, as they say, is no flower. Are we drinking in my room or yours?'

His mum would not have approved of her son having a woman in his room. She had been in rooms herself. They bought a bottle of wine and went to Constanz's room. She put her arms round him and began to sob.

He had been brought up by women. He knew about tears.

'I was so fucking scared,' she said. 'The job says I stay close to the old fake – I *need* to be close to him, you know that – but tricks like those farmers, and then the rifle shot —'

'What scares you is running out of drink.' He pulled her arms from his neck, sat her on her bed and kept well away. 'Who runs you?'

'*Newsweek*, I told you.'

'That's it,' he agreed. 'You're a stringer. You're not a correspondent. You're not a professional intelligence officer, either. But someone strings you. I wonder who.'

If that was a question, he'd have to find his own answer.

'I was fucking *scared.* You weren't fucking scared.'

'I was scared.'

'Henk wasn't.' Mentioning his name made her tears almost genuine.

'The General is used to bullets,' he comforted. He sat beside her on the bed. 'He's a pillbox, like de Gaulle. If he flinched at a bit of small arms fire he'd have to shoot himself.'

'How you rubbish us all.'

'You rubbish yourself. But only because you've got one or two bits in your brain that old Weiss is deficient in.'

She didn't like this topic either. She got away from it by unbuttoning his shirt. She appeared to do it absentmindedly, and if he hadn't been on leave he would probably have stopped her at once. That's what he told himself, but her hands were sharp. They went beneath the skin. Even so, he wasn't about to have sex with her. Turn your front to a woman and your back to the world.

At some time during this, he noticed her ankle. He didn't notice it immediately. He wasn't John Donne. He got to it slowly.

5

Constanz wore clean-cut clothes in tough fabric, the kind of expensive arty-cum-sporty that went with her shoulder bag. She was a lot easier to undress than dress, as they say – in his salary, anyway. And she wore boots.

She didn't wear boots in bed, not by the time he noticed her ankle. Her ankle was bound in pink plaster.

'How did you damage that?'

'It's my bangle,' she yawned. 'My hallmark. Like a priestess courtesan's in the Temple of Horus.'

He wondered what she kept under it. Bruised flesh? A strained tendon? Or something more interesting?

'He forgot to let go,' she moaned. 'I forget whether he was throwing me on to the bed or into the bed, but he forgot to let go.'

'I thought it was out of the bed.'

'He never threw me out of his bed. It's a trick in wrestling.'

146

Or in shearing a sheep or branding a steer. You hold them by the foot. He didn't say that. He'd been bitchy enough.

'You've got an old man's body. Corrugated.'

'Irish whiskey and the whip.'

'I thought Irish Whip was a throw in wrestling.' The General had given her wrestling on the brain.

'The whip was Libyan, not Irish.'

'Pleasurable?'

'For someone, I daresay.'

'Providing you can still get your jimjam up.'

'Took me a year to get the knack back. Surprised what a bit of violence will do to it. It wasn't even a lump in my throat.'

'What happened to your friend? The one with the whip.'

'He got between the light and a gun someone was holding.'

'Who was the someone?'

'One of those names you never find in history books. I'm not going to make love to you, Constanz. Sorry,' he said, a few moments later. 'That was awful of me.'

She began to cry, or to curse. It was all under her breath, and everything was getting so bloody dark.

He found their bottle of wine on her bedside cupboard, then some glasses, one of his blindfold accomplishments.

'Perhaps we shouldn't have begun,' he said.

'Perhaps not.'

'So why?'

'I'm so fucking lonely.'

He poured wine, sat back on the bed, and cuddled her. They drank and talked, then drank some more. They slept sitting up, holding each other like drunks against a lamppost. They slept for an hour. Matson was good at sleep.

He felt bad about her when he woke, but he was glad he'd made the effort to be companionable. He needed friends.

'Now make me laugh,' she commanded as she got off the bed. 'For fuck's sake, Matson, make me laugh.'

She didn't laugh. The lavatory flushed itself instead.

'I'm going to drown Henk in something like that,' Constanz said. 'Wet or dry, I'm going to drown him in one of those Croatian lavatory bowls.'

'I thought you loved him.'

'My love is like that.' She came back to sit on the bed. Or her ankle did.

6

They were late for the meal. It was an interesting occasion, even halfway through the second course. Everybody there disliked at least one other person, except for the child.

After half an hour's toying with his food and refusing the wine, the General picked the lad up under one arm, as if he were a duffle-bag, and carried him off to bed.

Constanz muttered to herself, stood abruptly and crossed the road to the sea. It was jet black, with fishing lights or island lights far out. This left Matson alone with Lotte Weiss for the first time. The tin table was uncomfortable. They hadn't been given cloths.

'Herr Weiss is quite the family man,' he began. 'Absolutely devoted.' You say things like that, across the languages, to a woman who disturbs you. A woman with a pretty, bruised face.

'My interest to the General is that I am the little man's mother.'

'His grandson.'

She hesitated. 'Yes, his grandson. For me, the boy is somewhat more.'

'Clearly. He's your son.'

'He's my pension.'

She touched Matson's hand quickly with her own, and he liked her doing that. Or he thought she touched him and thought he liked it. Reality or illusion, he liked it. The touch of their fingers, or the tingle of her thought, had been impersonal, though, as if she wanted to feel some younger skin simply to remind herself such things were there.

She carried on talking, but her talk had gone beyond him. He smiled at her, neither fondly nor befuddled, then watched Constanz walk back across the road.

He was growing sleepy with drink. He desired Lotte Weiss. He had a death-wish on him greater than the General's.

148

TWELVE

1

Next morning Lotte Weiss' face was better. Her cheek was inflamed, but it needed colour anyway. She looked no more damaged than she would after a sleepless night.

Had vitamin E done this, or an infusion of the General's life-force?

Matson tried not to think about her. It was too early for thinking. It was German time. The sea near in was dark with the mountains overhead. Only far out were there slats of fire.

A single forty-watt bulb swung on the street side of the bar. Its contacts were fickle, its light too meagre to watch them by. Or to shoot them by, if anyone had the mind.

He stood with the two women and sipped coffee. They waited for the General. The coffee was bad. It wasn't even neutral. It was downright and deliberately bad. The bulb was what it had always been, the colour of Matson's liver. It couldn't get any deader until its filaments went.

Across the road there were street lamps. They had switched themselves off in the pre-dawn glimmer, so their stems and wrought-iron cross-pieces were silhouetted against the brightening sea. Gulls used them as staging posts. They reminded Matson of the photographs in Lolly's book at the end of the chapter on the executions in Belgrade. Some of Weiss's early work.

The General said he had stopped here for a hanging. Matson guessed he would have used one of those street lamps. He mentioned the idea quietly to Constanz.

'Fuck you,' she said. 'And fuck the SS. And fuck where they killed the poor guy. All I know is this bloody shack makes its coffee from his bones.' She belched and pushed her face into Matson's but only because Weiss had arrived,

149

walking along the front from the sea.

Weiss nodded to Matson, as if he had just sold him a horse and was sorry it was playing him up. 'My path is the flash of lightning, as I promised you.'

'Providing you strike Belgrade.'

'Do you want some of this coffee, Henk?'

'Thank you, no. I saw him make it with water from the lavatory cistern. Rusty but perfectly hygienic. That is why I let you drink it while I went to check the car. It is full of bad thoughts just the same.'

'What about the car, General?'

'A handful of mud in the exhaust. One exhaust only. No more than a gesture.'

'Someone trying to cut your power on the climb out of town.'

'Perhaps. Now we are warned. You had better ride in the front seat with me, Hauptmann, in case these Croats have changed their allegiance.'

'Tito was a Croat.'

'Tito was different. Tito was a communist. I always knew exactly how I stood with him. And he with me. I respected him for it.'

'I daresay you'd have hanged him.'

'I've hanged lots of men I've respected. It's a waste of energy to hang anyone else. If you want to destroy a forest, Hauptmann, burn the good wood.'

Lotte Weiss went upstairs and came down with the child in her arms. He lay outstretched, with his limbs blanketed against the cold. And he slept. Children wake early, but not this one. Matson wondered if he were ill or drugged, or so full of his mother's anxiety he daren't face the day.

Weiss led them to the Mercedes. He didn't fetch it for them. He wasn't a chauffeur. He leant over its bonnet and spread his maps in the gloom.

'Orders at tank-light, General?'

'My daughter-in-law would like us to be riding in a tank, yes. I don't like tanks myself. You can't see the man who is killing you.'

Constanz got ready to laugh, but a gull did it for her.

'So here are my intentions. I am going to Belgrade, there

to be rid of Captain Matson. I shall retain Mrs Ehrenberg-Zanetti, for no other reason than I made her a promise. I shall move at speed, but by my zed. My zed is – let me see – my zed is by Knin, Bosanko Grahovo, Livno, Zenica, Samac Slav, and then by autoput to Belgrade. How does that sound, Hauptmann Matson?'

'Like Milton, General.'

A teacher in Camberwell had read them some Milton once. 'How does that sound, lads?'

'Like shit, sir.'

2

They arranged themselves in the car. Weiss placed his pistol beside him on the seat. Was it an invitation for Matson to grab it if necessary?

He didn't touch the thing. It was the ancient Luger Parabellum and it leaked oil like an old gearbox.

Weiss U-turned the Mercedes and drove north, climbing out of town the way they had come in. This surprised Matson until he remembered that the turn-off to Knin was a mile or two back. It wasn't the clever way to Belgrade, but it was the General's way, the SS way, his whoreson zed. Matson hadn't expected such a route. Nor, probably, had the people who doctored the car's exhaust.

Weiss drove fast, but a mite more comfortably than yesterday. If you must drive the Dalmatian coast with a maniac, then north is the way to go. The vertiginous drop to the sea is on the far side of the road.

Matson could hear bells, a persistent friendly chime. There was no village belfry, no village of any sort. The chime was riding with them. He listened to his own ears, the way you do after a hard evening's drinking. 'Have you got the radio on, General?'

'Don't be ridiculous.'

The belling became insistent. Matson knew what it was, and realized with horror he was probably too late.

'Pull over.'

'Again, don't be ridiculous.'

'Stop the car, Weiss.'

'Idiot. I stop for nothing.'

Matson had been promoted. He was being afforded equal status with the sleeping child. He reached for the handbrake and anchored it progressively.

The car was already skidding before he touched the brake. The General was unable to control it. The bells still chimed as the car spun and drifted off into a gravelled hollow against the side of the hill.

'I said pull over, Weiss. Were you waiting for God to do it for you?'

'God?' he mocked.

'God or Galileo.'

'Yes, it's a fair way down to the water. I think the front wheel is loose.'

'I thought you checked the car. They don't need to kill you with a bomb, General, they can get you to kill yourself with a tintack.'

Matson stepped out, and stood back while a petrol tanker brushed past on the wrong side of the road. It was followed by a long procession of cars overtaking a donkey cart. He didn't say any more. Presumably even Weiss understood how close they had come to death.

It wasn't a tintack, but something much more direct. As Matson levered off the right front hubcap, he decided to examine the tyres for nailing. It was clear Weiss hadn't bothered.

The cap came free. Matson held it hard against the wheel so as not to spill its contents. This was where the belling had come from, and here were the bells.

Three nuts spun loose in the rim, polished by their kilometre of rotation. The fourth nut was all that retained the wheel, and that one was on the end of its stalk. It had almost cut through the bolt.

Matson carried the three studs in their hubcap to show the General. The old man was searching southwards, through his binoculars, back along the coast. He took no notice of Matson whatsoever.

'I'll need the jack, Weiss. Someone loosened your nuts for you.'

152

'Loosened 'em?' the Ehrenberg-Zanetti shrilled. 'God, I'd love to tear them out by the roots!'

Weiss let that one pass. So did Matson. 'I thought you said you'd checked the car. You'd better leave the checking to me in future.' He was annoyed at his own lack of care.

'You're quite right, Hauptmann. I don't check wheels. I leave that to chaps like you.'

'You're supposed to be trained. Experienced, anyway. The books say you fought a war against those insurrectionists down there.'

'I fought a war against a partisan army, Hauptmann. I kept the insurrectionists tucked up in my bed.' He spoke for Matson, his women in the car and possibly for his grandchild. His women, at least, were to be insulted. He kept his binoculars to his eyes, his mind on loftier things. 'You were right about one little matter. They were waiting for me on the climb out of town. What a pity I climbed in the wrong direction.'

Matson's binoculars were locked in his wrecked car. He reached for the General's. They were an ancient pair of military Zeiss, with range-finding graticules.

'Whatever murderer tampered with my wheel, Matson – God can keep that one for Himself. The glasses are full of more interesting possibilities.'

Matson let his eyes be guided across the roofs of last night's town towards the far side of the re-entrant where the coastal highway rose to leave the treeline opposite and gouged its way along the crag and then the sea-cliff before disappearing south.

At about their own height there was a gritting recess, much like this one. Two groups of men crouched there. He refocussed the Zeiss.

Seven of them with another above the road to act as lookout. They had deployed two medium-to-heavy machine guns on tripods to enfilade the distant slab of highway.

'Partisans, Hauptmann, as I say. They've even kept me one of those Vickers your Churchill armed them with.'

'It looks as if they pinched one of yours as well, General. A German army Maschinengewehr thirty-four, unless I'm much mistaken.' He smirked. 'Manufactured in Austria, as it happens, by Stey-Daimler-Puch, especially for Prinz Eugen. Your men got careless, Weiss.'

'My men got dead.'

'This lot are hardly very brisk, either. What would you say the range is, General? Two thousand yards? You'd expect to engage a target at this distance, surely?'

'I would always engage rather than not engage. It's a matter of will with me.'

'Zen in the art of machine-gun deployment?'

'Not Zen. Will. This lot must be blind not to seize their chance to shoot at me.'

'They can see too well, General. They can see the other cars on the road.'

'If you want to bring down a giant you must expect to crush the little people who stand in his shadow.' He turned to face Constanz's derision. 'I do not speak of myself. I speak of war. To kill the giant is the essence of battle. If there is no giant to kill, then you have not properly formulated your objective.'

'Whizz,' she said. 'I think whizz is the word I mean.'

Again the sense of unreality. A combined cyclic rate of two thousand rounds a minute, so why slow the Mercedes by bunging its exhaust? Matson fidgeted his gaze to focus round a graticule. Even in tank-light he could see there was no belt in either gun, no ammunition trays either.

He didn't mention this to the General. The old man would be deeply hurt. They weren't trying to kill him, simply frighten him to death.

'I came the wrong way for them,' he kept on saying. 'It was my lightning-stroke, you see. My zed on the map will protect us.'

3

Matson jacked up the front of the Mercedes. Nobody thought to get out. Fixing wheels was men's work. It took a Matson to do the job, and a Weiss to see it was good.

Matson did the job. Weiss could see whatever he damn well liked.

Matson walked round the car. There was nothing under-neath, as the General had said. The two rear hubs were plas-tered in swarf from last night's storm. You can't fake a goo like that.

The left front wheel was different. The three-pointed star at the centre of the hub had been hand wiped. There was a bright smudge of cleanness from here to the edge of the hubcap.

Matson took a screwdriver and prised at it gently. Only checking. If someone had hidden a device with a rotation trigger, it would have blown within yards of moving off.

He saw the tiny loop of wire. 'Get them out of there, General. Get them out and stand back.' He could hardly speak. He tried to hold the cap entirely still. Salt dripped from his forehead and filled his eyes with pain.

The car rocked on the jack as they moved from their seats. He'd forgotten to unfasten the jack.

The jack collapsed. Matson didn't die. He assumed he didn't. The strain in his forearms and chest and abdomen was excruciating, but his brain retained its eyes, and its eyes blinked themselves clear of anxiety and looked at the hub in his hands. His hands were remarkably steady. The hub it was that shook and so did its loop of wire. Its loop of wire was clad in red plastic, and the plastic trembled in sympathy.

The child didn't speak or shrill, but it was upright at last, and on noisy boots. A child's footsteps are unmistakable. Matson heard them come sleep-walking towards the bomb.

'Idiot!' Weiss patted the lad away to his mother. Weiss himself stood closer. He had to be where the danger was. He was scared. He breathed noisily for once.

Matson's hands didn't like being breathed over. They were going very well without breath.

He let them get on with it. His face flattened itself against the bonnet. His body twisted and levitated so his right leg was planted in front of the radiator grille, while his left leg and his chest and abdomen lay over the hood. A hubcap can hold an awful lot of plastic, so lying over the cylinder block wasn't going to do him any good.

'Nervous, Hauptmann?' The old sod climbed into his mind. 'If that thing blows you can take comfort that your guts will be mashed by a very superior engine.'

'I know, General. I'll be fuel-injected.'

The device was fastened against the rim of the hub with adhesive tape. The stuff was so pink and mumsy, so like the plaster on Constanz's ankle, that he nearly choked on it. But it was the wire that held his attention. Did its circuit have to make or break in order to trip the trigger?

'Evens, General. Equal odds either way if you're a betting man. I'd like you to fetch me the pliers from your tool box. Your money, too. Fifty per cent either way.'

Matson looked at the pliers but couldn't free a hand to take them. Weiss would have to do it.

'My money says we cut it we die,' Weiss said.

'Then you won't live to collect, because we're certainly going to cut it, General.'

Matson examined the loop again, and what he could see of the device. He hoped the bomb-maker was not going to prove too clever for his own common sense. Sound but unsubtle would be exactly right.

The cap slipped from his fingers.

4

It seemed to fall for a long time, but it lay on the gravel almost before it left his hand. Time is like that and so are fingers. He tried to snatch it back, to return it to stillness. He couldn't. It tore out its loop of wire and left it hanging from under one of the bolts. Cutting it would have killed him. It was already earthed, so the circuit was made. He should have seen that and understood its implications.

The fall severed the wire just the same. The device was like a Croatian lavatory. It did not work.

'You're unfit, Hauptmann.'

'Frightened, General. You look rather moist yourself.' Matson got both legs on the ground and examined the hub. It lay face down, and could hide dangers; but he felt increasingly certain it was a dud. Bomb-disposal experts know this euphoria. Unless they take steps to deal with it they become dead.

Bomb-disposal experts deal with bombs. Matson picked up the hub and looked at the battery taped to the rim.

An ordinary two-cell battery and a piece of wire. Nothing else. As he stepped towards Weiss, his shoes sloshed with sweat. 'A trick, General. Somebody's trying to tease you till you run out of caution.'

Lotte and Constanz had got hold of Weiss's binoculars, and looked thoughtful at what they could see through them. Weiss snatched them away from Lotte and pushed her towards the car. He didn't approve of women playing with men's toys. He handed the glasses to the little boy, who found some sky in them, then something miraculous like a leaf or a tree.

Constanz glanced at Matson for comfort. He offered her a kiss for Weiss's sake. He thought it was for Weiss, anyway. Her lips tasted better unflavoured, but the kiss wasn't for her.

As he fondled her, he showed her the battery. 'Tuck it in your handbag, darling. It's where it came from, isn't it?' He rummaged among the hardware hanging from her shoulder-strap, and found the empty flat-celled torch. Empty torch, empty bottle, empty cartridge box. Her gun at least was loaded. The adhesive matched the stuff on her ankle. 'I trust the wheel nuts were somebody else's doing. Two people with a death-wish is more than I could put up with so early in the morning.'

Her teeth were chattering. Withdrawal symptoms, perhaps. 'They could kill us with those fucking machine-guns,' she said at last.

'That's enough fucking for today.'

5

After the adrenalin surge, the let-down. During the let-down, the extreme sourness of mind.

Matson watched Weiss wave his women into the car. The boy was once more asleep, seemed to sleep as soon as his mother touched him. There was something wrong about this, but not for now. Matson was a man for short-term trouble, not for children. He prowled around the Mercedes.

He felt the roof box. Fibreglass, impossible to booby-trap. The hand luggage was stowed as yesterday, up above the box, tensioned under a tarpaulin with three or four webs of rubber-sprung octopus clips. Weiss had reloaded the cases himself, so nothing could have been planted under the tarpaulin, any more than in the box.

All this had been bearing down on the jack while Matson had changed the wheel then struggled with the supposed bomb. At some time or other, it had collapsed it. It had also been weighing on Matson's mind.

If the General, Lotte, the child, and Constanz kept their spare knickers on the roof, what on earth did they carry in the boot? An inflatable power boat? A motorbike with side-car? A pack-howitzer? There was room enough.

He depressed the catch, and surprised himself by opening the lid. He also surprised Weiss, who came quickly round the car, having presumably released the electronic lock from the front. Weiss wanted to make sure his load hadn't shifted. Instead he found Matson, and slammed the boot shut.

There were spades, shovels, crowbars, and long-handled trenching tools, picks with their helves removed, all of them brand new, racked and as glitteringly tidy as a gigantic box of knives. Enough of them to bury an infantry battalion for a siege.

Weiss had locked his truths away from the retina but not the memory. Matson's curiosity was left with coiled power cables, extension lanterns and a small compressor. Impossible to know whether the flat wooden casket underneath them contained a pneumatic drill, the family Christmas presents, or a couple of the old man's ancestors; but the hydraulic compressor was indicative.

So much backweight had kept them alive when the front wheel loosened. The high-profiled front probably prevented them from nosing in and turning over. The unusual parallel-ogram of weight certainly stopped the bolts from shearing while they were halfway up the cliff road.

Matson said all this, then asked, 'Archaeology, General?'

Weiss studied him hard. 'Geology, actually. I have an instinct about this property of mine.'

158

Matson had told Weiss to expect trouble. Weiss had evaded it, and avoided more than he expected. So now trouble was over.

Matson's usefulness had lasted for a kilometre. He was in the back seat again, with Constanz. He didn't know which of them had made the arrangement, but he was glad of it. If he had to drive in a car with a maniac's foot on the pedal, he was happier in the back. Not safer, just happier.

They turned off the coastal highway and began to climb through the mountains. The route was on a map somewhere. So was the North Pole.

The old man's thumb-nail had found a road marked as a track. This in a country where the roads marked as roads were mostly tracks anyway.

They climbed steeply. They weren't yet flying. They powered upward through contours of forest. First a penumbra of tall cypress fingers interspersed among cork or red larch – Matson wasn't sure this morning; he kept his perceptions tucked in – then a deeper gloom of layered spruce that had been taken over by God and the winds and packed in tight. They rose endlessly through this, as if through some kind of dank cloud. Only it wasn't dank. It was dry and musty as a geriatric's sneeze, and the smell needled in through the Mercedes' air conditioning and through the unstoppered rifle holes. They rose endlessly but they had to end. They were powered by Weiss's ego, which always antici-pated conclusions.

They levelled out among mountain oaks. There are more oaks in the world than good wines, Matson found himself saying to Constanz, who wasn't talking to him, and certainly more than there are good beers. He couldn't see if these were sessile or pedunculate, and he didn't glance twice to find out. He was waiting for the bullet to come in or the grenade to bounce on the bonnet. Shrapnel made lovely exit wounds. They were pedunculate, all right. And his blood was sessile. It spouted straight from the heart.

They lifted into another climb so gentle it didn't change a gear, and came out into sunshine on a landscape of jumbled

159

bone. The track lost itself amid a huge amphitheatre of rock, white against the sun, black elsewhere. The Mercedes drove across tarns of dust, picking its way through a labyrinth of Weiss's metaphysical propositions like a beetle scurrying for cover.

Matson imagined the sniper's rifle. He saw the helicopter.

7

He watched it for some time. He watched through several changes of desolation. Sometimes they twisted up the boulder-snagged floor of a hanging valley, sometimes they followed a shelf along a cliff, a shelf that sloped outward and grew narrower against a rockface that stood higher.

The helicopter kept low, save that low was up here, and it stayed behind. It practised what the military call tactical flying. This must be the whirlybird Popovic had mentioned, here to pick up the pieces. Matson felt sure that the colonel's communications truck hadn't followed along a track like this – or followed them at all.

An intelligent surveillance helicopter should scan the road ahead, not the road behind, but even a low helicopter has a reasonable field of view. Perhaps the observer in this one reckoned he could see enough.

They were among trees again, or bushes with a bit of ambition. They had climbed to a flatness where the moss and lichen could make soil, so thorns could root among the stones. Perhaps it was a mountain top. Matson's memory of the map suggested that the central plateau was hours away.

Weiss spoke to Lotte. She shifted her grip on the child and began to scrabble among a box of cassettes. They were to have music. Matson objected. 'You'll need your ears, Weiss. You must know that.'

'I'm on holiday, Matson. Death didn't follow me up here.'

'I'd prefer silence, General, if I'm to do you any good.'

'You've tightened the wheels, Hauptmann. You've done your bit.'

Weiss gestured for Lotte to turn up the volume. He leant forward himself and twisted it louder.

160

The sky whirled. The roof drummed with dancers in hobnailed boots. For a moment the old man's ego seemed to burst into intolerable noise – the old man's ego then Matson's rage. It was the helicopter squatting overhead.

The thing had raced up and dropped down on the car, trying to tell them something.

Matson put his hand into Constanz's bag. Her hand was already there. The helicopter stayed close. What the hell was it trying to say?

Nothing could be waiting ahead of them, surely? It takes an army to seal every possible road, not a handful of fanatics.

8

Not even a holy idiot could outguess Weiss the way he was behaving now. He switched off the ignition and let the Mercedes drift to a standstill. He got out and left them. It was his car. He did things like that. The thump of the rotors invaded the open door, but couldn't beat back the treacle of the music.

The helicopter lifted, then dropped into an indolent circling hover. Perhaps it was only Weiss it was talking to. Perhaps it had spoken.

They stepped from the car in their turn. Where the great man is seen to go, little men will follow.

Lotte spread the child on the front seat. The tape was still playing. Matson switched it off.

This woke the child, who jumped straight into running. He saw a butterfly. They were fritillaries even up here, helicopter high, imaginary fritillaries.

Matson parted some bushes. There were higher mountains to come. They were a long way ahead, built of whiteness and halted cloud. This, underfoot, was the soft top of a sharp world. The sun was everywhere, but the air smelled wet, as it will when the wind blows in high places.

He could scarcely hear the helicopter. There was nothing for its rotors to echo against. It turned like a meat-fly, un-decided between plate and plate.

The child had lost its butterfly and now circled witlessly,

mimicking the helicopter. Always at such moments the bullet comes, but only in books. Matson knew there was no one here to send it.

Weiss continued to surprise him. He lit a cigarette and tossed the packet back into the car. Matson was sure he didn't smoke. He remembered the General saying something to that effect last night. The cigarette was a ritual, a gesture from the past.

'This is where the Bosnians killed their Serbs,' he explained. 'Or the Hercegovinians killed them. I forget which. Here they killed Serbs, anyway. Not many.' He threw his scarcely smoked cigarette away and filled the air with its breath. 'Ten, twenty, thirty thousand. That sort of number. Two army corps of Serbs. The military parallel is inappropriate, of course: they had their women with them, and in this case their children. Perhaps fifty thousand. It can't be more than sixty. This isn't a significant place. Most of the Serbs were sent up the railway line to Jasenovac, where the job was done properly. There's no railway on this side.' He became moody at the aesthetics of it. 'Mostly they marched them up from the coast, exactly the way we came. Some died along the route. Some ran off and had to be marched up again. Quite a lot came by truck from inland. There's a better road in a kilometre or so.'

So there could be an ambush ahead. Matson doubted if that was what the helicopter was signalling. He remembered something quite private. He stood against the side of the Mercedes and felt beneath the tarpaulin on the roof-box. He had another half bottle of Courvoisier in the case. He brought it back and offered it to Constanz. She looked furious, the way people do when you hand them a truth, but she took it.

'Yes, they did the job properly at Jasenovac. You can do the job properly once you've got trains.'

'Gas chambers, General?'

'These were Serbs, Matson. There are lots of ways to kill Serbs, none of them pleasant to talk about in front of the children.' He smiled at Lotte as well as the boy. 'It was the trains that were essential. Better for the kids, too. A lot were sent to Croatia for adoption, but none from this side.' He relished another memory. 'The Serbs have always felt doomed, so they overbreed. You've encountered the theory, perhaps. The Croats are Catholic yet they don't breed. They know their God will save them. The Führer recognised the conundrum. They are bourgeois, bourgeois to a man with the manners of old women. The bourgeoisie hoard their seed the way they count their money.' He kicked the soil. 'Anyway, this place wouldn't do. I made them put a stop to it.' He glanced towards the helicopter. 'Something else they won't forgive me for! You should put paid to people where you find them, or somewhere you can take them easily.'

He looked at Constanz. He acknowledged her stare. He was seeking the approval of a superior logic. 'Thank God it never became the fashion up here. A few thousand, as I say. There were no permanent hutments, no memorials.'

'Is that it?' Constanz asked. She hadn't drunk any cognac. 'Is that the whole of what you've got to say about it?'

Weiss always had more to say. 'I envy these people up here. I envy them the inaccessibility of this place.' He kicked the soil again, demonstrating with his boot. 'They've not even been removed for burial.' He turned what he had found. It was a caked skull. It looked like a flint with eyeholes.

'Jesus,' Constanz growled. 'It's a baby's.'

'Skulls are tiny.' Weiss was being gentle. 'It's the absence of meat and hair that creates the illusion.'

He went to the Mercedes and took out his binoculars. The helicopter was loud again, loud and low. It batted directly overhead, then went away east in a straight line.

Matson though he knew what it had been saying when it hovered over the car. Its pilot and observer and whoever else sat with them had said, 'This is the place, you bastard. You had to come here, didn't you?' Men can build a lot of rage in a helicopter, with their heads buzzing under the Jesus nut. Even men who report to cynics like Popovic.

Then he had a better idea. They had flown away as soon as they saw Weiss take out his binoculars. Binoculars in a razed extermination camp? The helicopter drifted away in the direction Weiss was searching.

At the edge of the plateau there were several sentinels of

rock, one of them black in the early sunlight. Weiss seemed to be using this as a datum point. There were graticules in the Zeiss. Matson had seen artillerists make a very exact survey with glasses like these. 'One degree subtends just under seventeen metres at a thousand,' he murmured.

'Quick answers are best, Hauptmann. One hundred at six thousand is the figure a soldier prefers to carry.'

Lotte sensed an indiscretion. She had a moment of social inspiration. She picked up the skull, considering it for her mantelpiece. Weiss told her to put it down. When the jackdaw rakes over its hoard, it always discards the bones from among its trinkets.

Matson didn't say this aloud. He was through with being cheeky. First Leonard, then the boot full of trenching tools, made him think of trinkets.

9

Weiss keyed the ignition. Lotte got ready for another cassette. Constanz sat looking at nothing. The child crouched on his mother's knee and hummed.

'I wanted him to see this,' the General mused. 'And the rest of you.' He didn't mention what it was that he had come to see; his binoculars were back in the glove compartment. 'I wanted you to understand what these people are capable of.'

Constanz breathed as if she was making love. So many extremes of emotion, so few ways of showing it.

Matson spoke for her. 'You set them off, Weiss. You and your Führer. Croat against Serb, Serb and Montenegrin against Slovenian, Bosnian, Albanian, and just about everyone else. Slav against Slav against Slav.'

'So did you, Hauptmann. A Vickers machine-gun was pointing at me an hour or two ago. You probably gave it to Dragoljub Mihailovich to shoot Tito in the back. I have no use for that argument.' He got the engine running at last. 'God gave Lucifer the first box of matches. So is *He* responsible for the fires of hell?'

'You don't believe in hell or Lucifer, Weiss.'

'Oh, I do. I do. I've seen them both. It's God I don't believe in.' The Mercedes crunched along the track, parting the overgrown bushes. 'You argue like a woman, Matson.'

They had Johann Strauss, the Younger he believed. 'The Blue Danube', anyway. Again it was too loud. Belgrade and its Danube were still two hundred miles away.

10

They were on a new road now, with proper metalling, running south-east for dozens of kilometres. It followed a ridge line that paralleled the coastal mountains.

Constanz slept. The child slept. Lotte shifted him from thigh to thigh. Then the tape stopped its noise, and he lay against her undisturbed.

Even asleep, he distracted Matson. Ridiculous of Weiss to place him in so much danger.

A wheel could wobble off its stalk, a piece of malice explode inside the engine. What you do for the perfect act of sabotage is remove a wheel, saw three-quarters of the way through the base of each bolt where it can't be seen, replace the wheel, tighten the nuts, and wait for a bump in the road to do the rest. Matson should have looked beneath the dirty hubs as well as the clean one. He didn't deserve to be alive. He had let the Ehrenberg-Zanetti deflect his attention with a torch battery and a silly piece of plaster.

Trying to understand her place in the larger scheme of things was a distraction he could not afford. For the moment, he chose to see her make-believe bomb as the delinquency of a woman disturbed by love. He knew this was a glib conclusion, sexist, and probably stupid.

He listened to the airstream filtering through the damaged Mercedes, the sough of its tyres. He was grateful for the improvement in the music.

Hendrik Reinhard Weiss ran on autopilot. The backs of his ears were pink. Everything between them was so bad that Matson ought to take Constanz's gun and put a bullet through it. Constanz would hardly thank him, but she wanted somebody to do it and she needed to be there when it was

165

done. She would love it to be with her own gun.

Matson wouldn't be the man. He only did what Leonard Fossit told him to, and Fossit had never told him to kill anyone. Surprising that several people had got themselves dead at his hands since he'd worked with Leonard. He couldn't bring himself to link cause and effect more directly than that.

The people who had died had been little men. Little men and mean-minded women. Their wickedness did not amount to a fraction of what Weiss was supposed to have done. Nor could the sum of their convictions, manic or perverse, match Weiss's for intensity. There was a moral there.

Matson had hated some of the people he had killed. For a moment, face to face, he had hated them all. Yet apart from a reflex disgust, an occasional rage, he had no feelings against Weiss.

He understood why Constanz was attracted to the old fox. There was his animal force, the glitter of his conceit. She also had her moralistic obsession with his past. Even smart people like her could fall in love with that kind of paradox. Weiss was famous. History had been relatively kind to him, much kinder than he had been to history. Try to unknot a noose like that and you can easily snare your hand.

Or find its coils become a serpent. The General represented the fake glamour of the original Nazis. He was a genial amalgam of Milton's Comus and Milton's Satan. Constanz didn't have Matson's advantage of a schooling in Camberwell, and of sitting among boys who had known to a man that Milton was shit.

You think of Milton, you think of hell. Matson thought of hell when he saw the tunnel.

11

The crest line ahead of them was steep. The road made no attempt to climb over it. It wriggled upwards for perhaps a thousand feet of altitude then plunged into an unlit hole as forbidding as the one under Loibl summit.

Blackness again. Darkness where there should be electric

166

light. Someone had switched off its neon strips the second they arrived beneath it.

The helicopter raced ahead to flurry against the entrance like a hawk whose prey has gone to ground.

Popovic had been cautious about tunnels, so much so that he had arranged for the Loibl to be closed. Tunnels were a happy hunting ground for the Serbian and Montenegrin partisans, he had implied, especially against Prinz Eugen.

What a pity he hadn't thought to close this one. There was something inside its enlarging tube of black. Something that clanked and rattled like the half-tracks of an armoured regiment – or the scales of St George's dragon. Something that flared with tiny flames.

12

Weiss braked. The sound from the tunnel was so intense they could hear it inside the car. So focussed they felt it now above the slide of the tyres. It smacked at them through the air. It pulsed up from the ground.

Here was where the real danger would be. Matson knew it in his gut.

The moment he realised the hole was full of yet another procession, fear became a rational certainty.

A procession in a wilderness is a nonsense. If it was a demonstration, it was aimed at them. Timed, and doubtless symbolically designed, to walk out of the earth as they sank into it.

A ritual resurrection to coincide with the Mercedes' burial?

Lights were bouncing up and down, feet were stamping; but they stayed in one place. There might be a few dozen of them. They might be the survivors of all the partisan brigades in their thousands. They were waiting for Weiss at the entrance of the tunnel. They were thronging at the mouth of the tomb.

Weiss stopping the car was the first entirely reasonable act Matson had seen him perform. Now he flashed his beams for the march to come on.

Shapes made of shadow began to move out at them.

The Luger lay on the seat again.

Matson felt for Constanz's fingers. He wanted to be sure they weren't doing something provocative, like wrapping themselves round her gun. He could stop the General loosing off, when the time came. Two fools would be more than he could cope with.

'Don't squeeze *any* part of me,' she hissed. '*All* of me wants to wee.' Her fingers were wet. So were his.

If the procession held the danger, then the Mercedes was the safest place. A choppy demonstration of hate is best ridden out in a vehicle.

The trouble with cars is that determined men can prise you out of them.

Weiss though along similar lines. He eased the Mercedes forward and reparked it firmly, hard against the right hand side of a wider piece of road. The procession could pass him by if it wished. Otherwise he had space to turn and burst free.

Perhaps the danger lay elsewhere. The hill ahead of them was huge. According to the map it was a three-thousand-metre mountain. The hole had taken his attention. Matson mustn't let it distract him from everything else.

The sun was high above them. It had not moved behind far enough to shine against the face of the cliff.

The cliff was in shadow. That was why the forms that burst from its tunnel were in shadow.

Further up the cliff, among rocks looking wet in an angle of sunshine?

Matson put his hand on Weiss's back. They weren't Vickers machine guns, not this time. Not Maschinengewehr 34. They were modernistic, flat-sided and therefore possibly home-made. They were on chest-high pivots manned by men who crouched alert in that wet drench of sunshine. There was even a van up there.

No: they weren't machine guns or Maschinengewehr. They were television cameras. Again the journey was being hijacked into the never-never land of video footage and peak-time viewing.

'Slick,' Constanz whispered. 'State Television is covering

these independence rallies as if they are protests against Weiss. That's one way to deflect them.'

'It won't work, surely?'

'Depends how much rage they can drum up against the old loop before someone puts paid to him.'

One little helicopter was all there was to keep him alive, a fragile perspex and struts affair with a four-man bubble. It was evidently puzzled witless.

If the TV company knew Weiss was coming this way, then plenty of people knew. It would only take one sniper up there in the shadow and Obergruppenführer Weiss could star in his much-deserved prime-time death.

Anyone can hire a television crew. This might be a private production.

People were leaving the tunnel in their hundreds. The helicopter made its mind up. Its rotors whirred it back into the sunshine. Glinting like a wet hen it came back towards the Mercedes.

Not before time. The procession was reaching out.

13

At a distance there looked to be as many women as men. This was an illusion. Some of the men wore caftans. So, further back, did a motley of young boys. These men and these boys carried flames in their hands and wore blood. The blood dripped from their burning hands and fell on their laps when they lifted their knees. These boys and these men who looked like women were dancing.

The caftans were made from white linen or buff unbleached cloth the colour of new sacks. They showed the blood well. Matson thought it was sheep's blood or dye. He was wrong.

The men in trousers had caps. So did the boys and men in caftans. The caps were blue or black, softer in outline than fezzes, fuller than skull-caps. Some were made of fleece, some were of woven or knitted wool.

Their trousers were black. The women wore black entirely. The women might have been blacks, so completely were they veiled. As they came nearer, they showed their hands. Their hands were not black, but had black ends, like candles. Their fingernails were varnished blue or mauve as for mourning.

The backs of their hands were the colour of beeswax or sour tallow. This, too, was the skin-colour of the men and the boys. It was more yellow than white, as if they chewed cordite or green tobacco. Their pale faces were still, and their heads were still, still but floating, like stones in a moonlit wall. Only their bodies danced.

Some carried staffs and some carried flambeaux. These smouldered. Inside the hill there had been fire. Now they danced it out of the hill.

'Creepers,' said the Ehrenberg-Zanetti. 'Creepers.' She went into her bag to find a camera, but came up with Matson's bottle instead. It was empty and she waved it dismissively. The car was surrounded by dancing men, and the bottle didn't go down well with them.

'Muslims,' Matson cautioned.

'I know. It's just as I said: another of those damned nationalist processions.' She examined a sign on a stick. 'Hercegovinian independence,' she triumphed. 'Or Bosnian independence. That Cyrillic script means as much to me as a donkey's dick, but it says independence as sure as God eats turkey.'

'Handschar against the rest,' Weiss exulted.

'I don't see any sign of the SS here, General.'

'They weren't SS, idiot. They were *of* the SS. They were Muslims, too.'

'History-geography,' Constanz agreed, 'with two fucking sugar lumps.' She handed Matson his bottle. 'Stick a ship in that one.' She found her camera and turned it the right way up.

The car became dark. The dancing men swayed around the Mercedes like a forest. As soon as they saw the camera they plastered the windows with their hands.

Then the hands blew away like so many leaves and doors were forced open. The windows were smeared with blood.

Really blood. Their hands bled. Blood is what looks like blood.

Women dragged Constanz and Lotte from the car and

170

threw scarves over their heads, blindfolding them. The boy had slipped from his mother's lap along the seat. They slapped him awake and made him stand outside by the open door.

Weiss did nothing when his daughter-in-law was taken, but he couldn't tolerate the threat to the boy. His pistol was in his hand, and levelled.

The dance did not stop. Its beat fell silent. The staffs no longer clicked, feet did not thump the soil, they hovered over the stones.

Impossible to halt so many hundreds of people with the nine shots in a hand-gun. It said a lot for Weiss's sense of timing that he was able to achieve even this much.

He stepped carefully from the car with the Luger outstretched before him. Matson stood watchfully beside him. The gun was at best a bluff. Unfired it promised something. With one shot pulled, all their hope would be gone.

The crowd continued its suspended dance. Then, directly in front of Weiss, the dancers parted. Not because of Weiss's gun. They parted to admit a naked man.

He was at least thirty years older than Weiss. He looked over a hundred. He had no hair, very little flesh, and – like the pig farmers beyond Kocevje Gora – no teeth. Unlike them, he did not look obscene without them. He needed nothing he did not have. He ghosted across the ground with a total absence of body weight.

He made himself as tall as Weiss and he smiled upon him. He did not smile with him, or at him. His smile did not suggest Weiss think again. His smile dismissed Weiss as of no importance. It brushed him from life altogether.

Weiss turned his gun on him, aiming it carefully at the cobwebs of the old man's throat.

'I know this lot,' Weiss said. 'They're some sort of Sufi – no, dervishes – from the monastery above here. This man is their memory. If I shoot him their dance collapses, their time will be suspended, the mutilated won't be able to recover, the blood will flow for ever, and many will die.'

Matson didn't believe that kind of nonsense. He had read about it, but he did not believe it. 'If you shoot him they'll lynch us,' he cautioned.

'It's you that'll be suspended, Henk,' Constanz was unawed, even in a blindfold. 'By the balls, old fellow. They're not as elastic as they were.'

Weiss raised his bid by soothing the cocking-hammer back with the edge of his free hand. He was within a hair's breadth of shooting them all into Kingdom Come. Less, if it was a sensitive trigger.

Still smiling, the old man leant forward and pushed his right index finger into the barrel of the gun.

You can't push a finger into the mean nine millimetres of a Luger Parabellum. Only a skeleton can. The weightless, fleshless dancer put his fingerbone into the bore, where it stuck at the first joint. His expression did not change.

It was then that the women pushed a young boy forward. He had taken off his caftan, so they turned away their eyes.

This was why Lotte and Constanz had been blindfolded. It was what Weiss and his grandson most especially had to see.

Matson did not believe what these people believed, but he knew their beliefs were not for women.

Or not this part of their ritual.

The boy wore a spur of blackthorn, straight through his face. It had been sharpened at one end and driven into his right cheek and out through his left. Through the palms of his hands were blunt iron nails. The nails were rusty.

This boy was not spattered with blood. His wounds did not bleed. He was frugal with blood. Blood was for the last of the lesser ones. Blood was for most, but not him.

He danced up slowly, with his eyes fixed on the old man, who still smiled at Weiss and forced his finger into the gun.

Weiss tugged on the trigger. Or pretended to tug. Or tried to tug. No shot followed. The finger had forbidden the gun.

'He's giving me the dance,' Weiss said. 'The swine is giving me the dance.' His voice was matter-of-fact. It always would be, however extravagant the hyperbole. Matter-of-fact whether he accepted a sentence of death or a million marks and the Knight's Grand Cross.

The boy carried a British bayonet. Not a sword-bayonet, not the modern dagger. It was a World War Two pigsticker, ten inches long, smooth and round like a straightened-out butcher's hook.

As he danced, the boy laid his left hand on the base of his stomach. He placed it horizontally with his outstretched little finger resting above his penis. He forced his fingers open, parting them to their fullest extent, and reached upwards with his thumb towards the apex of his ribs.

He danced for some time, while his hand continued to crab itself open, growing wider and wider.

When his thumb was as far up his belly as he could make it reach, he put the point of the pigsticker carefully above it, and danced there for a full five minutes with his left hand outstretched between the point of the bayonet and the base of his penis, confirming the measure.

The old man removed his finger from Weiss's pistol, and turned his back on him for ever. He looked towards the boy and the staffs stopped rattling, the dancing stopped.

The boy moved his left hand, and clenched it above his right on the catch of the bayonet.

Then he drove all ten inches of the blade into his belly.

It was the first time Matson had seen the General's grandson neither asleep nor fidgeting.

The old man stepped forward and pulled out the thorn from the boy's face.

He pulled out the nails, right and left.

He pulled out the bayonet and handed it to Matson with the same meaningless smile, but with his eyes closed tight.

He gave the thorn to the General by sticking it into his gun. He presented the nails to the blindfolded women.

The grandson gaped. The old man spat in his mouth, without looking where he spat.

Then he spat on the young dancer's wounds, and the wounds disappeared.

The boy's caftan was dropped over his head and shoulders, and he was whisked away.

Constanz and Lotte had their blindfolds removed, the women moved on, and the dance started up again.

'So what the shit happened?' Constanz asked. 'Did anybody see?'

'The old man gave life to little Hendrik,' Weiss said. He wasn't answering Constanz, simply talking to the air. 'He gave the child life.'

Matson believed nothing. He had witnessed some conjuring tricks, that was all. The best one was discovering the boy had a name. He was christened with a curse. That was why Matson hadn't heard it. Each time his mother said 'Henk', he had thought she was talking to Weiss.

Yes, the lad was christened with a curse. Too big a curse to be cancelled by the spit of a redundant wizard.

Weiss was above and beyond all this. Before restarting the car he was struck with a thought. 'I wonder what they were saying to me,' he mused. 'Can somebody tell me what their message really was?'

'"Welcome home",' Matson suggested. 'It must have seemed quite like old times, Weiss, what with the burning and the bayoneting. A pity the ladies were too ancient to refresh your recollections with an hour or two of rape.'

'Ah, but I remember them when they were young,' Weiss said. He invited Lotte to share the joke.

14

The helicopter was low overhead. Hard to believe its presence had any relevance.

Now it lifted straight up the cliff. It rose slowly, its rotors chewing for altitude in the thin air.

Weiss put his gun away and restarted the car.

'What makes that tunnel any safer than it was five minutes ago?' Matson asked.

He asked in general, so it was the General who replied. 'Something you wouldn't know about. Instinct. An experienced soldier has an instinct in such matters.'

Constanz did something with her notebook. She used it to hide her smile.

Matson said, 'You remind me of those stories about the old opera house in Dublin, Weiss. The shows were terrible, but people went to them because there was always a good chance the stage would collapse.'

'You think the tunnel will fall in?' Weiss was delighted at the idea. He asked Lotte for another tape. Matson expected Wagner, but they got Mozart as they entered the tunnel.

174

The Luger lay on the seat again. So did a box of Parabellum cartridges. The box was stapled closed, and there were no spare sliders or clips.

Mozart was too buoyant for the General's nerves. He asked for silence. Silence was Matson's kind of music.

It stayed silent all the way into the hill. Water dripped when they bisected the path of a stream. Otherwise they saw nothing.

The surprise was waiting for them as they left the tunnel.

15

Only the child was amused by it. It was nicely got up, as surprises went, for a hot afternoon in a wilderness. Its belts and its boots were sweetly polished, its carbines were at the shoulder when a purist would have preferred them at the slope. Henk Junior wasn't critical in such matters.

Lotte applauded gently. Lotte was the kind of woman who would applaud an elephant for dying.

The sun had moved enough to put this side of the mountain in longer shadow. The police were well lit just the same. Four large floodlights on stands took care of this. Their work on their belt and boots wasn't wasted, but the boot polish on the stocks of their carbines was a pity. They stood to attention with brown hands and smeared tunics. They lined the road beyond the tunnel in two ranks facing inwards. Matson felt as if he was coming out of church after a wedding.

In a sense he was. This was a further ceremony in the nuptials of Obergruppenführer Weiss and *Jugoslovenska Radiotelevizija*.

'You going to inspect them, Weiss?' Matson looked around for Popovic. He gazed into a hand-held television camera instead. The owners of the nation's nine point six million receivers were about to get their money's worth.

'Passports, vehicle documents, then open the trunk of your car.'

The policeman was some thirty years old, but the bags beneath his eyes were older. He had inherited them from his grandparents and they were stuffed with ageless wisdom. 'Let me see that gun,' he said. 'And the papers that go with it.'

'The gun is mine.'

'In which case it is not a gun,' the policeman agreed. 'It is part of an ancient monument. The bayonet is a more recent matter.' He confiscated Matson's souvenir.

He spoke to Weiss in German, and when Weiss answered in Serbo-Croat he switched him back to German. He spoke to Matson in English. He spoke wisely. He said, 'Good morning,' which was only wrong by an hour. When Weiss intruded his English, he ignored him by slamming both eye bags. He obviously loathed Weiss, and that made him moral and sensible; but he didn't kill the swine himself, and that made him smart. He walked round the Mercedes, fingered the bullet holes in the glass and grew wistful. He looked from each hole towards Weiss's head then back again, as if sympathetic magic might yet work. Weiss's head did not bleed, nor did the Mercedes bleed, but one of them would bleed soon, and he was an intelligent enough policeman to guess who it would be.

He examined the contents of Weiss's boot, and said nothing. He took out a cigarette and called 'Come out here, Mister Matson Paddy.'

Matson was pleased to come out here. 'My name is —'

'Your name is what I call you. Lesson one. I am making a big effort of diplomatic condescension to talk to persons best not in my country in languages not my own. You do not do my country the kindnesses of speaking its official language, Mister Paddy? Any of its languages or dialects? I thought not. I bet you cannot even recite any of our great nationalistic poems? A few verses of one of those on our glorious Battlefield of the Blackbirds? Even children in the village school can recite those end to end, Mister Matson Paddy. How can you travel so far and know so little?' He no longer smoked his cigarette. He gestured as if waiting for a cue. He was, of course, waiting on camera. He wasn't talking to Matson. He was talking to show off his English, which was like a conveyor belt in a quarry – efficient but full of lumps. He paused and gazed upwards.

Matson gazed upwards too. He saw floodlights and

176

shadow, and decided to stand closer to the policeman than at first seemed necessary.

The policeman handed him a card. He paused and followed it with two more. 'Don't look at them now,' he reproved. 'Read them at your pleasure. They belong to Colonel Popovic. He wants you to report to him where those papers tell you.'

'"Report"?'

'It's an order, Mister Paddy. What he calls a persuasive order. You are to be in no doubt of being persuaded.'

'Tell Popo I accept his invitation.'

'Tell his greatness when you get there. I never talk to Colonel Popovic. I am a general merely. Of police. I can only kick your arse. Colonel Popovic is much more —' Words failed him. 'Colonel Popovic is allowed to kick the inside of your head.'

Matson beamed at him. He pocketed Popo's set of visiting cards, turned and found Constanz beside him.

'Gigolos in drag,' she said. 'Talk about trying to whip up a cause.'

'You talk about it.' He wanted to be back in the car. He wanted the car to be moving.

'When a country's falling apart, central government needs a unifying war. Isn't that the historical European scenario?'

'It's a scenario.' He got her beside the Mercedes at last. He didn't trust the set up.

'They can't have their war, so they revive an old one, their only viable one.'

'Sorry, Constanz. It doesn't make sense.'

'It does if they can make Henk into a big enough monster, then keep the hounds from eating his guts until the situation has been properly milked.'

'It won't last them a week.'

'I don't give him a week, Matson. Nor do you. But a week would be enough. These people are poets. Poets and propagandists. Give them a rich seven days and they'll spin you a season. Time is what they need, for Christ's sake. Time is *all* they need.'

The production was running out of time as far as Matson was concerned. Mercifully *Jugoslovenska Radiotelevizija* had full editing facilities on tape and film. The sniper did not. He could only do it once. Matson pushed Constanz on to the back seat of the car as soon as he heard a rifle bolt go home.

There was no time to follow her. The long-anticipated sharpshooter put three aimed shots in a four-inch group on to the top of a stone across the road. The police had already stood aside to let him loose them off.

The rounds went ricocheting into the valley as they were meant to. First the bullet, then the bang, then the ricochet drowning out the echo. After each bang came the ponderous flick and snap of the bolt. Matson heard the cartridges eject. They fell as loud as beer cans, they were so near.

As he ducked into the car, he noticed that the floodlights had been switched off with commendable alacrity. 'Better drive,' he advised Weiss. 'Even though he's been trying hard to miss you. He's still got one up the spout.'

The General of Police crouched behind the bonnet of the Mercedes. He might have been waving a pistol, he might have been peeling a banana.

As they moved ahead and uncovered him, Matson gave him a present. It was a souvenir of Kocevje Gora. 'Don't bother to look for his empty cases,' he advised. 'They'll be just like this one. Three-o-three ball, old stock.' A similar weapon, though hardly the same one.

He knew it was a Lee Enfield right enough, but badly maintained: dry woodwork amplifying the muzzle-shock, a loose magazine giving its distinctive rattle.

Accurate enough shooting, but sloppy bolt action. Shots as uncrisp as the blur of their echoes. Lolly's ghost had kept on returning, but this bad use of a .303 banished his shade for ever.

Meanwhile a failed assassination attempt would be tonight's big news.

178

THIRTEEN

1

Belgrade's streets were full of people waiting for something to happen. Matson was reminded of his time in Beirut, after the first big car bomb and before the rockets came.

'Look at them,' Weiss chuckled. He did his best to plaster a couple of youths against the Mercedes' windscreen for closer inspection. 'The citizens are in a state of confident frenzy. They're in a frenzy because they're Serbs, and they're confident because there's no one here to contradict them.'

'They need someone like you, General.'

'They need *me*, Matson. There is no one like me.'

He drove fast for another three blocks, then slowed behind a procession. Not against its tail, as Anglo-Irish has it, more its backside. About forty buttocks' worth jammed cheek to cheek across the thoroughfare, then buttock beyond buttock from here to eternity, or at least as far as Kosovo and back.

The procession wasn't a feminine and festive affair, like the one in Slovenia. The marchers were male, or nearly all male, the young ones in jeans, the older ones in shiny-seated acrylic. Being male they smelled male, all hair-oil and moustache, even when they were bald and clean-shaven.

Weiss halted behind them, to let Matson out. 'I must find some petrol,' he said.

Matson thought the car ran on megalomania. It had drunk nothing else for the last five hundred kilometres, anyway. He unfastened his case from the roof and went round to the driver's window to say thank you. Constanz needed no persuading to stay where she was.

'I'll join you later, then, General.'

'You'll do as you have to do.'

'Where, exactly?'

'Buy a newspaper.' The window sliced his words. 'Or ask your friend Popovic.'

2

The ground floor was unfurnished and deserted, the lift gate padlocked. A new lift gate with an old padlock. Matson climbed stairs noisy with builders' dust to find two open doors. Beyond one, several young women sat typing. One of them searched a VDU for data while a colleague looked on. They wore uniform skirts and grey green blouses with buttoned pockets.

The other room held a large telephone console. Its mains light was on and a generator hummed. There was a two-way radio behind the door. Matson went to look in. He was headed off by a pair of women in full uniform – tunics, caps, leather belts. They each carried a sub-machine-gun, unloaded but with the magazine held flat against the stock, the first round bulging from the pressure of the feed.

A communist country. No need to feel surprised at a regiment of Amazons.

Armed women always frightened him – not, he thought, from any sexist reason. He mistrusted situations which were unsusceptible to blarney. Equip a woman with handcuffs, or a gavel, or the bank vault keys, and she won't listen to whispers; she'll do as her training tells her. And if she's trained to give you a clip of 9 mm straight through the buckle, that's what you'll certainly get before your dear old Irish gob is even halfway ajar.

He grinned and turned towards them. The move displeased them, that or his face. The girls snapped home their magazines and levelled their guns abdomen high. One half drew back her cocking handle, a nerve-stretching trick, then let the action spring forward, even worse.

Time to produce one of Popo's visiting cards. He offered it slowly. 'Colonel Popovic?' he asked.

They detained his suitcase, asked for his passport, tucked it into the handle of his case and pointed upstairs.

180

'Popovic,' one said. Popo was either being demoted or translated into legend.

The doors on the next landing would have been a disappointment even in a station lavatory. Only one had a nameplate. It read, simply, *Milovan Popovic.* Matson knocked.

'Come in, my dear. I have some very bad news for you. What is not bad is merely puzzling.'

Matson went in.

'Yesterday your embassy asked me to place you under arrest. They can't do such a thing, but they did. Today they merely request me to send you to meet them somewhere quiet.' Matson allowed himself to be hugged. 'Someone obviously wants to stick a knife up your guts. Better have a drink while your stomach's still waterproof.'

3

Matson saw no drink. He saw a composition floor with lots of new dust trodden in. Someone – Popovic himself? – had tried to clean it with a dustpan and brush. The dustpan was full; the brush dusty. The room held a large desk and a dozen wardrobe-sized filing cabinets, each of them as welcoming as a double coffin. The desk was loosely constructed from a Woolworth-style veneer. It had a ginger front and inadequate legs.

Popo was an old-world dandy. He obviously hated the place. He waved Matson to a chair and said, 'You should come over. Over is not very far, and since Yugoslavia is nominally communist nothing unpleasant can happen to you here.' Matson's eyebrows must have climbed, because Popo added, 'Nothing pleasant can happen either. Nothing *can* happen.' He opened a drawer or two in his desk to show they were empty, perhaps of tape-recorders. ' "I will give you nothing you do not want. I will give you nothing." That is not a Slav speaking, certainly not a Southern Slav. It is too abstract. It is the true voice of communism, I won't say at its most perfect but at its most pure. Do you know what "pure" meant in nineteenth-century England? I thought not. A

181

foreigner always garners the most interesting titbits. It meant dog shit. I did not waste my time while I was in London, you see.'

He stood up again to open some filing cabinets. They too were empty. 'Full of communism,' he explained. 'Some are full of the new communism. In some I store the old.'

His desk top was laden and untidy. 'That's where I keep my common sense. It will not have escaped your attention that nearly all communist countries manufacture wine. Russia, Cuba, Nicaragua and, of course, Romania, Bulgaria, Hungary and Poland. They manufacture very good wine indeed. If you live there you can't get any. The availability of wine is what makes Yugoslavia unique. It's why we are not full members of the Comintern, why we remain unaligned. We want to keep our hands on some of our own wine.' He opened another filing cabinet. It was full of bottles. 'It's what makes my country worth fighting for, Patrick, my dear. I would cheerfully die for the contents of this cupboard. Die a bit, anyhow, if the company were right.' He passed Matson a bottle and a corkscrew while he called outside for clean glasses and waited for one of the uniformed pair on the lower landing to bring them up to him. 'It's because you under-stand such things that I'm going to propose a deal to you. It'll be worth having someone watch your back while you meet this person Pilkington from your embassy.'

'Pilkington?' Matson began to laugh.

'Not Leonard Pilkington, my dear. London can send lots of nastier Pilkingtons than that.'

4

'No, Patrick. I'm not omniscient. I watched the man get off the plane, and then I phoned Graz. That Leodolter has the answers, once his friend lets him speak.'

Matson tasted the wine. It was good, but then it would be. He said, 'What do I have to do in return for having you guard my back?'

Popovic tried to look embarrassed. 'You seem to have the

confidence of my protégé, the venerable Kraut.' He spread his hands. 'I have my resources. I have – all sorts of things. But I cannot get a man in close to the Obershitbag. Or a woman, as it happens. I mean, he's susceptible to women but he already has women along. You see my dilemma?'

'One is his daughter-in-law – you told me that yourself. The other —'

'Women cannot operate while there are other women around. That's not a fact of surveillance I give you; it's a fact of life. But to know that a man like you is in close —'

'I can't possibly work for you, Popo. You must know that.'

'I shall be working for you, won't I? I and the whole office.' He scuffed the dust with his feet. 'You will be working, as always, for yourself. Not for London. Not for any of these Mr Pilkingtons. For yourself.'

'I work to London.'

'Of course, my dear Patrick. Of course. And of course.'

Popovic had been standing most of this time, standing and drinking or pretending to drink. Now he circled and stood whisperingly close. He had gold spot breath and a nice after-shave. He wasn't offensive. 'As I see it, this Weiss business, which is this Lippiat business, is turning out bad for you. Perhaps it was always meant to be bad, a career trap at least. Heads – you lose: tails – someone else wins. The softer the task, the harder the fall.' He allowed himself to tap Matson's chair. 'This man Pilkington is here either to take you home wrapped in chains, or to bury you in a box in the embassy yard. What else explains the complex of requests I have received from them?'

He moved away, gesturing with his half empty bottle. He was a puzzled man, a concerned man, thinking aloud. A man in this mood is always at his most mesmeric. Matson reminded himself of this, and kept on listening.

'I don't know how your people regarded Lippiat, or came to regard him. I have certain information about that. I make my deductions. Probably, in real terms, I know the truth of him better than any of you, his control included.

'What I do know, what I feel, is that for London, or for someone in London, someone in one of the funny depart-ments, you and this dead or alive Lippiat —'

'He's dead, Popo.'

'Yes, Patrick, he is exactly as you say he is. I feel it in my water. And I also feel that someone thinks you killed him. Or helped him disappear. Or helped him disappear and then killed him. Or took on his identity. Or joined him in his crusade to rid the world of geriatric Nazis like Obershitbag Weiss. You may be acting to orders, you may actually be here on leave, though I doubt it. But remember I know about London. Half my professional life is London. Its streets are full of pure, and none of those streets is straight.'

Matson saw nothing to say. Popo read the situation as Matson himself read it. As Willi and Albin read it. Or as they pretended to read it. Again, he wondered what inducements Popovic had offered in Austria.

Matson saw nothing to say, but an Irishman has to say something. 'I don't belong to one of the funny departments, Popo.'

'We know you don't, my dear. It's just your rotten luck to work to a decent man who's a long way out of his depth.'

'Splashing around in your water?'

'He won't be drowning in piss, you know. He'll choke on the best black wine.'

Matson chuckled, but the echo was ghostly. London had done nothing right on this one – presumably as a prelude to blaming him for doing everything wrong. He sipped wine, precariously.

So did Popo. They drank to keep truth at bay. They were benevolent neutrals, he and Popovic.

'Matson, my dear. I am bound to ask you to ask yourself a question that has troubled me for several days now. I take my cue from the Austrian press at its most lurid, but there's always poetry in the entirely fanciful.'

Matson was already wearing his obtuse smile. He wore it well.

'When you were sent to involve yourself with Gerald Lippiat, were you not in reality being directed towards the Obershitbag?'

'I ask myself, Popo. I assure you I do.'

'And?'

'I don't know.'

'Will you share with me the evidence on which you reach such a non-conclusion?'

'The answer, even to you, must be no.'

'Then you're telling me you're in even worse trouble than I expected.'

5

'Normally we can conduct out careers in private, you and I. By which I mean civil servants like you, intelligence officers like myself. In theory, men such as us do not even exist.' Popovic smiled sadly, the way the flogging headmaster at Camberwell did before unlocking the base of the grandfather clock and taking out the punishment book and the cane with the painful splits in its side. 'I expect the Austrians' scurrilous account of your misadventures has found its way into the British tabloids, don't you?'

If it had, then Matson wasn't going to give Popovic the satisfaction of asking him to bring out his clippings.

'Your troubles are very clear to me, dear Patrick, and no more than common sense would anticipate. You were thoughtless enough to be sitting near someone when he blew himself into *bouillabaisse*. That was an indiscretion, Patrick. The first real indiscretion in *l'affaire* Weiss. Why should Milovan Popovic also be punished for it?'

Matson was thrown completely off guard. He watched Popovic go back behind his desk and begin to rummage. 'I didn't blow anyone up, Matson, my dear. I didn't need to. My own people landed me in the pure. They landed me there without benefit of Semtex.' His desk was pleasingly untidy. He'd already said it was where his brains were. 'In my case, which may or may not be your case, there are leaks from the very top on this one. Here somewhere' – he pretended to find what he was looking for – 'is a copy of *Newsweek*. This is a fortnight old. A fortnight ago I was still in London. Some whore called Constanz Zanetti. Do you know her?'

'Almost as well as you do, Popo. You had her passport in your hand. So did your traffic police. She's travelling with Weiss.'

'Ah! Frau *Ehrenberg*. Frau Ehrenberg, sometimes Zanetti.' He clapped his hand to his head. 'But she already had *my* name by then.'

'She told me she didn't know you, either.'

'What women do, and what they acknowledge. No, I daresay you're right. I'm merely a name to her. But how did she get that name? Somebody gave me to her. I'm a secret, my dear. A state secret. I'm supposed to be Intelligence.'

'Personified.'

'I am sly. I am successful. I am sleek. I do tiny things in London. Suddenly, here is my name in every rag, world-wide. I am variously described as a "counter-insurgency wizard" —'

'She drinks a lot, Popo.'

'"One-time Tito bodyguard". Zanetti again. Unlike your Mr Lippiat, I never even met Tito. "Head of Yugoslavia's Secret Intelligence Service". Your *Sun* newspaper.'

'Not my *Sun*.'

'May it ever set, and may you get only daughters. That last is a sexist Serbian curse equivalent to demi-castration. If nothing worse befalls your heart lumps, you may take it as a friend's blessing. To be thus billed, in our profession, is never to rise further. I have bought drinks for *Sun* journalists. I have slept with several of their wives. "General Milovan Popovic" – here we have a New York tuppence coloured – "General Milovan Popovic, director of the mighty apparatus of Yugoslavian Military Intelligence, has assumed personal command of the operation. He guarantees Herr Weiss's safety, general to general". Know the headline on that one? *Ancient Kraut Goes Home*. I'm a colonel, Matson my dear. While I'm lucky. I liked London. I liked being attaché. I enjoy pretending to be a diplomat.'

'So how did you get this job, you old liar?'

'How does one get any job? As a punishment.' He rustled the wilderness on his desk top, again as if searching for something. 'I was caught with my pants down.'

'A lady, I take it?'

'Caught with *her* pants down. Naturally it was a lady. I don't collect boy scouts.'

'A pity. You might have got a badge and stayed put. You

186

don't appear to be very well organized over Weiss, you know.'

'Pig farmers. You keep on accusing me of those.'

'And riflemen. And people who loosen wheel nuts.'

'Mavericks, merely. Mavericks too stupid to rest on their hate. If such people finish him, he deserves to die. But they won't. They can't.' He passed Matson a piece of paper. 'No, my dear. This is what will kill him, and my career too.' He put the corkscrew to another bottle. 'Unless the pair of us can prevent it.'

'You can count me out.'

'Not until I've counted you in. I was speaking of myself and the Obershitbag. It's what's on that paper keeps me up at nights.'

The smeared scrap of paper meant nothing to Matson. He looked at Popovic and waited for an explanation.

6

'It is a photocopy. A photograph of a photograph. Dozens were sent. I suppressed them. They were sent to the press. We don't have newspaper tycoons over here. We have men with balls. Such men are susceptible to persuasion. *Radio-televizija* I can do less about. It's run by a woman.'

'So?'

'I told her to sit on what she has, and promised her an exclusive when the time comes.'

'Meaning when Weiss is dead?'

'Meaning when the time comes.'

Not Cyrillic. A western typewriter. Or a Japanese type-writer, which was much the same. There were six lines of what might be verse, followed by nine signatures.

'Look, Popo. I'm tired. I can't translate this. If I could, I probably wouldn't understand it.'

'Line by line it says roughly:

'We excuse you the hangings on the Terazija,
But Kocevje Gora we will not forgive,
Nor the wounded burnt alive in the Neretva,

187

Nor the children's bones in the hills above the trees.
What you did on the island till its skulls became a tower
We shall punish on Otok in the Lake without a name.

'It's not the verse that worries me,' Popovic went on. 'It's the signatories.'

Matson looked at the list. *Matija Gubec, Ivan Crnojevic, Jug Bogdan* – this one appearing firstly by itself then twice repeated with additional words that Matson did not understand – *Kosovka, Stefan Kotromanic, Banus Kulin, Primoz Trubar, Clement Slovensky.* The names were handwritten, and each was in a different hand. If they were signatures, then they were signed with an unusual lack of flourish.

'Aliases?' he suggested.

'Shit, my dear. Shit and brown sugar. Is that all you can say? Of course, they're *noms de guerre.* What else are they?'

'I suppose they're a code. *Stefan Kotromanic* is an acrostic for the mechanic or madman of Kotor, for instance.'

'No, no, no. Is it?' He became briefly interested in the idea. 'Not quite in English. Even less in Serbo-Croat. Stefan Kotromanic is the Bosnian who stole Hercegovinia from Serbia in the fourteenth century. Don't you read history books? These are famous names from the nation's past. From our mythology, even. Jug Bogdan is such a one, Kosovka the Maiden of Kosovo even more so. Poems are written about her. Bogdan died at the Battle of Kosovo on Kosovo Polje, the Field of Blackbirds, which became the Field of Flowers. Trubar was a famous churchman. Slovensky became a saint. Saint Clement. Now you see?'

'Perhaps if you twist the neck of that bottle, Popo.'

'Forgive me, my dear. Will you take coffee, or tea with peppermint?' This was a terrible threat. Having reproved Matson's impatience, Popovic uncorked the bottle he was holding. 'Yugoslavia is a federation, if you please. A federation of six new states that in turn overlie a lot of older ones. A jigsaw on a jigsaw, and the puzzles are laid on sand. *Screw* the old states. The new ones are falling apart.' He tasted the wine, rinsed his mouth with it, then tried again. 'Englishmen keep hooch in their filing cabinets. So do Americans. It's a disgusting habit.' Matson was being told his place. 'To drink

188

wine is to assure oneself of a clear head.'

'I'm absolutely clear about it.'

'Those names, those ancient, sometimes legendary names, each represent one of the states of the federation. And they've been chosen with considerable discretion.'

Matson accepted his wine. He had learned to be a good listener, especially to rigmarole. A man brought up by women has to be.

7

'Matija Gubec is a big name among the Croats. There are bigger names, but none so significant to the idea of revolution. He led a peasants' revolt in the sixteenth century, a bit like your Watt Ball.' Popovic enjoyed the moment. 'Well, he lost. They all lost. Some had their eyes dug out, their guts unwound on a stick – they were up to some odd things in Croatia even then. Matija Gubec himself was brought to Zagreb by his captors and crowned king. During the ceremony, the state executioner removed his gold crown and replaced it with one of white hot iron and cooked his brains for him. His tomb still sweats at the memory. It runs with dew. I do not want my grave to sweat, my dear. Especially because of Obershitbag Weiss.

'Then we have Ivan Crnojevic. Ivan sleeps in an ice cave up in Montenegro in the arms of the fairies. Sometimes he comes out to frighten the Turks and the Albanians. He does this by speaking thunder. He speaks a lot of thunder. You'll hear Crnojevic often if you get near Mount Durmitor.' He dried his lips, which were wine-smeared with talking. 'And you will get near the Black Mountain if you follow Weiss. Otok is there, and Jezero the Lake without a Name. It is his current address.'

'I thought Otok simply means "island"?'

'It does, my dear Patrick. It's what the Montenegrins call the place since that man went there during the war.'

'Crnojevic?'

'Don't try my patience. You bloody know who I mean!' He swallowed a little modesty, then added, 'We Serbs get in

189

twice, three times. No, four. It's to make that Croat bastard Kotromanic more acceptable, I expect.'

'Aren't you making rather much of this stuff?'

'I'm making what it makes of itself. You fucking listen you fucking learn.'

Matson listened.

'First we've got Kosovka, as I say. The Maiden of Kosovo who brings bread and wine to the bleeding warriors. Then there is Jug Bogdan.' Popovic put his glass down and said, 'I can't take any more. It's like drinking blood.'

Some things were harder to listen to than others.

'A lot of thought has gone into this, and it's thought I don't understand. Jug Bogdan, you see. Followed, as signatures, by Jug Bogdan's Widow and One of Jug Bogdan's Daughters-in-law.'

'Absolutely fascinating.'

'Jug Bogdan was a great warrior, doubtless, but he was most famous because he died in battle with his sons and left a widow and nine widowed daughters-in-law.'

After a long car journey this recital was more than Matson wanted. 'But if it's not a code, it's just a lot of poetry, isn't it?'

'You won't understand Yugoslavia unless you're accessible to poetry. You once told me you read poetry, anyway.'

'Only when drunk.'

'In London you're always drunk. I take this list *very* seriously, and its threat. If the Obershitbag dies on the end of some pig farmer's shotgun it will go hard for me, but it will not be the end. But if this Matija Gubec, this Stefan Kotromanic, this Jug Bogdan and the rest carve their names on his prick I shall look like every loser in Balkan history, and there's been too many of those already.'

8

Matson wondered what to believe of this, and what to make of what he believed. *A lie is like a Shakespearean play*, an instructor had said, long before he'd read any Shakespeare. *You can only unravel the truth of it by studying its images.*

If Popovic had let anything slip – or tried overhard to conceal something – it had been earlier, much earlier.

Matson would have to run it through in his mind when he had some peace and quiet.

Not now. Popovic stood himself up, sat himself down, began a grumbling fidget with his legs. 'One thing this document does confirm. It is an establishment plot, or the tip of an establishment plot, this photographed poem and this silly list. The Belgrade establishment have let the old man come here. Now they propose to kill him in their own way. Or let people they know kill him in ways they'll leave open.'

'Communist countries don't have establishments.'

Popo spoke a lot of consonants. Presumably he was swearing. '*Naif* as well as ugly,' he scoffed. The liquid Serbian syllables loosened his spit again. He made use of it. 'I say it's an establishment plot because the right people know about it. They mayn't know *what* it is, but they know that it *is*. The army knows. The security agencies know. That cow who runs the broadcasts knows. I bet the old partisan leaders know. They are the ones who will hold the young bloods back.'

'How very Balkan Byzantine.'

'Everyone – I mean the populace at large – everyone wants Weiss arrested as a war criminal. If he's arrested, I doubt if he'll hang. Even if he does, hanging's too good for him. So what more persuasive than to say, "Slacken your clamour for action on this one. We can't hang him for you, but you'll be reassured to know he's about to cook his own head in a gas oven after he's fallen into a crate of broken glass"? That sort of thing. That's not the Balkans, my dear. Not only the Balkans. It's clubland Britain. It reminds me of the Freemasons.'

'You weren't one of those, surely?'

'Several of my wives' husbands were. Sometimes I wonder if the whole business wasn't concocted back there, but by someone who understands us.' Popovic had worked himself up into a substantial lather of conviction by now. 'There are plenty of men and women with good reason to kill the Obershitbag, Patrick. You've already seen evidence of it. But they'll give that plot pride of place, because they respect the plot-makers. If the plot falls through, then the rest of them will have a try. I can stop those, *and* the mavericks – it's an ordinary police job. This is what exercises me.'

'So what exercises the plot-makers? Tell me what your so-called establishment expects to get out of it?'

'Outrage. A few days of outrage sticking deep in the national gut. Outrage is the one thing that unites us in these troubled times, now we've got the Slovenes and these bloody Albanians dragging us apart.'

9

Popovic finally corked the bottle – but which one? – and became business-like. He crossed to a tiny wall map of the city, and beckoned Matson to look with him. 'I have arranged for you to meet with your Mister Pilkington *here.*' His thumbnail covered a swelling at the end of a street, an embolism in the arterial flow.

Matson saw a cobweb of roads and squares, read names like *Boulevard of the Revolution, Marx and Lenin, The Proletarian Brigades, The International Brigade, The 27th March, The 14th December, The 29th November. March* and *November* went on for ever.

'When you get lost in Belgrade, you can always ask someone for a date.' Popovic smirked. 'That's an English joke.' He moved his thumb. 'You're to meet in the Terazija.'

'Where Weiss did his hangings.'

'Him and others. That's up above, my dear. Downstairs there are some very good bars. One of my ladies will take you there.'

'No thanks.'

'Not inside the door. She'll just point it out. When you leave, she'll take you to your hotel.'

'I haven't booked one.'

'It's my town. You'll go where I tell you.'

'Suppose I don't get away?'

'Suppose you have trouble and make a professional decision not to go along with it? Well, well, well. Then you punch your friend on the nose – or one of your friends on

192

one of their noses – and you shout "no!" in a loud voice and run into the kitchen. I have it arranged.'

'There's a back way?'

'Immaterial. You'll be arrested for soliciting. You'll be quite safe after that. No one messes with the police in Belgrade.'

Matson wasn't a fisherman – the Austrians were right about one thing at least – but he knew when it was time to tug on the string. He turned at the door, smiled sweetly and said, 'But I already have my hotel, Popo. And you bloody well know it. It's called the British Embassy.'

'Shit, my dear. Shit. Shit. Shit. Don't you believe me when I say you'll never reach it?' Popo's exasperation was genuine. 'Well, you might get there. In the drains, if your head will float that far.'

He came over to Matson, and let him see his bloodshot eyes from very close to. 'If you won't suck on sense, let me throw you some sugar.' His hand brushed at Matson's lapels while he tried to make up his mind about something. 'Shit, Patrick,' was all he could offer at first. Shit came easy. 'I hadn't intended to tell you this till you found your way back here tomorrow. The Security Police are holding someone for me. A most interesting character. I hoped to produce him to you once they'd had time to bend him about a bit. That was to be my inducement to you. Well, now you know. So look after your kidneys with this man Pilkington or you'll cause me more trouble than a nagging wife.'

'What is the name of this man you're holding?'

'He's someone who signed that list. How do we know? Thumb-prints, my dear. For topographical reasons, he's either Ivan Crnojevic or Jug Bogdan. I hardly think he's the widow or the daughter-in-law, do you?'

'He's a Serb?'

'In a sense.'

'A Montenegrin, then?'

'In a sense. Wait until tomorrow. Whatever he's got for us, he'll have coughed it down the plug by then.'

193

FOURTEEN

1

Thank God Belgrade didn't go to bed early. Not above or below the Terazija it didn't. Matson wafted towards the appointed place in a cloud of anonymity.

It was one of those self-aware grottoes you can find in any European city, full of dull blue light and the smoky aroma of good coffee and hot chocolate. Turkish coffee ladles hung on spindles behind the bar, and there was a huge iron dish of burning charcoal screwed to the far wall under a blackened copper chimney.

The blue light was what counted. So did the door that led out back, as Popovic had promised.

He recognised the senior Pilkington at once, sitting alone at a table close to the charcoal. The Royal Artillery all-ranks tie was an innovation and perhaps a fibber. The dark blue suit was one he had gazed upon often, but in colder climes where the material looked more at home and didn't cling to its owner so limply for comfort. Matson had clung there once or twice himself, metaphorically speaking.

This Mr Pilkington hadn't come alone. There were two men who could only be English sitting together at a strategically chosen table by the door. They were big chaps, dressed in contrasting versions of Foreign Office *chic*. He didn't let the wrapping-paper fool him. He looked them over carefully as he pushed past.

The nearer one wore a piece of Gieves and Hawkes suiting with a well-cut chin to match. The other came cheaper in one of those limited edition floppies that had probably only cost him seven or eight hundred quid in that gaffery along the back of Piccadilly that Matson used to tremble even to walk past – seven or eight hundred quid and the knowledge that

194

there were eleven other men in the western hemisphere who were dressed more less as he was. He made up for it with a hand-stitched shirt which, as Matson's mum would have said, 'shrieked quality, if only quality dare be loud'.

Popovic must have known who the senior Pilkington was. Ralph Dixon was visible enough in London. Besides, it was Ralph who had tumbled Lippiat and sent the whole mess dripping inexorably over the carpet. Popo probably knew this as well. He knew most things.

He could only have held back Ralph's identity as a way of scaring Matson. But to what purpose? Didn't he realise they were friends?

Or did he simply take the pragmatic view that this was a job where friendship counts for little once the dirt seeps out? It's not even worth a silver bullet.

2

Ralph's opening remark was frosty. 'There are those who say keep him running, and those who say bring him back.'

'What does Leonard say?'

'Leonard is unavailable for comment. They don't mind what you did to Lippiat —'

'I had nothing to do with poor old Gerry.'

'They care what gets into the press. The qualities have reported the Austrian papers in detail. The tabloids have stories of their own. Tabloids mean votes, so there were questions asked. You're a very bad smell just now, and totally unlikely to recover.'

'Mind if I have a drink, Ralph?'

'I ordered you a Turkish and slivovitz. I had them taken away once the slivovitz grew hot and the Turkish cold.' He snapped his fingers. The coffee came back. So did a tumbler of iced water. The slivovitz did not return. 'Where the hell have you been all night? Selling us to the Yugoslavs?'

Matson chewed some ice, and let the question rest.

'What worries the Foreigners and the rest of that gang is that the Austrians haven't complained about you. The suspicion is a deal was struck.'

'There's a better explanation. The Austrians know I didn't do anything.' The two by the door were pretending to read the menu. Ralph wasn't Foreign Office. That's why the others were here, to make sure he didn't creep off before Matson was back on the leash – or inside a nice padlocked basket. 'Doesn't it worry you, Ralph? First Lolly being moved on, then me?'

'It happens. It's happening.'

'Not a bit too pat for you?'

'Life can be like that. Chaos or continuum. This time we've got the continuum.'

'Repetition, merely. Lose an agent, and it stops on somebody's desk, Ralph. But a traitor goes down in some foreign clime and no questions get asked, do they?'

'You're not an agent. I'd ask even if you were. That's why I'm out here.'

'You carry no clout. Not with that lot.' A nod towards the other two. 'Catch them knifing me, actually knifing me, in Hyde Park and I daresay you'd ask someone to explain. But if they proved I'd kept bad company, you'd toddle down to the appropriate lodges and have the chief constables call off the Old Bill. You'd go hand in hand.'

'Meanwhile the cry is they want you out of the way.'

'You bet. Somebody made a mistake in asking me to move Lolly on. It stands out a mile.'

The two by the door stopped wrestling with the menu. They were acting impatient instead. Matson had things to say, and he needed time to say them. He stood up and took his coat off, draping it over the back of his chair. Then he sat down again. He looked like a man who was determined to drink his way through several buckets of iced water. The other two relaxed and ordered drinks.

'Either you weren't meant to catch Lolly, Ralph. Or you – or more likely they – weren't supposed to act on it. Somebody over in the Foreigners sent Lolly on a very strange job, or assented to what he was doing on his own account. Then somebody changed his mind, or found out that someone was about to stop him, and sent me to move him on. Or the somebody who sent me decided a death might be better.'

'No one would dare be so obvious. Not when it comes to

landing you in the pile. Leonard and I both know the background, for goodness' sake. We were there when you were briefed.'

'You and Leonard have been placed in baulk by being told I've been naughty since I've left. Only your nasty suspicious mind stands between me and damnation, Ralph – that and Leonard's eternal intellectual detachment, when he can be persuaded out of the cupboard. Now tell me when either quality has ever won a colleague an acquittal in an internal inquiry in the teeth of suspicious circumstance.'

Dixon glanced towards the Foreigners himself. 'Anyone can be turned – that's always the argument. It *is* the argument.'

'Turned by the Austrians? Turned where? Beat me on the balls and I'll squeak, Ralph. But I've not been known to cough.' He couldn't tell Dixon everything. 'Somebody arranged a nasty death for Lolly. Somebody put two bullets through a bedroll I was only just absent from. I hope it wasn't the same someone. I hope even more fervently it wasn't some oddball from HMG.' It seemed the best use he could make of facts he couldn't begin to understand.

'Rifle bullets?' Dixon asked.

Matson offered him his surviving cartridge. 'Three hundred yards, not much more.'

'You can't put a night sight on a Lee Enfield. Or not easily. *You* might cobble one on, Thump.'

Matson hadn't thought about that. There used to be a sniping telescope once upon a time.

3

If Ralph Dixon was back to calling him 'Thump' things were looking better for him.

The slivovitz arrived in a stoppered half-litre jar. He wanted to stay with the iced water, but to be cautious about drink would seem sly. He certainly couldn't offer his session with Popovic as an excuse.

Ralph poured for Matson, not for himself. 'Why did Leonard move you across into Yugoslavia? Sending officers abroad is way outside his remit.'

197

'He wanted me to stay with certain loose ends in the Lippiat business. He's curious to know why his department's been landed in the mire like this.'

'Leonard says you told him Lolly might not be dead.'

'Ancient news. The Austrians found a second stiff they're keeping quiet about. They showed me photographs. The face is a bit pickled in pond life, but they are certain on other evidence that this one is Lolly. They know I didn't cause Lolly Two's demise and the inference must be I didn't cause Lolly One's either. But if someone back home were responsible, then Leonard will need to know.'

'You're sure about that one?'

'The Austrians are. Tell me about Lolly in London.'

'You know most of it. I twigged him for drifting in and out of the Yugoslav Embassy too damned often. My lads and lassies in the electronic cars did the rest. They recorded him in some bloody McDonald's or other giving agents' names to Popovic.'

'To Popovic direct?' Matson couldn't picture Popovic in a McDonald's. 'Then what?'

'I told Pomeroy. Pomeroy conferred with whoever has the Balkan desk.'

'Who's that?'

'No one with a handle to his name. A consortium of second-generation expats or other ethnics, I believe. The Balkan desk is very sub-sub-sub. Not so much a desk as a box of nibs. Probably overseen by Pomeroy, like most things in the Eastern Med.

'And *there* you may have your clue, Thump. A man like Pomeroy is inclined to take the lofty view of international affairs – I daresay he'd call it holistic – but basically he's for the *status quo*, if not your actual stasis.

'But Yugoslavia isn't amenable to his thinking. It's clearly falling apart, and it's falling apart because its different tribes and prophets want it that way. Pomeroy's given the desk over to ethnics, as I say. And if they're Slovenians, Croatians or Bosnians, then apart is all right by them. Apart is their new religion.'

The Balkanization of British foreign policy was a novel idea to Matson. He took a sip on the strength of it.

'It's only the Serbians, together with a few Slovenian, Croatian and Bosnian *communists* – or old Titoites – who want to hang together; and coves like that certainly aren't going to find employment in the British Foreign Office. Or I hope they're not.' Dixon thought and added, 'So supposing Lolly, who was a pal of Pomeroy's —'

'And a pal of Tito's —'

'Suppose Lolly took the holistic view as well. And supposing he had a suggestion or two to make regarding your Mr Weiss. I mean, this Weiss thing is a pan-Yugoslav gut-jerker, isn't it?'

'I've heard the idea expressed.' Matson had evidence for a more cynical view of the matter. 'So what did this box of nibs do next?'

'They said send Paddy to tell Lolly to piss off. I translate, of course.'

'Why me?'

'Not one of them. Clean hands. Leave already booked. *Now* it looks bad. It looks as if someone was out to frame you for mayhem as previously discussed. Or for folly.'

'Or both.'

'I can count. *Then* it looked right.'

'That all?'

'What more do you want?'

'Confirmation that anyone among the Foreigners, Pomeroy or anyone else, told anyone outside – you, Leonard, anyone – the wider truth about Gerald Lippiat. That he's running a big operation.'

'He was too old.'

'Leonard says they told him. Did they tell you?'

'Much too old.'

'Then they suckered you as well as me. Here's something else. He's accredited. Leonard wasn't told that, as it happens.'

'I don't believe it.'

'At Berne. Leonard says the Foreign Office will claim it's an oversight.'

'The host country doesn't let that sort of thing pass. Switzerland's a tight-arsed place, very suspicious of diplomats. Prefers crooks.'

'So the Foreigners are lying.'

199

'I don't have to believe you, Paddy. About him being accredited.'

'True. You can go back to the embassy and pick up a diplomatic list.'

Dixon made a note – as if he'd forget. 'You know our job. Trust no one. Not even your unborn child.'

'In our job, the unborn child is very rarely our own.'

'Drink your slivovitz, there's a good boy, and tell me what happened when you met Lippiat in Austria.'

Matson decided to be frank about nearly everything.

4

Dixon didn't give him time. 'There's only one question, isn't there? Did you kill the bugger?'

'I have a somewhat odd reputation, but hardly as inter-service assassin.'

'Would you have killed him if you'd been asked to?'

'One of us? Even a bad one? Certainly not.' It sounded a bit too police cadet, so he added, 'I'd be bloody suspicious of anything like that. There are people for that sort of thing. Bring the lad in for a hearing, I'd say.' He swallowed his rage. The evening's alcohol was dissolving his common sense. 'You know I wasn't asked to do anything fancy. You were there.'

'I was there when Leonard and Marcus Pomeroy were there.'

'There *was* no other time.' Just like lovers say. 'And certainly not with anyone else.'

'You should have caught the first flight home from Graz, then our jobs would have been a lot simpler.'

'I didn't come here to be let off, Ralph. Still less to be told off.' Brave impulse. Improbable lies. 'I came here to get off and go on walking.'

'I'm not stopping you. The two gents over there come from another firm and have other instructions.' Their instructions made Dixon look broody. 'You're earmarked for sacrifice, Thump. I mean, yes, I'm starting to believe in you. When have I ever not? And when does what I believe in matter a toss? I can damn you. I can't save you. I can deal only in negatives or non-negatives. Positives aren't for the

200

likes of me.' The slivovitz sank in the bottle. 'You're earmarked for sacrifice, as I say; and that's the monstrous convenience of it. You've had a bit too much luck of late. No one thinks you'll go any higher, get a department and so forth; but you keep on happening. It's not as if you're either bred to it or trained for it.'

'I'm a late recruit. That doesn't cancel ambition.'

'There are chaps who do everything right and get nowhere. There's men like Marcus Pomeroy who do exactly as they've been trained to do, which is sit on their hands and do nothing, who do it and wake up smelling of fertilizer. Then there's you. You do everything wrong and wake up stinking of roses.'

'"Stinking" he says. I know my place, Ralph. No one need worry, not even Leonard. Certainly not Marcus.'

'You know your place. We know your place. But do the politicians? That's how the argument against you runs. Sooner or later we're going to be caught heads-down in the tub again, with our trouserless legs a-waving and no profit to show for it. Somebody's going to say, "Put someone new in charge. Make a clean sweep. Get a man who knows what he's talking about. This fellow Matson —"'

'I'm in *that* much trouble?'

'That's how I read it.'

'Well, I may just resign, Ralph.'

'Resignations please no one. Some fool will immediately clamour to have you brought back. That's why you've been fixed.'

He re-stoppered the slivovitz flask. It was empty. 'Besides, you can't resign your way past those blokes at the door.'

5

'If the villains *are* those Slavs at the ethnic desk – it's a big "if", isn't it, Thump? – you can bet that pair have a direct line to them.'

'They certainly have a direct line to someone who's demanding me home. Most probably that someone is quite legitimate, expressing reasoned concern. Unfortunately the

201

department wasn't legit on this one. Leonard wasn't legit. Nobody was legit. Pomeroy wasn't. You weren't. These things have a nasty habit of falling to pieces in front of a board of inquiry, especially a board one of the main actors finds himself conducting. It won't be me, Ralph. And it won't be you. You probably knew it all along. I knew it as soon as Lippiat's caravan went up in smoke. You'll have to hang together, as they say.'

'So what will you do?'

'I'll carry on running, Ralph. Running I'll be your best hope. I have to believe, as the Austrians believe, that Lippiat was aiming at Weiss. It's why I'm travelling with Weiss. I also have to believe that he might have been part of a larger, Slavonic plot pointing in the same direction. The intriguing thing' – time for a screaming lie – 'the idea which teases Leonard, is that the Balkan plot may also be a London plot, or even bigger.'

'Is that why the American woman called in at the embassy a couple of hours back?'

Matson wasn't up to that. Constanz was supposed to be with Weiss.

'She obviously knew what to say to get the embassy spooks out of bed.'

'Ehrenberg-Zanetti. She's not CIA.'

'Someone's taught her some recipes then. I'd watch her, Thump. I was told to tell you she'd be waiting at some hotel or other, in case you ever got there. Here it is.' Dixon fished a piece of paper from his pocket.

'Never write things down.'

'I'm not a spook.'

Matson liked to be angry before being truly nasty; and here he was – angry again. It was one of the beauties of alcohol. 'These private games, Ralph. Someone is dealing with us as if we're a pack of pictures on his private card table. So far they've dealt us two deaths in Austria. They've also dealt my name on to the hot list. So bloody hot that I'm soon going to be kick-marched back to the Embassy. If I'm lucky.'

Ralph Dixon was reflective.

'Are you detailed to escort me back to London?'

No answer.

202

'Looks as if I'm not meant to arrive there, then.'

Matson dried his hands on the linings of his trouser pockets, then stood up and put his jacket on.

'You know why I accepted this stand-off?' Dixon said. 'Because I don't want to take you home, Thump. You'll find it difficult to get past those chaps at the door, just the same.'

He had been offered an escape route. He would have to take it.

6

'Are those two ethnics or bona fide members of the diplomatic filth?'

'True-blue Foreigners. One Winchester and Cantab, one St Paul's and Oxon. Scraping the barrel nowadays.'

'Call them over, there's a pal.'

Ralph tapped his glass. He used the stopper from the slivovitz bottle. He only tapped once, as if by accident. They were already there.

Big men. They moved with the certainty of privilege and the assurance of those advantages Matson's Irish mum and even more Irish grandmum had failed to provide him with in Camberwell.

They didn't so much sit as stoop into the two vacant chairs. Then they watched Matson. They had intent, pre-occupied eyes, like chimps at a zoo tea-party. Unfortunately, they were larger than chimps, and growing bigger by the second. More like gorillas, but too well bred to be half as polite or a quarter as amiable.

'Which of you is the Old Paulian?' Matson asked sweetly. 'Or do I mean Pauline as in lady friend?'

His pronunciation was corrected. It was the deodorized lout in the limited edition floppy who spoke the necessary icy syllable.

Matson spread his nose with a knuckle-busting left he didn't know he still carried. If it was meant to look like a poofy punch it was a bit of a failure.

St Paul's used to have a good boxing team. Perhaps that was why it was the Winchester-bred Gieves and Hawkes who kicked Matson's legs from under him and caught him in a double armlock on the way down. He banged Matson's face on the ornamental table, liked the sound it made, and banged it again.

The tricks they can fit into a Cambridge Tripos now they've stopped them reading books. Matson wanted to say this out loud. Instead he obeyed orders.

'No,' he whinnied, in extravagant falsetto. He did it in Serbo-Croat, or perhaps in plain Serbian as Popo instructed, 'no' being one of the six or seven words he knew, and sounding even more billy-goat-like than in Anglo-Irish. '*Ne! Ne! Ne! Ne!*'

He was arrested by a posse of Popovic's uniformed ladies and taken into protective custody almost at once. Or he thought it was them. His cheekbone was painful, and he couldn't see very well close to.

Further off, innumerable policemen with sidearms and whistles knocked over furniture and stamped on glass to surround the remaining Englishmen.

Matson's face dripped. His arresting officer annoyed him by taking notes. His nose splashed the page with Popovic's blood red wine. She put her pencil away. She had evidence enough.

'Not Mr Pilkington,' Matson explained to the assembled uniforms. 'Mr Pilkington didn't lay a finger on me, not even once.'

'I warn you, Matson.' Ralph spoke sternly. He spoke for Embassy consumption.

The other two resisted arrest. They were modestly manhandled, so they protested. They did this fluently, in the local tongue. They waved their Embassy cards, their passports, but not yet their wallets. This amalgam of trans-sexual extravagance and tightfistedness led to them being handcuffed.

Diplomatic immunity is never easy to establish. It requires a trip to the police station, drinks all round, and much shaking of hands, before everyone is entirely certain.

By the time they were free, Matson would be tucked up in his hotel bed. He would be sharing it with his own increasingly bad temper.

FIFTEEN

1

The Ehrenberg-Zanetti didn't wait in the lounge. Lounging was not for her. Matson found her in his room, already in bed.

She wasn't what his grandmum called 'bone-naked'; Constanz had too much style for that. She wore a layer or two above her skin, but they were layers through which the skin was plainly in view; she was a fit girl with her bones barely tucked away. The place smelled of steam. She had been scrubbing them.

Matson went into the bathroom. There was only cold water left, but it was cleaner than on the coast. He cooled his face. He didn't wash with it. He rinsed his bloodstained shirt.

He came back and said, 'We'll leave –'

'Shit, Matson. What ate you?'

'As I said, we'll leave you and Milovan Drusan Popovic.' He stared moodily at the portable typewriter she'd so thoughtfully left a page of her homework in. An all-American Japanese Brother with the wrong typeface for Popo's poem. 'We won't even bother to ask how it is you're able to tell the British Embassy the name of the hotel he's going to send me to – and so ensure they know where to pick me up. And tell them you'll be here, thus making certain I'll come.'

'Shit again, Matson. You really know how to flatter a girl.'

'We'll even drop the fact that you and Popovic share the same brand of twanky talk. Never use a vicarage word when any old four letters'll serve instead.' Her silence surprised him so much he had to take a noisy breath before adding, 'Don't bother to answer that. I'm through with listening. I'm through with talking. I'm through with everything for tonight.' His nose began to drip blood again.

'You came here to fuck, I hope?'

Tonight was much too fraught with imponderables for him to grit his teeth and mingle business with business, so to speak. 'Get fed up with waiting for Henk to find another five minutes on his dance card, did we? Or did we simply get ourself chucked out of the Mercedes again?'

'We got our own self out in a black mood of rage and a pink to red fever of lust.'

'Lust for me?' He ignored the black mood altogether.

'Anyone with a dick, Matson. Anyone with half. Yours'll do at a pinch.'

'And a pinch is probably what it would need, in your case.'

'At least I can get you to wash behind its ears and dip its stalk in a vase from time to time. Things like that go down big with an all-American girl like me – even the tiny ones.'

2

'The cartilage is damaged,' she murmured. 'Not broken.' She was bathing his nose. She was better with it than he was. And with the rest of him, to be fair to her.

That didn't make him trust her. Nothing would, ever. He had to hope Popovic had some of his people in place. If not he'd better make a run for it while he was still alive.

She reached for her handbag but his own hand beat her to it. His hand was nervy tonight. His fingers found a bottle of cognac.

'Where's the Smith and Wee?'

'In my knickers,' she said. 'If you want to practise.'

It was under the pillow with six shots chambered. She wasn't the sort of lady to worry about shooting herself in the foot, obviously. He wondered what she was worried about.

She sipped thirstily but gracefully. She didn't wipe her mouth with the back of her hand. She touched his, 'I'm not letting you have any of this,' she coughed. 'You're limp enough already.'

He sipped her lips as a courtesy, not as a prelude. She

tasted of toothbrush, mouthspray and healthy air. No trace of dinner, not a whiff of alcohol, not even a whisper. Not even after the cognac. Today might be well into tonight but it was still today, so to speak, so where through her breaths and entrances had the grape juice gone?

The bottle looked familiar, and it would serve to distract him from passion. He took it from her and sniffed at it. 'Cold tea,' he said. 'My bottle, but cold tea.'

'I drank your bottle.'

'Can't you afford drink?'

'I can't afford *to* drink,' she admitted. 'Not as often as I seem to drink.'

'So why pretend to be piddled all the time?'

'Men. One man.'

'Men don't like drunk women, surely? They like the easy lay, true enough.'

'Got me in one. A guy lays me when he thinks he's got me skull-blasted and come tomorrow I don't even have to remember him.'

'Weiss?'

'My, we *are* working quick tonight! He's had me he thinks drunk. He'll *have* to try sober.'

'So you'll have your revenge and upstage him?'

'Yep. Maybe I'll stand him up.' She paused, then turned on him a look dark with hatred. 'And maybe I'll nod him into the bedroom and cat his fucking balls for breakfast.'

'They're not kosher.'

'Offal never is. I'll eat them and spit them out.'

'Are you Jug Bogdan's Widow?' he asked. 'Or are you playing the Fair Maid of Kosovo?'

The silence grew long. She gazed at the bottle with genuine but frustrated interest. 'The Countess of Bogdan never ate anyone's balls,' she said at length. 'And Kosovka never even saw any.'

He kicked off the rest of his clothes, as a prelude to sleep, then found her a genuine bottle, wedged in his case between Lolly's books and his own Marks and Sparks socks. 'There were nine other widows,' he said. 'One of them must have seen or done something.'

'That was on Kosovo Polje,' she whispered. 'I would never

say so to a Serb, but compared to Hendrik Weiss those legendary Turkish Generals were a joke – as widow-making machines, anyway.' She drank.

3

'And as baby-making machines too.' She'd picked the sentence up after an interval, the way people do when they're drunk or deranged. She wasn't either. 'Odd for such a sexual old warrior to be fascinated by Hitler.'

Talking of one person while making love to another was a North London habit he'd never grown really proficient in. It strengthened his resolve not to try.

'He absolutely adores those knights in *Parsifal* that Adolf identified himself with.' She spoke with the occasional dash and ellipsis, but not because she was beginning to glitter. 'Klingsor especially. Smooth between the legs, you see. Eunuchized by self-enchantment.'

She did things to him, between drinks so to speak. He thought she did them to deflect the general thrust of his questioning. She was a clever lover. Liars often are.

'I thought so,' she said. 'You've got nothing useful to add. He dreams of being Adolf who dreams of being Klingsor, but in fact he's got his gonads intact. They're like a sackful of cauliflowers. Old Henk's goddamned grotesticled.' She caught hold of Matson by the balls.

The scrotum is a curious fold of skin. Handled apart from its contents – with just the teasiest pinch between fingernail and thumbnail – it brings no great pain to the male animal, but a total absence of breath. Every farm girl knows that wrinkle. The Ehrenberg-Zanetti was clearly of the rural sisterhood.

'Uff!' said Matson, or rather he didn't say. His mouth was as voiceless as a bagpipe in deep water.

'There's a man in the bathroom,' she breathed, the way lovers do, holding him so he couldn't answer. 'So what the fuck are you going to do about it, Matson?'

4

She let him get most of himself away from the bed, while her disengaged hand swept beneath pillow then bolster for her gun.

A naked man is rarely at his best in a fight. A naked man with a crease in his bollocks is both timorous and devoid of intelligence.

There was a fanlight above the bathroom door, and beyond it the light was on, not brightly, but on. Not the ceiling light, but the neon strip over the wash basin. It hadn't been on.

Neon strips have uncertain contacts. Have been known to become inflamed in the dark, like other things he could think of.

He felt better for that witticism, and better for his trousers and shirt.

Mrs Ehrenberg-Zanetti had taken something from her handbag and was screwing it on to the barrel of her gun. The Smith was now silenced. He was suspicious of silencers. How did she know it was a man? The intruder had presumably entered via the bathroom window, not from the corridor.

He smelled man, now. Lots of man. The room was full to overflowing with the stink of overheated male imaginings. Her nose must be better than his.

Shoes would be a big advantage, but there was no time for perfection. The bathroom light went off and the bathroom door opened, just as Constanz switched the room lights on from beside the bed. Decent of her.

A smallish man in a black training suit and a pair of fire-soles blinked at them through the doorway, blinked but kept on coming forward. He came forward two-handed, and it was Matson he came at. He had a blackjack in his right hand and a syringe in his left.

This should have been funny, but it wasn't. Matson wasn't entirely clear where Mrs Ehrenberg-Zanetti's gun was pointing. The syringe looked big enough to kill horses or inject petrol in a death camp. The man swung and jabbed alternatively, jabbed and swung.

'Get out of the way, Matson, and I'll shoot the little fucker.'

Matson wasn't trained in defence. He took a forward

move himself. The blackjack shaved his face and deadened the meat of his left shoulder, but he'd already index-fingered the man straight in the eye. He chopped two-handed, left arm slow and numb, at the man's right elbow, as he would in the first stages of a knife attack.

The man already had one hand to his face and the syringe was slipping from his fingers.

Matson got a chin-hold and hair-hold on him, and kicked the needle out of reach, taking care not to impale his naked foot. Good to know Constanz was on his side. He was pondering whether to break the fellow's neck, or opt for some more reversible form of carotid inhibition, when it struck him that the syringe might offer a kinder sleep.

He felt for the thing, restrained the brute one more time and stuck him with it. A nice juicy jab on the upper leg, with the needle hard in till the barrel touched cloth. Brutal, but the fellow was unconscious.

The unconscious man threw himself backwards out of Matson's arms, in a wrestler's arch of amazing strength, head bent, legs stiff, like a toddler refusing its high chair. He threw himself backwards and puked up a clear stream of liquid over Constanz's gun hand.

Matson had no time to depress the syringe. No time and no need. The man was already dead, as dead as her gun would have made him and in similar time.

The human brain is a curious thing, almost as dumb as a testicle, especially after midnight, especially what Matson's instructor used to call 'the brain on the trigger'. Constanz's certainly was. She shot the bugger.

Perhaps her gun did it for her. Guns are self-willed like that. It had intended to shoot the fellow before he spewed on her shooting finger, so it did it.

She got in close, took care to angle away from Matson, and spread the poor stiff's thorax with a half charge.

Matson put him down gently. The gun had been entirely quiet. A lot of noise from his mouth, a mess of blood from his chest. Nothing had exited. Yes, a half charge into a dead man. Cyanide or some other hydrocyanic on the needle followed by a hot cliché of lead.

Having a corpse on your hands, or rather your bedroom

210

carpet in a foreign country, concentrates the mind wonderfully.

'You didn't have to,' he said. 'Kill him twice, I mean. I wasn't even trying to kill him once.'

'Now what?' she said.

Matson always knew what came next. What came next was putting his shoes on.

5

Constanz gazed at the dead man and wrinkled her nose as Matson laced them tight. 'God!' she whistled. 'The ultimate hot-shot. I thought you said Henk was the one with the enemies.'

'Only because I'm so modest.'

The wind through the bathroom window blew straight off the Danube. It was chilly. Or chilly on a damp back.

He eyed the darkness. 'There'll be a back-up man. A driver, anyway. Perhaps he'll remove the corpse for us.'

They were on the second floor: second floor English, not American or Serbian. Below him there was a first floor and a ground floor – say twenty-five feet. Thirty feet in Ireland. More in places where the air was thin.

The room was on a back street. Down there, and a bit along, was parked a Volkswagen Beetle. It was placed exactly between street lamp and street lamp. Otherwise, the night was empty.

There were supposed to be lots of Volkswagen Beetles in Yugoslavia. Matson had read the figures. So far he had noticed only one. This one.

The hotel was walled off at the back. There was a strip of grass between the hotel and its boundary. A square unlovable drainpipe rose beside the window. There was a gap between drainpipe and wall. No time to test it.

'Good,' he muttered. He flashed the bedroom light once, in case the car driver was attentive and looking for some kind of signal. 'See you.'

'How will you get back?'

He dropped through the window, taking his weight under

his left armpit, then on the fingers of his right hand hooked into the sill, his right then his left arm at full stretch. Less than twenty feet now, perhaps only fifteen.

Five or six yards of darkness below his shoes. Grass beneath the darkness. God knows what density of Yugoslavia lay beneath the grass.

He landed soft and crouched against the wall. Low stonework plus an imposing frieze of iron. Here and there a stone pillar of lofty gravitas, level in height with the iron bars of the frieze.

He crawled behind the low stone boundary until he was hidden by the pillar nearest the Volkswagen, then swarmed over the top. He sprung and grabbed at the stonework, crouched toad-like on the summit and jumped into the road.

The Volkswagen was facing away, so the driver was on the other side. He thought he had been unseen and silent, but the passenger door swung open invitingly.

Winkling people out of a Beetle is as hard as digging flesh from a frosted whelk. No time to go back home for his old mum's hatpin. Matson stooped inside the car, caught hold of a good handful of cloth and body flab, and jerked everything into the open. He recognised the smell of the fabric and the aftershave. It wasn't his chum of the designer suiting, it was Gieves and Hawkes. The man who had mashed his face on the restaurant table.

Matson slammed him back against the open door and hit him. He didn't stop to shake hands. He hit him with an unwinding backhanded chop, not just from the elbow, but on the full stride. He got shoulder and spine and all of his frustrated kinetic energy smack behind it.

He heard the bone crack, and cartilage give off that sliding sound it makes when it's well and truly unstrung from its anchorage. He threw the lad back into the car and pushed his head forward over the wheel. Then he opened his mouth and felt for his tongue. He didn't want him to swallow his own blood and suffocate on it. Nothing so neat. He wanted him to drip over that expensive suit and ruin it for ever.

He'd belted the bastard a lot harder than he'd hit Blondie a few days before. But Blondie had only tried to drown him. He hadn't tried to get him angry.

212

6

What Matson needed to do was dump the dead corpse next to the live corpse and drive the Volkswagen several streets away, thus leaving Gieves and Hawkes with the total conundrum.

That would be the end of it. At least as far as the local embassy was concerned. The whole office couldn't be dedicated to bringing him home. Or to chopping him down. There couldn't be more than two spooks on staff, and Matson had bent both of them. The ambassador would get to notice their bruised noses and missing faces; and they'd be asked awkward questions. They might find it best to lie. Ralph Dixon, though a visitor, might decide to even things up and tell the truth.

If Ralph told the truth, the ambassador would phone Pomeroy. He might even go higher. But first he'd phone Pomeroy. Matson might still go home, but hardly in a box. Meanwhile, there was the dead corpse, the upstairs corpse, to consider.

If Constanz had been more of an outdoor type, Matson would have whispered for her to chuck the problem down, or even lower it on a strand of her hair.

As it was, she'd need Matson's help to heave it over the windowsill. They would certainly have to drop it, and risk the noise. If they lowered the body on sheets the bedding would be dirtied, and some of it bloody.

Matson stood below their second-storey bathroom window and felt the drainpipe. He had already classified it as unlovable before jumping down. It was square and too fat to climb. There were few anchor points. Equally, there was a gap between drainpipe and wall, a fat gap.

Matson put a hand on each side of the pipe. It was like gripping an iron box. The lower section was firm, perhaps because it went into the concrete footing of the wall.

He placed the soles of his feet against the stonework and lay back. He wasn't fit enough, but it was a technique he'd practised in the gym and in the mountains. In the mountains, you can only put your hands in the same side of the crack. This was easier. That's what he told himself. Keep the body

213

dynamic. He walked up the wall and into trouble.

It's possible to rope climb even a weakly attached drainpipe, providing it's narrow enough, properly bedded, and secure at the top.

On a fat drainpipe you can only lie back, as the rock-climbing fraternity call the technique. Rock climbers climb rock. Lying back on a drainpipe strains the bolts in their least frictive direction. It lugs them straight out of the wall.

The first section held firm. The next was solid to begin with. The bolts began pulling out as he was halfway up it.

He reached a quick hand towards the bracket above his head and hung from it, his weight anchoring the half-drawn bolts. The intruder had managed the climb, but he was only a little guy.

No way Matson could progress to the third section from such a finger-hold. He would have to slip down to the full stretch of his arm, drop the six or eight feet remaining to the ground, and give up. Walking through the front door of the hotel might cause trouble in these bloodthirsty circumstances, but that was what he would have to do.

Something dug into his side. The sill of the first floor bathroom window. He put his free hand down on it, and pushed up. Standing upright with only a loose bolt to balance against was difficult.

Treading up on to that same bolt demonstrated the superiority of metaphysics over practical mechanics. Practical mechanics, brutish mechanics, were the basis of his day-to-day faith. He said one Hail Mary and reached on high. Hail Marys formed part of his nightly superstition.

The third section of pipe was a wooden surrogate, recently refurbished. It held, just, until he gained the fourth section.

This section was the last. The bolts were senile and the bolt holes geriatric. Matson heard rust shift inside dust, and dust grate around rust. He daren't lie back. He pulled down hard, grabbed for the windowsill, missed it, and fell.

He fell all the way down a grasping arm, the hand of which snatched hairs from his left armpit, pulled skin from his left elbow, then settled to a wristlock.

Lovely Rapunzel. Constanz was strong after all, strong as well as resourceful. He put his right hand on the window-

214

sill, and began to lift himself up, thanks to her masterly assistance.

Her hand had grown callouses since he'd last felt it, but you don't notice such things at once.

7

Matson tumbled through the bathroom window and sprawled on the floor. The hand let go of him. Several hands let go. Hands he hadn't even noticed. Discreet hands that had caught him merely by the cloth of his shirt and the baubles of his head.

Their owners weren't in uniform, but in a uniform mufti of mud-brown, double-breasted suiting. They looked and smelled like off-duty military, all gun oil, garlic and chicken fat. Garlic on their breath, chicken fat on their double-breasted suiting and gun oil wherever it could get. Matson wrinkled his nose, but only in generic recognition. His own army had smelled of aftershave and chips.

Popovic was present, and no more of a surprise than anything else that happens in a bad dream. Popovic stood in the bedroom, scolding Constanz gently and waving her gun at her. He held it in a handkerchief, perhaps to blur any fingerprints.

Constanz sat on the bed, dressed in a leather buttoned raincoat with epaulettes. It was obviously from her suitcase and presumably offered the only opacity she could think of in a hurry.

The corpse was on the floor, and still very much a corpse. Its spine arched backwards rather less than before. It straightened a notch at a time as the muscles unclenched their spasm. This gave it an appearance of life, in spite of the hole in its ribs. It made tiny noises as it moved, like someone stretching on waking.

'Your Mrs Zanetti and my Mrs Ehrenberg.' Popovic turned to Matson as if introducing them. 'She has appealed to me for help. Which is intelligent of her, not to say prescient. For this I forgive her much.'

'When did you two meet?' Matson asked sweetly.

'Just now when she presented herself, in distress, to my room. I made acquaintance with her voice only last evening, though I believe I saw her asleep a day or two back. In your Range Rover, was it? Or General Weiss's Mercedes? She is – what shall I call it?'

'Ubiquitous.'

'My dear, I told you no porkies. Or, if I did, only a tiny one with the merest curl to its tail. I like my eggs altogether, Patrick. Tucked away under the same chicken's bum. When Mrs Ehrenberg phoned me for an interview, I told her she would have to wait until it was convenient. I gave her the name of your hotel. Which is also my hotel. Where it is sometimes convenient.'

Matson's eyebrows had already climbed as high as they could be expected to go, so Popovic smiled and added, 'I *have* been known to sleep in the office, my dear. But never that one.'

'Don't talk about the weather during an earthquake, Popo.'

'It's *your* earthquake, my dear.' Popovic admonished the corpse with his boot. 'But Mrs Ehrenberg-Zanetti has per-suaded me I could also make it my own. So tell me what happens out there.' He pointed past his assembled brown suits in the general direction of the bathroom window.

Matson told him about the Volkswagen and its damaged contents. 'I'm afraid your people arrested the same Embassy gent earlier this evening, Popo.'

'In connection with yourself. I was frightened it might come to this. But chance works in very small numbers, or we shouldn't be able to recognise her for who she is. I shall not mention your name when I return him, nor when I ask for his recall. But your people will scarcely need reminding of you.'

Matson said nothing.

Popovic gazed at him with all the enthusiasm the hour could muster. 'On the other hand, you can stop looking over your shoulder from now on. At least, as far as your Embassy is concerned.' He made for the door and held it open for the chicken-and-garlic brigade to leave. 'Unless anything followed you from London, that is.'

'There you go a little fast for me.'

216

'Bullets, Patrick my dear friend. You spoke of bullets through bedrolls, bullets through cars. You cannot seriously imagine such things were set up from here, could you? You were scarcely known to have arrived. London is my bet.'

'Or Popovic.'

'I hope that's a joke, my dear. I really really do.' His English was so idiomatic, he even pronounced it 'reelly reelly', like a Woolworth's girl or television presenter.

He wasn't finished, even now; then nobody supposed he would be. 'You owe me, Patrick. You owe me now.'

'Perhaps. But I'm not allowed to pay you. We both know that.'

'Not for letting you walk free from a mess like this?'

'I'm not asking for any sort of accommodation, Popo. Not beyond what Mrs Ehrenberg-Zanetti feels able to arrange with you.'

Popovic didn't answer that one. Popovic had gone.

SIXTEEN

1

'This is not a prison. It's a detention centre.'

'There's a difference?'

'People are sometimes let out of prison, my dear. This place is run by the Security Police.'

They had come through a gate, a wire fence, a door in a windowless wall, a grille, an inner door. The frontage had been small, but the building had the smell of somewhere that went back a long way – in time, at least.

Matson and Popovic waited in a room roughly ten feet square. It was furnished with thinning cloth-backed linoleum and a strip light. It had a door in and a door that looked as if it would lead even further in the same direction. In Britain, these places were once painted glossy green. Now they are vinyl white. This one was grey, like grandmother's hair. It smelled of half a century of anxiety and cheap tobacco. You could see the air.

Popovic noticed the twitch of Matson's nostrils and said mildly, 'These buildings are all the same. They are designed to be ventilated by draught, but gaps that let wind in let protests out.'

The far door opened, and four men in crumpled suits came quickly into the room.

Popovic carried on speaking. He changed languages without changing voice or pitch.

The four men listened to him while he went on conversationally in those liquid vowels and explosive consonants that Matson's ear was always too slow to assemble. As they listened they caught Matson by the shoulders and wrists, forced his hands behind his back and handcuffed them there.

This took about three seconds and a wrenched elbow. Then they stood away from him.

'I meant to explain, my dear. You can only get in here with a security rating so astronomically high as to be unbelievable. Even my own is temporary.' He walked behind Matson to admire his friend's body-sculpture. 'Ah,' he breathed. 'The felon's pose, the final indignity.' He tested the link with the full weight of his hand, and it hurt. 'Or you can come in like this, as a prisoner.'

'And?'

'First I shall play my joker, as promised. I shall show you Jug Bogdan. That will leave the game even, I think. Afterwards, Patrick – well, I won't be so trite as to invite you to consider who holds the trumps.' The thought hurt him.

'Fastidious of you.'

'Let me deal instead in the symbolism of the original Magyar pack. There's a suit called 'keys'. Trumps or not, you can take it I hold those. Certainly since last night.'

2

'Jug Bogdan' was the joker. He didn't look too badly messed about. He was bare-chested and showed an area of pink bruising beneath the left collarbone, the sort of dispersed contusion a man gets from tripping against a security policeman's boot.

He could also have received the same degree of damage from the butt plate of a 'short' – or even a standard-snouted – Lee Enfield .303 fired left-handed or left-eyed with nothing more to protect his shoulder than a summer shirt and a few beads of sweat.

Especially if he'd emptied the shell-cases and repacked them with the kind of magnum load favoured by weapon freaks and snipers.

'I didn't know you were left-handed.' An odd thing for Matson to say, but even Lazarus must have heard a few peculiar remarks when he'd stepped from the tomb. 'If I'd known you were feeling so much better I'd have brought some grapes.'

Lippiat had died not once but twice. Matson didn't examine him really closely – ghosts never have to fuss overmuch with their make-up. At first glance, Lolly looked a whole lot healthier than he did when his body fell apart in Matson's and the innkeeper's hands. According to Willi's and Albin's photographs, he'd been in even worse shape the second time round.

'I'm not,' Lolly said. 'I picked up an eye infection that day on the lake.'

Matson remembered the bolt work of the shots close-to in the mountains. Not very crisp. They could have been fired by a man reaching left-handed over the stock to operate a right-handed bolt, especially a man not used to firing that way.

The two shots at Kocevje Gora had been different. Still, an infection takes time to develop.

Somebody started to laugh. It must have been Matson.

3

Two plain-clothes security policemen held his elbows with thumbs dug into the pressure points. The other two watched from the corridor, as if there were fears that he and Lippiat might kill each other. Popovic fussed between the six of them, like a photographer at a wedding.

Now they had him deep inside, the two spare policemen came in to unlock Matson's handcuffs. Not quite that. They unclipped the metal from his right wrist and fastened it beside the bracelet on his left.

Thoughtful types. A dangling handcuff can be made as dangerous as a mace and chain.

Only then did the thumbnail and bone come away from the sore spots in his elbows, and the four of them go out, to the usual sound of keys in iron doors and boots on stone. This was a place where the quietest men were allowed the hardest footwear.

Leaving Lolly and Matson to be soothed together for the bridal group.

'I don't know if this place is bugged, my dear. You'll have to ask Mister Lippiat about the internal economy. None of us is in any great position to complain if it is.' Popovic turned to Lippiat. 'I want you to tell Captain Matson what he wants to know, Gerald. Everything.' His voice was gentle. 'If you think it safe for you to part with anything, that is.'

Lolly read the sentence back in his mind to see how codified it was. His face stayed empty of expression.

'Captain Matson is going to do us a favour, Gerald. I am saving his bacon for him by showing him you. You of all people will understand how useful to him that must be. It is highly unlikely he will want to refuse me the tiny accommodation I ask in return.'

'And suppose this place *is* bugged, Popo?' Lippiat's eyes indicated that the painted stonework was in his view deafer than the dead, but he wasn't quite comfortable about the ventilation grille in the ceiling. 'Suppose these walls have ears and you get hold of the transcript, as you assuredly will? I may have some bitchy things to say.'

'Very hard to hurt Popo's feelings. Almost impossible, my dear. The fact is I've caught you out and locked you up.' He touched the man's shoulder. 'There was a certain amount of biting involved. It's only reasonable you should want to bark.' He gazed at the ventilation grille for himself. 'Yugoslavia won't stage a trial on this one. No one will know about you. Not now, not tomorrow, not ever. And it may well be for ever. That's never, isn't it?' He smiled like an old-fashioned headmaster about to deal out some pain, but sensing hope just beyond. 'But suppose it's not? You'll want to set the record straight with your own crowd, I think?'

'Captain Matson's in no position to help matters one way or the other. Is he now?'

Popovic smiled complacently, knocked on the door, and waited to be let out.

Not that 'out' was out. He had the authority to ask to be let in to some other place, that was all. Whether he could do as much for Matson might well depend on the ventilation grille.

4

'That Popovic is a clever man, Paddy. Very clever. I made the mistake of trusting him with my exodus from Karnten. From Carinthia. It seemed smart at the time. He found me the corpse.'

'Which one?'

'You're confusing the issue. The one in the motor caravan. I'll come to the other one later.'

'Popovic, then. Popovic and clever.'

'A moderately clever man who wanted me out of the way would have killed me and dumped my body in the lake. It's deep enough, for God's sake. A clever-clever man would have approved of my plot, then used me as the corpse in my own fireball.'

'Why didn't he? Knowing what you now know, I mean. That he wanted you out of the way because he had more pressing things on his mind.'

'As I read it, it was because he couldn't tell if I was kosher. If I really was a defector – no problem. He could lose me somewhere. If I was still running messages for any of the English or American services or agencies, then the fireball might be their plan as well as my own smoke-screen. No point in making enemies unnecessarily, so why not go along with it – no matter whose wheeze it was – and simply help me across the border then lock me up?'

'From time to time trotting you out on a chain?'

Lippiat chose to look puzzled.

'The last time no later than yesterday. Remember the scene? Fake dervishes. Fake protest marchers. A stagy shower of paramilitaries. Television lights. Cameras galore. A whole clip of bullets in a four-inch group, missing myself, missing Obergruppenführer Weiss and ricocheting all the way to technicolour heaven from the bonce of a strategic rock. He let you out for that, didn't he?'

'That wasn't out, Paddy. That was further in. I was being landed right in it. The cameras got me, you know.'

'So why not blow a hole in Herr Weiss's head?'

'What, on Popovic's say-so? When he's set me up and got me on film?'

222

'Well, at least he showed you Weiss's head.'

'I won't say Popovic is untrustworthy. I am saying I don't know anybody who can afford to trust him. He takes hostages. He never gives them. He's got me on film. He's got you on his payroll.'

'Bullshit.'

Lippiat grinned towards the grille. 'He told me he was probably going to bring you to see me. He told me yesterday.'

'So?'

'He said he'd bring you only if you were as deeply in the manure with our own people as I am. He *owns* both of us, Paddy. Any time we're naughty, he can give either of us to our Embassy and have an end of us.'

'I can go home any time I like,' Matson lied.

'Alive? Or in a bucket of offal?' The silence grew over-long, so he added, 'Shooting people like Weiss gives me no sort of job satisfaction these days.'

5

'I have other worries,' Matson said. 'Selfish ones, I agree. They go like this. There have been several bits of random tough and rough. Amateurish swipes that my own proximity to the gentlemen landed me right alongside.'

'My heart bleeds for you both.'

'Together with a number of sophisticated attempts to scare Herr Weiss rather than kill him.'

'Warn, Paddy. Warn not scare. I've got some tricksy friends. They like, a bit of cheek. It's part of the national character.'

'Did your friends send me some of your reading material? In Austria, then at Kocevje Gora?'

'I fancy the Austrian fuzz got most of my stuff – what wasn't burnt or drowned. Popovic has what little I brought over.'

'So why did Popovic bother – or, more likely, have his people bother?'

'If it *was* Popovic. Because you were *there*, Paddy. Incidentally, why the hell were you, and why are you? He would have to assume you were my contact, my courier, my control – perhaps all three. In which case, he would want to give you the feeling that I was still around. Going maverick, perhaps, haywire even; but around.'

'Shooting at me?'

Lolly played puzzled. Matson described the incident in detail.

'I'd say the books were his idea, the bullet someone else's. I don't believe in missed shots, warning shots or whatever. Nor do you deep down. Especially when they hit the bed someone has seen you sneak into.'

'Bullshit. You shot at me. You sent me one of your bloody books. You crept around at night, made sure it was me, then decided to maim me or warn me off. You've just admitted that other business yesterday.'

'Yesterday was different. Popovic helicoptered me there and made me an offer I couldn't refuse. I wanted to take a good long look at Weiss, in any event.'

'Why?'

'Stay tuned, Paddy. People don't know when I creep about them at night. When I shoot at them, they stay shot. Though, I must say, it's half a lifetime since I shot anyone.' He thought for a moment. 'My people back home knew about my Yugoslav ploy. I'm getting too old to carry lies in my head. I think I told you so back in Karnten?'

Matson had told Dixon as much.

'Somebody sent you after me, Paddy. Somebody could have been sent after you, too.'

'With a rifle?'

'Bullets come cheap. They're extremely able messengers.'

6

'I mean: dear old Popo-my-dear's had a number of chats at me. I understand what's in his mind, or what he wants me to understand. He thinks like the Austrians think. That I'm part of a Weiss plot. That somebody back home tried to stop me. That you came to cry halt, persuade me to go home or push right off. Even to kill me. You and I know what you actually did. Only you, Paddy, know what you came to do.'

'Is there a Weiss plot?'

'We're talking about you. Stay tuned, as I say, and don't waste your time. Popo thinks you were meant to drop yourself in trouble by following me across the border.'

'I've given it a certain amount of thought myself.'

'It won't stand up. You were intended to damage your reputation, I've no doubt of that. The snag with Popo's scenario, and I've told him as much –' This time both of them addressed the ventilation grille. 'The trouble with that little number is that only I, and then Popo, knew anything in advance about my faked-up "accident". For anyone to have been confident of getting you to follow me across the border, they would have needed to know I'd be dead, then demonstrably undead (which I never intended), and conclude you'd be suspicious enough, or dogged enough, to carry on. In reality, they'd have to foresee every damned thing that set you ahead, including a whole lot of factors I myself can't even guess at. Things you found out in the Austrian nick, for instance.'

'Agreed.'

'Now I don't know whether you really came to top me.'

'I didn't.'

'I didn't think so at the time. That's why you're still alive, Paddy. Or I'm still alive,' he corrected modestly. 'Somebody played chess with the pair of us. There's no "need to know" at that bloody Balkan desk. They steal each other's underpants and share shirts and socks. Whoever wanted to stop me thought, Let's send Matson. It'll be two birds with one stone. Lolly'll cut up rough. He'll try and wring Matson's neck, then Matson'll peck him back. If Matson triumphs, end of Lolly. If Lippiat wins one-nil, then goodbye to his immediate intentions. He'll be a murderer as far as Austria is concerned, and have badly mislaid a friendly, to his own firm's certain knowledge and displeasure. He'll know we know he knows we know. That's how they think, Patrick. And that's what they thought. It shows no confidence in their field officers' second-phase possession. Then we're both used to being undervalued.'

225

Matson nodded thoughtfully. 'When you appeared to have got yourself toasted, they made exactly the noises you predicted.'

'It's a pity you got involved with the rest of it, Paddy. It'll get you banged up or dead. While you're alive, try and listen.'

Lippiat was still fidgeting about. Hardly a good indication of honesty. 'A chap's love life is always a bit of a groan. It's what it ties into that counts.'

'You telling me your cradle story? Or are you telling me what you told them back home?'

'They listened, Paddy. They bloody listened. That's what makes it so risky for you.'

7

'Sometimes she called herself Vera, sometimes Anja – I think like that, and not Anna. We all had more than one name. Some of us needed a dozen. Her real name was probably Jovanka, even though she wasn't from the south. She was seventeen and married to a Montenegrin called Zarkovic, an older bloke whose name was Peter and who couldn't be with us because he had a crooked knee. Weiss treated him to a crooked neck the following year. See how the sod keeps on cropping up? Meanwhile, Peter was the name she used to mention while she was sharing my sleeping bag. Get the picture? An unusual girl. She had those Slovene looks – the most beautiful girls in Europe. She was a cracker.'

Matson heard this with considerable impatience. His face must have said so.

'We managed to get her pregnant, Patrick. Her and me, and a couple of dozen snowy evenings when the waterfalls froze, and not even the wolves got a bite. If they stuck their noses out we ate them.'

The cell was bare, and talk began to condense and drip from the painted stone. The overhead grille did what it could.

'There was love as well as passion. There was also the war and her old man. Common sense says one thing, but the heart does another. The body – God bless it – does what it can.'

226

A plastic tub squatted in the corner. It was yellow. It looked like a chamber pot. Lippiat held it out to him and, when he didn't take it, sipped from it noisily. It was a ewer full of cold water. Once again Matson had refused to drink with him.

'That was at a time when partisan women weren't allowed to get themselves pregnant, not by their husbands, not by the odds and sods, certainly not by me.'

Matson had a bruise or two. He had been manhandled last night and pushed around this morning. The cold stonework was turning him into an old man. Give him much longer at one degree centigrade and his body was going to die on him. God knows what it was doing to Gerry.

'They found them with a bun up, they got shot. That was how the story went. I never saw a pregnant woman shot, Paddy. Anja didn't get shot. She was sent back to Peter, and that did none of us any good. Weiss killed Peter, as I told you, and for Anja he arranged something rather worse.'

Matson's body got the better of his patience. 'So you told all this to the Balkan Desk?'

'Some of it.'

'Somebody writing a soap opera?'

8

'Let me do it my own way, Paddy. You're not going to hear it from me twice.'

Matson leant against the coldness in the wall. It kept him very still.

'I met a man in a restaurant,' Lippiat went on. 'In Berne.'

Matson groaned.

'No, it wasn't what you think. I wasn't being set up, not then. Not unless he was prepared to take twenty years and risk me snuffing it *en route*. No, no. We're professional, you and I, Paddy. We know how things are. They don't happen like this. He wasn't trying to egg me into any kind of indiscretion. Didn't know I had any secrets.

'He was a Slav. Half Croat, half Slovene – rather like

grandfather Tito himself. I had been pointed out to him as someone who had been with the partisans in the war, on the big retreat.

'I don't know what they told you, but I'm in Berne quite a lot.'

'They told me all about Berne.'

'Believe Berne. The "all" is certain to be lies. One time – and we met over the years – I told him about Anja Jovanka Zarkovic – I told him about a Yugoslav girl I had a baby by. We were rather drunk. We both cried a little. I believe we cried. He certainly did.

' "You never married," he said.

'I said no, but the wine had done its work. I said I'd lived a lot, I'd had a passable career as a regular soldier, and a fair-to-middling one as a civil servant, but that I'd known such an intensity of love as a boy scarcely out of his teens that it had lasted me a lifetime.

' "You never married," he said. That was our trigger. He knew what it meant. He knew I was a Jew and certainly not queer, so he knew I had taken a vow as he had taken a vow to sublimate our earthly love and replace it, quite literally, with a love of earth. Mother Earth. His earth. Yugoslavia.'

They both took water this time, Matson so he could stay awake.

'Well, my friend grew very quiet then. Asked a few questions. Answered a few himself. The conversation was deep where for years it had been trivial. It was like discovering we were brothers.

'Afterwards I didn't see him for a bit. He came back here to Belgrade.

'Then he came to London – oh, a couple of years since – and said he had need of me in a matter of honour. You laugh, I didn't. I'm too much in love with the code.'

'So you sold out.' Matson was appalled at the unworld-liness of it. The man was being untrue to something Matson couldn't define – possibly no more than his pension, but that was enough. He was reneging on his future at the end of a long career. It wasn't even Queen and Country. That was mere dishonour. To be untrue to one's pension was to be a bloody imbecile. 'No one,' he said. 'No one but no one but no one sells out to the Yugoslavs. I've said it before, and I'll say it again.'

'I sold out in 1944. I was parachuted in. When they came to get me out, they left rather more of me behind than any of us had bargained for.'

'I didn't come here for fairy stories.'

'Stay away from Serbia then. Let's say that while I was out here a number of people, too damn many of them, but one in particular' – his voice grew gruff at some memory or other – 'bought a certain obligation from me, and bought it in blood. The debt was never called in. How could it be? They were all dead. But a couple of years ago, I decided to begin paying it. *Not* by giving away anything of ours. I simply paid up.

'The Foreign Office doesn't like its underlings to owe debts to anyone. I'm not a traitor. I simply wish to be free to act.'

'They all say that.'

'My freedom was forbidden me, as yours is. Get yourself in the picture, Matson, and don't be so bloody smug about the frame.' He limped over and stood very close. His body was trembling, from stress, from duress, from cold. Matson couldn't tell, but he didn't think the man was deranged. He'd seen girlfriends look more glassy-eyed in a kitchen fight. 'When I was told the details of what was required of me, I consulted them back home. I kept them informed. I asked my masters for leave. When it was refused, I asked for a discharge – at *my* age. I asked for *time*. I told them every little jigsaw bit of everything. I'm a good soldier. But they said no, Matson. I shouldn't have told them. My boss is – *you* know Marcus Pomeroy. He's a Jew, as it happens. Like me, if it matters. How was I to know that even the Jews in the FO protect SS generals now?'

'You said you weren't after Weiss.' That was just to give himself something to say. Matson's ear had heard the coins start to drop. One penny first, and then two. Pomeroy hadn't said no, he was certain of that. And Matson was beginning to form a very clear idea of what he hadn't said no to.

9

'Of course I'm after Weiss. But not like that. Anyway, I'm in here now.'

'This bloke has a name, your friend in Berne? Not Popovic, was it?'

Lippiat laughed. 'No. Someone with clout. They'd have to use white-hot pincers before I tell them who. This lot won't dare. Popo certainly won't.'

'They found out you were "Jug Bogdan". They'll want the identities of the other names on that list.'

'Ditto. Bollocks and ditto. They wouldn't dare. The more they might guess, the more they'll be too terrified to ask.' Lolly was looking pleased with himself. He liked the direction their talk was taking.

'I take it your Berne pal is one of what Popovic is pleased to call the Serbian establishment?'

'Something like that. What I did with Popovic in London was really quite trivial. I merely sought him out and negotiated an accommodation.'

'Agents' names being the price?'

'Filth. Handschar and worse. Do you understand what that means? They lived by my say-so, and well they knew it.'

'They're dead now.'

'Perhaps. Their number's been on it for years, for damned near half a century. There weren't enough bullets then, that's all. Not enough ropes, not enough trees. No bloody time.' He sat down on the floor, showing fatigue at last. 'My people knew I was meeting Popo. What I was proposing to do, what I had to say. God knows why they went so white round the gills when Dixon discovered what I was up to.' He stretched out and seemed comfortable. 'You'd have thought they'd be reassured to encounter such total honesty in a colleague. Rarely can deed and intent have been such a perfect match – in our line of country, anyway.

'That was where I went wrong with Popo, just the same. We always kid ourselves. We behave as if we're alone and working to others who are alone. But none of us are. We play by the book, but we know there's no way we can write the whole story in it. All our deals are based on it.'

'The ones that go wrong.'

'All of our deals. Any simple sentence contains at least one lie. Three if it's in translation. Three times three if the speaker thinks in two languages. Popovic said one thing and I must have heard another. Or the promise of another.'

10

'So what did Popo say to you? I understand how he proposed to help you, but what was the deal exactly?'

'He said come across the border and snooker the Obershitbag for us.'

'He said *what*?'

'Verbatim, Paddy. And seriatim. Snooker the Obershitbag. You've met the old ram. It's purest Popospeak. One headshot with a high-velocity rifle. He offered Yugoslavia to provide the rifle and a fine back light. Weiss to provide the head. Well, of course, I pretended to accept.'

'Come on, Lolly. *You* proposed –'

'I'm not into revenge, Patrick. Not that sort of revenge, anyway. I keep on telling you. Vincenz Weiss cured me of that stuff, if ever I needed curing.'

'Was that one down to you? His death, I mean.'

Lippiat was silent for a moment. When he spoke it was to say, 'If I ever get my finger round a trigger, Paddy, the bloody bullet hits what I want it to hit.' For some reason he began to cry. 'Excuse my continued boasting,' he muttered. 'A bit of swank distracts me.'

'So you had nothing to do with the death of Weiss's son?'

'I had everything to do with it, in the sense his life was down to me. I was Vincenz Weiss's father. I was responsible for his birth, so you could say I was responsible for his death. And if you plant life in such a bed of death –'

'Was this before or after Anja Zarkovic?'

He blew his nose, and said, 'It *was* Anja.' Another tune on the handkerchief. 'Poor Anja. Bloody poetry, isn't it? A sonnet sequence, that lad's life. And his death? He was halfway to making quite a decent soldier, by all accounts, when Weiss's bad luck claimed him. Another victim. I was a proud man, Paddy, proud by proxy.

'Revenge? You're father of another man's child, it's about the best revenge you'll ever get. I mean, I owe Weiss a lot of hate and history owes him more. Vincenz's death cancels my share of it, and history must find its own way. Besides, a bullet through the head was never quite what I had in mind for that bastard. Forty odd years ago, we sat down there deciding what we wanted to do to him – when I say "we" I include Tito – and, by a large majority, a bullet in the head was not thought to be it. What do you say?'

'A mass of contradictions, if I say anything.'

'That's life, dear boy. Or so Pomeroy expressed himself.'

'What about this Anja and Vincenz Weiss?'

'When I heard what happened to Peter Z, I made my way – as soon as I could, which wasn't very – to find Anja and the baby. The child was a boy, and Weiss had taken him.'

'Taken him? Why?'

'He was convinced he was his own. A seven-month child, but it happens with shock or short rations.'

'Why didn't he think it was Peter Zarkovic's?'

'Anja never got back to Peter. Not till after the birth. Weiss saw her and took a fancy, you see.'

'Why did he take this child, and not any others? There were supposed to be plenty of girls he had here, willing and unwilling.'

The ventilation grille was like the lattice in a confession box.

'He was in love with her, that's why. He wanted Anja permanently for his own. She couldn't say no to him having her, but she could certainly say bollocks to marrying the sod – or whatever he proposed. Even Weiss would see sense over that. See sense and top poor Peter out of rage and revenge.'

Lolly was through with crying. He began to laugh. It was the first mad note he'd struck. 'What the Obergruppenführer and I have in common is our love for the same woman.'

'Popovic doesn't know this story, I take it.'

'He does now.'

232

'You've had your weep, Lolly. Can't say I blame you. Now let's get back to Austria.'

'Nasty hole. Sterile as Switzerland and twice as prissy.'

'Whose idea was the bonfire and bang?'

'Popo's. He said London was after me.'

'He said *that*?'

'Apparently Leonard Fossit started asking a lot of questions about Weiss. Too many, Popo thought. He came out to Austria, ostensibly to warn me. The Yugoslavs were giving a reception, and there was Leonard cheek by chop with Marcus Pomeroy. Leonard talking about Weiss and *The Times* articles, Pomeroy saying I was a Balkan freak, already out there, and what would I think once I got to hear Weiss was going south?'

Matson knew about Fossit. The rest was news to him.

'Popovic is a big fib. The Serbs are born that way. Anyway, that was his argument so I decided to push on out. He might have been lying. It suited his purpose to hurry me over the frontier. But he named names and they seemed good ones, because Fossit wasn't an immediately obvious part of the scenario. Mention of him made it smell right, somehow. Then you showed up – too late to be part of my motivation, of course – but you really frightened me. You work for Fossit, and there you were.'

'Why – starting in London – why did Popovic want to aid stroke trick you stroke string you along in this?'

'Cover his back, I fancy. I know Popo as a spymaster. So do you, I daresay. It's an open secret. No one worries too much about what the Yugoslav Embassy digs out of London, so it's only half a job. Suddenly – hey presto – he knows he's going to be called home. Promoted demoted to mastermind the security on this Weiss trip. *That's* a dodgy number to contemplate. We've seen the cameras, read the spread. His hands are tied. When Weiss goes down – and he *will* go down – Popo's career will be on the chalk mark. Wrists already fastened. Blindfold and noose waiting. But if he can produce me – someone, anyone – and say he might have lost the big one, but there were many incidental successes along the way . . . and then he produces you as well.'

Matson nodded. The two cases were different. He wasn't going to waste time on that. 'So the explosion was his idea? Where did the corpse come from?'

'Ditto.'

'He said what? "It just so happens I've got a stiff in my luggage"?'

'I didn't ask. The Yugoslavs must have their contacts in southern Austria, run all kinds of cells, I daresay. I assumed his people had wasted someone and were holding a body on ice – literally, as it turned out – and Lolly sniffed it out.

'I mean, it wouldn't make sense to one of us. You can't imagine Ralph Dixon asking Pomeroy for a favour, say. We don't know enough of what we're all doing. Out here, they have to share their secrets. Old So-an-so's got a corpse. Old Thingummy's put in for too much departmental toilet paper. A secret secret is bad communism. It suggests a traitor.'

Matson didn't believe a word of the explanation, though it was possible Lolly might. What was so numbing about his account was that the whole plot – with Matson as cat, mouse and cheese – was in place long before anyone suggested he leave London. It was ready and waiting in everyone's mind before Dixon's merry men reported Lolly talking to Popovic even.

Lolly would have played his little game, and Popo would have upstaged him, exactly as happened. But if Ralph hadn't explored his suspicions, then reported them as he was obviously meant to, Matson would be in the clear and enjoying the polluted waters of Italy.

'That's one corpse,' he said. 'What about corpse number two?'

'Günter Lenz. General Lenz. I had him on my hands as well, you see.'

12

'It can't be. It was recently dead. Lenz had been dead for ages.'

'Who told you that? The Austrians? It's their nasty suspicious minds. They always get goose-pimply when I turn up.

'I knew they were on to me. They have a good man called Leodolter. Good men are not invisible, Patrick. Merely more discreet. I noticed the young rotter noticing me. I'm not invisible, either, but I'm even more bloody discreet. Then there was Inspector Kaub.'

'Kaub is part of the local –'

'Kaub is a Fed, seconded for the duration. The duration of what? I ask. The duration of me, I answer. Another thing, if Kaub is only an inspector, I'll eat my tosh. That man runs half of Austria. What half? The efficient half.'

'They think you've been killing off their Nazis, Lolly. That's their efficient half for you.'

'Nazis, you say? Since the war? I've never gone in for it, Paddy. As I keep on saying. Well, only once, and certainly not in Austria. I suppose the suspicion stuck to me, even so. Nothing clings more tenaciously than an unsolved crime.'

'Let's confine ourselves to Lenz. I won't ask you to talk about the other thing.'

'I will, willingly, given time. Stay tuned. It sounds as if the Colonel is going to keep you here. Good chap, Günter Lenz. Salt of the earth. Well, he is by now, anyway.'

Matson noted the change of tone. There was a sinister bonhomie about Lippiat, as if he knew the hard part was over. He wondered if the lies and the shameless contradictions were over too.

'I went to see him. More than once. I made no bones about the fact I was dead against men like Weiss. Well, I found him to be a nice old ... not buffer: there's no way you can ever call an ex-Wehrmacht general a buffer. I found him very good company. Of course the police can tie me to him. I went there several times. He even had me to dinner. Freshly caught salmon, a haunch of wild boar that had been pickled in red wine till it fell off the bone. Better than venison. Not so black on the tooth. The talk was agreeable, too.'

Matson was hoping he'd come to that.

'Said he disapproved of men like the Gruppenführer. It was one thing to be a Nazi, and a pretty beastly thing at that. But to boast about it after forty years – get his drift? He even made out a fairish case for that toady Waldheim, as well as a

Kraut ever can for a riker. Said reticence was at least becoming. What he had against Weiss – beyond the fact he was SS, and, as an old-time army man, Lenz couldn't stand the SS – was his current noisiness. "Get someone to ask him how bloody loud he was when he was working for the British," he suggested. "More, ask him how much mouth he shot while he was with the Yanks." "You ask him," I said. "I can never get a word in. Nobody can."

'Then I invited him to the wagon to have a return match. I cooked something or other, and I had some nice tins. Told him I was going to Bogenfeld later that week. He asked to come with me for a day or two, nice and private. He didn't have any live-ins, just a daily cook and weekly cleaner – that sort of thing.'

'He wasn't constrained?'

'By me? No, he was an old man, and pretty poorly. Legs, circulation – you know. He'd have thought it awfully *infra dig*, not to say non-U, to go up to that chintzy bloody *gasthaus*. So would I. They're for the Trojans, and people like you from London. Like a lavatory without the shit, those places.

'He didn't call it a motor caravan. Said it was his command wagon. I've got two bunks. I cook well when I fish. There's always good wine *chez* Lippiat at the dear old Lolly *schloss*. He was as pleased as Punch. Then the old fart's ticker went.

'I assume it was something like that. He refused to let me call a doctor. Said let him lie up with me till he was fit to travel – liked the ambience, see? – then I could take him home. Then he died on me. I'd been about to drive him back anyway.'

'When was this?'

'Evening before you showed up. Night before my bonfire.'

'Why didn't you use *his* corpse? Squeamish?'

'Figured he'd be missed, and they'd put two and two together. Besides, I'd already indented for the other one, so to speak.'

'It doesn't sound likely, does it?'

'Truth never does. You can see I'd be tempted to reverse roles, dump the chilly one in the lake and cook the general.

For reasons already given, I rejected it. Also, the frozen bloke turned up incomplete. No head, no guts.'

'Did it look like an expert job?'

'Removed through an incision, but not by a doctor. Nor a medical student. Don't ask me how or who. More like the cut you'd make in a rabbit's fur with your pocket knife.

'Decent chap, Lenz. A four-square Prussian soldier. One of Marshal Blucher's sort, I daresay. Mad like Blucher, but bloody good company. I'd say he was straight. Like those old Indian Army colonels. Screw your missus, without a doubt, but never cheat you at cards.'

'It'll show up on autopsy.' Albin and Willi had claimed it was Lolly's corpse beyond question.

'Maybe. But I got his lungs nice and full of water, see. Used a hose. Half like drowning. Half like foul play. Half like – well, I've run out of fractions, but enough to keep Kaub, Leodolter and Co guessing.

'I did a couple of tender bits of surgery on his features with a flat stone. Makes you wince, what? But we've done worse. Then I had a go at the old pickers and thieves with a piece of pumice I keep for me geriatric hard-pad. Totally erased the prints. I mean, they could prove it wasn't me if they really wanted to, but I don't think these bloody Austrians care. They mightn't believe corpse number one. I didn't believe it myself. They'd put it down to my low cunning. But corpse number two made a nice little scenario, don't you think?

'Anyway, it's shallow round the north side of the lake. I dragged him along the bottom by his ankles, before casting him adrift. Did it at night. I daresay the gravel did the rest.' He raised his voice to the ventilation grille. 'You can come and let one of us out, Colonel Popovic.'

13

'I tell you why I can't top Weiss. Apart from Vincenz, I mean. It's the one suspicion the Austrians have got me on file for. And the Krauts. Name Ulrich Raum mean anything to you? No reason it should mean anything to anyone, except for the couple of dozen people his particularly nasty shadow fell across during the Fifth Offensive, Operation Schwarz. I lay in a ditch one time with an empty gun and watched that bastard at work. Kids mostly. I won't bore a sophisticate of your generation with the details.

'He came in first with the Reich, I believe. Just like Weiss. A posh crowd of unposh people, the Reich. Good soldiers. Like Weiss he got injured, sent to Austria to lick his wounds, then to Romania when they were forming Prinz Eugen and wanted some proven people as stiffeners. He was a sturmbannführer, I think, nothing exalted, one of those boy scout SS titles but from an originally élite outfit. Prinz Eugen weren't élite, but they were bloody good in the mountains. Plenty of spunk.

'Especially the bits Weiss got hold of. You know his sort of officer. Leads from the front, but somehow persuades the slackers he's behind them with a pistol.

'Raum survived. I had a little list in those days. Weiss was on it, of course. Raum was the only one I ever met up with.

'Have you ever been to Berchtesgarten? So's Hitler. You'll know the lake then, in that funnel of the mountains. Take everything bad in Austria, transfer it to the FDR and drop it down a deep hole and you've got the place. I went there a couple of times because Morecombe gives me rheumatism. I don't go back, not since I met Raum staying at my hotel. It was always raining anyway.

'First time I got a reasonable chance to catch up on him, I did it.

'It was raining, as I say. I mean mountain rain, raining the weather's head off. But he had to go on his walk, you see. It was a religion with them, to walk where the Führer walked. So he had to go. A man like that has a wife, she's got to go. A man like me sees a man like that, I have to go. Follow me?

'Not high season. Neither summer nor snow. It was as lonely on that wooden walkway above the lake as if we were at the Reichenbach Falls.

'I killed the woman first. His sort always keeps his woman behind him to tell him what his digestion's like. I didn't do anything naughty. I hard-edged the poor cow and tipped her straight into the drink. Not a moo. He didn't even look round at the splash.

238

'The monkey of it is you just can't kill a slime like that. What would be the point? That gristly bastard didn't just kill people, take it from me.

'I said, "Ulrich Raum", and he damn nearly jumped out of his trousers. "Stand to attention," I said. "I've a warrant from Milovan Djilas and the Third Brigade. You were sentenced to death twenty-seven years ago in your absence. I am your appointed executioner and it's bloody well on you."

'He wouldn't utter. He didn't say a word. Not a word. He let the rain fall on his brolly, then his brush-top haircut and looked at me as if I wasn't there. I'm always there, Patrick.

'Any time I meet one of those bastards I'll put it to him.

'I wrung the sod's neck. I started, I stopped. I stopped, I started. But he wouldn't put up a fight. I got him on the deck, he still wouldn't fight. Then I hung him from one of those under-logs – you know, the props – I hung him in his braces. Military unelasticated. They didn't break. Nor did his neck.

'It stopped raining. People came along. A couple even canoodled right above where he was hanging from the footway. I hope they were Slavs, but they wouldn't be. Not there.

'I went long ways about. It's not easy country to go long ways about in, believe me. Not even then, when I was twenty years younger.

'The State Police said it was suicide. They came to no conclusions about his wife. Bavaria, see. Down there, they find a Nazi dead in suspicious circumstances, they give him a decent funeral and hush it up. Save they wear leather trousers, and they squeak. Nazis don't exist, especially dead ones.

'You tell them you know where there's a live Nazi, they give you a decent funeral and hush you up, too. There's a lot of hush in Bavaria, Paddy. I used to sit out there and listen to snow fall on a still night. Snow's the loudest noise Bavarians ever make about anything political. The place is run by neo-Nazis, but everyone belongs to the party, so there's no need to quarrel. Lots of oompa oompa in the beerhalls, but total silence otherwise. They've got consciences there that jump a mile if they hear pine needles crackle in the fog.'

239

'Fine. So what do I put when I get myself home –'

'If you get yourself home –'

'And file my report?'

'Tell them the truth, Paddy. Say you're too young to understand. Or tell them a better truth. Tell them I'm dead.'

'So Weiss is safe?'

'Certainly not. I'm not the be-all and end-all. Men like Weiss are always at risk. It's just that I have a new hate and a new purpose. The hate is for what my beloved Balkans are doing to themselves. The purpose is to put it right.'

'Why aren't you and Popovic on the same side over this?'

'He has other ideas about the way it should be done.'

'Certainly not by listening to this nonsense, my dear.' Popovic was already in the room with them. 'Such stuff. You speak such stuff.'

14

Popovic's jack-in-the-box entrance was easy to explain. Cell doors open more quietly than they close. He wore soft shoes. The loud ones approached.

The four security police, or some of them, one of them, grabbed Matson from behind. He was held less vigorously this time. They had made their point earlier. He scarcely felt the cuff being removed. He waited patiently while it was correctly reapplied.

Keys came out of the cell door like teeth being drawn. Popovic had handled them gently. Someone was reasserting his authority.

They had already shackled Lippiat. His wrists were linked in front of him. The police had plans for him.

One of the suits hopped on to another one's neck and shoulders, so that they balanced together like a pair of tumblers in a circus. The mounted one threaded a piece of cord through the grill in the ceiling. This he let hang double-ended. The other two lifted Lippiat's arms above his head. The cord was knotted under the chain of his handcuffs, taking the weight of his uplifted arms, but not his body.

They spoke softly to Lolly as they did this. They

murmured to one another. The top man hopped down. They stopped being busy and went back to looking important.

'We don't suspend him,' Propovic said. 'We don't even stretch his arms. They're humanely supported.'

When interrogators want fast answers, or simply decide to incapacitate you, they lift your arms behind your back, and hang your body-weight from them in that position.

'It's the circulatory system that does it for us.'

Torture was not a good topic with Matson.

'Never inflict pain, my dear. It's barbaric and unnecessary. Let pain inflict itself. The body is its own best rack.'

Gerald Lippiat settled his legs, inching his feet wider apart. He yawned affably.

'Thanks, Lolly.' Matson touched a foot with his outstretched shoe.

Lolly pretended to go to sleep.

15

Interrogators are secretive people. Torturers even more so. They don't do the rough stuff in public, or before a witness – unless they want to soften up the witness as well. Matson waited for trouble.

To his surprise, he found himself unhandcuffed and outside in the street, he supposed in that order, much as Popovic had promised him.

As they walked towards Popovic's car, he said, 'I do wish you wouldn't lay these demonstrations on for my benefit.'

Popovic didn't smile. 'It wasn't a demonstration,' he hissed, urgent for accuracy in any language. 'Demonstration implies a degree of the actual. It was a charade. And it was for my benefit.'

Matson was now awake enough to notice the splendour of the Colonel's staff car. It was an executive Ford, the one with leather upholstery. Both the marque and the logo had been removed to deflect totalitarian envy.

Popovic waved the driver into the back seat. 'Stick to the truth,' he warned. 'She speaks English almost as well as I do.'

Matson recognised her as the woman who had driven him

to and from last night's rendezvous with Dixon, but in a much smaller car. She was an attractive thing, especially in uniform. He had been in no mood to notice her yesterday evening.

As Popovic drove towards the hotel, he said, 'They haven't roughed Lippiat up. They don't dare. If he spoke one word of truth in there, that was it. I do dare, as it happens. But he was also quite correct when he said I lack – what was it? – "the clout". That was why they chose me, my dear. I mean, I'm powerful enough, but I understand there are those I must not go up against.'

'I find that odd. In Nazi Germany, for example, no one was exempt. Nor in Russia, even now.'

'That's because torture comes from the top in some places. Here the more equal ones are exempt, unless they fall from grace.'

'Lolly's in *that* category?'

'Perhaps, for historic reasons. Perhaps. He is also well acquainted with Balkan politics. All he needed to do last night to make that lot back off was hint at whose names he might drop if they started twisting his kneecaps.' He put his hand on the car horn and left it there, screeching dolorously and illegally in a public place until a policeman moved towards them, notebook in hand.

The policeman performed a little pantomime. He slowed his stride, then came on uncertainly, head on one side. Was it? ... Yes, it was Colonel Popovic. He stopped, came on once more, his head on the other side, eyes gazing archly, to demand, no: ask, ascertain, what it was the colonel required.

Popovic required to break the law. The policeman let him get on with it.

'I am one of the more equal, my dear. Illustriously more equal when it suits them. Not more equal enough. And *you*, Patrick, you have wasted our time this morning. You did not push Lippiat hard enough. The police got nothing, but that is because they didn't try. To you he spoke lies and then fairy stories. He twisted you round his little finger.'

'I got exactly what I wanted from him.'

Popovic gazed at him oddly, the way you look at a drunk or an imbecile. Then the traffic moved forward, and he concentrated on driving. 'Clearly we don't want the same things, my dear.'

16

Back at the hotel, they had breakfast.

'Breakfast,' said Popo, 'will be bad. But there will be moderate sausage, tolerable bread and clean tea.'

Clean tea sounded excellent. Matson drank it and got ready to refuse any request he couldn't lie his way out of later.

Popovic surprised him. 'In return for what I have done for you, I need one thing. I need what I asked last night. I want you to stay with this man Weiss, and tell me what comes of it.'

Popovic held up his hand. 'You say you are on leave. It does not matter how strictly this is true. I have shown you, and therefore London, exactly how things stand in their direction. I have closed the file on their Mr Lippiat. And on Mr Lippiat's Mr Lippiat. What happens to this lout Weiss belongs to the world quite as much as it belongs to Yugoslavia. But it belongs to Yugoslavia first. Tell London what you like, when you can. But tell me also. Is that too much to ask?'

Matson didn't think so. Not in these vexed circumstances.

'To make up for my ongoing reluctance to provide you with a firearm, and you to accept one, I daresay, I'll find you a Yugo. That's another kind of weapon altogether. Don't curl your lip. The engine will be good. The brakes will be good. It will stick to the road like spearmint and burn no petrol.' He smiled and added, 'The rest is a heap of tin can. Here you will witness the advantages that proceed from technological backwardness. Yugoslavia makes stalwart cans.' He paused long enough to place a slice of the nation's moderate sausage on a crust of its tolerable bread before adding, 'Besides, you must ask yourself how much good a more expensive car will do you if someone shoots its tyre out again.'

243

'So the Range Rover *was* blown off the road?'

'About seven millimetres of vindictiveness in your front left Firestone, my dear. Which is point three hundred, isn't it. Or shall I say point three oh three?'

SEVENTEEN

1

The Yugo was fast. It didn't so much hold the road as caress it. Like love it was softest on the curves, and like love it threatened to come unstuck.

'Jesus,' Constanz sighed. The engine made a noise like stones in a pressure cooker, so words were hard to hear. 'This is beautiful. Truly beautiful.'

Matson agreed. Weiss wasn't driving. There were no bullets, no arrogant vibrations. He didn't have to peep at the road from behind the smug pinkness of the Obergruppen-führer's ears.

When he came this way before, it was summer. He remembered maize and black corn with sunflowers; flocks of geese so fat they looked like marauding fruit. Two drinks, and two was enough in those days, and goose fields became waddling melons. He saw lots of those. He dreamt of ripe melons walking towards him with schoolgirls in their beaks.

Today it was early spring. The corn plains were wedge-wood blue, so black was the soil, so thin the green.

Later, the tarmac ribboned away between slopes of white dirt, and the green grew jazzy with calcium, sick as dishonest sex. It plunged among wooded hills, then it climbed. His liver held up well in the sunlight, but the stuttering shadows of the pine trees were bad for his lack of sleep.

Beyond was no better. Glistening ridges of karst or even marble, then mountains of fissured whiteness, the rockfaces groined so deep they looked like pyramids of dice.

'Crna Gora,' she called. 'Montenegro.'

You don't come to it at once. You climb. That's what you do.

The Yugo liked climbing. It was noisy but nippy. Matson could do with a lot less noise and a little less nip. Circumstances made him keep his foot down.

2

The lorry was one of those big-snouted tractor-trailers. He'd had it in his mirror for an hour at least. He saw first one side of it then the other as it articulated its way round the bends behind him.

Its klaxon let out one of those banshee wails that make you wonder whether you've got a two-hundred-piece orchestra tuning up in the back of the car, or something unusual has happened to your scalp, like a church falling on it with a steeple full of bells. 'Stay back,' he said to it. It was travelling fast, so he needed to be faster. 'I don't want the sod getting past before we reach the big gradients,' he explained.

'You fucking poet,' Constanz answered. She wafted a make-believe kiss at him, like a goldfish eating bubbles for breakfast.

The lorry kept closing on them. The Yugo threw itself forward.

The road straightened out along a two-mile cut. Karst rising sheer on the right, forest tops like a dream of bracken a long way down to the left.

The truck gave another blast on the siren and began to overtake.

There was an opening ahead in the cliff. They were clearly about to run out over some kind of ravine, where the side winds would be fierce and uncertain. He slowed and hugged the cliff, and let the truck draw level. Then they were on the viaduct, with vehicle shock from the left, the mountain wind strong from the right, strong but not gusting. The Yugo flew ahead like a bird.

'There's a belvedere!' Constanz shouted. 'This place is sensational. Why don't we stop and –'

He didn't see the belvedere. He saw the iron uprights of the viaduct's fence strobing beside Constanz's face, the

246

stressed metal of the guard rail snaking past so quickly that the minuscule blemishes in its construction made it pulse and blur. Beyond it there was rocky space and a huddle of dark water a long way below. Constanz's face grew large with fear, wide-eyed and urgent as she gazed at what was happening beside him.

The truck wasn't past him. He saw orange hubs, tyre walls grey with speed. The rear wheel of its tractor drew level with his door, and that was when Constanz screamed. He stole another look. The wheel was moving in on them.

He wasn't in control of the Yugo any more. It had lateral energy, manic powers. Remarkable car. It became a tank, a biscuit box and aeroplane more or less simultaneously, as it burst, collapsed and flew its way into the ravine. Constanz's side was the tank. It kicked a big hole in the guard rail, or perhaps merely bent it outwards and downwards, while his own door was buckling in on him in a terribly namby-pamby manner but doing spiteful things to his knee.

Before it fell apart it was airborne, on Constanz's side first, hence her consternation – airborne and rotating into a slow wingover.

Then it was a car again, spinning as it fell.

The guard rail had done a first class job. It hadn't crushed them underneath the truck or fractured and impaled them. It had simply become a rupture in a strip of bubblegum that punctured to let everything through.

What an inadequate thought to die on.

'Shit!' somebody said. Certainly not him.

3

'The door's locked!'

Death was pitch dark, wet round the ankles, and only moderately painful. Then it was deepening green tinged with black.

'I can't get it open.'

Noisy woman. He reached for the courtesy light, and there she was with water up to her waist and a dab of blood on her chin.

The Yugo was submerged and sinking, going down engine-heavy but approximately the right way up. She had her seat belt on. His was unfastened. His foot was jammed. The light was a miracle which was abruptly withdrawn. She continued to jerk at the door.

The water crept in slowly. It pushed up from under the pedals. It seeped round the window seals and dripped from under the fascia. Cars should be built better than that. It had only fallen a few hundred feet into mountain water. You can buy the stuff in bottles.

Now it was settling into some dank Sargasso of the soul.

'Tuscarora,' he corrected. His own soul was like that. It was his very own.

4

While Matson was in the Thugs he attended a course at the underwater tower at Portland. Everyone in Special Forces did.

The course was devised for submariners. The snoggers' car in the reservoir was only an instructor's joke. The snogger wouldn't know how to get out. And if he did he couldn't get his girlfriend out. And if he could they'd never make it to the surface. And if they did they'd be crippled with the bends for however long it took them to die from massive embolism of the brain. Ha! Ha! Ha!

Matson had matured since then. He had grown up to become an instructor's joke.

Submariners have escape suits. They have the traditional cylinder and mask, supplanted by the ultra-modern simple-to-operate two-piece hood and apron. 'If you can't find one of those, you can always come up with your head in a bucket.' But to be successful with a bucket you need a flo-tation jacket. There are any number of those in a submarine, and plenty of buckets lying around for anyone, like Matson, without an escape suit.

The Yugo might be built like a bucket. It might even have been built from buckets. There were no spare buckets lying around.

You can die or you can get it right. If you get it right you'll probably die anyway. If you're going to die it's still a point of honour to get it right.

He felt for Constanz, and kissed what there was of her above water. He kissed her neck. 'Can you hear me?'

'Sure as fuck there's nothing better I can listen to.'

'We've got to go out by your door. Mine's distorted.'

'I've already told you it's –'

'Wait. We've got several atmospheres of water on top of us. In a minute the water and the air inside'll balance out. You'll see.'

If the Yugo doesn't crumple like a tin can first, crumple and crush us, or wrap us in a half-ton straitjacket.

He didn't say that. He said, 'You've got to breathe air. Keep breathing this air. You've got to have fat lungs if you're going to float.'

'Fat lungs?'

'It's a technical –' He didn't have time to explain how a lady under so much water should think to behave next, what to do with her air, how to breathe it out slowly, because at that point the pressure equalized and the silly cow got her door open, which was what she had been struggling to do for the last ninety seconds, and in a single slamming instant their air became water, their air rushed into water, all breath had gone, there was no air to breathe.

5

'Pressurized air,' he said to her through buttoned lips. 'Pressurized air,' he said in his head. 'Use it. Rise gradually. Go up with me. Matson knows how slowly you must rise. Stay right beside me, and breathe out as you go.' All without a word leaving his head.

His boot had come off or the pedal had snapped or he was short of his left foot. At whatever cost to his future, with one bound Matson was free. He pushed her through the door.

She didn't wait for him. The water was dark and had a restless muscle. He grabbed at her legs, but only caught her skirt and a kick in the guts. Breathe out, he said. He breathed

249

out, right enough. He breathed out everything he had. At this pressure, you always have more. That's the beauty of it.

How deep were they? How deep and how deeper than deep?

Breathe out too much and you achieve negative buoyancy.

Don't breathe out at all and you blow your brains, your joints, your lungs. You mustn't take that pressure up with you; but you need pressure to take you up.

At this depth, without escape kit, you can't win. And it must be deep. Things were so dark.

Constanz had gone straight up. Which was one way to die.

Matson wasn't like that. Matson was good. Matson rose as indolently as a tank-fish in the window of a Chinese take-away. He could see even less than the fish. The water was nightmare black. Perhaps he had concussion, brain-damage from the fall. He could not even see the bubbles of his own explosive breath.

You feel them. You feel them as hard and alien as cauliflower-sized globules of quicksilver, as stupid and unhelpful as worry beads. You feel them with your nostrils, your chest, your forehead, your chin.

They do not all of them gout through your nose or lay themselves like ostrich eggs already hatching tails from the mummy-sucking orifice of your stretched-open mouth. Some of them seep through your skin. This isn't the bends, you pray, not yet sweet heaven the nitrogen boiling off from your joints. They disturb you, these little ones. They come from unlikely places like the bush beneath your arms, but your body hasn't punctured: this is just your old life looking for its gills.

Contrary to expectation they do not rise very fast. They drift up like children's balloons that have grown warm by the fire. Their way is always higher, but they do not seek to go there with any conviction. They know about cross currents. They lend themselves to eels.

You follow them with your nose. If you feel them on your chest you are rising too fast. If you feel them sliding past whatever you've left of feeling lower down then you're on the way to dying.

Avoid General Death. Stay behind your bubbles. Keep

your breath well in front of you, advises Obergruppenführer Death.

How far had the Yugo sunk? How fast does iron drown itself in water? Perhaps he wasn't rising but sinking, the nails in his remaining boot grown strangely magnetic, its laces already mating with the deep-water worms.

Constanz had cheated, gone rushing up. Black mark, Constanz. Even at Camberwell the bloody girls were first, halfway down the page before he'd read the question. Hands up in the air to tell tales to teacher before he'd got his finger an inch above their knee.

Her boot in his gut had made him spill his air. He needed that air at three four five atmospheres' pressure to keep his chest buoyant. What had his instructor said?

Somewhere between twelve and twenty feet beneath the surface, the submerged human body develops negative buoyancy. It can spring-heel up from the bottom of the deep end. It can power up, perhaps, if it's got strength in its muscles, and oxygen. But plunge more than twenty feet, and only God can help you.

Unless you've gone down in a pressurized bubble, which he had, and retained enough of it to sustain you while you return, which he absolutely hadn't.

He struggled for half a minute. Then for half a lifetime more.

Why was it so deep? Had he fallen down a well? Was he trying to rise sideways? Did his brain become so waterlogged it lost its sense of direction? This was a mountain river, either that or a mirage born of drowning his burst-open skull in the outfall of his blood. Such rivers rush downhill, tumble over stones, are whitewater shallows or cascades of froth. They are never remotely deep, never anywhere this deep.

There must be a damn great dam. Perhaps there was a series of dams. The whole ravine was dammed. This water was laid in deep-rooted steps.

Matson began to laugh. The whole thing was another *stausee* like the ones in Austria. He heard Willi's shrill and Albin's dusty chuckle. He was drowning in a *stausee*. A German blond couldn't do it to him, not even with his roller skates, but a Serbian lorry could. A Serbian lorry had! The

251

water was so damned deep, because the water was dammed. What a lovely joke. He laughed and laughed. And laughed. You need air to laugh.

Yes, laughter needs air. He opened his water-blurred eyes, and there was fresh air. He saw it.

6

The air wasn't empty. It had a bridge in it, a single span viaduct. The viaduct was long. It stretched all the way across his bit of heaven, its arch directly overhead. There was blueness above it, a stone-white sunshine on its belly.

Down here, and for most of the way up, things were dark. Rocks were dark. Bird-song was dark. He heard beaks chatter, sensed wings, saw nothing.

He had crashed so far he should have killed himself. Hitting water from that height above was like a dive on to concrete.

His murder had been carefully planned: the right time, the perfect place, the exact circumstance. The lorry driver might even report side-swiping the guard rail. A gust of wind, perhaps. An unfortunate puncture. Mercifully no other vehicle was involved. The Yugo was drowned in deepest ink, lost inside the blackness at the bottom of the world.

Dear little car. It must have hit the water nose-first and gone plunging under, decelerating in feet or even fathoms without pulverizing instantly.

Thank God for the deepness he floated on. A normal mountain river would have been the death of him, with its shallows, its rockslips, its boulders.

This one was dammed. He couldn't see the dam; he was too close to the margin, but there must be a dam. He'd reached a decision about that.

The shout came about now. Or perhaps it was earlier, like a telephone ringing while he slept. He couldn't be certain.

What he noticed was the head, stuck beyond the bridge. A head like an ant dot. Then an arm for antenna.

Matson lay crumpled on a water as soulless as Popovic's composition floor, and wondered what he looked like. He

252

wasn't even wet. He felt ripples graze the bruising of his skin like sand against sunburn, and he burst into thought. It was the head that did it.

He thought: the lorry driver's up there. It's him peering over. He'll see I'm not dead. He'll find a way down to finish the job. I'll be easy meat for a rock or even a lump of drift-wood, busted like this. He's on his way now.

It wasn't beaks and feathers he heard. It was his cold body chattering.

Not him, but a somebody else.

He'd forgotten a somebody else, that there might be some other person. Did that mean he was busted up bad, or grown complacent through shock?

7

There wasn't a bank, not as such. There rarely is in a flood pool. There was a place where an older trackway sloped down along the cliff, then broke among trees and drowned in the water.

Constanz clung there and dribbled. She dribbled a rich green liquid that might be pond weed, might be bile.

His muscles were too numb to lift him to her. He stopped himself thinking about muscles and crawled from the water with whatever was left.

Constanz wasn't unconscious. She was drowsy drunk. This was much as normal, but where was her angry wit? Or even its absence? She wouldn't talk.

'Constanz!'

She breathed from a soggy head.

'Constanz, old darling, please say "fuck".'

She was presenting the first signs, or worse, of embolism of the brain.

The rich green liquid was neither here nor there. Matson was clear it referred – he liked that word – referred to some lesser medical emergency, like rupture of the spleen or being scared shitless.

It might be alcohol-induced. It might be mint julep.

If she had an embolism, she needed to be hospitalized. She

253

would be brain-damaged, brain-dead, dead, according to factors he couldn't work out.

The hospital needed to be here, and she already in it. Anything else was hopelessly too late.

Diving barges, and submarine rescue vessels, have pressure chambers. At the first sign of grogginess, in the victim goes. Hospitals don't have them as part of their normal furnishing. The hospital behind him certainly didn't. They weren't even building it yet.

Suppose she didn't have an embolism. Suppose she was stunned, short of oxygen and shocked. What about the bends?

Constanz had surfaced from what sort of depth? At least eighty feet. At least. It felt like eight hundred. She had bobbed straight up with hyperinflated lungs from four atmospheres of pressure into skullbursting normal and nil.

The nitrogen would be bubbling through her lovely blood, boiling away to siphon into her knees, her hips, her elbows, her neck, blowing her limb-joints one by one, fusing her neurones, stripping the sheath from the nerve-bundles in her spine, assaulting and destroying her central nervous system. Even without an embolism the same pressurized gas would be steaming inside her brain like gravy in a bag pudding.

Constanz in her puke and her tights and her pants and somehow not much else was likely to die or become crippled, here on a piece of shingle at the bottom of this ravine.

'Matson –' she started to say. She got as far as 'Ma –' like a lamb calling for its mother.

He caught her under his arm, his elbow in her stomach, his hand flat on her naked ribs, and dragged her to the water's lip. He found a large, loose rock and hooked himself to it with his other arm. 'Breathe,' he croaked. 'Constanz, take a good lung full of air.'

'You prick,' she said.

The toppling of the rock took them in fast. It also removed skin from Matson's side and thigh and outside leg as it dragged them under a hundred times more abruptly than the Yugo could ever have done.

He clung to the rock and to Constanz. They tumbled together like twins against the placenta, until their piece of

254

mountain broke from his grasp and from the clench of his knees and took tiny bits of him with it to the bottom of nowhere. Leaving them forty foot under.

What do you do when a person has the bends? You put them in a pressure chamber.

He and Constanz were alone in the dark waters at a pressure of two extra atmospheres.

Constanz couldn't swim. Constanz was properly unconscious.

If he could rise up slowly with Constanz drowning sweetly in his arms –

He couldn't rise. Not this time he couldn't.

Matson had been taught the truth. Men have it from their ancestor who stole it in the garden. They have it but they remember it only a bit at a time. Wasn't that what his grandmother said the Reverend Father had said to her?

Matson had risen up from the Yugo, and Constanz had swirled up like a rocket, because they were buoyant with water-packed air. They'd breathed air at extra atmospheres of pressure. Their lungs were inflated, too inflated in the case of the girl who'd refused to breathe out.

This time they'd gone down with the stone, and the stone had no air in it. Their lungs were only packed with the outside air, and the water was squeezing them flat, deflating them as certainly as if they were locked in a python's coils.

He remembered it now: somewhere between twelve and twenty feet deep a suddenly immersed body achieves negative buoyancy. There is nothing to bring it back, so it continues to sink till it finds its level – say about here.

Then the lungs become flooded and it sinks a bit more.

Meanwhile the pressure in the chest is intolerable. Carbon dioxide aching to get out?

No: the black wet serpent of the depths crushing it in.

Sink away, Matson. Sink while you think.

Constanz was cold as rubber in his arms, but nothing as useful as an inflated tyre. His poor drunk, dying two-night-not-quite-stand stand, he was drowning himself trying to save ...

All this time kicking with his legs, frogging up and down, his blacked-out brain talking close-lipped into her ear to tell

255

her flopping body to kick her knitted tights around, shake half a leg.

A high diver rises by swimming. Matson swam, he climbed no-handed up the rope of his bubbles, he swarmed the endless ladder of the dark, which like a bad dream collapsed on him slowly.

The first inner-tube was pink. It rose past him inflating as it went. It was followed by the second and the third and –

The Yugo was down there shedding its tyres. The pressure compressed them, that way they came off the rims, then their tubes rose ripening through his gut and banged against his mind. They kept on passing through as fat and unanxious as goldfish. Good old Yugo. Who would have thought it had so many wheels, so many tyres, so much blood?

Constanz caught at one, Matson caught one. That slowed it down a bit. The one Matson caught was entirely without substance, a bubble at best. A bauble certainly. That is how you drown.

8

'I'm very sorry to see you here.'

'You dishonourable bastard. Was it you tried to kill me? Someone from your lot certainly did.'

'No need, dear lad. You're killing yourself.' Pomeroy glanced at his watch. 'In half a minute's time you'll have succeeded.' He poured himself a second-class brandy, disguising it as coffee inside a paper cup. 'Well, here you go, old chum. I wish I had something better to offer you.'

'Dishonourable bastard.'

'There's no such thing as dishonour, not in my business.' Pomeroy sipped noisily. 'Honour is as jealously guarded as – what shall I say – your sister's virtue? No, let us choose a simile of more durable value. The label on a bottle of champagne. The whole thrust of diplomacy is to get your eager lads – Lawrence of Arabia would be a good example of those: he's a bit non-vintage, but he'll do – is to get your eager lads to make promises on your behalf and overlook the certainty that some other lad will break them.' He lit his paper cup. It burned brighter than any cigar. 'Rising in the Service – something you always accuse *me* of – is a very different art. It's a bit like yeast. It escapes definition, so let me define it for you. It's the art of being neither the man who makes the promise nor the man who breaks it. They're the little twerps who go under. Look at your Lawrence. Look at Gandhi.'

'Gandhi wasn't a diplomat.'

'My point exactly. He went under.'

Matson went under. In very deep water.

9

He didn't swallow fishscales. He swallowed thirst.

He was choking in the waterworld of salmon, the excrement of fish, so there was no way he could swallow. He brought up his breakfast in a good deep gust.

No more air, but his chest felt better.

Drowning doesn't taste of weed. It tastes of women. He tasted the women his life hadn't tasted. He wasted several years counting countless women. They seemed much the same. Lotte, call me Silly, his salty piccalilli. Counting them, courting them, shuffling them off.

His chest ached again.

He encountered Constanz's tights. Sometime, while drowning, she had kicked free of her tights. Here they were, empty of her legs and quite devoid of conscience. They hung on a branch of water, and kicked their empty heels at him. Weiss had seized the woman and was hanging her by the neck.

His chest, or perhaps his heart.

They continued dancing upward. The gallows sprung her upwards. There were street-lamps overhead. In his skull, overhead. Weiss hanged his enemies from street-lamps. His eye followed her upwards and burst.

Matson had his head inside the light. He broke the pane of water and dragged his body through.

Constanz lay naked in the sunshine of heaven.

No: she sprawled brazen in the hot flames of hell. A

257

black-headed grizzly-haired South Slavonic imp knelt between her legs and handled the capacities of meat on her chest.

'Stop meddling with that woman. She's dead.'

'I do what I damn well like. I'm the damn well doctor. I'm giving her the kiss of life.'

'Life has already kissed her.'

Matson lay against the shoreline. He retched. He was back where he started, on the lip of broken track. Constanz still wore her tights. He must have made it to safety on the tail of an illusion.

The doctor, if doctor he was, knelt down beside her, not between the witless sprawl of her legs. Someone had covered her with a folded cloth. it was old and worn, scabbed with oil, blanched by battery acid, but it looked as if it had started life as a military blanket. The man spoke in Serbo-Croat, or in Serbian pure and simple.

Matson was no good at either. He waited till he was standing upright before he said, 'Didn't you speak to me in English?'

'Yes, I can do English. Why can't you do Serb? Better yet, why can't you do common sense? This woman here tells me what you do. Which is neither English nor Serbian. Is heroic but a fool.'

'Asshole,' she managed. Her voice sounded sweeter than love.

'Never swear by saints or pieces of human body,' the doctor cautioned. 'Each piece of the body is as useful as one another, and that organ more than some.'

'I breathed out while I surfaced, you witless shitless fool. I came up from hell and deeper, and I swore at him all the way up. Why didn't you follow me? Too much lead in your pencil?'

From her, that was a compliment.

'Shitless is another matter,' the doctor said. 'Especially in a hot climate.'

10

The doctor's presence was interesting. So was the army-surplus blanket, if such it was.

Matson heard boots on the track overhead, and looked for a full chorus of Popovic's ladies to follow. His imagination was overheating, but not by much.

Two uniformed legs beneath two stacks of folded blankets bobbing precariously downhill. These blankets were also slim, but folded narrow and high, as for kit inspection; so there weren't many of them. Smoke oozed from their folds, and they came with a strong smell of tobacco. They flopped themselves on to the water's edge, to fatten with mud and dust.

This left Matson two policemen, or soldiers, or something in between. A lad of eighteen or nineteen with a nicotined moustache. Beside him, a full-grown man of about twenty-two who had become alarmed by the public health warnings and shaved off his bristles but not yet his fingers. These were as unsavoury as last year's bananas, and about the same colour. They handed Constanz blankets, picked up one at a time. They passed them over wistfully, unhappy to see the rest of her nakedness disappear like this.

When the senior youngster had got his last year's bananas free of further obligation to duty, he pulled a cigarette from the top right-hand pocket of his tunic and lit it from the one which was just about to burn its way into his mouth. He was wise not to wear a moustache.

He smiled apologetically and tugged his opened pocket towards Constanz, Matson, the doctor and his friend with the facial hair to show it was empty. Unfortunately his free hand gave an involuntary tap of the bananas to his other top pocket. It bulged like an Amazon's breast. He had enough in there to kipper his head for another hour or two.

He had an afterthought. He removed one of Constanz's blankets and handed it to Matson. He chose the blanket carefully. It wasn't the most convenient one.

Then he backed off hurriedly. Matson wondered which part of the Slavonic body Constanz had blistered him with. He didn't go pink; only the other lad did that. He went

259

white. Even the doctor found it hard to smile.

Constanz readjusted her poncho. Matson tried to help her up the track.

Once they walked alone, she comforted him. 'Jesus, Matson, I'll not bed with you again. And I'll certainly not bed you. I'll dream that you're drowning me, then wake to being fucked by a merman.'

'Mermen can't –'

'You asked for that one. I won't even dot its eyes.'

Best to keep quiet. They walked bare-footed, on water-softened skin. The soil was all stones.

EIGHTEEN

1

Popovic took hours. They had risen at dawn and drowned at noon. Now they had to wait. Matson was glad it wasn't for St Peter.

They waited in the back of the doctor's truck. It was about the size and shape of a World War II military fifteen hundredweight. It was parked on the viaduct by the shattered guardrail, masking the mess. There were no skidmarks, nothing. There hadn't been time to touch a brake.

It must have been the doctor's head Matson had seen, looking over. His or that of one of the two uniformed lads who accompanied him. The three stood there now, smoking. Smoking was what the younger two did best. The doctor only smoked a cheroot of the finest Macedonian tobacco every quarter of an hour or so. His companions darted through five-puff squibs by the packet, then spat what was left of each cigarette into the drinking water below the bridge. Matson was glad not to be standing with them, watching things forever fall down.

Then Popovic arrived. Not in a command vehicle or staff car, but in the other truck's twin. If the Yugoslav special forces were limited to fifteen hundredweight lookalikes, then the exercise had the appearance of being run by an army of ghosts.

Popovic examined the broken guardrail. He liked it. He was as gleeful as a surgeon faced with a particularly intriguing wound.

'Come to see how dead we are?'

'I told you to take a little drink while your guts were still waterproof.'

261

'A shade too prophetic, don't you think?'

Popovic turned away to ask for something in the back of his truck. He was handed a silver-cased quarter-litre flask. Matson saw varnished fingernails. He carried it first to Constanz, then came back to Matson. 'Don't be silly, my dear. If I'd wanted you immobilized, I'd have kept you in clink with your chum.'

'What about doing someone a favour?'

'Someone in London, perhaps?' Popovic stroked his upper lip between finger and thumb, waiting for wisdom to grow and communicate. 'If I'd wanted to kill you, or someone else had wanted me to kill you, I wouldn't have killed you like that. I don't believe you even half think it of me, or you'd be cutting up rough. I'd have got someone reliable to stick a knife in your rhubarb. Someone like the doctor here.'

'The doctor is a doctor.'

'Yes, and reliable. He's a Serb and sixty-five.'

'What the hell is that supposed to mean?'

'It means he learned his best tricks before he took the Hippocratic oath. He was twenty when the war finished.'

Popovic turned away with the gesture of apology Matson had come to know well. It meant he wasn't through with the discussion, but other things must come first. Politesse, for example.

He had some of his ladies with him, the ones Matson was acquainted with.

Matson's driver of last evening gazed from the strangely dressed Constanz to the water-soiled Matson. Her look spoke volumes, but hardly of might-have-been.

The other two didn't wave their sub-machine-guns this time. They'd left them in the truck or behind their ears. One of them had two sets of fatigues, socks, mountain boots and some lumberjack shirts for Matson. The other had a whole lot of clothes for Constanz. They weren't quite her style. They were a mite too garish for that. But the boots were of good leather, and the blouse she chose to put on was full in the sleeve, after her fashion. None of them looked as if they came off an ordinary peg, not in a ready-to-wear or *samoposluga*, anyway. An interesting fact, but it suggested no more than Matson already suspected.

262

Time to ask for their blankets back. The two lads grinned closer. Constanz was pulling her pants on. It was better than spitting on water.

Popovic shooed them away, then returned to his main theme. 'A lorry accident. It's an English death, my dear. Or a French death. An Irishman would take no pleasure in it. Nor would a Serb.

'To have a lorry brush you off a bridge into deep water. What imagination! It is either blind fate or quintessentially British. It gives a fellow a sporting chance, which always means an unsporting chance and often no chance at all. Like the notion of divine intervention, if God thought the wrong man was standing on the gallows.'

'Or the wrong gal,' Constanz said.

'My money's on your lot, my dear.'

Matson said nothing. He had regained Popovic's flask. Constanz, after maximum delay, was at last wearing a skirt.

Popovic liked women in skirts. He liked women. His eyes said this before he added, 'Someone wanted gravity and deep water to kill you. Kill *you*, Patrick. Not the American lady. Or to see if God and the water nymphs would spare you. Someone who believes in neither. In all of Europe, only the English fall into such a prosaic category.'

'Or the communists.'

'The Southern Slavs believe in the spirit world, take my word for it. As for God in His heaven ... if you want to cast doubts on the orthodoxy of the Serbian Orthodox, we'll be eating sabres for breakfast, you and I.'

'I'll keep to kippers, if I may. The driver of that container lorry was presumably a Southern Slav?'

'And he prayed for you on the way down, believe it. His prayers saved you. They won't save him. We shall have him soon, never fear. And shake what we can from his mouth.'

'If the loop knows anything,' Constanz said.

'He'll know a man who knows a man. I shall know too. I don't take this matter lightly, believe me, Patrick. I'm embarrassed. I am embarrassed and ashamed. I had my three best fellows behind you by not more than a kilometre.'

'An ancient billy-goat and a brace of lambs.'

'Dogs, I assure you. One of them a wolfhound. When the doctor saw the truck hurry you up, even then there was no more than a suspicion. Trucks have a low speed limit, true. But there are few police out on these mountain roads, so this is where a driver makes his time. It didn't seem over-sinister.'

Age and youth. It was parochial to be prejudiced against either, but Matson belonged to a service that was dismissive of both. He hadn't asked for an escort, and he didn't like the one he'd got.

Popovic seemed to read his mind. 'The doctor may be an old man. But in these mountains he is *the* old man.'

'Like Ivan Crnojevic?'

Popovic was delighted Matson had remembered that bit of folk history. His hugging was getting to be a painful habit. Matson had picked up bruises by the day on this trip.

He didn't get to count them.

3

What he heard was Popovic whisper in his ear, 'Talking of geriatrics, my dear – *and* of the spirit world. Your old man has been raising spectres, damn him. Your old man and my old man.' He gulped against Matson's brains before letting him go.

'Weiss?'

'The venerable Obershitbag. He didn't get up here till late last night. Very late. As you may imagine. It was twelve o'clock when they reached the lake. Wagnerian midnight almost to the teutonic second. There was, but naturally, a demonstration waiting for him. Nothing vigorous, you understand.'

Matson understood.

'Two or three dozen of the locals with pole-lanterns – fishermen and boat people – under police orders to be well-behaved, but determined to shuffle their feet and spit. Picture the scene? Weiss, the child, the woman –'

Matson could picture it.

'Surrounded by a gang of louts and lads hoping things

would get out of hand so they could dump him under the lake. A couple of Montenegrin village policemen who would gladly mind their coats for them, and let them get on with it.

'So what does the old pig do?

'He jumps out of that car and walks up and down the whole line of them as if he's inspecting a guard of honour. He says to them how good it is to be home among friends and family, asks them to remember him to their mothers, then tells them they're surly and undisciplined and that he expects a better reception from his sons and grandsons next time around. He detains the nearest and youngest to boat him and his belongings over to Otok, has the police mind the Mercedes and dismisses the rest of them.'

Matson was reminded of Weiss dealing with the pig farmers. This insult to a community's womenfolk was another matter.

'He speaks the language, you see, my dear. He speaks it fluently. No doubt they're cursing themselves now, but they weren't expecting to understand him; so they fell under the magic. Luck of the devil.'

4

Popovic went to the doctor's truck and used the radio. He spoke a few words of sing-song radio-speak – presumably the call-sign – then listened. First he listened with the headset held against one ear, the rest of it flapping in the wind. The he looped the thing over his head, and shut himself away to listen properly.

A helicopter appeared above the lip of the ravine, sidled out until it was midway over the gap, then let down slowly until it was only a few feet overhead.

Weather howled down from the mountain, gusting it twenty yards to one side and dropping it below their eyeline – this under a clear blue sky. The helicopter picked itself up and sidled back to them – back to Popovic, anyway, like a dog sniffing close to its master.

Its pilot didn't like the ravine. He rotated, lifted, put himself nose down for maximum power, then went away fast beyond the lip of the dam. In a second, the aircraft lost itself inside an abnormal silence. Even while it stooped overhead, the wind had vacuumed off the racket of its rotors, and siphoned it away.

Popovic was a sleek man, glossy of cheek. Now he was bone-faced. He spoke a few sentences, hissingly, at the doctor, like a wife rebuking her husband. Then he came snarling back to Matson. 'This must be the closed season for old men. The season and the weather. Our other old man has spirited himself out of prison.'

'Lippiat?'

'Hesse is dead, my dear. So is the Birdman of Alcatraz. Yes, Lippiat. Who else but Mr Slippy Lippiat?'

Matson stepped away from him. He went to the broken guardrail for the first time. 'From that detention centre and from your Security Police?'

'Someone opened doors, you may rest on it.'

Matson looked down at the water. He looked into it. He couldn't see the Yugo. Nobody could. Nobody would. It was gone into the silence. He heard the breeze come up the ravine. He saw a wind-sock stiffen on its post at the end of the viaduct. There had been no traffic on the road, not since he and Constanz had climbed back to it. He wondered if it was always like this, or if Popovic had arranged for it to be sealed off. He wondered about many things.

'Last night I said this was an establishment business. Well, here's your proof. The war is where our new establishment locates its pedigree. They remember half a dozen Englishmen from that time, and Lippiat is one of that half a dozen, probably the most famous because – like the doctor – he was so young.'

'I thought he was only a wireless operator.'

'Yes, but young. Look at Kosovo Polje. Listen to what the *guslari* sing about the Field of Blackbirds. I tell you a great truth, Patrick.'

'Truth is like the jungle, Popo. It's neutral.'

Lippiat wasn't neutral. Not now. Not if he'd won the argument with the Security Police, and was on his way to the hills.

266

5

Popovic stayed with the doctor's truck and gave Matson to the women. They moved off in convoy, Popovic leading.

The ladies rode up front. Either they needed to be in radio contact with the other truck, or none of them was happy to ride with strangers.

This left him alone with Constanz, and some better-smelling blankets. He settled himself near the open back, so he could see out.

'How safe are we, Matson?'

'Very. Nowadays, scarcely anyone can afford the money to have a chap killed twice.'

'Don't joke me.'

'I'm not Obergruppenführer Weiss. There isn't a queue of bloodthirsty amateurs out there waiting to excavate my chitterlings with a pocket knife. I'd worry if a nutter was following me around with a gun. I'd worry till they'd caught him. But this wasn't a nutter. This was a professional job. I doubt if the driver was a professional, but somebody orchestrated him and paid him some money. He didn't muff it. He put us through the parapet over a ravine. He mayn't be able to collect his second instalment, but you can bet his employers aren't going to ask him to return their down payment. They had perfection.' He coughed modestly. 'It's just that in this case perfection wasn't good enough.'

'What makes you think anyone gives a shit about you?'

The truck slowed, but didn't stop. Presumably Popovic up front had slowed without stopping.

They moved ahead at about fifteen miles an hour, while first a house then a roadside bar dropped behind the open back of the truck. Both buildings had wide eaves, and the bar with its cedarwood flanks and stone columns looked enticing.

Popovic hadn't slowed for this. A parking area began to unfold itself into their rearward eyeline, a rubbled hollow as big as a football pitch, part natural, part quarried into the side of the hill.

Several trucks and high-sides were parked there, eight- or ten-wheeled tractor combinations like the one that had swiped them.

The one that interested Popovic was away to one side, looking strangely dislocated on the broken ground, like a lizard that's been hit with a stick. It interested Matson, too. He was intimately acquainted with the hubs of its front wheels. They had tried to get into his life.

There were two police cars beside it, and a helicopter, another bubble-and-pylon job but not the one they had seen before. It was open to argument whether the lorry had parked itself there or whether they had told it to pull over, perhaps long ago on a ground feed from the doctor.

The radio would have told Popovic what there was to know. Since they were picking up speed again, Matson could only guess this wasn't much. The police presumably had the driver, as Popo had promised; but no more. They'd have to take him somewhere to sweat him. A back room at the road-house would hardly meet the case.

Popovic wouldn't consider the matter important enough for extreme measures. His duty was to protect Weiss, and his own reputation. Hunting down Matson's would-be murderers was a secondary matter.

Unless he believed, as Matson believed, that Matson was being nobbled to stop him interfering in whatever was intended for Weiss.

Matson dozed till the cold woke him.

6

The ravine ran beside them and was deep, full of fog and the smell of bonfires. There were trees on the far side and storm-broken wood on this side, then copse boles and cut saplings in a widening band as the road curled back from the edge.

The roadhouse was on the lip of the ravine.

It was built of slate, or cemented scree. The roof was low, without eaves, and plastered in bands of concrete. They were at the very top of the tree-line; and where trees are reluctant to stand only a fool builds with wood. The place was shuttered like a blockhouse.

A vehicle was parked here. Matson noticed it stood on a long scud of compacted snow, blackening to scree. It was an

268

Audi Quatro, he thought, but with the squared-off rally trim and a battery of floodlights. A man stood by it clapping gauntleted hands.

The Quatro was painted matt grey, like a mint-edition Wehrmacht scout car waiting for the camouflage blobs to go on. This was odd in itself, so much ugliness tipped over such an elegant vehicle. The man's identity was even odder.

Matson's eyes weren't functioning too well. They'd had two immersions in freezing water at multiple atmospheres of pressure. They probably sported a capillary rupture or two. He was certain he knew the man, even so. Even at a distance.

It was his naked wrestling companion of a week or so back, he of the slimy thighs and slippery roller skates. Matson wasn't recognized in return. He encountered no answering blink, no shock. The fellow was searching for something else, thinking other thoughts. He didn't expect Matson to be dead or alive, or know or care anything about him. One day he might, given the chance, but not now. The death plot wasn't down to Weiss. Weiss was involved in his own megalomaniac processes.

Weiss might be alone on his island, but he had an outer guard in place. His fighting patrols were out.

NINETEEN

1

Matson climbed uneagerly from the back of the truck.

So this was Otok, Island, on the Lake without a name.

He saw a sky-blue stillness of water, streaky round the edges where conifers looked in. The island was a golden lozenge of rock, not the grim raft of karst he had expected. It had trees and a lawn, and shrubbery in as many nasty shades of green as a mashed cabbage. The leaves were meaty and still. There were rhododendrons, bush peonies, oleasters, exotica Matson hated because they always looked foreign wherever they grew. They had never seemed more alien than now, in this bleak but sunlit basin in Montenegro.

Otok was only six to eight hundred yards off-shore from where the vehicles had halted among the trees, but the water went on a long way behind it; and the lake twisted away out of view to left and right among the hills.

If there was danger, it would come from this side. It might already be in place and waiting. Popovic sensed as much. He sent his two smokers along the shoreline with carbines at the ready. A watcher could scent them for miles, so they weren't to be taken seriously, but they might keep a few heads down.

Two of the women checked their sub-machine-guns, walked back among the trees, then turned parallel to the men. Beaters on the lakeside, hunters in the wood. Matson couldn't hear the second pair move. He was impressed. He looked towards Otok again.

The house was awful, at least in elevation. It was vaguely oriental, with verandahs all round, verandahs overhung by an upper floor and enclosed by the supporting pillars in a kind of colonnade. It resembled a squashed pagoda.

Constanz reacted with a very short sentence. 'Ugh!' she said.

'It's a house with something on its mind,' Popovic agreed.

Matson wondered why Weiss was drawn to it. Then he rememberd his other monstrosity on the Austrian *stausee*. They were two of a kind, both gloomed in by trees, both standing near still water.

The house was roughly in the centre of the island. At the right hand end, nearer to where they stood, there was a windowless tower of grey and white stone. It was as tall as a factory chimney, but fat. A bit like a round castle keep with the rest of the castle missing. It was too ponderous for the tapering flatness of the island. If it had to be built, it should have been sited at the centre where the house was. Even so, it would have made Otok top heavy above the water line, like a dredger.

'What's that monstrosity?' Matson asked.

'That's Henk Weiss,' Constanz said. 'With some woman or other.'

Two figures had come from the house and were waving. At six hundred yards a standing man is only two thirds as tall as the foresight of a rifle.

'Love must have keen eyes,' Matson muttered. 'I was talking about the tower.'

'Better not ask.'

'You been here before?'

'I do my homework, Matson. And the reading's not always nice.'

2

Left to himself, Matson wouldn't have moved for at least ten minutes. He was never in a hurry with a forest at his back, and pines were a special problem. Even when they grow in an empty plantation they are full of noises. Even when the wind is still. Noises not of feather nor of claw. Conifers are their own sound, and he needed time to tune in to it.

Popovic was in no mood to give him any. 'The Ober-shitbag is calling you, Patrick. Madam.' He gestured for the

271

driver to carry the bag they had provided for Constanz while he picked up Matson's hold-all himself, again courtesy of the Yugoslav government.

The road ended here. Leaving the doctor to listen in to the radio net, they began to pick their way along the shoreline. To their front, a jut of land reached much nearer to the island. It tapered off into a scatter of rocks which someone had converted into a landing stage by laying pine bark and crusty planking on top of uneven balks of wood.

'This is fine water,' Popovic grunted. 'Fine water makes fat fish.' He didn't look like a man for fish. 'The place needs better associations, my dear. A less bloody history, a decent owner.'

'How bloody?'

'What the Turks did, I can talk about. Him I leave to books. He cancelled everything.'

Weiss was on the water now, in a boat plainly too big to belong to the island. There were other figures on board it, so many it could scarcely stay afloat. It was a craft almost without freeboard, and laden, gunwales awash, with white stones. Cries followed it across the lake as it hurried slowly towards them, cries like the mouthings of mad children. Weiss crouched amidships. Standing oarsmen sculled or quanted it stern and bow, grotesque and slow as any damaged insect. Popovic's party would beat it to the landing stage, and Weiss was not a man who enjoyed being last.

'Names are our history. Names in Montenegro more than most. After *he* got here, these waters became quite simply Jezero, Lake. That place Otok, Island.'

'There are other islands in the lake.'

'They keep their names. But their location is still Jezero, the Lake with no name.'

'That old man can't take your place names away from you.'

'We took our names away from him. Where Weiss is, no other name remains. Weiss, is *that* a name? It is the colour of snow. The colour of leprosy. The colour of nothing.'

The colour of lilies, Matson thought, as they reached the archipelago of rocks and picked their way along the planking. 'Even lilies are a kind of death,' he said aloud, making Constanz glance at him sharply.

272

The white stones it was that cried from Weiss's boat. The white stones that jostled it to overloading and almost capsized it. The minute Matson saw this, he realised that Weiss was crossing over with a cargo of goats.

The goats did not enjoy the water. The boatmen, or the goatherds, did not enjoy Weiss.

One thing about water, you can speak across it. Weiss spoke to Matson from a long way off-shore. 'I said they might keep half a dozen sheep on my lawns. Not a hundred goats in my shrubbery. These men can't count any more than their parents could count. I had to shoot them in batches of ten at a time before they would notice.'

The boat was against the jetty now, and discharging goats. The goats kicked the planking half to pieces in their hurry to be on dry land, and nearly had them all into the water. The goatherds went to run after them, but Weiss had not dismissed them. He had a use for them. He made them come back. He knew how to dominate people who hated him. He worked them a command at a time. No need for giant imperatives. He was the giant. His was the imperative. He placed them amidships with their poles. The stern seat was now his own.

Before this, he welcomed Matson. He welcomed him in German. He intercepted Popovic's handing over of the hold-all. Constanz's case he ignored, though his eye took account of the driver who carried it. His eye and a raised eyebrow.

Popovic tried to step on board. Weiss did not let him. Popovic explained he had to inspect Otok's security arrangements. Weiss said there was no room in the boat. It was not Weiss's boat, but he saw no place in it. He said some of this in German, some of it in English.

Popovic gave his answer its answer. He was himself a man of power, never more than now. He kept his voice down, his gaze calm and hard, and he insisted he come to the island. He insisted as of right. He spoke in Serbo Croat for the sake of his dignity and the benefit of the boatmen and the driver. It did him no good.

The boat made faster time without its flock of goats. When Matson first trod on Otok, Popovic was still speaking from the jetty.

273

3

The woman waited for them. She stood upright and still on one of Otok's lawns and waited for Weiss to leave the island and then for his return. The jetty was closer than Matson's first glimpse of the island, perhaps only three hundred yards away. Even at three hundred yards Matson thought the woman was Lotte. But Lotte was not a woman for waiting, not Lili Weiss.

This woman was brown-faced. She dressed entirely in black. The black had lost its freshness, but the brown was firm and unlined, except around the eyes. Matson guessed she was in her late sixties, but she might have been younger.

She watched quietly while they got themselves out of the boat, and then she stepped forward and held out her hand, first to Constanz and then to Matson. 'I am Anka,' she said. 'You speak English, you are welcome.'

If this was a dig at Weiss, he ignored it. 'She speaks English,' he explained, 'for some reason best known to herself. Speaks it or tries to speak it. German I made her speak as a condition of her staying on.'

Clearly she had some long-term connection with the house. She led them to their rooms, Weiss carrying Matson's bag, Matson carrying Constanz's.

It was only now, with Constanz carrying nothing, that Matson realized she wore no handbag. She had left it in the Yugo, a dozen fathoms under. She could do without her bottle. Could he do without her gun?

4

Matson didn't like the place. If more than three or four hostile people got themselves as far as the island – and who was to identify them or stop them? – then the house would be indefensible. He was viewing it with a soldier's eye. There was no other way to view it: it was as dismal as a barracks.

He walked over the bare wooden flooring and came downstairs to flagstones. The voices were outside.

No need to cross the water. Weiss wasn't going to bother

274

with defence. He proposed to get himself shot in the open air, at the shortest range possible.

There, right at the water's edge, on the margin closest to the shore, was where he had stood himself. His trousers were intelligent and dark; but his shirt was radiant white.

The setting was a rough wooden table, with benches planted into the rock. Lotte perched there, while Anka served Turkish coffee and iced water. Lotte treated Constanz like a long-awaited friend. To Matson she offered nothing. She played one person at a time.

'What do you think of it, Hauptmann?'

'Not enormously much. I envy you your pleasure in it, but wonder is it worth the risk.'

Weiss not only stayed standing, he kept decently to one side. He held his coffee against his lip and flashed his shirt towards the trees on the shoreline. His guests need have no worries, his gestures implied. Their heads would never come between his laundry and its bullet.

Matson found himself watching the distant trees. Trees, when watched, come closer.

'Tell me why you should want such a place.'

'Because I could buy it for nothing.'

'It's a damp house on a cold lake.' Fear makes for a certain rudeness.

'There's a old Serbian proverb. "If vinegar is free, it tastes sweeter than honey."' He gazed at Anka, as if she were a garden gnome.

Matson watched her too, struck by her dignity and, he supposed, beauty. He saw where her stillness came from, her reticence of gesture. She had a damaged leg. She could stand on it, she could walk on it, but she spared herself sudden movement.

'I signed papers in 1943 or 4. It was in the autumn of the big offensive up here.'

'Compulsory purchase?'

'No. The owner brought me the deeds and pressed me to buy.'

'How much did you pay him?'

'He wanted his wife back. She was a valuable woman, so a fair price.'

The General watched Anka pick up the tureen of charcoal and tuck up the empty coffee-makers against the handles, then totter back to the kitchen with them. She looked weary.

'You see,' he triumphed. 'His house was made to last. It was built of Mount Durmitor. The Slavs all have bad joints, the Montenegrins and Albanians worse than anyone. I had the best of the bargain.'

'It was Anka? You kept her on?'

'Only when her husband was shot by an *Einsatzgruppe*. I tried to intercede for him, but the people who killed him were a Hungarian wolfpack from some *Freiwilligen* division or other. Fellow animals. They used to kick heads first and write the execution warrant second. In his case, I was lucky enough to be able to pick up a warrant. Posthumously, of course. But I owed it to the woman. It's hanging on the wall somewhere.'

'And you dare come back here?'

He wasn't listening. 'Some people frame their commissions, their academic honours, their certificates of merit. She framed her husband's death warrant. Quaint of her.' He clapped his hands for more coffee and sat down at the table. 'She stayed on till now, and she can stay till she dies. I kept my bargain, even with a dead man. She looks after my kitchen. My bedroom has always been able to look after itself.'

'You're lucky she doesn't serve powdered glass.'

He laughed and watched the woman shuffle towards him, crippled though ten years younger than he was. 'Powdered glass is too quick for these people. They go in for far more imaginative revenges.'

Anka bent over the table, and his hand explored what he could find of her bottom, just as he had done with the woman at Kocevje Gora. 'She wasn't altogether reluctant, believe me. Very few of them were. Women admire success in a man.'

They sat a long time in silence after this, Lotte trying to speak but finding nothing to say. As an epilogue the General said, 'Sex in wartime is an odd business. The Americans had the money, too much of it. I'm told that is what the Tommies complained about. But we Germans were in East Europe a

276

whole lot longer, and we had the uniform. The SS had the best uniforms of anyone. The British, by and large, had nothing.'

'We didn't make so many widows, either.'

'Making widows helps a man's sexual advancement. Making widows is a good practical step.'

The General didn't drink the coffee. He wanted to go inside. It was growing dark.

Matson bet he was going to light lots and lots of lamps.

5

He did. He had Anka light them. They were oil-burners, with glass chimneys and incandescent mantles. Sixteen glowed in the huge room downstairs, sixteen and a log fire. In such numbers they were brighter than electric light, and much better to shoot by. If you sent one flying it would burn and, with a wooden ceiling overhead, hard luck to the besieged wounded.

You can smell sixteen oil-lamps. They would be uneasy on the nose even if they burned pure alcohol. The partially refined kerosene in their tanks spread a faint blue haze in the air and dulled what was left of Matson's five wits as the night shut down.

They ate fish cooked in pine nuts and garlic. Fish and paraffin don't go, not for Matson and Constanz they didn't, so recently nearly dead in the water.

'These fish are bad,' Weiss said, reproving Anka, who wasn't invited to her own table. 'They are doubtless female, and too early in the year. They wring themselves out with spawning,' he explained to the child.

Little Henk liked fish. He did not like his grandfather's explanations. He preferred the mess he could make with breadcrusts and bones.

'Tomorrow we'll eat meat,' Weiss promised himself.

'No meat,' Anka said.

'We'll eat wild pig if I have to swim over and shoot some myself. There are bears in those woods – do you know that, Hauptmann? Bears and, I insist, wolves.'

277

'There always are, especially, after wine.' The wine was pale and resined, but exceptionally good. 'Do you have a hunting rifle with you, General? A spare gun of any sort?'

Killing pigs gave Matson no pleasure, nor did killing any animal, but he had been hearing sounds outside the house for some time now. Footfalls soft across the lawn, footfalls gritty on the verandah. The goats had gone away. Sheep do not sound like this.

Weiss smiled his tolerant smile and asked, 'How is it in English – "the patter of tiny feet"?'

'The expression applies only to children.'

'They are children, believe me. They creep about in the dark merely to assure themselves I am here.'

'Do you want me to send them away?' Matson watched a face glimmer against the windowpane, heard other sounds at his back.

'Do they bother you, Hauptmann? It is me they have come to look at. They have certain claims on me. I mixed my seed with their grandmothers.'

The women sat very still.

'You don't have a gun, Hauptmann Matson? A pity. The warrior needs his weapon.'

Matson said nothing. Earlier, he had gone into the kitchen and taped a knife to his leg. He knew about killing with knives, how to kill and who. You choose a man who hasn't got a firearm, preferably with his trousers down and his back turned. He didn't expect to find too many of those, not pattering about Otok in the dark.

Weiss laid his Luger on the table. It had been hiding on his lap, but perfectly visible from some of the window angles. 'In certain circumstances you may borrow it.' He slid it along the table. 'You've already seen it. It's my wartime pistol.' He spoke to impress them with his calmness. The gun was for the watchers in the night.

Good old Luger Parabellum. Matson handled it briefly. 'Do you keep it in grease?'

'Grease? I keep it oiled and ready for action.'

Matson was frightened of that. He emptied it, shook it, cocked it and fired a dry round. It rattled like a can full of

278

pebbles. 'I'd rather you kept it in grease,' he said. He'd rather have a new gun.

He reloaded it and slid it back to Weiss. ' "Borrow"? What does that mean?'

'If I am incapacitated, you may need to shoot. Do you know how to shoot? I say "borrow" because, again in certain circumstances, the gun would come to belong to little Henk.'

'Well, I shan't need to borrow it tonight, General.' He listened to the deepening silence, and then to the drip and splash of oars ill-managed in water.

'Children,' Weiss agreed. 'It's the one you don't hear that gets you.'

Lotte did her daft laugh. She laughed as if Weiss had said something funny. As if Matson, just by being, was funny. Then she stopped laughing and was attractive again.

'They left something for you, Herr Weiss.'

It was Anka shuffling in from the door, Anka carrying a fruit basket and handling it with the long-fingered disdain one reserves for objects not one's own, that have come from other places, been soiled by other hands.

She walked around the table to the head and placed it in front of Weiss, setting it down on his gun.

It contained two poisoned rats, plump from their greed for water, the haemorrhage drip from their noses glowing red as the brightest berry.

It was Constanz's turn to laugh. 'You asked for your fucking meat,' she said. 'Myself, I'll stay with the fish.'

6

They didn't leave the table. To leave and go outside would convey the wrong message to the men on the water. It might even suggest alarm. Weiss did not let himself be alarmed.

Besides, the child was drooping with sleep, and Lotte had a new trick. Lotte felt at home. Lotte began to crochet.

Women do not crochet at table, not at Weiss's table, with the meal not yet cleared and dead rats still in their basket.

He poured himself a brandy, or some amber spirit from a

decanter, then pushed it at Matson, knocking Lotte's wrist and dragging her thread.

'Thank you, General. Not until I've looked round the island.'

Weiss was delighted with him. 'Ah, Hauptmann. You soldier like a fox.' Delighted with Matson, even more delighted with himself. 'You seek to retain your sniff.'

'Like a dog, General. But otherwise as you say. Spirits get up my nose.' Matson needed more than his sense of smell. Like any other animal of the night, he needed not to be smelled.

Constanz didn't mind being smelled. She wore a perfume rich as Indian oil. Presumably she had begged some from Anka or Lotte. Now she enriched it with brandy.

Weiss had broken Lotte's thread when he passed the decanter, exactly as he intended. Crocheting isn't like knitting. It is very hard to repair.

Lotte took out a pocket-knife, a strange object for a woman's bag. Its handle was over-ornate, almost vulgar, but its blade was brutal in size. It would sharpen poles as well as pencils.

She laid out her shattered trellis of thread, then unpicked her last circle of work, using the blade to cut the end clean. It wasn't quite as sharp as it looked, and she dug into the table top. She closed the blade and prised up a tiny marlin spike. The knife wasn't one of those Swedish miracles. It had just the double function, the blade and the marlin, like a standard service knife.

So far she had crocheted lace-fine, using a tiny hook. Now she used the marlin to knit a series of loops, radiating out from the fragile core. She did this quickly. Weiss watched her in annoyance, Matson with total attention.

When the loops were finished, she took up her hook again, and began to crochet finely, making an outer circle to collar the loops. The whole effect was beautiful, but mad. Quite mad. It looked like the doodling of a schizophrene. She didn't put her knife away, either. When the collar was complete, she intended to weave more loops. Even if Weiss hadn't disturbed the pattern, this was what she planned.

Weiss didn't like Lotte claiming so much attention. He

280

clapped his hand for Anka to bring him a burning stick from the fire. With the cool end in hand, he contemplated his basket of rats. 'If the Hauptmann needs no cognac.' He laced the corpses liberally with brandy, and used the burning stick to set it on fire. It did not catch at once. Then it leapt with a darting blue flame, a black smoke of fur, a disgusting stench.

Somebody gasped in horror. It was Anka, choking on emotion, discovering a terrible significance in what he did.

'You bastard,' Constanz said. 'You Grade A Kraut bastard.'

Weiss had Lotte's crochet-work in his fingers. He spread it lovingly on the pyre. He muttered to himself in German, then translated to Matson: 'To each death its appropriate winding sheet.' He breathed in the smoke, until the burning basket began to singe the table. This was too much even for him. He swept it to the floor.

Matson had seen Weiss push himself towards extravagance at last. Was the Obergruppenführer breaking down, or coming magnificently into his own?

The little boy slept.

7

Most men are heroes in their own story. It was Matson's luck to be a hero in Weiss's. He had to take care not to let it cloud his judgement.

Weiss encouraged him. He wanted him to feel loved. He sniffed the ghastly air. 'There are those who bring me rats, Captain Matson.'

Captain Matson was an improvement.

'Then, when I set them on fire, it wakens memories for them. They can recall my treatment of rats, and the smell I made at their burning.'

Constanz's hatred was palpable. It did no good to know that Weiss could muffle it with a kiss. A kiss only lasts in time.

'What do you say, Hauptmann? Or doesn't your experience run to such matters?'

Anka kept herself busy. She began to refill the lamps. She

tipped kerosene from an open jug, without extinguishing the flame.

Lotte started another loop, on a new crochet no bigger than her thumbnail.

'I only know about armies and soldiers, Weiss.'

'Don't bandy definitions with me, young Matson. I *was* in the army. I *was* a soldier. I've seen more soldiering than a man of your generation will ever see.'

'My regimental history does not run to murder, I'll give you that.'

'I was a soldier,' he repeated. It was his honour code. He sat above the smoking rats and needed to be liked. 'I was not in the Wehrmacht, true. I was SS.'

'The formation that did the army's dirty work?'

'No, Hauptmann. The SS did the army's *work*. Wherever there was work, we did it. Where there was failure we brought success.'

'You lost.'

'The SS didn't lose. Europe, World-Europe lost. The Reich was overwhelmed by historic catastrophe. To that catastrophe the SS brought fortitude.'

Matson needed brandy after all. The decanter was empty. That, at least, was a diversion.

8

Weiss had Anka remove the rats. 'Take them,' he said, 'and bury them. Unless you can think of a better place.'

He was hinting at matters unknown to Matson, but painful. She scuffed the mess with her shoe, then kicked it towards the kitchen as she went to find more cognac

'I understand your opposition to the SS, young man.'

Did Constanz snort at this, or at something earlier?

'There is much you will hear me affirm. Very little I ever deny.' He flashed his teeth, but the signal stopped short of a smile. 'I am not ashamed of what I did. But at this distance, what I was – well it sometimes puzzles me. Take my rank. I spent months as Obergruppenführer. Months. A month in wartime is an eternity, and when one is young even more so.'

He did smile this time. At Lotte, who was young. And at Constanz, who was seething. 'No one of that rank ever set foot in Yugoslavia. Yet that is what they called me. Gruppenführer was too much. Certainly too much. Something between a division and a corps. You will know it is over exalted for so insignificant a place.' He pretended modesty while he was boasting, then boasted about his modesty. 'No one of such a rank ever came here, but I was here. So I became Obergruppenführer. It made me a what? Army Commander almost. I was never that.' Again the flash of teeth. 'I wasn't being made up. I was being chosen for blame. Not even that. I was being blamed. I embraced the honour gratefully.'

'Let's forget what you were,' Constanz suggested. 'Let's get back to what you did.'

Weiss had enjoyed his cognac. Now he enjoyed his words. 'You are probably even less of a historian than you are a soldier, Hauptmann. But one thing is apparent to even the most casual student of warfare. Generals advance to more and more preposterous titles the faster their armies diminish.

'I even became Oberstgruppenführer at the end, for all of nine days. They let me lose the war for them. The most miserable nine days of my life. Then I was in clink in Austria.'

'And lucky to be there.'

'A prisoner is never lucky. Let us just say I was less unlucky than some in our army.'

Matson reached for the fresh decanter, but Weiss wanted to be outside.

9

A full fat moon had risen white on the water, blackening the undersides of trees.

Matson did not seek the shadows. There might be watchers on shore, identifying them with a night glass. He saw no reason to teach them how easily he could lose himself.

Weiss had worn a dark jacket for dinner. He left it unbuttoned. He made no attempt to cover his white shirt.

Constanz and Anka walked with them. This might be Weiss's island. It was Anka who laid claim to it by showing them around.

The child cried out in the house. Lotte was putting him to bed.

Matson saw no chance to protect Weiss, or his *impedimenta*, unless the old Nazi was prepared to meet properly with Popovic and accept an adequate number of his people onto Otok.

Impedimenta when alive, *detrita* once dead. Wasn't that what Bigmouth had said two nights ago on the coast? Mason didn't know Latin, hadn't read Caesar, didn't care whether Weiss was right or wrong. What he did was remember things.

They had reached the wooden table by the water's edge. It would be a romantic place to sit, but as foolish by moonlight as it had been this afternoon.

Weiss didn't stop. He turned to his right, and led them along the edge of the water. They had shrubbery at their back now, then rocks, then occasional trees. They didn't stand out as they had in silhouette above the moonlit lawn.

Anka's limp grew more pronounced. She lagged behind. Between landing-stage and house, house and table, she was keen to lead the way. Not any longer. The terrain was too rough for her.

Matson smelled perfume, saw blooms, petal clusters jammed open by frost, others half-opened, part closed as they reacted to shelter and starlight. Weiss had led them almost to the end of the island. They were in a place of roses, a whole acre of bushes and ramblers with one or two unsticked standards. These last were not yet in flower; nor were many others so early in the year. The ones that were did their best, and they were here in plenty.

Even after dewfall they smelled like the meat on a woman's chest. They smelled like Constanz's borrowed perfume, wholesome and strong.

'Excellent roses, Weiss.'

'I planted them a long time ago.'

'I thought peonies were the natural as well as the national flower?'

284

'You are thinking of Kosovo Field, Hauptmann. The soil was different. It was a liar's soil, for one thing.' He stooped and lifted grit in his hand. 'There they had blood. Roses enjoy blood, true. But here there is no blood. Once I decided this was to be my place, I shed no blood this end of the island. Fortunately roses also like potash.' He opened his fingers, and the dirt melted in the moonlight as it fell. It was as thin as snuff.

Matson looked at the lake's rim of trees, the bright climb of the hills to the stark heights beyond. Surely Jezero was the wrong shape for a volcanic tarn, the island too big for a magmatic core?

Weiss watched him for a second or two as if following his thoughts. 'Tell him,' he said to Anka.

10

They were back at the table. Weiss paced widely about, Matson kept himself low by the water's edge and counted the minutes and degrees before the moon sank behind Durmitor, or whatever the name was of the huge mass of peak.

It was Constanz who got herself ready to deliver. Hard to tell if she fancied herself gypsy or Jew or some avenging angel from Slavonic folklore. She certainly fancied herself.

'Two things happened on this island,' she said. 'Two things over and beyond the festive screwing and the obligatory bouts of vestal rape.'

'Some people have flock-lined souls,' Matson grunted. 'They encourage history to stick to them.' He wanted Anka to speak, not the Ehrenberg-Zanetti.

'Fuck you, Matson. Fuck your tumble-dried, fragged out and free-falling little brain pan. Fuck it and fuck it again. Two things happened, and *she* can't bring herself to tell you about them any more than Henk can. For once.'

The silence grew heavy. The moment was so bleak Matson decided to set about making it bleaker. 'You should meet Popovic, Weiss. Meet him and treat with him. For your own peace of mind. He's a soldier, not a policeman.'

'I thought for a moment you were promising me a priest.

285

Mrs Zanetti here thinks I'm in need of everlasting confession.'

'He has a poem, Weiss. Written by a fool, he says, but he takes its madness seriously. It says you will be punished for Kocevje Gora, for the Neretna, and for here.'

'If I am to meet him, so be it. But not to discuss poetry. Kocevje I have spoken about. We are never going to make peace over that.' It grieved him to be misunderstood. 'On the Neretna I shot prisoners, as I was ordered.'

'And had hundreds of their injured thrown into the ravine.' Constanz spoke quietly for Constanz.

'To save bullets. In a war of movement they're always at a premium.'

'And what about Otok, Weiss?'

'Here I saved bullets as well.'

11

The island was innominate. The Lake had lost its name. Hard to tell whether this was the place *SS Commanders Against the Southern Slavs* spoke of when it fastened its only out-and-out atrocity on the then Brigadeführer Weiss, and came as close as its reticence would allow to branding him a war criminal.

The authors' peculiar even-handedness was in evidence nonetheless. They began this chapter, as they began many, with Kurt Waldheim's excuse that the Yugoslav campaign was a 'dirty affair' a 'bitter business with excesses on all sides'. ('All' was a poignant word, so much more intricate in its possibilities than 'both'.)

The authors also pointed out that on Otok – if it was indeed Otok – Weiss butchered no children and killed no women, though he had taken women prisoners in circumstances which rendered it mandatory for him to execute them.

Lippiat had spared the margins this time round. There was not a single word of complaint at the implication that Weiss, *in extremis,* had kept clean hands while everyone around him was blood-soaked to the armpits.

286

Operation Schwarz was the second offensive to begin by encircling Tito's partisans in Montenegro, then proceed to a search-and-destroy campaign on the high plateaux surrounding Mt Durmitor. This time the preparation was much more detailed. The Axis were able to deploy a whole army group, including SS and Wehrmacht panzer divisions, and over fifty thousand Croatians and Bulgarians of the by then notorious 'freiwilligen' formations. Einsatzgruppen, allegedly of the Waffen SS (although SS historians deny this), were to be used in 'mopping up' operations against Montenegrin villages judged to have been sympathetic to the partisan cause.

In all, the Axis had over one hundred and fifty thousand front-line troops in the encirclement, and almost as many again in the attack. They were able to reinforce substantially and resupply continually. The partisan army numbered nineteen thousand, though – in a sense – all Montenegro was in revolt, if not in arms.

After several days of confused fighting, a brigade group under the command of Brigadeführer Weiss broke into the area of encirclement, close to the point where the partisan main body was concentrating prior to breaking out. Brigade Group Weiss consisted of elements of SS Prinz Eugen, of Handschar der SS, as well as formations not yet identified. It is likely its composition was Weiss's own brigade from SS Prinz Eugen, a battalion and perhaps some independent companies from Handschar, a mountain regiment of artillery and an Einsatzgruppe or an Einsatzkommando.

Once he had broken in, Weiss proceeded with characteristic flair. He ordered his unit commanders to operate independently; and freed as many troops as possible for combat by establishing group headquarters on an island, making Brigade staff and B-echelon units responsible for their own defence. The island also served as a natural compound for prisoners.

German High Command and the Officer Commanding Second Army Group had both issued written standing orders that all partisan prisoners were to be executed. Field Marshal von Lohr, the officer in command of Operation

287

Schwarz, had also insisted that the offensive be pursued 'with the utmost rigour and severity'. However, a compound was required for intelligence purposes. All prisoners were to be interrogated, and prisoners of rank, or of significance otherwise, sent to Army Group Headquarters.

The island was not of many acres' extent, and after the partisans broke out to the north-west, it was found to be holding upwards of a thousand prisoners, whether partisans or Montenegrin villagers.

Three prisoners were selected for detailed interrogation at Army Group. The rest were executed immediately. Weiss was present at these executions – that is, he was on the island so could scarcely claim to be uninvolved. More culpably, he countermanded the proposed method of execution. The men were to be shot, and their corpses disposed of by incineration on wooden pyres ignited by flame-throwers.

'To kill a thousand men with one shot each to the head is inhumane,' Weiss advised the officer in charge of the execution squad. 'Consider how long some of them must wait. You will also expend at least one thousand bullets. Pistol ammunition is in short supply. To kill them with a machine gun or machine guns will require at least ten thousand rounds of belt ammunition, perhaps much more. You could fight a battle with that firepower. Since you are going to incinerate the bodies anyway, why not use the flame-throwers to kill the men in the first place? It may seem inhumane: it will merely be noisy. If the troops hesitate, remind them they use the flammenwerfer *in battle without a moment's thought.' The troops, as it happened, did not complain. They were an Einsatzgruppe of the Waffen SS.*

12

Constanz wasn't done yet. 'Some things pass into folk history among the Southern Slavs,' she said. 'And when they pass into folk history, books show a curious reluctance to touch upon them.'

288

Matson began to see how even a man like Weiss could feel overwomaned.

'Like the tower,' she said. 'I've heard Serbs talk of it. I've heard men talk of it many times. Your biographers don't mention it. Has Lili seen it yet? And what about young Henk?'

'Henk is asleep,' Weiss said, 'and Lotte makes spider's webs from pieces of string.' He stood up. 'You will need to bring a torch,' he instructed Anka.

The woman didn't move, and this suited Matson. He had no desire to call further attention to their presence by flashing a torch.

'You'll have seen the tower at Nis?' Constanz asked sweetly. 'It's the sort of thing a dick-head like you would go and gawp at, Matson.'

'I saw it when I came here on a cycle trip as a boy,' Matson admitted. 'I took a look at the Sultan's tower then. Good God, Weiss,' he added, as he realised what was being said.

'Mine is better,' Weiss said. 'I had need of an ossuary, you see.' He spoke the last sentence for Constanz, then turned and walked swiftly to the house.

Matson didn't think she would manage to insult her way back into his bed.

Weiss wasn't running away. He came back at once, carrying the decanter and some glasses. He brought one for Anka, but she wouldn't drink with him.

'What do you think of me, Patrick Matson? I did not kill men to make the tower from their bones. I made the tower because it gave me something useful to do with the bones I already had. Also –' he hesitated – 'I have made this point to you before. Is it wasteful of a man's life to leave his death unmarked. Kill ten men, kill a thousand. In a mass grave they mean nothing. How is insurrection to learn its lesson? By counting widows' tears? Weeping makes for imprecise counting, Hauptmann Patrick, believe me. Besides, these Slavs are always weeping about something – a poem, a still-born calf, a dead cat. Weeping or laughing. When they really grieve they clench their faces at you and go grey about the cheekbone. You do not know whether they are in mourning or chewing cordite to make a bottle bomb.'

'I never mourn,' Anka said. It was the first time she spoke unbidden. 'For you I chew cordite.'

These weren't words to stay on. She had a torch in the pocket of her overall. Perhaps she would always feel the need of a torch in the dark. She stood and said, 'Come on, Englishman. I'll show you, and only you. Because of my husband.'

13

'Yes,' she said. 'His skull is in the tower.'

The tower was a hollow place without floors, a tube that lacked windows.

Matson stood inside the door. Hundreds, perhaps thousands of skulls grinned in the torchlight like so many flints. A bird flew from a mouth and raucoused about, trapped by their presence in the doorway. The place was bigger than that horror at Nis, and more terrible because it was more recent. Matson couldn't rid himself of the feeling that if it weren't for Weiss most of these bits of bone would still be alive. It was like standing in a scaled-down version of Dante's Hell, a hell that smelled of berries and bird droppings, and kept itself innocent and neutral, the way hell is.

'His skull is over there,' Anka said. 'But my loss is elsewhere. First there was the loss of my son. Then there was the loss of the father of my son.'

Matson felt a prickling of the skin, as if he stood naked under the pines.

'Then I lost my son again.'

He knew what she would say next.

'My son was the man known as Vincenz Weiss.'

'Known as?' He had no reason to disbelieve this part of Lolly's story, but he had to ask the question. 'Wasn't Weiss the father?'

She paused. 'It was convenient for the General to think so – yes. I have no idea what he really thought. Who knows with a man like that?'

'Who knows?' he asked. 'When did you last see the father of your child?' Matson put an arm around her, knowing she

290

was too old to take it amiss. 'Not your husband over there. Nor the General who thinks he owns your husband's house.'

'What is it to you?'

'I knew Mr Lippiat,' he said. He couldn't see her face, but he could tell the name didn't register. Yet Anja, Jovanka, Anka. This had to be Lolly's woman.

'Gerald Lippiat,' he prompted.

'We had many names. *He* certainly did. But none of these.'

'Lippiat.'

'He told me, once, that his family name, in English, was the Serbian for lime tree.'

'And is Lippiat?'

'A little. A very little.'

'What about Lolly? Or Gerry?'

She clapped her hands in delight. 'Geri,' she said, pronouncing the G hard. That's it. That's him. That was my man. Mr Gerilac Lipa, Geri Lipa, my little Guerrilla Vine. For years he would not come to me. Then I saw him ten years ago. Just now they told me he was dead. Is he here?'

'I saw him in Belgrade,' Matson here. Here? Of course he was bloody here. 'He spoke of you, Anja. He spoke of you both. When he spoke he wept.'

What graceless words one gives, and how people grow grateful for them.

As they left the tower, and the bird still flapping, he said, 'You must want to kill General Weiss.'

'Kill is too easy. We saw too much of kill. If only Lipi were with me, he'd find a way what to do.'

At least he knew why she'd bothered to learn English, even if Weiss didn't.

14

The moon was almost set. Constanz's perfume lingered by the water's edge, but she wasn't here. Weiss was smoking a cigar. Matson had only seen him smoke once before, on the mountain. Then it was merely a ritual gesture, a puff for the dead. Now he clenched a cigar in his face and sucked it till it

291

made his eye sockets and thin cheeks glare like a lamp in a pumpkin. Or an aiming post.

'I sent your woman for my cigars, Matson. Then I sent her away. I may need her for other things.'

'Mrs Ehrenberg-Zanetti is her own person, General.'

'They're never that. Not even this one.' He watched Anka shuffle off then indicated the darkened hills. 'These are a pure people, Captain. That's why I came back. I want their understanding. They are warriors like the Germans were before we were corrupted by kings. Warriors like the kings were before the Industrial Revolution made them greedy.'

Matson could either listen or leave the island. There was no middle way.

'I have killed them by the hundred. Once, no twice, in headlong clashes with the Partisan Brigades, I have killed them by the thousand. I have seen their dead lie down like a field of stones. Then they have got up and thrown the mountain at me.'

Matson did not comment. He was watching the shoreline. Three lights that might also be cigars glowed and faced them in a horizontal row beneath the invisible trees.

Weiss saw them too. 'The Slavs are mad. They have the battle madness. They fought us as if they could win. And, just possibly, they won.'

'You certainly lost, anyway.'

They weren't cigars. They were masked pocket torches.

'That is how I prefer to see it, Captain Matson. We seem to have lost. I am not sure about certainly.'

He might have left things there, but Constanz and Anka came back from the house. Now he had an audience. 'If we lost, it was only in the mean world of arithmetic.' He smiled at Constanz and, yes, he knew. 'We killed the Jews because the world would be a better place without them.' He did not smile at Anka. 'We killed the Slavs because they existed in such impossible numbers. In neither case did we kill enough of them.'

Matson noticed that the three lights had grouped themselves one above the other now, as if signalling the attack.

'And then there were the people like Captain Matson.'

15

Weiss's gaze was enigmatic. 'We took no pleasure in your death, but we killed you, and millions like you.'

Sometime soon his world was going to end. This gave him an enormous advantage in debate. 'There is too much soldier in you, I think, and not enough warrior.' He struck a match and dropped it, searching for a cigar. He struck another one, as if tempting the bullets to smash into him.

'Churchill makes the same distinction, when speaking of ourselves and you Germans.'

'Quoting Churchill is surely the last resort of an inferior mind. The Americans – the new Americans, today's Americans: not the real Americans, the ones who defeated me – the Americans always quote Churchill. The war here, this scrap in what you call the Balkans, was an affair between men. Not Churchillian men. Not soldiers. But men.' He lit the cigar for the benefit of his murderers. 'Men of both sexes, Captain Matson. It was, you may believe me, truly adult. Soldiers are an odd race, you know. You, of all people, *must* know. They have their codes, they have their systems of honour. Warriors are not like soldiers. They have no codes, no honour. They exist in absolutes. They kill. They rape. They loot. They massacre. They desecrate.'

'That is a description of the Beast.'

'It is the description of a man in wartime. It is the description of the warrior.'

'It's certainly not the description of the soldier.'

Weiss drew the night towards the end of his cigar and said, 'Soldiers are boys, not men.'

16

The child had stopped crying long since. Lotte came cross the lawn at last, making the General's audience complete.

'Now let me tell you about that tower, Matson. Women, I think, understand such matters. So do most men. Boys don't.'

'I take it as an honour to number myself among the boys, General. In this instance, anyway.'

Constanz snorted. Lotte applauded as if Matson had done something clever, like falling on a knife.

'A warrior fights the world he finds himself in. He fights the enemy's world entire. His world includes his women.'

Lotte's mouth fell open in a kind of ecstasy now, as if she did so want to be included. Matson wondered if there was a simple explanation for her, like drugs, or premature senility.

Weiss wasn't talking to Matson. He was lecturing the darkened shoreline as if arguing with his own death. 'There are two things a warrior can do to the the man he has defeated. He can kill him, then take his woman. Or he can take his woman and kill him.'

Constanz clapped her hands, but slowly, like Mrs Punch patting the baby.

'Both have their rewards,' Weiss said imperturbably.

The cigar coughed, then crackled back at one edge like a burning thatch. Someone whistled on shore. The lights had disappeared.

'A recent widow is generally so mopish – is that a word? – she's generally a very dull bedfellow. Once in a while' – he indicated Anka – 'she craves the implantation of the domi-nant gene, but that is only when she is at her most brutish, because the slaughter has been absolute. Otherwise women are very rarely as intelligent as beasts in the wild, Balkan women certainly not. No, Captain Matson, the most piquant sex is *always* with a woman who thinks you have it in your power to reprieve her man. The more aloof you are, the more remote, the more expressive her attention. I have even enjoyed such moments with a woman who has begged me to cut her fellow down from the hanging tree before it is too late. You have a poem in Palgrave's *Golden Treasury*, I think. "The nymph died more quickly but he died more slow".'

'You're a disgusting bastard, General Weiss.'

'I'm afraid my English isn't up to that, my dear fellow. Your German certainly is not.'

He had his arms round Lotte and then Constanz, hugging them fondly and without desire, in friendship rather than passion. His hand began to explore Constanz just the same, groping her gently, enjoying the newer ground.

She shrugged at Anka, then grinned at Matson. 'Don't

294

look so sulky, Patrick. He's bound to kick your balls from time to time. It's what you both expect, and I daresay you like it.'

'You remind me,' Weiss said to her. 'I spoke of the two things a warrior could do to a man. Kill him and have his woman. Or have his woman and kill him. In fact, there's a third.' He gave her a kiss. 'I kept it from you, but men will tell it hereabouts if you mention my name. Or if you say Turk. You can remove a man's manhood, Captain. Either his testicles or his possibilities entire. And then have his women. His women grieve less, you see. The warrior achieves balance. Also a man without his *je ne sais quoi* is firstly so sore, and secondly so sad, that what you do to his women doesn't bother him for a very considerable time. A man who has just had his leg off is rarely in the mood to mourn the death of a favourite cat.'

He sent Lotte to look after her son. As Matson had said, the Ehrenberg-Zanetti was her own woman.

17

Matson was slow to go upstairs, but he needed to be there. He wanted the world to think the house was in bed.

The polished boards did not creak. Most doors were closed, and Constanz's room was empty. He heard Weiss laugh somewhere, and realised laughter was what he'd first heard of him, back at Rosental. This time, as last time, his laugh was too hearty and overlaid by the voices of women.

An oil-lamp had been left glowing in Matson's room, presumably by Anka. He had no kit, only this afternoon's issue garments. Still, the boots were soft and good. One shirt was dark.

The kitchen knife was loose on his leg. He retaped it as best he could. Tomorrow he would ask his last night's sleeping partner for some of her elastoplast. No, he wouldn't. It was down there in the Yugo, like the rest of her.

He extinguished the oil lamp and stepped to the window. He peered outside, waiting for his eyes to grow accustomed to the darkness.

His door opened, letting in light.

It was Lili Weiss, dressed to transcend the language barrier. She wore a slip-over housecoat and a lot of pallid skin. The housecoat was barely opaque, but where it folded, it became blue with a mauve ripple, calling attention to what was left of the bruise on her cheek. She followed her shadow quickly into the room.

To be fair to the language barrier, she did say something, but he was in no mood to listen. Unexpected women turning up in your bedroom may be all right in foreign films, but even there they're scarcely credible. Otok, on two swigs of brandy, was not quite foreign enough.

'Thanks,' he said. 'I don't need any back-up.' He would make his own dispositions, not the General's.

It was a rude enough response, but he'd had an exhausting day. Seeing the hurt in her eyes, he had the grace to try again, this time with the hindsight of his Irish eloquence. 'Thank you for looking in,' he smiled. 'I've been well taken care of.'

When she'd gone, and she didn't go at once, he went downstairs and out into the damp starlight to search the island. He wasn't looking for Weiss's death. He was checking up on his own.

He found nothing at the end that held the rose bushes. He wasn't expecting to. There wasn't enough cover. Back at the table and benches, Constanz's perfume just lingered, in spite of a dew he watched dribble from mist banks rolling in from the water. Those Indian oils were tacky things. He must remember to stay away from them.

There were a thousand dead men in the tower. He stole in to them, to make sure they were still alone. Their bones did not stride forth and strangle him. He blessed them for their tolerance. Even to be alive in Weiss's company meant he was on the wrong side.

The bird did not complain this time. That was a bonus, because just beyond the tower he found what he was looking for.

18

There are two sorts of cover, natural and prepared. Matson had been trained to make his prepared cover look natural, to 'bamboozle the eye and not baffle it', as his instructor had said. When the eye is baffled it looks again.

The bushes beyond the tower were thick to the water's edge, but they 'let the mind through', again to quote his instructor in the Thugs. As he crouched to one side of the tower, he could sense the darkness steal through them, see rustlings of leaves less dark, and now, flat on his belly, detect the leaden shine of the lake beyond them.

Except for one place where the bushes were still only bushes, but grew as thick as a gun turret, as thick as a shed.

Matson breathed out and smelled brandy. He moved back a hundred yards, noting that the breeze blew against him, from the tower. This was good. He sipped lake water, but not enough to rattle in his gut, and forced himself to be sick. He paid back the fish for their total lack of excellence. He drank more water from a cleaner bit of lake. He breathed a lot of air through his open mouth. He breathed like an ancient serpent, drying his throat on air. The air, alas, was moist, and so was he, with dew.

Damp clothes chafe. They do not rustle. He bypassed the tower, and entered the bushes from a fresh direction, slipping branch from branch as deftly as a crochet needle. Then, in a place without leaves, he lay down.

There was nobody there. His nose told him that, his nose and then his ears. His brain followed. His brain had been wrong at Kocevje Gora, but his instinct had been for alarm. Tonight instinct felt as calm as his stomach without the fish.

On toe and elbow he inched towards what had baffled him. It was a hide of plaited branches, springy and still growing, but much too thick. It was entered front and back by two low crawlways. There was no one at home.

Matson sat inside it and made sure of his knife. He laid aside the stick he'd brought along in case he needed to lock off a windpipe or make, as a different instructor said, 'a capacious crater in an epigastrium'. He practised silent

297

breathing. He needed a lot of silent breath tonight. His nerves weren't what they were. Or did he mean his nerve?

Two RGD-5 anti-personnel grenades, two more unknowns with smoke vents, and four nasty phosphorus scorch-and-blinds such as the British army had withdrawn when it had last deployed his grandfather. These were wrapped in environmentally friendly oilcloth. He found them by sitting on them, not without damage to his peace of mind. He identified them by touch: he wasn't into grenades so he didn't know their types or countries of origin.

The guns were laced inside industrial polythene, the sort builders drape over roofs to keep out the moths. Two Kalashnikovs, no – honest mistake in the dark – two Czech VZ58V assault rifles. Two Beretta Model 12s. A pair of pistols, one Tokarev TT-33 and one Makarov. Assorted boxes of Togagypt 9, centre-fire 7.62 ball, and 9mm Para-bellum, presumably for the Beretta sub-machine gun. So what about the Makarov? Parabellum again? He'd never fired a Makarov, though it was a usual enough gun.

The temptations were enormous.

Meanwhile he was sitting on an arsenal of weapons suffi-cient to equip six villains; though he was willing to bet on only two of them.

19

He had to assume the weapons, and the painstakingly constructed hideaway, were nothing to do with Weiss's contingent from back home. There was no sign of the men on the island, and the predominance of Eastern Bloc weapons – this included the RGD-5 grenades – suggested not. They were good pieces, but even the excellent pair of Italian Beretta sub-machine guns had a proven terrorist pedi-gree; and he assumed the Rosental crowd would be armed with mainstream German firepower.

His instinct was to confiscate the armoury entire. Dismantling the enemy's dumps was a perfect principle of war: Fuller and Liddell-Hart were entirely in favour of it. This wasn't war, though. To leave it intact and keep watch

298

over it might provide him with the best intelligence, if he stayed alive long enough to use it.

The assassins were either going to pose as innocent visitors – shepherds again? – in which case they would have to pick up their arsenal, and might be intercepted by an attentive soul such as himself. Or, more likely, they intended to swim in.

The wrappings were lake-proof as well as weather-proof. They had probably been delivered by swimmers in the first place, rafted and pushed after dark, say.

It was only between landing stage and lawn that the crossing was near. From landing stage to the end of the island would be nearly half a mile. Pythagoras insisted on it. The landing stage was on a peninsula. The rest of the shore-line lay further back. He'd estimated the distance at six hundred yards when he'd first seen it, and he'd stick by that, in spite of being jolted by the truck and by Constanz.

They would need some pretty good kit for an underwater swim of that distance, so the betting must be they intended to arrive on the surface at night.

The comfortable way ahead, the cuckoo's way, would be for him to toss the grenades into the water (at the risk of eructations from the antique phosphorus) and borrow a gun or two for himself. He would sleep a lot more comfortably with one of the Berettas beside his bed and the Makarov under his pillow.

Unfortunately, he wasn't a cuckoo. He had to assume the nesting pair could count.

He stripped the guns and remade them, one by one. They were well maintained, but no automatic weapon can ever be quite as reliable as a revolver. He sabotaged them reluctantly but thoroughly.

He assumed the killers would check the actions when they were reunited with their weapons, so he left these ungritted and concentrated on the vents. They were wet enough with oil to accept dust gratefully. He sealed them, dug out the first millimetre of his dirty work with the peduncle of a leaf, then polished the external surfaces with his lovely new shirt, spoiling everything about equally.

This took a long time in the dark, but he was more at ease

with the underside of guns than of mermaids, so when dawn broke properly he saw that all was good. When they were fired, none of them would re-cock. They would each manage one shot, though. He hoped not at him.

20

He walked into the house, across the stone floor and up the wooden stairs. He smelled fish and oil-lamps and sleep. Constanz was reassuring Weiss, and the Obergruppenführer was merely profit-taking. Weiss had won a trick or two, but Weiss was Weiss. Women were part of his war game.

Matson looked into her empty bedroom. If his fingers itched for anything it was to have them snuggled round the comforting old-fashioned slide trigger of the Tokarev he'd left so reluctantly behind him.

When people stash up that kind of firepower, it's hard to resist the conclusion that they intend to blow everyone away.

The movement behind him startled him. He must take some vitamin B. Lili Weiss again, fully dressed this time. She looked awful, the way a truly beautiful woman can.

'You're a night animal, Mr Matson.'

'Someone's got to be. Your father-in-law is in deadly peril here.' He didn't tell her about the cache of arms. He didn't, on principle, tell anyone anything.

She followed him into his room. 'I had a lonely night,' she said.

'I had no night at all.'

She held her face to be kissed, the way a child inclines its head to be comforted.

After the excitement the testroglandin, the excess in the thigh.

He kissed her cheek, then her lips.

First the parachute jump, then the glitter. He owed Weiss several.

Lili had no scent. She was like a flint. No, flints smell. She was like a stone.

'No,' she said. She pronounced the word like an Australian, as if she was choking.

He pushed some of her clothing up, pulled some of it down. He mauled. At first he didn't think he mauled. She made him think it. So he mauled.

'That's enough for now,' she said. At least she didn't say 'no' any more. He didn't know whether the rest of her was grunts or German.

'A woman like you can be *terribly* weakening,' he whispered.

She glinted. Her smile was like a beer can under water. The image was good. It finished him entirely. He didn't think he'd earned himself an ally, and certainly not a friend.

21

Breakfast happened almost at once. The two women looked at each other in triumph. Weiss gazed upon him with uncharacteristic compassion.

TWENTY

1

Days begin after breakfast, especially days following nights that haven't ended.

Matson's day began with Weiss shouting. The man was outside and some distance away. He was shouting with his back turned, in slow and as-for-idiots Serbian. He was calling to someone, or to several someones, on the shore of the lake.

Decent of him not to shout in German, in spite of his insistence that the local population were to a man descended from the apex of his jackboots and trousers; but he could sound just as overbearing in Serbian, and with even more consonants.

Matson pottered around the downstairs room, examining the reading matter. He tried to understand what was going on. The replies were high-pitched and multiple, like gulls quarrelling for garbage; he could tell Weiss was getting nowhere with them, whatever they were.

Weiss came brusquely into the house. He wasn't pleased. He wasn't a man to lose his temper, so his displeasure hurt him.

'What's up, General? Your children growing disobedient?'

Weiss poured himself some coffee. 'There are no boats,' he said. 'I want a boat over here, *now*, and they tell me this friend of yours, this Popovic, has broken every boat on the lake.'

'Broken?'

'It does not take much to immobilize a wooden row-boat, Captain Matson. These people are fishermen, fish farmers at least, and they need their boats.'

'So do your enemies.'

'So do I.'

'I'd say Colonel Popovic was showing an admirable thoroughness, wouldn't you, General?'

Teutonic thoroughness was the phrase that sprang to mind. He hoped Popo wasn't merely being spiteful. He picked up his reading matter and took himself outside.

2

Anka had copies of Lolly's books. Not from Lippiat's hand or by his gift, but the Serbian originals of both volumes that had sunk in the Yugo.

Matson sat with them away from the sunshine. He had read them closely in English. Now he intended to use his memory of them to improve his Serbo-Croat.

There was also a 1:25 000 map of the terrain for ten miles about. He spread this first, using the books for table weights, and began to do his homework.

The map was a two-metre fold-out of divided card on cloth, overprinted with an artillery grid. A remarkable number of its squares were empty. Each of them proclaimed a kilometre-sided slab of nothing. Unfortunately, the landscape in front of his eyes consisted of kilometre squares of crag and tangle, backed by chutes of snow and the occasional windy glacis of ice. He saw dark escarpments, black vegetation and white scree beneath an egg yolk of yellow sunshine topped by a glittering migraine of frost. Cézanne had painted it with bird lime on his palette and a bad hangover, and some of it had dripped off the canvas.

Back on the map, even the empty squares had contour lines. These were big, bold and erotic. They flowed wetly and wildly from some junior cartographer's dream, and owed nothing to stadia rod or theodolite.

Matson used the peaks as datums and drew his own map. Like the other, it was full of nothing, but it was a nothing he could see, a nothing he could remember and rely on. Ravines and watercourses were matters he could only guess at, so he didn't. This only took him a minute or two. Then he reached for a book.

303

'Ah, Hauptmann. You're planning to run out on me? You'll need to swim, then.' Weiss didn't want to be unangry alone.

'I may yet need to retreat, General. Or to liaise more closely with Colonel Popovic. As you yourself should. I found a substantial arsenal of weapons in your shrubbery last night.'

'Disregard it. I did.'

Matson offered him a face. It belonged to his grand-mother.

'My nights are for other things.'

Matson's face persisted.

'I didn't even look for it, I confess. I reason like this. If anyone is intent on killing me after forty years, they will do it from among those trees on the shoreline over there.'

'Revenge has its flavour, Weiss. It needs to be tasted on a short spoon. I forget who said it, but you'll recognize the sentiment.' He stood and stopped the old man by catching his sleeve. 'I sat with those weapons for three or four hours. I took them apart. I put them together. I treated them to a certain amount of cautious sabotage and a great deal of thought.'

'And to my daughter-in-law, what did you say to her?'

'Nothing. These people might not want to kill you. Or not at once. Not right out. They may intend to seize you. They may plan to hold a trial. They might want something neither of us can guess at.'

'Guess on, Hauptmann. You're writing quite a story.' He gave Matson the whole of his attention now.

'They may intend to extort money, or demand the return of the island.'

'Somewhere in the first of your words, perhaps.' He turned, and was determined to take Matson with him. 'These fools who planted the guns – they may begin in a minute. They may take days. It may be never. Whatever it is, the hours must be passed.' He smiled. 'What do you do when you've been with a woman, Captain Matson?' He let Matson savour the moment. 'I always go for a swim. Even your Wellington could not fornicate all the time.'

'Not while he was on horseback.'

'What shall we do with this brace of females, then?'

'I think we should pick them some flowers. "Brace", General? Isn't the Serbian lady Anka one of yours as well?'

'She closed her legs. As I've said before, such a gesture should be respected.'

3

Matson did not consider that Weiss, at his age, had a nerve to strip off and go for a swim. He thought that anyone, at any age, had a nerve to strip off. As for swimming, Matson had seen enough of that recently.

Weiss didn't look bad for a man of seventy. Old men without flesh generally look presentable. A bit like skeletons, perhaps; but no one quarrels with skeletons. Weiss himself had known plenty, and one of Matson's own discoveries in the last twenty-four hours was that the thousand sets of bones in that tower belonged to the only people on the island he could really trust.

Weiss didn't have buttocks. He had a skinniness and a something less. He had a buttockless left profile. His right profile was an aberration, gluteally speaking. Presumably that sniper's bullet in Belgrade had removed quite a lot of him. Shot in the backside is even more of a joke than shot in the foot. Shot anywhere is pretty awful. Matson knew.

'Ah, Hauptmann. You're admiring my demotion? From Panzer commander to commander of Prinz Eugen.'

'I didn't know you felt like that.'

'The Reich was a great unit. The greatest.'

'I never met it. I got shot in the backside once myself. It's an unsavoury story. I was shot by a diplomat who was defending two naked women.'

'You turned your back out of *délicatesse*?'

'I dived under his gun.'

'What happened to him?'

'He needed a face-lift.'

Matson found himself swimming with Weiss in spite of his best intentions.

305

4

Jezero was cold and threatening. It had been fed by so many slabs of ice it felt like the water from a glacier.

Once they were in, Weiss said. 'There are scars on your back. Whips, I think.'

'I was a felon, Weiss.'

'Where? No, that's intrusive. Tell me about your leg.'

'I lost a chunk of calf muscle.'

'Mercury in the bullet?'

'A penknife on the jacketing more like.'

'Where?'

'Somewhere people were shooting.'

'You're a secret one, Matson. I shall call you Patrick. I could trust you.'

'In these limited circumstances.'

'You wouldn't stand back.'

'Like yourself, I'm trained not to.'

'You might stand forward on the other side?'

'I certainly might.'

'I can trust a man who says that.'

This came with a deal of shivering and shouting, and an ache in the jawbone always dulls the hearing.

Neither of them saw the motor boat until it almost hit them.

5

Matson's first thought was, *God, I go swimming, only to dive straight into a plot to attack me in the water.* This would represent a considerable coincidence, but sleepless nights are full of them.

By this time the boat had missed him, thrashed its screws into reverse, rammed the lawn, then powered itself backwards and properly afloat again. The frothed-up dirty water looked as ugly as canned ale. He had already recognised Popovic in the stern, so could be forgiven the domestic metaphor.

Popovic wasn't pleased. He was surrounded by unfamiliar

uniforms – from below the froth line they looked an unlikely combination of police and navy – and he intended to be in control of them as well as insist that at least one of them was in control of the boat. He did not apologize to Matson or to Weiss. The ugly truth was probably that neither of them had been noticed in the water: the pilot had only spotted the island itself at the last moment before holing it amidships.

Popovic eased away at half astern, then took his new command round the inshore waters of Otok in a slow anti-clockwise circuit of inspection, no doubt intending to arrive properly when he had re-established good military order and discipline.

Matson and Weiss were now nearly ashore, wading knee deep in muddy water, then calf-deep in watery mud. Matson wasn't bashful, but his nudity was suffering from the chill factor, so he was glad to see Popo had left his women behind.

'Ha! Ha! Ha!' They had Constanz instead. 'Mandrake and the angle worm, guess which is which.' Constanz laughing in inverted commas from inside the house, Constanz running outside and hooting freely and frankly without punctuation mark at the miracle of her own wit and the wonders of God's invention. '"Weary Willy and Tired Tim", or was it' – she strode closer, pulling Lotte after her by an odd limb or so – 'or was it, is it, "Weeny Willy and Tiny Tim"?'

Matson was relieved her camera had drowned in the Yugo. The General dressed at speed, and had just got his boots laced when Popovic arrived at the landing stage for the second time.

6

Popovic disembarked and saluted. This was impressive.

'*Gospodine* Weiss,' he said to the General, stripping him of rank.

'*Gospodo* Weiss,' he offered to Lotte, making the native point.

'*Draga gospodico* Ehrenberg-Zanetti.' This was cheeky, since Constanz was at least a widow. Matson wasn't sure about the vocatives, either. Weren't they a shade too formal, in speech nowadays? He must ask Anka. '*Vrhovni zapovjed-niki* Matson.' God knows what that meant, but it was bound to be excessive.

'You have broken the row-boats,' Weiss said.

'A plank in each. And I paid.'

'I use those boats as ferries.'

'*Dragi drugi* Weiss –'

'I am *not* your dear comrade.' Weiss didn't like being nettled, but he clearly was.

'*Dragi drugi*, tomorrow two naval speedboats are being brought up from the coast, by lorry. At set hours of the day, one of them will be at your disposal if you will only make a small contribution for the gas oil, the diesel. For the moment' – he gestured towards the partially moored pleasure craft with its three sailors and four policemen standing approximately to attention – 'for the moment, there is only one powerboat on the lake, *gospodine* Weiss.'

'I know. I am negotiating its purchase.'

'Alas, no longer. It now belongs to ... well, never mind that, *drugi*. In effect I own it for the duration of your stay.'

'Then I shall have to arrange something else.'

'My ambition, General, is to frustrate you in everything. I have the will. I have the power.' His cough was modest. 'I almost have the ability.' He smirked, but it was an expression not without tinges of melancholy. 'No one official is going to say this to you, Obergruppenführer, no one from the Ministry of the Interior; so you'll have to take it as from one old soldier to another. Go back to Austria. Leave now. Leave this minute, and I'll guarantee to protect you.'

'Unthinkable. This island –'

'This island will bury you, my dear.' His eyebrows offered Weiss the chance to reject this further endearment. 'A wise man would know that and be content to leave such a place to the enjoyment of his grandson.' He clapped his hands and the policemen disembarked from the boat. 'I shall now search Otok.'

'By whose leave, Colonel Popovic?'

'By mine own, *drugi*.'

'You will need some sort of warrant.'

'I write the warrants in such matters, *drugi* Weiss.'

308

This went beyond Popo's usual hyperbole, but any examination of it was interrupted by Anka's arrival with coffee, iced water and biscuits of rice and caramel, enough for policemen, sailors, all Yugoslavs, both Germans, Constanz and Matson, this without the least hint of permission from Weiss whatsoever.

7

Popovic was one for the revenge of the short spoon. Matson hoped Weiss would take note of the fact. Before inspecting the island, the Colonel used his glove to dust the Nazi's shirt free of biscuit crumbs. He said mildly, 'Yugoslavia was created by a benevolent despot, *drugi*. The despotism persists. It is all around you. I am sure you will not waste your time disputing the fact. The benevolence is limited in your case, and lies entirely within my gift. I am playing the reluctant policeman in what is, even now, a police state.'

Weiss gave no appearance of listening.

'So, *dragi* Hendrik, since you are merely a civilian, have the good sense not any more to piss me about.'

Popovic led Matson to one side, decided he had not done quite enough, and returned. 'If you do, you will swim ashore for your provisions, my dear. And for your funeral.' He stood back to admire the white blots that drained the colour from Weiss's cheekbones. 'You're a skinny man, Herr Weiss. I doubt if your corpse will float.'

To Matson he murmured, 'And dead he will assuredly be. Unless we get our act together, the pair of us.'

'You've frightened the ladies, Popo.'

'So long as I've frightened someone. Something bad will undoubtedly happen here by tonight at the latest.'

'At the earliest.'

'Then it will happen tonight, my dear.' He listened to Matson's reasoning about the cache of weapons, and said moodily, 'Yes, they will swim, and it will be after tonight's moon, say midnight or later, and it will be brutish.'

'Why not some other night? Why shouldn't they prefer to fray the old man's nerves a bit?'

309

'Because of my good news and my bad news, my dear. Most of my good news and some of my bad news.'

They stood by the tower of skulls. By daylight it was a much nastier monument to cruelty and to Weiss than the one at Nis was to the black Turkish Pasha.

Popo looked at it and shrugged. 'They ask us why we don't forget.'

They approached the hide in the branches. 'My good news, Patrick, is what I told the General – namely that I shall have two more boats on the lake, and a battery of search-lights. A battery sounds impressive. As you know, it means two. Still, Otok will be floodlit. Part of the bad news is that neither boats nor fighting lights will be in place until tomorrow night. Whereas I requested them, from London, as soon as I knew I had this assignment.'

'Still the establishment plot? Is that what tonight's timing rests on?'

'It rests upon various parts of the remainder of my bad news. Even without which –' he examined the outside of the hide. 'I see nothing to suggest these people are amateurs, do you? ... Even without my news there is the moon, my dear. It rises later each afternoon; it sets later each night. It approaches full. In a night or two we shall have moonlight until sunrise. I should expect such people to take account of this simple matter, wouldn't you? Fishermen plan for such things. So do thieves and even soldiers.'

By daylight it was possible to part the branches of the hide without crawling into it.

'You should have hidden yourself one of those Berettas. You should have taken a Beretta and be damned to me, Patrick. If they get to the Obershitbag, I want you to promise me you'll stand well back.'

'I'm breaking his bread and drinking his wine.'

'"When time flies with bullets in her beak, lead is all she can eat".'

'An old Serbian saying?'

'Irish, Patrick. The doctor has left me.'

'Is that bad news?'

'The worst. It was he who alerted me to the true nature of my problem. I only rounded him up for duty, the day you arrived in Belgrade. He laughed and advised me to go sick. Very, very sick. Incontrovertibly sick. He offered me a needle full of meningitis, the lesser strain, but an illness of undoubted gravity.'

'So *that* is your evidence.'

'That old man knows the real scene, and he knows I cannot win. Now I have him against me, even as I have your Mr Lippiat, and everything they represent.' He whistled, with fingers in his mouth, for his policemen to remove the arms cache.

'Tell them to be careful with those gas canisters, Popo. I don't believe the labels any more than you do, but I could be wrong.'

Two pressurized steel bottles, each looking like fire-extinguishers, one painted yellow, one black, each with red bands and the international skull and crossbones marking for danger, both with the black-on-orange cross for lethal toxicity.

One was stencilled with the letters $(CICH_2CH_2)_2S$ for mustard gas; the other $CICH:CHA5A12$, for Lewisite. Time-honoured killers both.

Matson watched two policemen pick them very gingerly to their tunics and handle them blanch-faced to the boat. He didn't believe anyone could obtain such gases in a laboratory pressure-bottle instead of in weapons form. And if they could, he didn't see how they could hope to use the stuff.

He said this to Popovic several times, and Popovic said it back to him. What he didn't say was that neither canister had been there last night.

8

The removal of the arsenal to the powerboat left Lotte agitated and Constanz unusually thoughtful. Weiss demonstrated his interest in the details of his assassination by looking bored. The child ran in circles through the shrubbery, exactly as he had done on the mountain top. This time there were no butterflies to chase. He saw circles so he ran them. Pursuing the invisible soon made him tired. Anka was more successful. She seemed to have disappeared.

311

Popovic had his policemen take an inventory of the firearms. He made them log the weapon numbers. He insisted every man in the boat witness and sign the list, including the sailors. Matson found that odd.

To Lotte Popovic said, 'Tell your nurse not to let your child run in the bushes. They are full of snakes at this time of the year. Early snakes are poisonous.'

Lotte shrieked.

'That was a lie,' he explained to Matson. 'But the Obershitbag must keep his party in some sort of order. His ego has taken charge of his common sense.'

'Right.'

'As for yourself, you cannot trust any of these people here, *any* of them. You are the only onion that does not belong in their soup, Patrick. Why should they not toss you straight in the fire?'

Popovic wasn't a sailor. He got his shoes wet. But he boarded and told his crew to cast off. He didn't salute. He backed the boat slowly into really deep water, then turned it to patrol the lake.

As they turned, he tossed the guns overboard one by one: two pistols, two subs, two assault carbines. He did this himself, to make sure they didn't stick in the hand. The bombs and the gas didn't worry him, any more than they had Matson, so he didn't pollute the lake with them.

He was a fine one to talk about trust. He clearly couldn't trust his own headquarters staff to prevent their booty from being recycled in the enemy's direction.

9

Matson knew he was foolish not to retain a weapon. He had felt naked this trip. The trouble was he had nothing against the people who wanted to kill Weiss. Not yet, he hadn't. And to be effective in these circumstances he would have to strike early, against people who hadn't declared their hand.

He could be too early or a long way too late. So what role did he envisage for himself if he chose to inhabit the time in between? Was he proposing to play umpire, peace-maker, or Hendrik Reinhard Weiss's bullet-proof vest?

Hendrik junior was lying in the shrubbery when Lotte found him. He hadn't been bitten by one of Popovic's imaginary serpents. He was asleep.

Matson watched his mother gather him in her arms and asked the world, 'Why does the lad sleep so much?'

'He's dying,' Lotte said. She hurried him past as if somewhere upstairs she could wind him up.

'She's mad,' Constanz offered.

'Was dying,' Weiss conceded. 'But this expedition is curing him.'

'Bullshit.'

'The old man blew life into him. You saw that dervish blow life into him.'

'I was blindfolded. What I saw otherwise was a lot of unhygienic activity.'

Weiss grunted and followed after his grandson, but he smiled at Constanz in passing.

Matson turned to her. 'Leukaemia?'

'I doubt. I don't think he's ill. He was active enough in Austria, and there was never any mention of a doctor. She drugs him.'

'You reckon?'

'Only for this trip. Not booze. One of those narcotic elixirs for kids. They aren't allowed in the States. She's scared out of her wits for him. She wants him in check.'

'Laudanum?'

'Not pink gin anyway.' She favoured Matson with a kiss. 'Stay in line, gingernuts, and don't be jealous. This is one story I'm going to cover from really close to.'

Matson had identified the principal villains now. He still didn't know what the villainy would be.

10

Sleep was becoming a deep necessity. He excused himself from lunch, which looked like being another Weiss lecture anyway, and went upstairs.

313

He undressed and washed himself in the bedroom basin. The water was cold, but it was better than the lake. The swim had been bracing, but fish water and the mud from Popovic's propellers would have coated his skin in enough micro-organisms to breed odour by moonset. Men who hunt in the dark must smell only of starlight.

He retaped the kitchen knife to his leg and lay naked under a duvet and a giant fur. It looked like bleached bear. He heard Weiss lecture Constanz. He heard Constanz's scoffing laugh. He heard Weiss scold her, and Constanz laugh again. He heard Weiss's tongue go strutting on and on, this time in German. She no longer interrupted. The game was being played according to the General's rules and in Constanz's half.

He dozed, then woke to hear them coming upstairs. They went into a room, he thought the General's, and shut the door. He hoped she'd remembered her notebook, then realised that even that was sunk in the Yugo. He experienced a moment's sympathy so deep that he drifted off again.

He slept until Lotte Weiss came into the room. She neither woke him nor let him be. She pulled the covers from his face and cried on him.

Tears are always attractive, even when they hit your face from a great height, but sobs are never very private. He pulled her quickly into bed to shut her up. She didn't argue. She had been here before.

She was, he decided, quite mad. Lost inside stress or mania. Her lips tasted odd and her cheeks smelled of her son's face flannel, but she knew about naked men, all the way down to the knives on their legs. All the way there and back.

When he was a boy Matson used to play in Myatt's Fields Park. There was a statue there, a statue rather like Lotte Weiss. It was called Androgyna or Hermaphrodite. The name was the product of his adult self, pretending to remember it as he lay in bed while Lotte undressed beneath the covers with a sound like newspapers tearing. The statue had been sculpted in stone or cast in cement, weather-coarsened stone or pimply cement. It had long hair, blind eyes and a woman's breasts, and its mind was on other things. It once had, allegedly, a fig leaf, this to conceal the primary sex between the legs or disguise the fact that there was no sex there. The fig leaf probably hovered on an illusion, the illusion that young trendies now call 'ambiguous gender', thus misusing two more words in their parents' language. The fig leaf stood proud of the body, or perhaps what the fig leaf concealed stood proud. So this nether and composite appendage, which was missing, had been fashioned separately and fastened to the main stone or concrete of the lower abdomen with a metal pin. Androgyna, once jewelled in every hole (or pinned, at least) had, in Bob Cherry's immortal phrase, been reduced to the lesser platonic order of 'jewels now missing, holes still there'.

Many a small boy boasted he'd fucked Androgyna. Boasted and lied.

Being with Lotte, even when she was naked as a Lily, was worse than being with that statue. At least the statue was serene.

'The bitch,' she said. She sobbed some further insults in German.

Matson did not ask who she meant.

She found the scar in Matson's buttock, the bullet-torn tissue in his calf, and became briefly excited. It wasn't a big excitement, what with his need for a fortnight's sleep, but they were able to push their barge out on the flood.

She pretended the sleep of satiety while he pretended to look at the ceiling. The ceiling was ancient and dark. Now he knew what it was like with that statue.

Didn't Carew have a word for this? Probably. Ovid did. Poets are such indelicate bastards.

11

'Your Colonel Popovic thinks tonight will be rowdy.'

Weiss skipped a stone halfway across the water, skimming it flat-armed and with a young man's vigour. 'What do you think?'

'It will be at night. He believes not later than tonight.' Matson did not compete with the stone. 'I found his reasons persuasive. Tonight there will be an early moon, followed by a long dark.'

'So what do you suggest, Patrick?'

'Supper while we may. Only one lamp above and below, so you can douse them quickly. After that, you inside with your pistol to protect yourself and the rest of them.'

'You?'

'Outside. We'll arrange a signal. I don't want you shooting at me when I return.'

'Can you throw that knife Lotte says you stole from the kitchen?'

'I'll work close.'

'Why don't we all hide out here?'

'Too big a party. They'll have glasses. They'll be watching us.'

'I don't like fighting from houses.'

'It'll be a hard house to get into. A hard house to burn, provided those oil lamps are left empty.'

'We shall eat by candlelight.'

'I believe you're enjoying yourself, General.'

'I know *you* are.'

They turned back towards the house and met Anka. She was carrying a bundle of wood. 'Fire,' she explained to Matson. She ignored Weiss. 'We cook everything here by wood.'

'You should try gas,' he advised.

12

'My death,' Weiss chuckled and raised his glass. It held some kind of local firewater, *mastika* or *vinjak*. He touched Matson's, which held wine diluted by the tap. The women hadn't come down yet, so he added, 'My death promises to be an interesting evening.'

The fire was small, as Matson had insisted. He couldn't tell if it was hot. His blood was deoxygenated through lack of sleep. As for Weiss, it wasn't quite that elderly men are low on corpuscles, because this one probably wasn't. He had ordered fire, and he proposed to enjoy it, even if it turned out to be too hot to bear.

316

Weiss wore an ordinary dinner-jacket and black tie. Matson knew the General regretted not having any mess kit on Otok, but guessed he wouldn't wear it anyway. Not because he was timid, still less ashamed. He was ashamed of nothing. Simply because he would have thought the gesture vulgar.

Not the uniform, which was sacred. The act of putting it on among women and Matson in a shirt but no jacket. A dark shirt, folded and slept on, and buttoned tight at the neck.

Anka had been cleaning the silver with soot from the fireplace. Weiss watched her lay the table, and said, 'The Slavs had to go, without doubt.'

'To be killed, you mean?'

'To be killed or to rush headlong into the sea. There are many Slavs and not much sea, so – yes – there had to be a deal of killing.'

'And you liked that?'

'Rather less than you seem to enjoy interrupting me, Patrick. I dislike its smell, I dislike its mess. I dislike its pain. More than anything I dislike its pain. Do you think we are monsters? But the SS, as I say, does the work. A man does his own killing, even so. A civil servant lifts a phone or signs a paper. A man gets on with it.' He lost himself for a second. 'A man gets on with his life in the certain knowledge that one day his death will get on with him.'

Matson added more water to his wine. Weiss wasn't a fanatic – perhaps none of them was. He was a man whose soundness could only be defined in terms of disease. His body wasn't youthful. It was merely not old. He wasn't sane. He was unmad. The morbid frontiers were irrelevant in his case.

'I used to call them dogs, but they're not that.' Weiss crossed the room and examined Peter Zarkovic's death warrant framed on the wall. 'The Slavs are an inferior warrior breed that had to move over.' He smiled at Anka. 'A man who rushes at you brandishing his spear must expect to be carried away on his shield. The Spartans knew that. They inherited our culture.'

'Your thinking is too fast for me there, General.'

317

'I began life as an officer of panzers, Patrick. Not as a pedestrian.'

Anka came back round the table to set glasses by the silver, and his hand rested on her thigh.

She smiled, not at him, not at Matson, but through the wall.

13

'The Slavonic women should have been put to a better use by us, Patrick.' He took his hand from her body, and his hand looked sad. 'We should have used them to breed warriors, not slaves. As I did myself.' He held out his glass, and she filled it for him. She leant over him slowly, as if this was the last time so let it take for ever, as if she was driving a nail into his head.

Weiss seemed pleased by her closeness.

'You don't believe in brothels, then?' Matson remembered his prison in Graz, and reminded Weiss of it.

'Yes. I sometimes went there. I had a friend who was there for a time. It wasn't a brothel. It was a place for officers to keep their ladies. As for the so-called slave brothels, and the houses of experiment – sex is a complete process.' He shuddered. 'If you cannot see birth in a woman's eye –'

'And death?'

'Death, too. But what a woman begins in her bed should be ended with a sword in the field. Not with a scalpel and a bottle of ether in some back room.'

His smile irritated Matson, but only because of its assumptions. That's when the death camps begin, he thought, in assumptions of privilege. Once you think you're privileged, the fox and the farm girl and the screaming in the gas chambers, they're all the bloody same; and the decisions are for you. He got his backside against the fire again. Matson mustn't grow short-tempered with a man intent on dying.

'Do you know how many divisions the Americans had in the field, Patrick?'

'In Europe?'

'World-wide. Forty-two. And the British Empire? Forty-

318

three. Smaller divisions, but a piece of pride for you. Be proud for a moment, and then I want you to contemplate a gigantic multinational war machine mustering some eighty divisions. Eighty.'

'I boggle at it.'

'Then you boggle at us. Do you know how many divisions we had to deploy in Serbia and Hercegovinia alone to hold the partisans in check and stop this miserable nation of barbarians from disrupting our lines of communication and threatening our entire right flank?'

'You know he is deeply ignorant of such matters, Henk.'

Constanz had come on to the scene, as drunk as she often pretended, yet as elegant as if she were flying on the plumes of her breath.

'Fifteen. Tito's ruffians tied up fifteen frontline German infantry divisions, nearly one fifth of our war machine. If only we could have used those fifteen divisions against Russia or in Western Europe.'

'Bully for Tito, Henk.' She was, Matson hoped, joking.

Weiss had gone beyond Constanz. His mind was homing on Anka again. 'I only shot prisoners because we would have needed another five divisions to guard the men we captured in this part of the war.' He still made absolute love. He reminded them why they were widows.

'So what did you do to the Jews, Henk? Did I tell you I was a Jew?' Constanz held out her glass to Matson. He filled it up with water.

'Personally, I did nothing. They're a people, you see, like us. And, like the SS, they are also a religion.'

Either the words stopped Constanz, or the water.

'I kept a rabbi once.' Weiss spoke as one might say rabbit or dog. 'Someone was supposed to shoot him, but I stepped in. I was always stepping in.' Another thunder of modesty. 'I kept him to explain his people to me, and their beliefs. He wanted to be out with his own kind. Said he had things to do. I told him I would guarantee his life. He continued to insist he had better things to do. I said he could be certain of my protection for as many days as he would diligently attempt to convert me. Do you know what he answered? He said Judaism was not a proselytizing religion, and even if it were

319

my conversion would not be high enough among the prioirties of his people for it to occupy any of his attention.'

'So you shot him?' Nice of Constanz to take up the questioning.

'No. He's alive. I don't think he ever forgave me for keeping him alive, but he's alive. I'e seen transcripts of various of the dozens of sworn depositions he has lodged against me, in Austria, in the United States, in Israel. Such people are vengeful, and so is their God.'

'And was your God a forgiving one?'

'Which God is that?'

'Didn't you swear allegiance to Adolf Hitler? You spoke of commandments.'

'I swore, yes.'

'And isn't he dead?'

'Certainly not.' He stepped away from the fire to look through the window and across the darkening water. 'The Führer is alive, here.' He was facing Matson now, not Constanz, his right palm flat against the pocket in his jacket where most men keep their hearts.

Lotte came in. She was wearing the silly dress Matson remembered from Kocevje Gora. 'Little Henk is asleep,' she said. 'I thought you'd be finished by now.'

320

TWENTY-ONE

1

They sat formally, Hendrik Reinhard Weiss at the head of the table, Lotte Weiss at the foot. The General had the windows and the doors to his left, and Matson to his right, facing them. Constanz was across from Matson, with her back to the danger. Save there wasn't any danger, not yet. Danger's hands were tied by the clock and the almanac to the sinking moon. They sat a long way apart.

They heard the motor boat circle the island, turn away up the lake, come back again. Popovic was doing his bit, or having someone do it for him. The boat had a spotlight, Matson remembered. If Popovic kept it on station, or at least the threat of it, then it would be a powerful disincentive to violence.

He wondered at Popo's pessimism. It had been the same in Belgrade. Did the old jester really think he was beaten? Or was he like many another soldier – buoyant over the sherry glass, less confident when the blood was carved?

Weiss wasn't a cocktail commander, Matson gave him that. There were men out there, and women, who were proposing to have his head for breakfast. Except for an interval of water and the seven shots in his pistol the odds were on their side. Yet Weiss sat disguised in total calm and amused his intellect by considering how they proposed to get it.

Matson had to admire the old murderer. He had integrity. His was an evil that refused to hide its face, still less excuse itself. Brutishness apart, he was one of those quintessential military intelligences that exults over the perfectly executed flanker and disregards the corpses it strews in its wake and the villages burning.

321

The gunshot was single and distant. It sounded through the doorway directly opposite Matson, but from the far side of the lake. It was throaty-muzzled, a baritone of a gun.

'A fowling piece,' Weiss said.

But a signal, Matson thought. *There have been no hunters up here. Popo has stopped that.*

They heard the boat turn to investigate, this within the space of two or three seconds.

Constanz cried out. She didn't scream. She put her hand up slowly to the back of her neck. The rest of the discharge spread itself out to hiss among the bushes, and ping against the window.

It would take heavy gauge shot and a high angle to reach this far. Possibly a hand load as well.

Weiss walked round the table to gaze at Constanz's back. Constanz looked at the blood on her hand. She laughed.

It wasn't one of Constanz's more pleasant laughs, but it was easier to live with than Lotte's nasal shriek. Lotte threw back her head, with cheeks pinched in and nostrils flared, and made a noise as if she expected to be dead.

2

The shot was lodged in Constanz's neck between tendon and surface bone, a bloodied lump trapped by her skin, about a third of the size of a salted peanut.

Weiss snuffed it free and held it against a candle flame. 'Bigger than buck, and no good for bird,' he considered. 'I'd say pig, wouldn't you, Patrick?' Removing the pellet had hurt Constanz, but that was in accord with his scheme of things.

'I'd say you'd better go home, Weiss, as Colonel Popovic advises.'

'Well, the gun has fired. We can sniff the powder.'

Weiss anointed Constanz's neck with brandy. This second pain stopped her hysteria. 'Antiseptic,' he explained. 'And sweeter than that other filth you're wearing.' He smacked Lotte back-handed on the mouth. It was a better gag than brandy. He kissed her to make it better.

'I think we should live somewhere else,' she mumbled.

Weiss resumed his seat, and gestured to Matson to do the same. 'Remarkable that,' he observed. 'First the detonation, then the strike of shot. Like a *minenwerfer* or a field piece. The trajectory is so high and slow you can actually hear your fate discharged before Nemesis hits you.'

Matson thought of the other rifles they had encountered this trip, the ones with flat trajectories that would scarcely be subsonic at this distance. What made him and Weiss so sure that a sniper's bullet wouldn't come their way? Especially now Popovic had destroyed the weapon cache and their other teeth were drawn?

A sniper's bullet through the door would have smashed Constanz's head and killed Matson with the pieces.

The motor boat circled on station. Popovic, or its current commander, wouldn't realize the shot had been directed against the house. Matson wondered whether to go and signal it. Weiss had done nothing about signals. Nor had Popo. Yet Otok was without radio or telephone.

'And if I do not choose to run, Patrick?'

'Then we sit it out until they show their hand.'

'My instinct is always to make something happen. Stones are forever falling from the high tower. In battle the choice is between being up there pushing them down, or underneath and having them smash your head.'

'We can always go away,' Lotte said.

'There are other towers, my dear. Some of them we don't see. Their stones are real, just the same.'

Lotte nodded, and decided to go mad again. She opened her bag and began crocheting. That is, she took out her hook and her knife and her ball of thread, and used them to tie knots with lots of air in them.

3

Meanwhile they ate meat. They had marinaded wild pig, a dish that Anka cooked exquisitely. Was this because Weiss had suggested it to her, or because it was her Lippiat's preferred meal for Nazi commanders shortly to be dead?

Weiss smiled and raised his glass, 'I'll give you ghosts,' he said. 'Ghosts of people not yet dead. Friends long since underground – life has a lot of those.'

Matson took wine without water, and looked for Anka to drink to that one. She wasn't there.

Jezero was without its motor boat now. And, much too early, it was minus the moon.

They stopped breaking bread. They no longer ate pig.

Behind Constanz's back the waters caught fire and blurred Matson's retinas with inverted flame. Otok glowed pink, glowed red, then was smothered in black. The flame had been doused, and with it the stars.

The flame was a mistake. The burning was what mattered. The burning had been going on for some time, at a well-considered angle in a clearing in the trees.

Burning makes smoke which, with the addition of diesel, thickens into towers, and the towers rise up to blot out the light.

4

The smoke curtained off the lake from the pathway of the moon. It drooped across Otok with a smell of smouldering vehicles, sour oil, singed tyres, then the sweeter forest-flavour of resinous woods.

'Like an aircraft going in.' Weiss poured more wine. 'They start early.' He sniffed appreciatively. 'No. Not like an aircraft. Nor a tank. No flesh.' He hadn't produced his pistol yet. He went back to the pork. Matson's place was to be outside, he thought, via the back door. He hadn't reckoned on taking up his station in such a hurry.

He heard the squealing first. They all did. He felt the footsteps. Felt them run across the turf, felt them jar the flag-stones and vibrate through the chair into the bones of his back. Someone running fast. He still faced the door, but it had grown too dark. He dropped his hand to his leg and reached for the knife.

Weiss chuckled and slid the carver to him, gliding it along the table as if he'd been asked to pass it and was too drunk to

324

bother. Matson watched his own hand touch its handle, then rest.

Snapshots only. He saw Weiss's chuckle. He could not hear it. He heard squealing, felt footsteps. He saw Constanz's startled eyes, the blood which oozed round the front of her neck, not by itself but in a spread of sweat, the squealing was so shrill. Inside it Lotte was crocheting, building holes in bits of thread with knife and needle, marlin and hook. She was scared out of her teeth, his nymphomaniac nut, but not out of her middle-European social graces. Death must go on. The squealing was all.

An amplified screech like the tuned-up cry of a bat, now stationary outside the door.

Anka had not been seen since she'd served the pig. Now she made her entrance.

A basket, another damned basket. The basket held the screech, the basket was the screech. And the basket grew louder. She carried it in, head held high. She served it with more reverence than she'd served the pig. She served it with a glint of triumph as well. She set down the squeal before the Obergruppenführer as fastidiously as if she were bringing him a bomb. Then she clasped her hands and stood back. She was praying for the finish, the explosion, the silence.

The rat was white, presumably bred for captivity. It was crucified in its basket. Tied outstretched with fine wire that had been twisted so tight it almost severed its outstretched limbs. In the way of rats the animal had tried to get free by cutting through one of its own front paws with its teeth.

'White,' Anka explained.

'Weiss,' Lotte hissed.

Constanz dabbed her blood in silence.

The crucifixion was a convenience. There was no other way a live rat could be presented.

He thrashed and frothed, spitting blood.

They supposed 'he'. Whatever its sex the rat's genitalia had been excised from its loins in a wedge-shaped slice. The cuts were scalpel sharp. The flesh gaped open in an unstitched T.

No more squeaks. Weiss had been decisive with the carving fork.

325

'Ever merciful.' It was Anka who spoke the commentary.

'Now set that one on fire.' Constanz at last.

Weiss didn't hear. He held a cylinder of paper between finger and finger. It had slid from underneath the mess. He unwrapped its tracery of blood.

Not paper. Card. It was loud in the silence.

'Henk!' he said. He shouted his grandson's name, then again. He swore, leapt clear of the table and started upstairs.

Matson's back grew chill. The child was the target, not the man. The child would pay the dues of the man.

A morsel of warning, castrated in its basket. Now this threat to a dopey little boy.

5

Weiss like a bull upstairs, hammering about on the wooden floors.

No, not a bull, a man. Throwing open doors, wrenching hasps off cupboards, chests. Trampling linen, dead papers, cobwebs, shoes, till the top of his house held no secrets. The child was gone.

Matson found the note on the lad's empty bed. Weiss was beyond finding notes. His rage sought flesh or nothing.

It was useless to Matson. Useless to Lotte. Constanz stayed downstairs. It was written in Cyrillic if not Glagolitic. They intended Weiss to choke on their past to the last sacred stone.

Weiss took it and calmed himself. He made an effort and read it. 'We have time,' he said. He knew.

Matson looked for explanations.

'Orders in ten minutes,' Weiss said. 'My orders group downstairs. First we'll search the island.'

'No orders, Weiss. Council of war. And I'll search the island. You stay inside. They'll have calculated you'll go blundering about in the smoke.'

Weiss howled. No longer in grief, nor in rage. He was psyched up for the charge. His life had been a charge. Now he must make another one. He howled his way downstairs, checking his pistol.

326

He heard Matson at last. There was nowhere to charge. This time it was personal, but there was only frustration. He shut his mouth and his mind, and held the pistol out to Matson.

'Keep it,' Matson said. 'You're still the target.'

'No, not me.' He wanted it to be him, but they'd got to the boy. He shouted again.

'How are you going to hush the old stud? Slap him one, for Christ's sake.'

Matson touched Consanz's cheek. She sat with an untasted glass. 'You've had a rough time,' he said. 'Give him a drink.'

Constanz looked awful, all cheekbone and tooth. 'Lili's all right,' she said. 'She's got her fucking knitting. Her fucking too, I'm told.'

She was giving Weiss a drink as Matson went into the kitchen, then out through its open door.

6

His first thought as a neutral was to warn Anka to make herself scarce. She had already disappeared.

She knew Weiss's ways. He would nail her up by the ankles and hold flame to her eyes.

A ladder stood propped against the back of the house. Had the boy been taken down it when the shot had been fired, or earlier?

The answer scarcely mattered. Not while there was a chance he was alive on the island.

The smoke had not settled on Otok. Only its shadow. The moon moves quickly when it is low, and by the time Matson had reached the tower he was in full light. He made quickly for the bushes. Quickly and, he hoped, quietly. The carving knife had a hefty enough blade, but the moonlight favoured men with pistols.

Nothing. Only the polythene wraps of the confiscated weapons.

He wondered how long to spend combing the bushes for anything more bloody.

No time. A thought took him back towards the tower. Popo had spoken of symmetry. He hoped no one had thought to make a balancing sacrifice here.

The door faced up the island, sideways on to the moon.

Matson took it at a run, shouldering it, rolling through. He lost the knife on the way.

He leapt to his feet and sideways. The bird smashed into him, flustering towards the door.

He had no torch, no matches, nothing. There was no enemy here, no one alive. The boy could be hanging above him by the neck and he wouldn't know.

'Henk!' he called. 'Henk Weiss!'

He felt for the knife. He had been taught to roll with a knife, but not with a Montengrin carver. He found it and checked the knife on his leg. Two-knife Matson.

His motives for running to this end of Otok were excellent. The hide had been here. The best cover was here. The tower was here. The presence of the hide suggested that a good way to and from the water would be here.

Also, since the smoke column was on the nearer land to the south, with the moon behind it, and since the moon moves west, then the east of the island would be longer in shadow.

He was wrong. They had gone off at the other end, from among Weiss's historic roses. Symmetry again?

The dinghy was more than halfway across when he saw it, a rubber boat with four people paddling, one of them probably a woman. Anka.

He looked but couldn't tell. He only had moonlight. Only had eyes.

A rubber boat in red, orange or brown. It was like trying to guess colours on a black and white screen.

The running steps had come from that end of the island.

There was no sign of the child, and now the boat was hidden by the spit of land where the jetty was.

He heard him cry across the water. He was with them and alive.

Unless they'd brought a goat as a mascot.

7

'You're late, Hauptmann. Late for orders.'

'I'm your only action, Weiss. You'll run on my time.' He went across to Lotte. 'Your son is alive. They've just taken him ashore.'

Lotte was making loops of thread with her pocket knife.

'She already knows,' Weiss said. 'You keep me waiting for stale news.' He flourished the paper Matson had found on his grandson's bed. 'They say they'll keep him unharmed in his basket for three whole days, and then they'll cut bits off him unless I do as they say. At the worst, I'll meet their demands, so the child will be well.' He gazed at Lotte in a kind of hangdog triumph.

Matson wasn't so sure, never mind the reference to baskets. 'What demands?'

'I'm to get rid of Popovic and his people from the lake.'

'And?'

'They'll send a messenger tomorrow.' He became morose. 'I'm dealing with madness here, not soldiers.' He looked to the women for support. 'They add a list of silly names.'

'Nine of them?' Matson glanced at the paper, now unrolled to the end. Its Cyrillic was beyond him, but one word was written three times. 'Jug Bogdan, Jug Bogdan's Widow, Jug Bogdan's Daughter-in-law,' he recited. He completed the list from memory. 'National heroes and martyrs, I believe.'

'Failures. I defeated the lot of them.'

'You must be older than we thought, General.'

'I can't ask that fellow Popovic to move. He'll hide away if I explain the circumstances. Then he'll be out there somewhere, spoiling things behind my back. It's me these criminals want. They'll get their messenger to me whether the lake is policed or not. I'll tell them I've arranged it this way to keep Popovic out of the hinterland.'

'You can't ignore their conditions,' Constanz said.

'If they harm the lad they'll have lost their hold on me. It's like any piece of military planning, a question of probabilities. I'd venture a motorized division on less. Are you

329

saying my own blood is exempt? Well, what do you think, Hauptmann?'

Weiss was too stressed to be argued with. 'I'd like to show you something at the back of the house,' Matson said quickly. 'Alone, please, General.' He took Weiss to the kitchen door and out of earshot.

Weiss bounded back inside to shout, 'We tell Popovic nothing. We tell nobody nothing until we know their conditions.' Then he was back again, high on the threat of action, and in a frenzy of frustration at the same time. A dangerous mix. 'Well, Patrick. What have you got for me?'

'Advice. You've got to calm down and stay watchful. There may be gunfire tonight, not messages tomorrow. We both know that.'

Weiss nodded.

'More important, you can't indulge in too much talk in there. You can't rely on those ladies. Or trust them, even. If you can, I can't. If I'm going to help you, I need to be private.' No need to damage Constanz further, or explain his doubts about Lotte. 'You have men out there, Weiss. I saw one yesterday. What will they have done when that shot was fired? Or the fire lit?'

'Nothing, I think, of use in this case. I had not envisaged it.'

'Our only hope is the other people's messenger, then. Not for you to hang him by the heels, General. For me to follow him.'

'He may not return to base. He may use a radio.'

'I doubt it. They'll worry about Popovic's – or Belgrade's – electronic resources. If I'm wrong, we'll have two whole days to come up with something better.'

Back inside the house, Lotte, said 'What was this secret –?'

Weiss had taken his pistol out. Someone was crossing the lawn.

8

'Don't shoot me in the chest. I'm wearing a new medal ribbon.'

'Colonel Popovic.'

'General Weiss.' As it happened, Popovic was ablaze with several rows of ribbon, as if he were at an embassy reception. It was a good entrance line.

'You took your time. There was very nearly a catastrophe. Mrs Ehrenberg-Zanetti has been shot.'

'So long as it wasn't by a bullet, General.' Popovic examined Constanz's neck, then helped himself to some cognac from the table and watched Weiss hide his gun. 'Have you anything to tell me?'

'No?'

'Anything else? A pity.' He indicated the disappearing moon, then closed the door on it. 'We have an enemy who lights bonfires and plays tricks with time. I have decided to damage my reputation, General, and save your life. This will render me unpopular in these parts.' He smiled at Lotte, who was at last showing signs of breaking up. 'I shall remain here until dawn. So will the boat and a sizeable contingent of my people.' He didn't seek permission. 'Now I must say things to Captain Matson.' He opened the door again. 'Captain Matson is not a talkative man. Your secrets will be safe with him.'

'He has given undertakings.'

'A Catholic saint, I'm sure.'

Matson followed Popovic through the front door. Popovic wasn't a target.

'I take it the boy has been snaffled, my dear. I deduce it from the abnormal degree of hush, and from something I will show you down at the fleet.' He led Matson towards the motor boat. 'The Hunbag is stupid, bringing women and infants,' he added. 'Any Serb could tell him that. He writes their scenario for them. The Croats would be frying the little bastard's ears by now.'

The motor boat was a pleasure craft. It had too many windows and too much light. It made an excellent target.

It was being guarded by Popovic's ladies and its full contingent of sailors. Matson climbed aboard, nodded to the driver and her pals, and realised he'd got Popo wrong about this. Women might be equal combatants in a post-revolutionary army, but the rogue had enough of a western eye to know that glamour makes convenient casualties. Slavs are sentimentalists anyway. If one of these stopped a bullet Jug Bogdan and Company would have an uphill public relations exercise on their hands.

'You said this was a newspaper plot, my dear. Remarkable acumen. I hear from Belgrade that an American newspaper already has the kidnap.'

'It only happened an hour ago.'

'I don't have the newspaper, but my people don't make mistakes in a matter of such consequence. Believe me they don't.' He handed Matson a résumé of the report. 'That is what I have to show you.'

'Constanz Zanetti, Mrs Ehrenberg-Zanetti was alone for the evening in Belgrade.'

'Indeed. She phoned me, as you now know.'

Matson got ready to leave the boat. Popovic spoke in Serbian, before returning to English. 'I'm saying tread carefully, Patrick. Even a woman can put powdered glass in your soup.'

9

'What did you tell him?' Weiss shouted from the porch.

'The world press did it for me. Think about that in the context of my earlier caution.'

Weiss looked vengeful. Or his nostrils and earlobes did in a thin shaft of light.

'No use banging heads, General.' He led the old man away from partially lit windows and prying night sights, and round to the kitchen corner. Weiss didn't want to be led. If he were shot it would solve everything for him, even sleep. He keened as his daughter-in-law had done before he slapped her.

'She's not a villain, General. She's simply the liar who invented the plot. Journalists do it all the time. If they're good at their job, their stories become attractive to people.'

Weiss was calm again. 'I've been speaking to Lotte. We can't accept that you go.'

'So the women are in on the plan.'

332

'The one I can trust.'

'The one who dopes the boy's drink.'

'I can't let you go. I don't fight by proxy, Captain Matson.'

'Then you're not fit to command. A three- or four-hundred-metre swim in a near-glacial lake'll kill you.'

'This is my kind of country.'

'Your ego may make it ashore, but the rest of you won't. Besides, you can't be in two places at once. Talk to them as they demand. Find out what it is they want. I'll be ashore and waiting to follow them when it's over.'

'You think it will be that simple?'

'No. But I can't see another way.'

'I'm mindful to shoot the messenger, Captain.'

'Then they'll kill your grandson. The messenger is only the dog. *Their* dog. Why not make him ours by letting him lead us to his masters?'

'If you're not here, they may think they can kill me.'

'I'm not your bodyguard.'

The General didn't like it, but that's how it had to be.

'When will you go?'

'When it suits me.'

Weiss loitered, came back to him. 'The boy's her child, Patrick. *Her* child.'

'Perhaps she thought the less trouble he gave to everyone, the safer he would be.'

10

The kitchen was primitive, but its roughness served a fastidious overlord. Matson found what he was looking for: a stack of polythene bags, rubbish bags, storage bags. There was string. There was bread. There were bottles.

He was securing a bottle inside a black rubbish bag with a brace of elastic bands when he smelled the Zanetti perfume.

'What you got there, Matson? Does Dreamsleeves make you wear a condom?'

'How's your neck, Constanz? Your mouth's in tune.'

She began to cry. A splash of sympathy in a jugful of bitters and here were the great tears rolling.

333

'Shit, Matson.'

The trouble with tears, his grandmother used to say, is you need a good jeweller to tell what they're worth.

She blew her nose. 'What happens now?'

'We help you find a notebook, then you can finish your story.'

'I mean what's going on? I'm being treated like pig's ribbon here.'

'I'm not privy to anyone's thinking.'

'So what's your plan exactly?'

'To stay alive. I'd think along similar lines, if I were you.'

'Bastard.'

He offered her half an arm. 'It's sound advice I give you.'

11

There were hours of darkness left. So many he might even sleep. Upstairs he went through his obsessive active service routine of scrubbing his body with soapless water, then rinsing and drying his hair.

He used the bedroom toilet soap to wash the clothes he had been wearing. He didn't need them now, but he might have to make the trip again. He soaked them free of the smell of soap, and hung them near the window. He dressed in the remaining shirt and some jeans from Popovic's hold-all, and went to find more water.

He heard Lotte's crying. She had been living through a great depression. Perhaps it was always there, perhaps only for the duration of this trip. Now, and at last, she was worried about her child. The kidnap had got to her. Weiss wasn't there to stone her brain, so she cried.

The General was sitting downstairs by a darkened window. He held Constanz, also seated, with his left arm round her shoulder as if he was hoping to break her. In his right hand he held an ancient two-barrelled shotgun with its butt ordered on the shoe of his outflung foot. Matson had seen a photograph of Billy the Kid looking like that. Or was it Jesse James?

Ancient was a glib adjective to apply to a shotgun. Matson

glanced again. The chasing on the barrel was definitely nineteenth century. Older than the General's Luger, anyhow.

'I found this in the larder,' Weiss explained. 'No food, but this and a box of cartridges.'

The cartridges looked all right. 'Let's hope they're cordite, not curry powder,' he said, to encourage Constanz.

'It will be an excellent gun close to, if those criminals try to storm the house.'

'Popovic is here with half a platoon. You won't need it.'

'An excellent gun, Hauptmann.'

'Save two bullets for the women, General.'

Weiss wasn't a cowhand. He didn't understand the joke. He had medieval ideas about rape. Principally that there will be no need for it, once women learn to do as they are told.

12

Upstairs again, Matson took off his shirt and trousers and put them in one of the kitchen bags. He put his boots in another and some spare underclothes in a third. He sealed them with elastic bands, and put the three bags inside a fourth, which he also made airtight with elastic bands.

He lay on the bed. Four o'clock would be early enough.

He woke almost at once. Someone's hand on his shoulder in the bullet-proof dark. His sleep reached out for Constanz. He'd find it hard to forgive her, but her body was better than blankets.

Lotte.

'I do not do it this time because I want to,' she said. 'I do it because he tells me to. He says because you go out you should have a present.'

And a future, he thought, and a better past.

'Henk says you will find him.'

'Why isn't the General with you? Why is he spending so much time with Constanz?'

'Because he doesn't trust her. Besides, it is not like that, him and me.'

'No?'

'Henk is an old man.'

335

'That's not what he thinks. He thnks he's *the* old man.'

It was lost on her. She began to undress herself, standing by the bed, but reluctantly. He heard her fold her clothes very slowly, patting them with deliberate hands. She was like a woman about to be flayed alive, but meanwhile desperate to leave everything in proper order for the executioner's daughter.

'You have me,' she said. 'And then you find my little one.'

'Why do you keep the boy sedated?'

'So you can find him. You can go tonight. You are trained in such things, General Weiss says.'

'Are you on any form of drug, Lili? Medicine?' He added encouragingly, 'I think you ought to take a sleeping tablet.'

She got into bed with him. She knew about men and Matson and beds.

'Put your clothes on,' he said. 'If you're feeling bad we'll talk. Put your clothes on first.'

He thought she was beautiful when he first saw her. She was beautiful. But she was about as attractive as a mad horse.

'I'll find your son,' he promised. He didn't believe it. What he believed was that a man uncontaminated by madness would leave this place, and Weiss and his women, and hitch out of these mountains and back to Belgrade. There were daily flights to England. 'Why did you let that villain become your lover?' he asked.

She sighed and stretched, as if at the end of an enormous contentment. 'Henk and I were always lovers.'

'He's your husband's father.'

'He's little Henk's father,' she said.

Matson felt sick.

'Anka says Hendrik was never Vincenz's father.'

'He was,' Matson said. He sat up and left the bed. He wondered how much more he could take of this. 'He was Vincenz's father for thirty-five years. He mightn't have been Vincenz's father for that significant five minutes, but he played father to the boy for the rest of his life.'

'Anka was Vincenz's mother.'

Perhaps he should leave earlier. Perhaps he should go now. Swimming in the lake would be less complicated than talking to her, the pine needles gentler.

336

She corrected herself. 'Anka says Vincenz's father is with the people out there. That's why I know little Henk won't be hurt. She gave me her word.'

It sounded like a jaggering non sequitur to Matson.

'That's why I lent her little Henk in the first place.'

'You let her take him away?' It's not the blood that runs cold. It's the brain.

'He's been over there the night before. While you were talking. He knows he won't be hurt.'

She circled about in his bed like a dog, yawned and fell asleep.

He picked up his bag, went out and knocked on Weiss's door. Weiss was with Constanz. 'Get up, Weiss. I need you.'

The General was fully dressed. 'I'm keeping watch,' he said.

'The bedrooms only face one way. Into the pillow.'

They went downstairs to the kitchen, Matson incongruous in vest and pants. The kitchen door opened on the side of the house nearest to the tower. He had used it previously. This time, no one with night binoculars must know about it.

Matson opened the door, and told Weiss to hold it open. He dived on to the ground and rolled sideways into the dark until he fetched up in the nearest bushes, then he got to his feet.

He heard the door close behind him. He held the polythene bundles against his abdomen and went through fast. He wasn't entirely silent. He was evading long-range detection by night scope, not from people nearer to.

If anyone nearer heard him, Popovic's boys and girls for example, then his rapid change of position would confuse them.

By any standards he was pretty silent. He knew that. He visualized the positions of the trees and larger bushes and avoided hitting anything big.

He did not check the tower. He could scarcely see, but a vision enhancer could, and the foot of the tower was in open ground.

He did check the hide again. Nothing.

He went by the crawlway on its far side, and then he was in the lake.

337

13

It was cold. He was already cold. It was colder.

He lay his cheek against his bundle of plastic and searched for stars. Orion would be nice, but it is always too low to be useful in the mountains.

Aldebaran offered, but only just. He took two or three kicks guided by the bull's red eye, then the eye was closed, snuffed out by cloud or the plume from a peak.

He found a planet, he thought Jupiter, not where he wanted a marker. Anything bright in the sky was good enough. It was on his left shoulder. He kicked for the shore, and met trouble.

There was a current flowing left to right. The point of the island divided it. He struggled to stay south of the point. The water tried to press him the wrong way, round the back of the island.

He had no flippers and he was trying to be quiet. He made no headway. After five minutes he had got worse than nowhere. A slimy hardness against his right shoulder. A rock. It was one of a cluster of stones extending the point.

Swimming with Weiss off the front of the house had been simple. Popovic was moored there now, but it would be easy to find a way past him.

He took a grab and a heave at the rock as a means of working his way ashore. Impossible. He couldn't get out. He'd allowed twenty minutes for a discreet, no-splash swim. Six or seven minutes had gone. He was bone cold and going backwards.

The current pushed him round the back of the island. If he let go of his bundle he could do it easily, but he needed what the bundle contained.

A current of only a knot or two, perhaps no more than the windspeed against his head and his over-buoyant package of clothing, but it was proving too much for him. He turned and went with it.

In no time he was round the back of the house, but yards off-shore.

They weren't burning many lamps. They would have been better without any. He saw Weiss upstairs with the heirloom

338

shotgun, Constanz downstairs by herself. He couldn't hear Lotte's crochet hook and marlin.

Funny what you can see on the way to a watery grave. He hoped Popovic had posted a picket or so round this side, and told Weiss they were there. He didn't want the General bagging another brace of women, this time with a ten or twelve bore.

Off the other end of the island he was out of the wind. Or the currents came together and slowed, like air round the surfaces of an aeroplane's wing.

Twenty minutes gone of a twenty-minute swim. He heard a fish jump, God knows what for after dark. He heard his teeth. No, not his teeth. His whole head was rattling with cold.

14

A cold man can't beach quietly. An exhausted man can't even crawl ashore.

After half an hour of frog-footed silence he sensed trees overhead. He was further west than he'd planned, but he'd had absolutely no help from Jupiter at all.

No trees yet. He had simply lost his planet. Whether behind cloud or the angle of a peak, the big gas was gone.

His plastic companion of the last fifty minutes, his flexible over-buoyant friend, let out a lungful of air in a drowning gurgle and began to swim underwater, then drag him back.

It was then that the mist came down. Vapours already in the air closed in and dripped, thickened until he saw nothing.

He mustn't panic. Rain was splashing on his head. The joke about getting wet indicated a miserable deterioration of morale. He thought that was the phrase.

He struggled to swim in a straight line. He hadn't managed very much straightness so far. Question. If God is blind does straightness exist?

Swimming was impossible with his head in a fleece of frost. His bundle, so recently under his chin, was back there under his knees. He reached for it and grated his knuckles. He put down his hands and touched dry land. Correction. He

339

touched wet land, the sort you find at the bottom of the water.

He'd over-swum his bundle. It was grounded. It was less buoyant because it had snagged and ripped.

Not rain. The drops were too big and too lonely. Mist water dropping from overhanging trees. A bird woke above his head and started its pre-dawn chorus, a male claiming its territory. Then it realised that Matson didn't smell of feathers, so shut up again, but didn't bother to turn off the tap.

The other birds knew nothing of this. They heard one sing so they all sang. The male birds, that is. The hens were in bed.

Matson crawled quickly ashore. He had terrible fears they were about to wake the sun.

If he had been keeping watch back there instead of waving and drowning, the startled birdsong would have alerted him. Even if it did spread to full chorus. Any good infantryman would have cocked an ear. Why should seasoned partisans be less alert?

He moved through the lakeside tangle until he was among the pillars of the pines. It's possible to move silently on pine needles, even in the dark. But not at speed, not when you're devastated with cold, not in the dark. He would do it later.

He groped for the line between two trees. He lay down and scooped aside needles and cones along his body length. His hands dug deeper, into the leaf mould of bushes and humus of weeds, into ten years' rot. This would be black stuff, so he piled the spoil at one end of his top scrape where it could be concealed.

He undid his bags. One only inner bag had punctured. His shirt was wet. He wrung it silently, close to the ground. Then he dressed in dry trousers, dry socks, dry boots, wet shirt and lay down in his trench on two plastic bags.

He put his feet and lower legs into a third and began to cover himself up to the waist in mould. Then in needles. On his wet shirt he laid needles. On his face he laid his humus-stained hands till his head felt as tacky as a newly dubbined boot.

Matson was now invisible. In daylight as in darkness, he

340

was Rotman. Morning began to tingle under the pines, but Matson was a ghost and his ghost was elsewhere. Matson was where he'd tried to be for nights and nights and nights. Matson was asleep. Cooking like a worm in a compost heap but undoubtedly asleep.

Four hours later he shifted position. He went uphill, moved a thousand yards east, came downhill until he could see the jetty and Otok but was too far back under trees to be seen, then buried himself again.

It took time, even for a somnambulist. But his second sleep was even better. It was virtuous. It was drier. It was immediate.

TWENTY-TWO

1

Sleeping in the open air is a science, sleeping unobserved an artform.

Sleeping out in cold weather silently is a multi-disciplined masterwork. Frost gets to work, then the dust of the forest and the must of its micro-organisms. The nostrils start to whistle, the jaw gapes open or rattles ajar.

Creep around the average platoon in their slit trenches at three a.m. (Matson's favourite hour for a creep) and you can hear the palatal snore, the nasal snore, the pharyngeal snore, the epiglottal snore, and the tongue-behind-the-tonsils oeso-phageal snore – an instrument so intriguing it has led to the invention of the bassoon.

Matson didn't snore. He breathed recycled air. He lay the right way up, which is down.

At eight o'clock in the dew-light a male roe-deer, noisy as a pair of boy scouts on stilts, came down to the water, then up to Matson's nearest tree, which he sniffed, then nibbled, then staled to show it belonged to him. He didn't see Matson.

At ten past eight a man with a smoky voice opened a radio net about twenty yards away from Matson, yammering for thirty seconds in a repetitive two-word singsong that could only be the station ident and call sign. Then he finished his netting call and lit a cigarette while his outstations checked in and reported signal strength. Armies do it the whole world over and it is bloody annoying.

Matson couldn't see the signaller, only smell him. He could smell the deer, and hoped the deer's smell was stronger. He didn't want humans making smells round his part of the forest, thank you, and attracting attention to it.

The man who brought the signaller coffee nearly trod on Matson's head. He sat himself down with the signaller and lit another cigarette with a smell.

Matson was irritated. He could have picked anywhere along this bit of the lake for a kip, and he'd chosen Popovic's regimental headquarters. Nothing he could do about it now.

As his instructor in the Thugs had said, 'If you've hidden down the lavatory and somebody sits on it, it's too late to move.'

Thirteen outstations checked in. That's a lot of outstations. Two more didn't check in, so signal pads rustled and more cigarettes were lit while thirteen outstations not only checked signal strength with control but they checked each other's signal strengths as well. Thirteen outstations checked each other fifteen times, and were able to report that the missing two were not dead, merely partially deaf. They could hear the other stations, or some of the other stations, but there was a mountain in the way so they couldn't hear control. Or they could hear control but control couldn't hear them.

How did Matson understand this? He understood it because it was keeping him awake and there was nothing else to think about. He didn't understand enough Serbo-Croat but he understood radio nets. He operated radio nets in his dreams of power.

He drifted into snoreless sleep, then was awake again. The signaller re-netted, perhaps on his reserve frequency, and the replies were really loud this time – someone had dug up the mountain – but there were only nine of them. Someone had dug up the mountain but thrown the dirt in the wrong direction.

His friend went for more coffee, passing close to Matson's head. Shouts floated across the water. Popovic's people were being summoned from Otok and back into the boat. Matson could see Otok, he could see the boat. He could see the man who shouted Popovic's orders. He couldn't see Popovic. Popovic was in the cabin eating shrimps on toast.

Matson counted eleven troops on the island, including the three women. Two of them carried section machine guns. Popovic meant business or the appearance of business. He

343

wondered if Popovic had left anyone back, or had even given Weiss a radio, preferably on net. He wondered if his driver knew how not to snore.

The motor boat backed off, turned, and came straight towards Matson's bed, then veered towards the jetty.

Popovic sited one of his section machine guns thirty yards in front of Matson, where it could cover both the jetty and the island. It was an M60 type of gun, probably Czech. Popo deployed it in its close-support mode, hull-down on a bipod. That meant he was serious about the jetty, less serious about the island.

At nine fifteen he walked to the water's edge to inspect his lines of fire.

At nine fifteen and a half he took something from his tunic pocket, stooped to pick up a handful of lake and began to clean his teeth.

At nine sixteen he picked up another handful of lake and rinsed his mouth.

He walked to within four or five yards of Matson, told off his signaller whom Matson still couldn't see, then took off his jacket and his shirt and hung them on a branch and began to shave. He used cream but shaved dry. He swore.

He called to the signaller's friend to bring him some hot water. The signaller's friend handed him the coffee he was bringing for the signaller.

Popovic shouted and sent him back again, but sipped gratefully.

Matson's driver stepped past Matson's feet with a bucket of boiling water. She was wearing legs instead of trousers, and of course she didn't snore.

He watched her go away. Then watched Popovic swill the coffee grains from his cup and dip it in the bucket and begin to shave in earnest.

At ten o'clock Popovic called a muster parade down by the jetty. About sixty people, say two platoons, appeared from along the shoreline and stood informally about while Popo spoke words to them. He used the word Weiss, he used the word Matson. Was he telling them Matson had gone? Were they to kill him or kiss him?

There was no sign of interest or agitation to indicate that

344

Popovic had mentioned young Weiss's abduction. Matson didn't hear the boy's name. He reckoned his Serbo-Croat was up to words like 'son', 'grandson', 'boy', 'child' and so on.

Weiss picked ten men from among the ranks, choosing them individually and not from a list, and embarked them on the motor cruiser. The sailors had stayed on board. He sent the boat up the lake to the west. He didn't go with it.

He divided the rest of his visible command in two roughly equal parties along the shore, and sent them off to the left and the right.

His visible command. His headquarter signallers stayed. The machine gun covering the jetty stayed, along with its gunner, its number two, and three or four other men, perhaps a half section in all.

None of these had paraded on muster, nor had the women. Nor had whoever was manning the other machine gun, which was presumably on the boat.

Popovic himself moved upshore to the east, followed by his two signallers. They lugged his headquarters radio between them, straining at a pair of bucket-sized grab handles. Two days ago he had parked his vehicles along there where the road finished at the lake. Perhaps he was going there now.

Last night he had spoken of two more patrol vessels being trucked up from the coast. It could be they were due.

This took till eleven a.m. Matson dozed and watched Otok. He'd burn his eyes staring at the intensifying blue of the lake now the clouds had rolled back, even though he was facing north and the sun was behind him. Otok was easy to watch, even while half asleep. Otok was where it would be at.

The most significant event was exactly at noon by Matson's watch, and like everything else it happened right beside him.

His driver came through the trees, walking towards him hand in hand with the smoky-eared young pongo from the viaduct above the dam, the one who had groped Constanz's blankets.

The driver had no blankets to grope, but the pair of them put themselves down on the pine needles without word or whisper within spitting distance of Matson – save Matson was too dry-mouthed to spit – and heartlessly began to spoil another of Matson's dreams.

Yugoslavs smoke, and Smoke Ears smoked enough for a regiment of them, even while making love. He nearly set the forest on fire with one of his cigarettes.

Matson nearly set the forest on fire with no cigarette at all. When he could bear it no more, he forced his gaze towards Otok.

He would have to move, or be ready to move. The messenger was arriving.

The couple sprawled across his eyeline and showed no inclination to move ever again. His driver wasn't into cigarettes, so her partner would take twice as long to smoke the ones he'd got.

She was into chewing gum. She wore varnished fingernails. They were breaking open the biggest packet of spearmint Matson had ever seen.

2

On Otok the main door opened. Out stepped Lotte, followed by Weiss and then Constanz.

Constanz seemed uncertain on her feet. She carried a chair.

They advanced side by side down the lawn and waited. Obviously they could see something on Matson's side of the lake that was invisible to Matson.

He couldn't make sudden movements of the head. Not only was he up to the neck in it, he was adjacent to the sprawl of the amorous pair.

Binoculars would have been handy, or handy if he had enough elbow room to use them. Eyes are not bad on bright blue days, eyes polished clear by sleep.

Lotte was wearing a khaki bush shirt cut outrageously short so as not to spoil anyone's view of her jodhpurs. There was no room to tuck anything into them except her thighs and her bum. She carried the shotgun broken on her arm, with the cartridge brass catching the sunlight. Matson had

346

seen her with a gun once before, frightening pig farmers. Impossible to guess how much of a deterrent she would present to the ignorant.

Constanz sat to one side. She leant unsteadily in her chair. Had they been slapping her around, or had she done it to herself, or pretended to do it, with drink?

He saw no sign that Weiss had trusted her with the Luger Parabellum.

Weiss had armed himself with a box of cigars. He placed it on the waterside table and went through the unmistakable pantomime of selecting, sniffing, trimming and lighting one.

The cigar was the badge of his composure.

Matson couldn't watch any more, not for a minute or so. Smoke Ears stood up from the driver and put himself away, including his cigarettes. Then he pulled a combat cap from under his epaulette, turned it inside out, beat it on his knee, turned it right way out again and put it on his head.

He helped the lady to her feet and they picked pine needles from each other, front and back. Then they left Matson to his view of the lake.

A boat was halfway to Otok, drifting with the current from Matson's right to his left. It had set off perhaps a hundred yards to the east, and it was being paddled firmly enough to make the landing stage in front of the table.

3

Popovic had smashed the boats on the lake, but you can't smash an inflatable, especially if you can't find it.

It was a biggish example, perhaps eight or nine feet long, built like a rubber escape dinghy from latex and canvas, with thick ballooning edges and a fabric hull. It had a backboard, but it wasn't being run with a motor. It would fold like a moderate-sized tent and inflate in five minutes with a foot pump.

No one was going to take a second look at it, not even Popovic unless he knew the whole story, and presumably he didn't. It was piled with kitchen essentials: a gas cylinder, bottles of water, baskets of onions, potatoes and something green.

347

The real inspiration was its crew. It was being paddled and steered by Anka, sitting straight-backed in the stern.

It was a hard craft to keep lined up. Once she drifted broadside on. She inclined her head slightly, as if talking to the vegetables.

Then she was abeam of the landing stage and again sideways on. She stood and tossed some vegetables ashore. One bundle rolled into the water. She didn't seem to mind.

Weiss spoke to Lotte, who moved across and examined the vegetables with the muzzle of her shotgun.

Something attracted Weiss's attention in the bottom of the boat. He leant forward and spoke to it. He disliked its tone of voice, waved his hand dismissively and lit another cigar.

Anka bent down and picked up a glint of white from her accomplice in the boat. Matson supposed it was the listed details of the conspirators' demands.

She held it out to Weiss, but he refused to take it. Once more he called to Lotte, who came forward and took it instead.

Lotte didn't read it. She tucked it fastidiously into the pocket of her shirt over her heartbeat.

Then she closed the breech of the shotgun and smashed Anka across the face with it. She had obviously come to realise the stupidity of her actions, and the danger to young Henk.

Anka sat back in the boat, but she didn't fall over.

She turned and paddled shorewards, her face a mask of red.

Lotte's action had been understandable, but not very helpful. Nor were her screams of anger that came flying over the lake.

Matson had tended to suppose the boy would be safe with Lippiat, and with Anka even more, since both of them were his grandparents and both without other descendants. But if Lotte had confided in Anka what she'd told to him last night, then the certainty was no longer there.

A swipe in the face with a gun barrel does no good for anyone's temper, especially the people who have to shut up and watch it happening.

The man concealed on the floor of the boat couldn't have

been pleased. Enraged but unable to show himself because of people on shore.

Lotte's action would look odd from there, if there were anyone on hand to notice it. So would her manic shouting. It would do her cause no good if Popovic chose to act on it.

Weiss must have thought so as well. He walked towards her and she stopped.

Matson climbed out of his nest and went into the woods.

The boat was halfway to shore, with Anka staunching her blood in her shawl.

4

Three o'clock. Two hours' sun overhead, mountain sun with the shadow on his side of the lake. So rather less sunshine than that, but long and serviceable twilight. Say two and a half hours. The moon would be up before sunset, tonight setting a whole hour later, again behind the tops at his back. He wouldn't be hindered by direct shadow.

Anka brought her boat in along the eastern side of the jetty, with Matson shifting through the trees to his right in order to keep level with her.

She passed the jetty and paddled alongside the rocky promontory it jutted from.

The land ran back here, two hundred yards into a tiny bay. She turned across it and beached on its other arm, well forward of the lakeside path, which avoided the spur. Two men sat up from among her crates and vegetables, jumped out of the rubber boat and dragged it up among the trees.

One of them returned and drew Anka after them. Her face looked badly hurt.

Two men made three too many.

Matson had hoped to follow a single messenger. Three people can separate in three directions.

Once he'd known there was more than one person in the boat, he'd tried to arrive at a plan of action.

Anka was the confusing ingredient. Her use as the go-between was obvious. But what about afterwards? Surely she would be sent to look after the child?

She knew the kid. She had an interest in him. It would be human and convenient for her to be used in this way.

But if someone local were needed to provision a group of strangers, or openly to carry messages between people who needed to remain in hiding? There was no certainty, nor even probability, that her messenger role was at an end.

Save for Lili's silly trick with the rifle. It had altered the status quo, and damaged both sides of the equation. A woman with a busted cheek needs to explain it away, and men like Popovic aren't easily convinced. Nor is village gossip.

A woman with broken bones in her face needs to see a doctor, needs to lie down. Bruised or broken she would find it difficult to soothe a traumatized child crying for its mother.

Matson's brain could not deal with this, not at speed. So it made a committee decision. What it couldn't solve it would ignore. Whatever was beyond it simply did not exist.

That felt better.

There were settlements around the lake, and villages and towns elsewhere on the mountain. The child would not be there, because children are noisy. Even drugged children are noisy at times. The conspirators' HQ might well be in such a place, but not their crèche and detention centre.

The child would be up in the big country. Tito had hidden an army there for months. Surely it could contain a small boy for three short days.

These were word-of-mouth people. They proceeded according to partisan traditions. A messenger would go to the group that held the child. He would be the one who went uphill.

Too bad if no one went inland straight away.

Matson's brain had got this far, and given his face a drink from the bottle he'd floated over with his boots, before the three of them reached the lakeside path.

6

Anka's face was bruised and bleeding. This meant it was cut rather than burst open. Lotte had caught it with a gun muzzle, or with the blade of the foresight if there was one. She leant on one of the men's shoulders, and they turned west along the path, moving to Matson's left.

The man was in his sixties, and presumably local. The path was well used and there were Popovic's people to consider as well as the curiosity of anyone else they might meet.

The other man was younger. He surprised Matson by going to ground on the far side of the path. He dropped down quickly and he found good cover. He might be intending to lie up, as Matson had done, somewhere adjacent to the island. He might be detailed to deflate the boat, but Matson didn't think so. He would have been better off staying back along the point. No. This man was the messenger who would go to the group with the child, or to some other rendezvous of significance.

He was simply casing the landscape before he got moving. Matson wasn't that well concealed. He was in shadow, but the other man wasn't in the sunshine. Matson had shifted ground quickly, intent on pursuit. He was placed to deflect glances, not an inch by inch scrutiny of the very small area of woodland that was all either could see once they looked away from the lake.

The man surprised him again. He stood up twenty yards from where Matson's eye expected him and began to whistle. Not a signal whistle. He was whistling a tune.

Then he moved quickly forward, going directly uphill. He passed very close to Matson. He was whistling because he had heard or seen someone, and wanted them to be curious enough to follow him for a bit, confident he could dump them. If they were hunting for him, they couldn't question Anka.

Or he had spotted Matson, and was playing the I-have-noticed-nothing-my-life-is-free-of-care-game, until he could dump Matson ditto, or step out from behind a tree and strangle him.

The former, surely. The man moved too well to pull such a

corny act as the latter would imply.

The gradient steepened quickly to a forty-degree slope, that worst of inclines. It knackers yomper and fell-runner alike. You can't put your hands out to climb it, or adopt the sharp-angled stork-legged zigzags of the fell-runner. You've got to put your head down and storm straight up it.

Unless you're following a good man who might treat you as an adversary. In which case, better to hold the chin high.

The man was in his middle thirties, the best of ages for tutored endurance. He showed good field craft and he was clearly a practised mountain man. This was evident in the rhythm of his walk. He moved relaxed and long. The bloody man continued to whistle.

Matson didn't whistle. His knee perhaps creaked a bit and there was a wheezy half inch of frost at the bottom of his lungs. He was too long out of England for it to be froth.

The whistle stopped abruptly. The man floated sideways in half a dozen bounding strides along the contour, taking him into cover.

Smoke Ears meanwhile stepped out from behind a tree, having evidently been attracted up and across the slope by the whistle. He pointed his sub-machine gun at Matson, holding it one-handed with butt folded over like a machine pistol, which was exactly what it was designed to be. Smoke Ears had moved well too. Matson hadn't heard him coming.

He recognised Matson, in spite of the leaf mould. This fact dropped his mouth open and lost him his cigarette. It drew him two steps forward in query, and kept him two steps speechless.

This was most fortunate, as you can't do an elbow roll uphill, and the last time Matson had tried one he'd been shot in the bum. He didn't want to go uphill, anyway, not into his quarry's eyeline.

Sweat dripped into his eyes. He smiled, caught hold of the sightless spout of the sub-machine gun, which was a standard Skorpion VZ61, dragged Smoke Ears towards his arms and filleted him with a chin jab.

That was an overstatement. Impossible to execute a chin jab properly while you're tugging on someone's Skorpion, and trying to guard against after-noise, like the gun firing twenty-five rounds automatic and bodies crashing to the ground.

A well-executed chin jab kills people. Matson didn't want to kill young Smoke Ears.

They danced drunkenly together. Matson didn't want to dance with him either. The young lout was a biological factory for the conversion of poisonous leaf tobacco to toxic ash, and his body was made up of the inevitable industrial odours. Matson wondered what the driver saw in him.

He lugged the lad a few yards downhill and was grateful the driver hadn't presented herself instead. He would have treated her the same way, and firearm-rated women tend to have faster trigger reflexes, as well as brittle bones.

Smoke Ears breathed evenly but not over-deeply. He took single breaths the way healthy sleepers do, not cyclic fours or sixes such as betoken heavy damage. He would wake in the next few minutes with a very sore head, neck and jaw. Matson wanted him to stay here, not going crying to Popovic. If one of Popovic's men were involved in an incident, Popovic would be bound to pretend to take action.

How to gag him? He was in field order, so there was no military necktie.

Matson emptied the young man's tunic of cigarettes, stuffed his mouth with a half empty soft pack of ten, and bound it into his face with his bootlace.

Then he removed his belt.

To tie an unconscious man leg-to-back-of-neck is life-threatening. So is grape-vining him, unless you can support his hands.

Matson found a suitably slim tree and folded Smoke Ears' legs around it, tucking one behind the knee of the other then slumping him down on them so his body weight locked him in place.

To stop him splitting apart his abdominal muscles by falling or throwing himself back, kind Uncle Paddy pulled the young fellow's arms in front of him round the tree and fastened his wrists together with his belt.

Then he was inspired. He raided Smoke Ears' pockets once more and lit a cigarette. He didn't smoke it – perish the

353

thought. Just a reassuring scrape of match on box, followed by the armpit odour of fresh leaf tobacco.

The young man was smoking. He had given up the chase.

The cigarette made Indian symbols among the pine needles for a long contented minute. Smoke Ears began to stir. He wondered who he was whiffing with.

Totally reassured, his man broke cover. Matson didn't hear him move. He saw him striding upwards some fifty yards ahead.

7

The forest suited Matson. He could stay close without being seen.

He thought he could.

The trouble was he wasn't fit enough. The target kept to his own relaxed rhythm and went fast. To keep him in sight, and himself out of sight, Matson had to stop, dodge behind trees, make ground by running. Twice he dived full length to one side, taking his weight on outstretched hands and collapsing arms so his tumble was silent. His man turned round, or started to turn round. Matson didn't know. He was already sprawling earthwards and damaging his stamina. Like being floored in the boxing ring. He had to rise slowly and treat the next minute cautiously.

His man was always out of sight before the referee began counting. Out of sight before the bell rang. Glimpsed and out of sight again.

Old forest, not a plantation in Cumbria. The trees weren't in neat rows, decently gapped. Giant trees make their own space, and there were plenty of giants. Firs, and most pines, manage to kill the competition; Matson was grateful for that. But struggling trees have roots to trip over, and they don't bother to bury their dead. The corpses leaned crazily among new growth, blocking the way. Sometimes he would bypass a tree whose roots had been denuded by storm water. Still growing, but dizzy, it would lean its branches on its pals' shoulders like a drunk at a party.

The angle of the mountain kept the vegetation in enough

354

order to let Matson through. The same angle proved he wasn't fit enough.

His weekly workout in the gym wasn't adequate for this sort of caper. He used to spend his weekends in the hills, but when had he last done that?

This thought kept him going for another hundred yards with his guts knocking and his tongue like a bib on his chin.

He wanted the trees to last until twilight, prayed for open ground after dark.

Wasn't there a wooded plateau up on top, in a basin of tilted edges? Or was Jezero on the plateau, and were the heights as wild as the map down at Otok suggested?

Another hundred yards.

A climber keeps an eye on his feet. Matson kept an eye on his feet. Popovic had kitted him with modern feet, lovely processed leather you needn't break in, leather supple as skin.

The way was up a dead watercourse now. The stream had gone under the tree roots and down into karst; but sump holes and pots still gaped. They could snap a man off at the knee, so Matson watched both his feet in turn, careful to plant them and cautious how he picked them up. The rock was loose, and he didn't want to send any downwards in a shower of noise. Yes, a climber keeps an eye on his feet. He should have kept an eye on his brain.

8

When you run in a lonely place, or even when you walk fast, you hear the other presence. It may be on a mountain, it may be among buildings after dark. The stranger keeps beside you, or behind you, or ahead. You stop and his footsteps stop, his breathings stop, his heartbeats stop, but not quite stop. None of them stops or goes much further on. They are yours, perhaps. Your echo, maybe. Who else's, then? Who can tell?

Matson knew his target was ahead. He thought there was someone behind him. Several someones. He knew about his ghostly companion. His companion had shadowed him over

355

the ice cap, followed him through the aircraft door on solo free falls. He discounted his ghostly companion as rigorously as he excluded his own body pain now. If you can't do things that make your body hurt you, then you may as well be dead.

No doubt about it. Someone was coming up fast behind him, a someone and a someone more. They did not move as well as his target, or as well as Matson. They moved rather better than his ghostly companion, so they slowed him on his scramble up the watercourse, they distracted his attention from the rocky ladders in front of him.

What was there and around him, in a torrent, was goats. A downpour of goats. Goats coming from ahead of him, not behind.

The buckgoat, the first buck, was brown. It stood up from nowhere, from a hole in the rock, and nodded Matson aside. It didn't butt him. Matson was already leaping to his right. The billy merely shrugged his surprise and helped Matson outwards with his head, which was wider by his horns, and hard.

Matson scrambled up the bank of the watercourse and watched its rocks metamorphose into goats. A shifting ladder of stones became an uncoiling rope of milch goats and little billies, black, white, brown, mostly brown because mountain goats, as the whole damned flock of them tumbled from the lip of the sky, saw Matson run and came clattering after.

That is, the lead billy saw Matson run and chased him. The rest of them followed their leader.

Matson wasn't frightened of goats. Nobody is. He'd learned to speak their language in the Lebanese hills.

A buck in a pen can be wild, but a buck with his women is a very decent chap. If you treat him with respect and dignify his senior wives he'll let you chew a stalk with him, nibble your coat, and piss upon your head as a mark of esteem.

Matson ran because goats mean people, a goat herd or goat girl at least. For a flock this big perhaps several. He didn't want the locals to see him, for all kinds of reasons. The best was that they'd greet him, and possibly delay him. His target would know he was there.

Run from a flock of females and they'll rarely follow. Run from a billy and the running triggers him. He'll think you're either a stud he must fight or a doe he must ... Matson was too out of breath to remember the word. He heard a hundred goats chase their stud goat chasing him. He ran in a spray of their saliva and he heard herdsmen swear. He hoped they made no reference to him.

Out of sight among the trees, and nearly over a drop, he turned. The billy was behind him. He decided Matson wasn't a female, or if a female wasn't nubile; he was angry with sexual frustration and spoiling for a fight.

Matson hit him. He wasn't as big as a horse, nor as big as a pony, but Matson had to hit him to discourage the flock. He hadn't brought his horns along, so he hit him on the nose with a large piece of tree.

The nose burst open, the way noses will, and the billy rolled downwards, to his brides' consternation. Matson ran uphill. He knew he had transgressed. He hoped the old fellow's reputation wasn't ruined or, worse, his legs broken. Goats never fall. It's against their religion. When they do they can easily suffer damage.

Three minutes later he was above the top of the watercourse, but he'd lost contact with his target.

He heard the herdsmen shout again. '*Medvjed!*' they called. They told someone to bring their rifle. They thought he was a bear. He hoped the billy wasn't dead.

It was good to be a bear. His target would have heard the hullabaloo and thought he was being followed. Then he would have heard 'bear', and been reassured.

Matson decided to be prudent. Even bears are prudent. He decided to get his breath back and put his mind about the landscape.

Half an hour to sunset. He found some coal-black shadow and crouched there while the upward cool from the pine needles soothed his pulse.

It took him a minute before the pressure slackened in his arms and twilight cleared from his eyes to give him back his sense of colour.

More than half an hour to sunset. Give it more. Give it ten minutes more. Save forty minutes.

He must have panted quietly. His target had been resting too, crouching above the watercourse listening to goats and

357

men, the scramble after the bear, and to his own ghostly companions. He rose from between two rocks not twenty yards away. He soothed his hair with his hands and went striding upwards.

9

There were no flies, and it was early in the year for mosquitoes. There were spiders, tiny red spiders tickling the nostril with the dampness of their threads. Their webs dried across Matson's face like the salt of perspiration. This was what the target had been combing from his hair.

For a hundred, two hundred yards he was easy to track. He had been forced to thread his way across a roof of mushrooms, shattering their slates. Not exactly mushrooms but a pine wood variant of stinkhorns, tortoise-backed toadstools that oozed black juice and a terrible smell.

Halfway across the noisy squelch of them Matson heard people following again. They had cleared the top of the watercourse. They were a hundred yards away, too close for comfort.

It wasn't the goatherds. It was the noise from earlier. The same number of men, the same footwear. Was it a patrol of Popovic's, some heavies from the kidnap gang, or Weiss's people?

He was tempted to wait and see, but he wasn't here to solve riddles. He was here to find a child.

He knew the answers to all the riddles in the world. He knew Popovic was ambivalent about his task, that Weiss shouldn't trust his women, and that one of them was mad. He knew London had many heads and he'd be better off in the Falklands using his pension to stock a fish farm. There was nobody he could rely on, except a few cronies far away and most of them were dead. None of it should concern him. His task was to rescue an average little boy whom Matson didn't know because he had been doped with some fancy elixir to satisfy the whims of his mother.

358

10

The slope steepened, and leant back on him.

He stopped because his quarry had stopped. The man ahead turned and moved quickly to his left, so Matson skipped forward by a couple of trees to see where he had gone, only to find there were no more trees, only beetling cliff. He was winded, and his eyesight suffered again. An overhanging line of escarpment running roughly east and west. It was probably the main skyline south from Otok, with the high peaks beyond; though he couldn't be certain. The overhang didn't worry him, not till he got his breath back. He knew that if you approach a scarp from a covered glacis, the difference of perception is so dramatic that the mind can turn a ninety or even an eighty degree wall into a hundred degree fit of dejection, particularly if the wind is moving the sky.

There was no wind to look at. No clouds. The sky was thin blue, growing empty of sunshine.

A brown bird of prey with the sun on its belly drifted off the cragline and hung there, eagle-huge, then crumpled like a gull and went back in.

His man had disappeared.

Several yards to his left a gully split the cliff. Matson edged along the rubble of white stone and let himself take a look.

His man was halfway up, or halfway up what could be seen of it. His kneefolds and the crease of his backside were wet with sweat. Matson was glad to see that. Matson wasn't wet with sweat. He was sweat itself. He was a bundle of bones in a bucket of brine. The bones were dissolving fast, and the bucket was beginning to drip. There'd be enough brine for an hour or two, even so.

He didn't start climbing at once. Gullies are bad places to follow in. The man might glance down past his sweaty crotch, glimpse Matson's sweaty head rising beamish beneath him, and decide to anoint it with a boulder or two. Gullies are what the trade calls a dirty climb, so why not climb dirty and kick a bit of the mountain down, or all of it if necessary?

Matson examined the face of the wall. Compacted lime-stone, friable in places, but mostly hard as marble, tricky as a stack of dice. He told himself he would be too visible to the following pack below. This was true, but the greater truth was that as climbs went the wall was a Rubik nightmare, and much too good for him.

He wondered about Popovic. Popovic was probably beginning to act. He hadn't queered Weiss's pitch with the kidnappers because officially he didn't know. On the other hand, that newspaper report, or report of a report, had been burning his pocket for some eighteen hours. He would be bound to investigate, even if Weiss fobbed him off with a story he knew was a lie.

His target had climbed out of sight. There was no sound behind. The other party had stopped for a breather.

Inside the gully it was dark. Matson's eyes adjusted as he climbed, and he climbed fast. To get his hands on some rock was a relief after the upward grind on his calf and thigh, the sapping of his abdomen involved in his erratic progress upwards.

He thought of the Scafell scramblers' gullies. This one was harder than the main Lord's Rake gully, easier than the exit from the West Wall Traverse. A bit like Red Gully, steeper but with firm rock to compensate.

He looked back towards the sunshine. The sky was tinged with mauve, though the tops beyond Otok glittered. Only the tops. The tree slopes were dark.

Otok was dark. Nothing glowed in the house. No one had lit the oil lamps. Perhaps only Anka performed such a menial task. Anka's away was not a joke Weiss would care for.

Easy climbing, but even that takes time. You look at a gully like this and if you've never done one you think, 'Three minutes.' If you're experienced, you say, 'Twenty minutes, half an hour,' because you can't bear to be bored by it any longer. It takes an hour. It takes an hour and a half.

However long it takes, the sky grows dark while you climb it.

At the top of the gully, in its bricked-up midnight, he heard men climbing below. They were only just starting, so they were well over a half an hour behind, no matter how good they were.

They weren't climbers. They swore. They swore in German.

11

The gully narrowed at the top, narrowed and steepened into a chimney.

What there was first was a chock stone, a common case of geological constipation. A boulder had slipped into the chimney's gullet and failed to exit from its bottom.

Matson discovered the chock stone with his head, so had to pause for a moment or two. One thing to climb a chimney in the dark, quite another to grope blindly inside it while his skull was on fire with imaginary stars.

One, perhaps two minutes earlier, Matson had heard the sound of cloth on rock. Say two minutes before he bashed his head. It was the only sound he had heard the target make, except for that whistled tune.

The man had been waiting, silently, checking on the climbers lower down. Matson had heard his mantelshelf heave over the chock stone. Most men mutter and grunt at such moments, expel breath. The target had done no more than catch cloth. A wood pigeon makes more sound shifting its claws on a frosty branch.

Someone below had a torch. Matson reached up to the chock stone, feeling with his hands this time, not his head, got a nice wide grip and leant backwards into space and pressed his body upwards with his legs. He had the edge of the chock stone against his chest.

The chock stone rocked. There was a tiny smell of splintered chalk, that dusty sputter that means a boulder has shifted off its hinge.

By definition, a chock stone can't be pulled down. Elephants can be suspended from it, elephants if not towers.

But it can be shifted out by a climber pressuring past it, for that first upward thrust is also out, and the chimney may only be locking it in one direction.

Matson shifted his grip. He let his legs swing back and hang free. He forced down with his arms and tried not to think of the several hundred feet or yards or miles of nothing under the soles of his feet.

He didn't have to try very hard. The nothing was dark, except for the occasional residual flash of concussion.

The torch flashed again. Softies. Matson was already levering a leg past the chock stone, then sitting sideways into the chimney, backside against its right hand surface, both feet against the other. Then one foot back as it narrowed even more comfortably. There was a star overhead, a pain inside his total lack of oxygen. Nothing moved against it. No-one got in its way. The chimney was safely empty.

He really must get fit again.

12

Chimneying is safe for anyone with a residual muscle. Matson had lent most of his to the girls in the office. But in a chimney as narrow as this, all he had to do was sit and shudder. He couldn't fall. He could only become a chock stone. He shuddered his way to the top.

It was the top, too. Almost the top of the world.

He lifted his head into diffused moonlight. He was on the edge of a trencher of land, a flatness among crags or trees.

The air was cold as a dip in the lake. A passing damp was congealing into frost and blurring his eyes. Waterdrops furred his lashes. He shook his head to clear them.

The sky grew colder and clearer as the mist finished falling from the air. The moon was in low trajectory, but the night was big with stars.

His target was a hundred yards ahead, perhaps less.

Matson went to ground and lost him. Stood up, and there he was, moving slowly onwards. He was scuffing his boot, as if uncovering something. Searching like a best man who thinks he's dropped the ring down a heating duct. Then he disappeared.

Matson ran after him.

The stink of an animal. Not a man, but a bear.

For the last couple of minutes he'd been stalking a bear.

'Hold it, Paddy. Don't even move. You're too damned easy.' Lippiat's voice came from off to his left.

It wasn't bloody Lippiat he'd been following. His target had disappeared even so.

Matson hadn't smelled bear, but cooking odours and bad

air smoking in the frost light from a fissure in the ground. He was looking at the sinkhole of a karstic cavern.

His view of it was blocked by Lippiat's legs and Lippiat's rifle. Mostly his rifle. Lippiat moved closer to give him a better sight of it. An original 'long' Lee Enfield, complete with sling.

Matson gestured towards the pothole. 'Is that where Ivan Crnojevic sleeps with his band of fairies?'

'Guided tours start in May, Paddy. You'd better get in a queue for a ticket or you'll miss the bus.'

'I'll take a look while I'm up here, if I may.'

Lippiat thumbed a silent safety-catch and gave a gracious flick to the bolt. He was holding the rifle right-handed, presented from the hip, so his eye infection was irrelevant.

'No stopping-power, Lolly.'

'That's what pistol salesmen are supposed to have said between the wars. You think this has got no stopping-power, try me and see. I guess it hasn't got stopping-power if you're up and running, Paddy. But you'll be running dead. Killing power's what I'm after. I've tried this gun on men. Men and SS. And vermin like your host. It only takes a couple of steps to kill them. You want to call that slow poison, it's a matter of perspective, I suppose.'

'You've got the boy, Gerald. I'm bound to come on past, bound to try.'

'The lad's not going to be hurt.'

Matson tried to get near enough, but Lippiat kept his distance then halted him dead with a tiny flourish of the gun.

'Weiss will understand the asking price. It's certainly one he'll remember paying.' Again the slight impatience with the rifle. 'The lad will be all right. He'll be spared in any event, I promise you. Now turn around, and get marching.'

Matson turned around, but not to get marching. The gun blew the top of his head off.

He lay on bracken and blood. He thought blood. His head had been hit or shot, presumably by Lolly's rifle in one of its functions.

Shot was the best conclusion. The air was brittle with recent cordite.

You start with the face, first making sure of the eyes. Two eyes. Face in place, body sensations missing. His brain was steaming gently ahead, but in the middle of a huge bruise. Steaming ahead in slow circles.

Water would be nice. He was lying on wet. He sipped a few mouthfuls of blood. It was crusty, the way blood is. Stone cold, like blood in a mortuary. Chewy as a mouthful of salt, then wet underneath like scum on the edge of a tide. But there was no taste to it. Blood and salt taste. Blood tastes of salt and, when it is cold, of death. So he wasn't drinking blood.

He was lying on frost. He was sipping snow. There was no bracken. There was only his own wet hair.

He got his hands free of his face. He felt thorax and abdomen, crotch. All unpunctured.

So why the smell of cordite, the smell of recent discharge?

He crouched up. He didn't stand. He felt too weak to stand. But even if he had been strong, he would have stayed low.

Three of them were there, just ahead of him. He felt for the knife inside his shirt. No one had taken it. It was warm from his body, and solid. He pondered how to do the most damage. He wanted a decision.

Only three of them, down in the starlight and frost about twenty feet ahead. He glanced round for Lolly. Lolly was gone, unless Lolly was one of them.

They lay with legs interlaced, the way infantry do on a patrol. You need four men, and eight legs, to make the best interchange of signals, but three would do.

He guessed they hadn't seen him lying here. They'd have done something otherwise.

When they saw him, he'd throw the carver at the one on the right. It would stick him or stun him.

Matson would rush the middle one, using the knife on his leg. If he didn't strain too hard for a kill, he might incapacitate the third one as well.

Then he'd roll to the left, and into the shadow of that piece of rock. It would have to be very fast in case he missed with his throw. He didn't expect to miss, but the throw would be a distraction in any case.

He might grab a gun on the way. That would be a bonus. Impossible to attack three men like this. They would know it too. That's why the odds would favour him.

First he had to analyze their intention. If they were Weiss's men, they might have been instructed to help him. They might be a happy band of gypsies warming their legs.

He wasn't going to say hands up and walk over and ask them to surrender either. Not with a knife in his hands.

His brain wasn't in bad shape. It remembered his training. It couldn't think yet, but it could remember.

It could remember that infantrymen exchanging signals lie face down, not face up like virgins on their wedding night.

Or whenever it is virgins lie face up.

Three stone-white faces, no camouflage, not even a dab of soil or mould from a ripped off section of tree bark. Weiss would be displeased. Three white faces, but with how many shadows on them? The shadows glittered. Extra mouths, misplaced eyes, little ponds that gaped with blood.

Matson crawled over. What he saw explained the smell of cordite. Lippiat wasn't here. But Lippiat had company, immediately before or after Matson's arrival – after, else he'd have niffed the discharge, heard the shots from the gully. The company had spelled trouble, but no trouble for Lippiat.

Head shots. Matson's training disapproved of head shots. But stone-white faces in the moonlight made easy shooting for a man of Lippiat's calibre. Easy shooting at clear aiming points.

Three shots and not a breath between them. At close range the Lee Enfield is a weapon of distinction and grace, such as mortuary beauticians approve of. Punchy entrance wounds, no enlargement at exit, unless the bullet takes something with it. And these lads were too young and well kept to need artificial teeth.

365

Matson nearly didn't recognize them, holes in faces being a distraction and the moonlight always odd. It makes ugly girls beautiful and cows become tigers. It even helped Lili look briefly alive in his arms, when she'd obviously prefer to be dead.

What a pity they hadn't been in their SS lookalikes. Lolly would have enjoyed that, but he'd known who they were when he'd said 'SS and vermin and men like your host'. He'd seen the Weiss chauffeur, Blondie and the handyman gardener stealing down on them; that's why he'd spoken those words. Then he'd fired past Matson's turned-away head and nearly blown his brains out.

Lolly hadn't looted, old warrior though he was. The bodies wore standard Walther P38s, probably at Weiss's expense.

His erstwhile naked swimming companion also carried something extra, probably as a love gift. An Israeli Industries Desert Eagle magnum with the short barrel. The new .44. Matson had ordered one, but it hadn't been delivered when he came on leave. He couldn't resist it. He took this, and some bloodied ammunition.

He should have picked up a Walther P38. It would fire Weiss's parabellum cartridges.

The big magnum was too much gun for a man about to go potholing.

14

Matson didn't like caves. He suffered acutely from common sense.

This would be more of a pothole, a dead and eventually alive watercourse cut out of karstic limestone. The direction of the surface fissure suggested that the gully and, lower down, the dried-up stream where he met the goats were part of the same system. The cave would reach thousands of feet down inside the mountain. Inside it he could break limbs, drown, suffocate or simply be lost. People went mad in places like that, and frequently they starved with only the blind to console them: blind rats, blind bats, blind fish, blind snakes.

366

He didn't suffer from common sense. He suffered from claustrophobia. He needed a companion, a light, a rope, a marker cord and some protective headgear.

The Germans had a torch. Rummaging among their packs and clothings started his headache again. It was cold up here.

He had crawled or been dragged some distance from the fissure in the ground. The Germans lay between it and the gully. Once he'd found their torch, he stayed on his hands and knees, turned through one hundred and eighty degrees and began to search for the entrance to the pot.

No more moon but an abundance of stars. He must have been unconscious for at least an hour. No, longer. The moon set after midnight. He might have frozen to death.

Surely Lippiat hadn't left him for dead?

If Gerry wanted him dead he'd be dead. He was too thorough for anything else. Matson had been in the way of an exchange of fire. The men were lying together. Lolly must have aimed close to his head more than once.

A crack in the ground widened and deepened. It didn't widen much, but it deepened dramatically.

The torch was a necessity. Underground he couldn't cope without it, but if people were sleeping without light down there. . . .

He lay with his head above the lip of the crack, held the torch down inside it and switched the thing on. Six feet below him nestled a dead sheep.

Fleece, horns, a frosty mess like old jam. The place was too cold for the dead animal to smell, but death always does its best. He buttoned his torch inside his shirt – more potential bruising – and lowered himself on to the rotting fleece.

No more cooking odours. The feast was long done.

He heard voices, heard metal on stone. Not a firearm. Something less solid. A tin cup.

The voices were not distorted. They weren't echoing up from the depths of the system. They were near.

Above him there were stars. He ghost-walked with his hands to make sure there was nothing for his head to bump, then edged forward on his backside, his feet feeling the way in front.

No more stars above. He had moved about three yards. Try another three.

The cave stopped. Solid ahead. Solid above. Solid to his right. To his left then. Feel to the left. Still solid.

A wind blew. Not a wind, a draught of air from the entrance. Draughts can't blow in unless they have somewhere to get to. This one was blowing out. So were the voices.

He saw a lightness above him. He hadn't used his torch so his eyes were now accustomed to what little illumination there was.

The lightness had a star in it, a star visible to only one eye. It shone through an extension of the crack in the cave roof. He winked, out of instinct. The star disappeared, but a tiny glow remained then disappeared in its turn.

A gust of laughter and the tiny glow was back again. He put his left hand down to the floor. There was no floor there, only draught. The floor had divided into two levels, one forking downwards in a rubble of stone, one shelving straight ahead and stopping against the end of the level. He was sitting on the shelf.

He shuffled backwards, made sure of the way out, and then came forward to drop down a level.

15

No torch. The torch wasn't necessary. He slid down with the gun on his lap, and he didn't slide far.

The chute spilled into a larger cavern, a place he would have to drop into or stay out of, because the chute steepened and disappeared.

The light and the people were at the far end. The light was a gas lantern. There was also the remains of a cooking fire. Or a warming fire. This end was ice cold.

The child was there. He crouched on the floor, pink faced and with eyes wide open. A cave and a camp fire were probably the best things he'd seen in weeks.

Hard to describe a cave in real-estate terms. Matson knew that its architecture was against him.

368

It was at least thirty feet long, perhaps fifty. It was ten feet wide and fifteen feet high. Matson was at the top of those fifteen feet, with the slide of stones going only a third of the way down.

Three of them, including today's messenger. Lolly wasn't one of them, so he could presumably arrive behind him. As could any number of other people.

Three of them for now. Matson at last with a gun.

He should have brought one of the Walthers. Did the magnum have a double-action trigger? Or could he only hand cock the first round? The reviews said it had a very heavy pull. He tried the hammer. Heavy again. It had been set up for some other work than fast active-service shooting.

Matson wasn't a murderer. Like other men who have been trained to kill efficiently, he looked for at least a hint of moral authority. He had no quarrel with Weiss's enemies, and with these three men least of all. One of them had raced him up the mountain and deserved his total admiration. They had no right to the child, true. They were his kidnappers or at least his gaolers.

One of them, a man with a beard, was covering the boy with a blanket. The third man cleared away a plate from near his head.

Little Henk was never far from sleep. Lotte's drugs saw to that. The lad would have to wait. He had to believe Lippiat that no harm was intended. Far better alert Popovic to arrange a proper rescue.

The best Matson could do against these people would be to demand the child at gunpoint. That would give him the moral authority. Equally it would squander the moral advantage.

Forget that he would have to fight his way down the mountain. What would he do now, if they bluffed his gun?

It would take aimed shots, in a burst situation. It would take him six or seven seconds even with a familiar gun. Six or seven seconds would give one of them plenty of time. The place might be booby-trapped. There might be a determination to kill the boy if anyone attempted a rescue.

Matson didn't consider the chance that any of the men might have a weapon to hand. He already knew he would

369

never fire. In a cave of compacted limestone, jacketed bullets might ricochet. Soft noses and snubs might bounce. He could get the boy dead and himself dead from this bloody magnum. And from a Walther P38.

There were four men there, suddenly. One of them standing. Matson heard his own name.

Lippiat, now stooping to join his friends, speaking their language and joking in it as easily as if it were his own. There was obviously another and better way in than by the shoot of rock.

Lippiat told Matson's story with his hands. He gave the Germans their obituary. They were *kaputt*, he said. Universal word. It travelled well. Matson? Matson had Lippiat's hand on his head, heard his brain leak away through the men's laughter. Matson was a thicky, a lunk. He'd had a sleep in the frost, wouldn't know the difference. Now he was gone howling away down the mountainside. They laughed. They showed no sign of packing up and leaving, no anxiety that their hide had been discovered.

Matson filed that away for later. Gerry's arrival clinched things. He wasn't going to shoot Lolly in cold blood, whatever he had against him. And cold-blooded it would need to be. He'd have to take him out immediately because he was too bloody handy with that rifle of his.

Matson inched away, back into the outer darkness. Lolly leant forward and stroked the child's face. He was his grandfather, of course, or he thought he was. That was a factor, too.

16

Failure depressed him. Failure or frustration. Depression is a sloppy emotion, and sloppy emotions make for sloppy deeds.

He slid backwards along the rock shelf, until he was no longer able to see into the cave. The palms of his hands found the rotting sheep. The sheep that had died down a hole. The sheep's plight should have warned him.

If this had been an active-service mission in the old days, Matson would have been properly briefed. Someone would have cautioned him *watch that hole, be careful how you climb from that bloody hole. In triumph or disarray, fit or with a bullet up your bum, be extremely careful of it.* If the Thugs hadn't known all the angles, they wouldn't have sent Matson. His thuggery only showed tinges of alpha. On a blind assignment, they'd have sent someone with a better balance of adrenalin and caution.

The emergent male is at risk. Like any animal in the birth-drop he is in danger from jackal and crow. The sheep should have warned him. He straddled it and stood up.

Something kicked his head. It might have been a hobnail. It might have been a meteorite. He was only unconscious for a second's falling, but he didn't fall. His assailant took a thoughtful grab at his windpipe. Matson hung from his Adam's apple and his cranial notch, his neck cosy in a nest of thumbs. Then the arms on the ends of the thumbs lifted him skywards and dragged him clear.

Matson smashed out. He did it from reflex reinforced by training. He led with his foot, and then with his elbows while he still lolled in space. *If your enemy rips your guts out or holds your head in the furnace door, kick him in the teeth,* more than one instructor had advised him. *He won't be expecting it.*

His assailant wasn't expecting it, but it didn't worry him. Something, somebody, the thumbs or a JCB powerdriver, began to beat his head on the ground.

'*Dummes Soldatchen,*' a voice said.

Matson recognised the voice almost immediately. He had wrestled with it once. He was aware of the smell. It was Auntie Goliath, sky high on the mountain top. Auntie was not with the patrol. Auntie was too big to patrol, and therefore not dead. Auntie was too big for death. Auntie Goliath wasn't saying, 'Aarh!' this time. Not with Matson at his feet. He was having his revenge. And his revenge was extremely painful to Matson, because one of Auntie's feet was bandaged in a plaster of Paris that had set as hard as concrete. Bandaged over the damage that Matson had so recently inflicted on it.

Auntie should have killed him at once instead of almost at once.

Auntie wasn't like that. Auntie had a trick or two to play.

One trick, actually.

Auntie Goliath picked him up again. Men like Auntie who've thought a lot about killing with their hands, and dreamt about it, and perhaps done it, tend to have a preferred way.

With his big belly as a fulcrum, and pectorals to apply the necessary bone-busting pressure, Auntie fancied the bear hug. He pushed Matson's head into the dirt and encouraged him to fill his face with it. Then, still holding him by the scruff and a fistful of scalp, he scooped him clear of the ground and into the air, turning him as he fell. He didn't let Matson's legs touch the ground again, oh no. Auntie Goliath didn't drop twelve-stone Matson any more than he would have let slip a romping child. He caught Matson shoulder-high with his arms round his waist, and stuck his chin into his abdomen and chewed his mouth to and fro, it seemed against Matson's spine. Then he locked his hands and tightened his grip.

Matson grunted with pain, would have screamed if he had the lungs, and began to kick his way down the giant's body.

This was according to plan. Auntie Goliath chuckled and began to climb up Matson in turn, settling him lower, till with his feet six or nine inches clear of the frost, he could increase the pressure and snap him.

Matson tried to lift a knee into a crotch, feel for a testicle or so, but his knee was nowhere he could lift it, and the Weiss entourage had been warned by Blondie against offering him any further genital inducement. His hand was clenched between bone and bone, and quickly lost the wit from its fingers.

What else was there? Ears. He could still move one arm from the elbow. All things were possible, every permutation of flesh, now his skeleton came unstrung.

He fingered Auntie's ear. Auntie's ear was an illusive concept. Wrestlers are like boxers, are like the essayist

Charles Lamb. They have no ear. Cauliflower is a misnomer. Bean would be better. Auntie Goliath's bean was in need of an overnight soaking in cold water before it would resemble anything so soft as an ear. And tonight, dressed truly to kill, Auntie had denied it the glory of diamond or pendant. Matson had nothing to swing on. Matson gave up.

His chin now rested on the top of Auntie's head. His neck was wrenching backwards, and inside it the bone grew longer. His mouth was full of blood, vomit, and whatever slice of mountain Auntie had so recently fed it with. The vomit was a bad sign. It meant something was on the point of snapping.

'*Dummchen*,' Auntie murmured. '*Ah, dummchen, dummchen, dummchen.*' With Matson so nearly done for, he treated himself to some breath. '*Ah, dummchen*,' he crooned.

Still humming to himself, he jerked his head from beneath Matson's chin. He gazed fondly upwards. There was longing in his eyes. Longing for the neck his traction was about to separate. Auntie was half in love with easeful death.

Matson didn't notice the gesture. Not at first. If only there were moonlight. The fat moon had set. But there was mountain starlight, and Auntie's eyes shone brighter in his skull than egg-whites in the holes of a mask. The rest became suffused.

Matson tried to speak to him. He strove, and Auntie loved him for it.

The word was never uttered. Matson choked instead. He choked on Mother Earth, he choked on Auntie's strength. He choked on a sooty mouthful of tooth chippings, peabugs and frost. Then there was Black Mountain grit, gone salty with blood.

He cleared his throat. He cleared it from the stomach. He cleared it straight into Auntie's face, lacking time to be decent, aiming mostly into one or the other of Auntie's eyes, but gumming up Auntie's crooning, all the way to the voicebox, possibly by the nostril.

The grit would be bad enough, the blood a salty worse; the spew acid and intolerable.

Auntie gagged and tried to wipe his eye on Matson, but

Matson was covered in yet more Matson, was producing it by the heartbeat.

Auntie didn't scream or let go. He set about killing Matson properly. It was like holding on to mud or melting butter, like wrestling in last year's offal. He tightened his grip, but the soap slid away and out of reach.

Matson didn't thump the man, kick him, or risk getting near him again. Should have felt inside his own mucky shirt, and used the Desert Eagle. He doubted his grip on a magnum, or even his strength to pull the trigger.

He left Auntie Goliath blind in the starlight, and set off on a jolting, loose-boned run for the lip of the crag.

18

The glacis was dry, the rock chimney dusty. It ate the slime from his hands and pullover. He shivered, heard Auntie come howling after him, so dropped quickly down to the chock stone.

Auntie climbed too. Matson went out and over the chock stone, nearly skidding on his own muck. His hands just held.

Auntie did not follow further. The chock stone was not for Auntie. Auntie was all chock stone himself.

Matson crouched underneath it, left heel behind him, right leg thrust forward. He couldn't sit back and jam, even though the width was right. He might need to shift position quickly. Auntie Goliath might grow wings or come back with a helicopter.

He heard a grunt up above, then a large wrenching of rock. The chock stone dragged lower with a sound like a tooth being pulled. A tooth with a thunderous root. A tooth in his own head. His face flooded with light.

Auntie had found the torch, was squatting on the chock stone and searching the void with it. He didn't find void. He encountered darkness visible. He saw Matson, clinging at the top of one of the mountain's natural waste-disposal chutes. He saw Matson and purred. Matson remembered the three Walthers up there, and pulled his head out of the light. He

374

huddled under the chock stone, dripping sweat. He glued himself on like a snail.

Auntie began to sing. His poor old foot in its iron hoop skidded around, and his heart beat noisily – sorry, that was Matson's heart but it was Auntie Goliath who sang. He got himself out of the chimney and began to collect rocks. Matson could hear him packing them together like a hod-carrier loading up with bricks. *Steinschlag* was taking on a new meaning.

So when he came down again, Matson would have to shoot him, if only he could see him beyond his torch, supposing Auntie hadn't picked up a gun or two for himself.

The Desert Eagle was a two-handed affair, unfortunately, and so far Matson couldn't spare even a finger.

He pressed himself more deeply into the chimney, and kept his head against the chock stone. While he stayed here, he was perfectly safe. If he moved he was dead. Auntie was preparing a suitable avalanche of Montenegro's natural scenery for him. And Montenegro was built from some of God's best masonry.

The chock stone moved. Something nudged Matson's back. The light shone briefly and he saw a spar of wood, whether a spruce pole or a rail from a sheep hut, he couldn't tell. Auntie was levering the chock stone away.

It might be impossible to displace, it might not.

The bullet and the muzzle flash were simultaneous. Something – jacketed lead or a scab of rock – looped and butted around the chimney like a wasp in a jamjar. Matson's leg flared with pain. He wasn't hit, not directly. Not yet. His calf had merely been peppered skinless by blowback.

Auntie fired again, again aiming at the slot he had made between chock stone and chimney. The ricochet went off a flake of rock and away into the night, deafening Matson with its clap of air. The flake glowed red-hot from impact.

Too damned close to his head. Matson waited until Auntie strained again on his piece of pole, put a hand out of the chimney, felt the face of the cliff, and went with what he found. He made two moves sideways in the dark, one on faith and one on nothing. Then he found a good, gritty ledge against his knee, and stepped up on to its shelf, all six inches of it.

Three more shots into the chimney. Then the levering and grunting with the pole.

Matson adjusted his grip and heard the chock stone fall towards Otok.

Light flashed. Auntie began to tip down his lovingly assembled arsenal of limestone and granite. The light flashed again. Auntie had detected rather than seen where he was.

Matson heard the man move away, shuffle back somewhere overhead.

Nothing happened. Either there was a glacis too steep for a lame man to risk, or Matson was sheltered by an overhang. Brill, as the teenagers say. Megabrill.

The voice came from very close, much too close for comfort.

19

It sounded directly above him, speaking Serbo-Croat brusquely and with some surprise. Lippiat, as distinct and snug to his ear as if there were a megaphone drilled through the rock. Not surprise. An ascending urgency of enquiry.

Auntie didn't answer, not in his give-away German. Auntie was not the man for it. Auntie was above there and unseen, for the moment unheard, but as immanent as a tummy rumble.

No more silence. Auntie took a shot, or somebody did, a shot whose echoes racketed above Matson then returned faintly from in front a dozen seconds later. The bullet went out beyond him and drooped towards the forest. A revolver bullet that had missed or a rifle bullet slowed by bone.

He heard the shuffle, the grunt – no, the grunt and then the shuffle – but it was the pistol that came down first, in a hot fart of cordite like a blackbird drunk in a powder shed. Liquid dribbled down, blood or some other heat.

Then came Auntie – did he fall or was he pushed? – a great wheezing shadow as huge as a tumbling bull.

He struck the cliff some fifty metres below, and went out

again voiceless. After that he spoke, but only the way balloon bags do when they've suffered a puncture. The crash was a long time coming, or a long time coming back.

Auntie didn't need to come back. Auntie stayed with Matson, his aroma still in the air.

TWENTY-THREE

1

'You'll never make Queen's Scout, my dear. Only a fool walks off a mountain at midnight. They'll withhold your Bushman's Thong.'

Matson reeked of dried sweat, wet sweat, leaf mould, German blood and his own blood, stale and fresh. He was as revolting as a week-old massacre. Mostly he stank of failure. He had done everything, achieved nothing.

'It was that or freeze to death.'

'Ah, death!' Popovic got himself out of bed and called for coffee. Instead of pyjamas he wore a commanding officer's active-service compromise: string vest and boxer shorts. He slept on a bedroll in a tent, but the bedroll was on a bed, and the tent had a slatted floor with carpet. It also held a pine wash-stand and one of his filing cabinets. It was a ridge tent as big as a room and it looked a lot more comfortable than his office in Belgrade.

'Fresh coffee takes time.' He unlocked an oval flask of Serbian brandy from his filing cabinet and found a pair of tin mugs inside his wash-stand. He poured generously. 'We old soldiers learn to be comfortable. It's a British notion, but universal in its application, my dear Patrick. God knows what it says about you boy soldiers.'

'The urgent fact is –'

'Your G. Bernard Shaw wrote a play about the Balkans, my dear. It contains a useful truth. Never make plots in a tent.' He received a bucket of coffee at the door and a baling spoon. 'Not until the squirrels have gone back to their trees, eh?' He listened to the boots go away across the pine needles, then added, 'I take it you found the boy? So did I.

378

Or I assume so. I have a photograph of your friend Lippiat and my friend the doctor walking into the earth together. Legendary figures performing magical acts. Jug Bogdan for sure, old Ivan Crnojevic perhaps.' He smirked. 'They are so pleased with themselves, the rascals, they forget how much detail can be uncovered by a good military stereoscope. I've had a helicopter up there for days, flying photographic patterns. Never overhead, you understand. Always round the edges of the mountain.' He rummaged in his wash-stand drawer and uncovered some glossies. 'Does this look like the place?'

It did. Lolly was wearing his Lee Enfield behind his shoulder, loose-slung in its sniping web. He also sported an unlikely looking pouched bandolier. The doctor was dressed as Matson remembered him, save for a woollen cap.

'Encouraged by this geographical certainty, I went for a ride up the mountain myself while you were strangling my lad in his braces.

'I took my binoculars, dear Patrick. They flaunt them-selves, these ancient conspirators. They are in Montenegro, our most secure state, they have a little pit-hole on top of its safest mountain, and they think it prudent to forget their partisan good manners. These are famous men, Patrick, well known among the stupid as much as to me. Jug Bogdan is no use. His relatives are in England. The 'doctor' is clearly Crnojevic, and lacks family ties. But I also have the true identities of Stefan Kotromanic, Banus Kulin and Primoz Trubar. Who Clement Slovensky is remains an unimportant mystery, given that a very good candidate of Matija Gubec is not only holidaying in these parts but was seen walking a broken-faced Jovanka Zarkovic through the woods yesterday.'

'The older man from the rubber boat. I saw someone of Weiss's age helping Anka.'

2

'Let me summarize my position, Patrick.' Popo brisk and persuasive now. 'I am certain the child is in no danger.

Kidnapping him was a mistake. No one likes kidnappers. Nobody believes, in a case like this, that the sins of a monstrous parent should be visited upon the innocent child. Vincenz Weiss was old enough to satisfy the Serbian notion of the blood feud. Perhaps. This is a little boy. In fifteen, twenty years' time, unless some of us change our thinking down here, then he may be considered eligible. Not now. If I am wrong about the larger view, well, the conspirators have given me hostages of my own. I know too many names, and I'm letting them know I know. No one is going to murder junior Weiss.'

Matson nodded his understanding. Agreement was something to be chewed on.

'The Hunbag is another matter. I can guard him. I cannot protect him. You pull your face at me again. I am not being defeatist, my dear. Merely liberal with my common sense. On the lake I now have the two naval launches as well as the one I snaffled. I have a helicopter. Around me I have my own people. I have closed Jezero right down. I have most of a regiment of infantry. Still, the Obergruppensniff does not want me on the island. I have been there. He insists I do not stay. From his point of view it's reasonable, no matter what reassurances I bring him about the kidnap. The child dominates his thinking. He doesn't want to transgress the conditions imposed by the people who hold him. Perhaps you can change his mind. Perhaps we can move towards more serious matters. Such as the matters you still refuse to talk to me about.'

The darkness beyond the tent flap was thinning. It had taken him the whole bloody night to blunder downhill into another of Popo's verbal traps.

'There is going to be a catastrophe and I can't see any way to protect him from it. I can't even protect him from his own women.' Popovic anticipated Matson's exasperation by saying, 'I respect that list of names, my dear. Now more than ever. The men are a perfect demographic fit. So what am I to make of the two ladies Bogdan, the Widow and the Daughter-in-law? And what of Kosovka, the Maiden of Kosovo herself? Or are these in fact ladies we do not know about? Are they still lurking down the hole or painting their

380

toenails in Belgrade? Is it likely?'

'The Ehrenberg-Zanetti is too strident to convince me she's a murderess,' Matson said. 'His son's wife is at worst mad, at best stupid.'

'Aggression and derangement. I could find murder there, couldn't you? My government would be entirely delighted if one of that pair – *foreigners*, my dear, and his own playthings, not to say family – were to top the Obersniffbag. And *if* it were *domestic* murder, dear Patrick –'

'Or were to look like a domestic murder.'

'How *quick* you are, and so early too. I doubt whether the local police will have anyone as sharp as, say, Inspector Kaub, do you?'

Or a second echelon staffed with Willis and Albins, Matson thought.

It was a mountain dawn, late and moist with fog from the water.

'Suppose there are two plots,' Popo said. 'Suppose there is a public plot and a private one. In both plots Weiss gets dead. In the private plot, Jovanka and Lippiat acquire their grandson, Jovanka regains her island.'

'How can that possibly be?'

'Because of who gets arrested for the murder. Arrested and perhaps executed.'

'That's not possible.'

'Not likely, I agree. But there may be an extra-judicial execution, my dear – a beautiful English phrase. It is, after all, *un crime passionnel.* A man may defend himself with his pistol, even against a woman, if he is an old man. I do not know the *mise en scène* because, like you, I am not *au fait* with the plot, but it may encompass corpses galore – all of them conveniently foreigners. With young Weiss, Jovanka's grandson, who will inherit the property anyway, being held in safety while the bullets fly.

'So much for the private plot. You see how it needs the public plot, how each depends upon the other? You perceive the *symmetry*? It needs the kidnapping of the boy both to attract public sympathy and to distract attention. To make sense of it. Weiss dies. You, I, or *somebody* rescues the child. Apart from the child, who does not belong to Weiss anyway, the entire Weiss clan is meanwhile swept away. Wouldn't that have appeal? The media would be content, but then – much more important down here – the whisperings would start, the whisperings and the songs. Their message? Jovanka has regained her island, her grandson, and, yes, perhaps regained one of her men who is the child's grandfather. The partisans will have triumphed. At a time when separation is rampant, famous men from each of the autonomous regions will have united to achieve a new balance. *Le coeur a ses raisons que la raison ne connait pas.* What do you say?'

'I'm glad you're full of so much French this morning, Popovic. You need something to wrap all that bullshit in.'

'I did not say the Weiss women will kill the old man, my dear. *Merely that it could so easily be made to look that way.*'

3

Popovic allowed himself to sit back on his bed so he could luxuriate on his next words. 'What keeps me awake at night is the old lady, Patrick. This Jovanka Zarkovic, widow of Peter Zarkovic, whose head holds up that tower. As I lie here, I can see the tower at dusk and at dawn, my dear. As the sun sets and as it rises. And I think of Jovanka Zarkovic with her hatred, alone in her house for forty years among her peonies and shrubberies and rose beds, knowing that sooner or later Weiss is going to take possession of it all. He has a piece of paper that gives him title to everything, including each and every skeleton her castle is built from. He *even owns her horror.*'

'She can't go back to the island, Popo. Not for moment. Not while Weiss is alive. And, as we both know, she's injured.'

'Mightn't it be possible in forty years, I wonder, to prepare a hideaway somewhere, a kind of monk's hole? A place where some of the other people whose relatives have been used for building material could smuggle themselves to wait?'

Matson was already on his feet. He had missed trains by listening while the porter gave too many directions.

'The messengers who delivered the rats, where did they get to? Perhaps Jovanka delivered the first rats by herself. Not the second, by all accounts. And the child. You saw him taken ashore. But was that directly? Directly after the rat game, perhaps. But directly after the kidnap?'

'I'll need some water transport, Popo.'

Popo was now safely inside the contents of his bedroll. They were unusually sybaritic for a soldier. 'Not while you're holding out on the larger truth, Patrick.'

'I don't know the half of it yet. And what I know would take an hour to make any sense of.'

Popovic turned his back and grinned, 'You'll all be dead before then.'

Matson went wearily towards the lake.

TWENTY-FOUR

1

Matson had buried his automatic before going to hear Popo's version of things. He had hidden it in yesterday's hollow beneath the trees. He didn't intend to exhume the gun, not yet. He needed one of his plastic bags.

He dumped his shirt, socks and trousers inside the bag. He'd lost his kitchen knife and its leg strappings somewhere on the mountain. The carver was still with him, but it was too much knife to swim with this time. He wrapped it and buried it beside the pistol. Full-calibre magnums are cannon. A full-calibre magnum automatic is a cannon encased in a steam-engine. He didn't propose to float this one to Otok, or have it drown him on the way.

He pulled his boots back onto bare feet, callouses and all, and carried his plastic bundle towards the jetty. From here to the landing stage was the shortest crossing, however public.

Beyond the last plank there was a flake of rock and then deep water. Matson sat on the plank with his foot on the rock and unlaced his boots once more. Nobody tittered. Nobody was awake to see him.

His head was full of Popovic's latest neurosis, that the threat to Weiss was already on the island. There might be a 'stay behind' team in place, prepared to involve the women in some calculated ritual of mayhem and then rig the evidence. Something was missing from the argument, but he was too tired to think it through.

He bagged his boots and secured enough air inside the plastic to give him a buoyant package. Then he saw the apparition.

His eyes were tired, his body exhausted, a skein of after-

384

dawn mist ghosted above the water. In those conditions of mind and light he glanced towards Otok and was surprised to see a statue.

It was of a naked woman, seated eyes down and pensive by the water's edge. At three hundred yards he couldn't see eyes; statues don't have eyes, they have positions of neck and head.

Not a statue. The nude was Lotte, poor Lili Weiss. He could see her hand move, a small stirring at her lap like the flutter of a bird's wing.

How had he mistaken her for a statue? Because the eye expects statues on lawns by lakes. Even Casanova must have seen more statues of naked women than naked women themselves.

Lotte wasn't naked, not quite. Her flesh was too blue. She must be wearing that ridiculous bath gown. The dew had pinned it against her and made it transparent.

God knows what drama of grief or jealousy had left her sitting like this, dressed like this, there in the thin dawn light.

Matson got into the water. He didn't wave. He didn't drown. He swam economically. His body seemed to lack moving parts, and the ones he had were short of blood.

Lotte was at her crocheting. Nearly naked or not, she had remembered her hook, her ball of thread and her knife.

A cramp took hold of him. First the cold, then the exhaustion, then the immovable pain in his damaged leg.

2

Cramp wouldn't kill him, not this trip. His bag of clothes was buoyant enough to hold chest and mouth above water while the rest of his body tied itself in knots. Cramp cures itself if you can wait long enough. Oxygen cures it quickly. Carbon dioxide cures it sooner than that. Carbon dioxide was what this cramp got. His body had plenty of that. It stopped breathing for a long harsh minute while it knotted itself up with the ecstasy of it.

Eyes without air grow long-sighted. They record miracles of star-form and leaf before going blind. Matson's own eyes

385

got their red corpuscles back before vision deserted them, and reached a conclusion well ahead of his brain.

Lotte was outdoors waiting for him. Her anxiety was for his return. Her dementia was his alone. He was expected. She was hoping for good news but her pain was nothing, or not entirely, to do with her absent son.

Fifty yards from the island he knew he was pushing towards catastrophe. Something had taken place, was happening now or was imminent. He wasn't psychic. He read it first from Lotte's posture, now from her face.

Weiss was waiting for him too. While his leg had been cramping, his long-sighted eyes had seen Weiss appear at an upstairs window, Matson's window.

Now Weiss was waiting by Lotte at the foot of the lawn. The whole island was waiting. Weiss was waiting so much and so hard that when Matson had thirty yards to go he stepped down on to the landing stage. He stood there and smiled and flourished with his hand.

He didn't extend its clasp to Matson. He unzipped his fly and piddled at length and with casual largesse through all of his arrogance into the very waters Matson would a second later be swimmimg in.

3

Matson had swum in the Western Mediterranean, where the transparent sections of water are one hundred per cent urine, and the thicknesses only occasionally fish. There such matters are catholic, warm-hearted and impersonal. Here they were aimed at him.

His face fetched up against the landing stage and Weiss's boots.

'Where is the boy?'

Matson rubbed wet hair against the General's trousers, and heaved himself out. He spat, missing the boots. Spitting was an achievement for a man with a dry mouth. Missing was the unfortunate product of exhaustion.

'Where is Mrs Ehrenberg-Zanetti?' That was quite a mouthful after a long swim.

386

Weiss and Lotte exchanged glances. Lotte's was sulky. She fidgeted her damp mauve gown like a broken wing.

'Asleep,' Weiss said. 'Asleep.' He took comfort in the word. Perhaps he was boasting again. 'Where is Henk?'

Matson told him, in detail.

'So you left him there. If anything goes wrong, if anything happens to him, I personally shall pick you to pieces.'

'You'll need strong fingers.'

'I shall use pliers.'

Matson took his not-quite-nudity indoors.

Lotte followed him. Weiss was ahead of him into the house, stopping him from taking his bundle upstairs.

4

'You neglected to rescue him.'

'Too much risk. He could have been hit in an exchange of fire.' He broke open the plastic bag and dressed in his shirt. 'Also I couldn't discount the idea that he might be deliberately sacrificed.'

'So. You found the odds too great.'

Matson stripped off his dripping drawers and kicked them through the door on to the lawn. Then he pulled on his jeans.

'Where did you acquire a gun for this supposed exchange of fire? Did Colonel Popovic provide it?'

'I took it from one of your people.' Matson explained the circumstances as he regained his socks and laced up his boots.

'First you damage one of them, then you break them all.'

'I didn't kill your men.' He felt easier now he was dressed. 'I couldn't have done it so well.' He found himself a chair by the table. 'In abstract, what happened to them seems unnecessary. Of course, I don't know what instructions you issued –'

'I issued no instructions. There is no telephone here.'

'Every night you were over-elaborate with cigars. Your men flashed torches from the shore. That was when I could see you. God knows what signals you sent when I couldn't see you – from your bedroom window, say. In any event, regrettable though their death is, the fact is they would probably have ended up getting the boy killed.'

'Suppose I believe you. Your story is no better than that they were killed by this other Englishman, this associate of yours.'

'Your old enemy, General.'

'The Austrian papers said you were friends,' Lotte said.

'Cronies,' Matson corrected. 'That's how my *Collins Gem German Dictionary* translates it. Cronies.' He pushed his hands against the table and made to stand up. 'I don't have to discuss this, Weiss. I can go to bed right now, if you like.' In a minute or two he'd fall asleep on the bloody floor.

'Later.' Weiss had taken his Luger from its holster and was turning it in his hand. He stood at the foot of the stairs, and from time to time kept glancing upwards.

'If there's going to be a council of war, I'd like Constanz to sit in on it,' Matson said.

'She's drunk,' Lotte snapped. 'All night drunk. She is now ill.'

'She wasn't drunk,' Weiss said. 'She's doped. This has become a family affair. Some things I do not wish her to concern herself with.'

Lotte giggled. She liked the idea of Constanz being doped, or drunk, or anything except here and available for comment. Her giggle made her sound drunk in her own right, but Lotte's giggle was Lotte's giggle, even before breakfast time.

'I'd like some coffee,' Matson said. Lotte's shock and Weiss's frustration at the continuing absence of the boy were natural enough. What he couldn't understand was the General's change of mood in the last thirty-six hours. The arrogance was there, but it was undercut by mistrust and indecision. Anguish was making him human, and it wasn't a pretty sight.

Weiss declipped the Luger, checked the Parabellum, reloaded it with a flourish.

Matson should have taken it from him in that unguarded operatic moment. Instead, he said gently, 'I'm not frightened of that bloody gun, Weiss.'

388

'I don't use guns to frighten people, Captain Matson. I use them the way you do. This gun especially.'

Matson hadn't shot schoolgirls in the head, not yet, or not in great numbers, but this was his time of reconciliation and light.

'Where is my man's gun now?' Weiss asked.

'I buried it. I needed to talk to Popovic.' He might as well have come by boat.

'You reported to Popovic? You reported to Popovic, not to me?'

'Neither of you runs me. Things have moved on since we last spoke. I've found the boy for you. Popovic has elaborate and convincing reasons for deducing he is safe. He is sure he can extract him without pain. If you decide otherwise, then the pair of us can go up there this evening. First, I'll need to rest.'

'Lotte said you would be the viper. What are you suggesting? That you lead me there for them to cut my balls off?'

'That's a strange image, Weiss. You're seeing the wrong traitors.'

Weiss gave a final glance upstairs, then placed his gun on the table. 'Coffee,' he said. 'All right, make us some coffee, Lili.'

Matson stayed slumped in his chair. Weiss could be as chauvinistic as he liked. Matson was merely tired.

As she heated water and milk in the kitchen, Weiss called, 'Or cocoa. Let's have some of that cocoa.' To Matson he smiled grimly and said, 'Cocoa's an ugly word. She'll know I mean drinking chocolate.'

5

Drinking chocolate it was, oversweet with honey already in the cup, but with an undercut of bitterness that cleared the mouth.

'Mrs Ehrenberg-Zanetti is a raucous woman,' the General said. 'An irreverent woman. I too judge the boy will come to no harm, no immediate harm anyway. However, the position

389

is ambiguous enough to make me wish you had been able to retrieve him for me.'

Lotte did not quite speak. She served Matson with more chocolate and sat at the table making a breathless noise in her throat.

'A young man should have his adventures,' the General said to her gently. 'And I am sure he will live to look back on this as an adventure. Unfortunately –' again to Lotte – 'old men cannot always endure the price. And women too must sometimes do more than weep.'

Matson wanted to tell him to make his point, so he could sleep, so they could all sleep. He felt so sleepy himself that he didn't care whether he slept or not.

The General took a piece of paper from the pocket in his shirt. 'I am reassured by what these kidnappers write to me,' he said. 'I have not yet shared the matter with Lotte,' he explained to Matson, 'beyond telling her to be easy that the boy is well.'

He unwrapped the paper and read it slowly, as if for the first time. Matson would not have thought he would show emotion, but he did. First he recited the names of the signatories, finishing with the three Bogdans. 'The boy will remain unharmed,' he said. 'That is the promise, so you can forget those hideous threats of the first evening.' He spoke to her quickly in German, then said, 'He will never be hurt, but after three days he will not be fed.' Again he spoke in German. Some words are easily translatable; some meanings can only be guessed at.

Matson guessed much too slowly. He was doing everything too slowly now.

'If I am prepared to emasculate myself,' Weiss said, 'then they will exchange Henk for the pieces.' He walked round the table to stand over Matson, who found himself unable to move. 'The women, you see. They can't forgive me for their women. And it seems some of their women' – He gestured towards the kitchen, as if Anka might still be there – 'it seems some of their women can't forgive me either. So they have demanded the historical revenge. One of the revenges.'

Matson said nothing. He noticed the gun was no longer on the table, but the gun was immaterial. He would need more than a gun to prop his eyelids up.

'It had to be a test, you see,' the General went on, and it will remain a test as far as I am concerned. But then life is my test. As for Lotte, when you left us the evening before last you said I was silly to trust her in this. Silly because she had so clearly drugged the child for the kidnappers.'

Lotte began her giggle again.

'I considered the matter, Hauptmann. I balanced it. I weighed it. I still do. All I can add to what you already know is this. Lotte drugged Mrs Ehrenberg-Zanetti with a splendid dish of percolan in hot chocolate. I did not ask her in advance. Even so, she has done the same for you. She did it before she knew the demands of these Serbian ruffians –'

'And Croatian,' Matson mumbled. 'And Slovene and –'

'What she does now is a matter for her own honour and judgement. If I am called upon to act in the boy's release, I shall feel bound by my obligation. She will know that. For the moment, I will simply leave her with the thought that one spare part is much like another.' He did not smile now. 'Or so I am reliably told,' he snapped to Lotte. He helped himself to chocolate. Not Matson's kind of chocolate. Chocolate from a jug.

Lotte continued to giggle. Lotte was gone and her giggle was behind him. The blow on Matson's neck was a sound, not a pain. Loose, oil-eaten gun. Loose, cocoa-numbed skull. A lot of light, a sort of darkness. Lili's hysterical giggle filled both of them, and stayed with him long after light and darkness had gone.

Funny how Lotte Weiss always became Lili whenever he closed his eyes.

6

The blow didn't knock him out. Or that was the first thought. It made an ongoing noise in his head. The noise quietened into an ache.

He struggled to get up. It was the hot chocolate. In other words, the bloody cocoa. The General had said it was drugged.

She kept drugs for the child. Children's elixirs have a syrupy base. Together with two or three adult sleeping tablets.

Chocolate was good for headaches. The pain cleared almost immediately.

'What did you hit me with?' You have these questions for someone who has been rough in her love-play.

'The truth, you smelly great lout.'

It wasn't his fault he smelled. It was hers. He had climbed a mountain for her, dabbled in dead men's blood for her. Gone down holes for her. Drunk Popovic's unspeakable cognac, all for her and her child.

He had swum lakes for her, lain in leaf mould, unavoidably watched his adorable little driver in the arms of a lad who might more properly be described a lout. If Frau Lotte Weiss wanted someone smelly she should have a word with young Smoke Ears. Matson would tell her so when she came back.

She hadn't gone away. Meanwhile Matson did smell. He had to be fair to her. Exhaustion and a good bash on the head made him crave to be fair. He smelled of last year's sweat. And the year before's. This year's had washed off in the lake, leaving wrinkled bones and a patina of freeze-dried pondwater. It was a pretty decent smell as such odours go. You could bottle it to spray on cats.

Lotte examined his face with her fingernail, pinched his earlobes, did something painful to a nostril. 'I am prepared to take time,' she said. He loved them when they spoke like that, stroked like that in dusky foreign voices.

He couldn't move his hands, which were outstretched and ached on the ends of his arms.

'Why should Henk pay such a price?' she mused. She combed his belly with a claw or two.

That woke him up a bit. But only in the mind. She had fed him woozy chocolate. She had clubbed him with the edge of an enormous German truth, then manoeuvred or persuaded him to where he now lay with outstretched hands tied to the legs of her bed. He wasn't on her bed. He never had been on her bed. He had never been in her bedroom before. That was why he had only been admitted as far as the floorboards on this occasion. Lotte knew what was appropriate in a bedroom.

She bit him. She found some meat on his collar-bone and bit it to wake him up. It didn't, so she bit him some more. Tenderly. That was the word. Only with her teeth. They didn't wake him up.

What woke him up was realizing that five minutes or five hours ago he was downstairs listening to Weiss talk about castration and here he was upstairs with a woman who had somehow got him tied and with his shirt off, and was laying her penknife, which wasn't so little, which was quite big enough, on the coldness of his naked abdomen. A woman who was stark, raving mad, who had been out of her wicket ever since he'd known her. Castration or total emasculation had the General said?

'Did the General help carry me?'

She put her arms beneath his backbone and lifted. She lifted Matson off the floor, she lifted most of his arms, and the end of the bed. When she gave them back to gravity, his wrists were cut, his back was hurt, the bed ached. Weiss hadn't helped her. The mad need no help in matters like this. Weiss had merely left a naughty suggestion floating in the air.

She unfastened his trousers.

'Jug Bogdan's Daughter-in-law,' he offered. 'What made you change sides?'

She tried him in Serbian, then went back to German. He thought she was making love to him, Jug Bogdan's Daughter-in-law, especially in her liquid Serbian.

When she spoke to him in English she was holding her knife to his throat. 'Perhaps I'll remove your voice box as well.'

'It's only making small talk.'

She laughed. She liked small talk. She put the knife back on his belly and inched it down.

7

'Does the General know you're doing this?'

She wore her superior smile. 'He could not bear to inflict his destiny on another man.'

393

'What will happen when he finds out what you have done?'

'He will treat you as a casualty of war.'

'We know how he felt about those.'

Matson kept his eye on Lotte Weiss, and not on the knife that laid its coldness on his belly.

His hands were throbbing. They felt swollen. She had tied his wrists too tightly. She did everything that way. Ruthlessly and too well. The cord must have been cut and waiting, perhaps already fastened to the bottom of the bed. It felt like the stuff they use for fishermen's net, but not lake net. Its thinness might be an illusion caused by tightness. He couldn't see it. His hands were under the end of the bed, his wrists hidden by the counterpane.

Matson knew what he had to do to get out of here. Unfortunately, a lot of mental conditioning from his past was being undone by the lapse of time since he was last on active training. He could no longer block out the negative thinking. He knew what he must do. He was pretty sure it wouldn't work.

What he must do was maximize the blind terror, the spasm of panic, the anguish at expected terrible agony, to try to burst free.

What stops you from breaking bonds, cords, straps, even chains, is not their strength but the pain the attempt causes you. Blot out all thought of this pain. Seek both to burst the bond and to slip your own hand through it.

Your brute force will break the bond or loosen it. You will break skin, peel tissue. This will give you a second's lubrication and help you slide free.

When the moment came he would lift his legs on to his chest, ignoring her silly knife if it was there and not yet in her hand, then kick forward and out, using the abdominal and thoracic leverage to smash himself upright, wrists free, and if they still weren't free, to hurl the bloody bed through the f......g window and into the s......g lake, if not into actual orbit. By which time his wrists would be free.

Why are you spelling *fucking* and *sodding* with extra dots like that, Matson?

Because the western alphabet does not stretch.

Why are you swearing? It is not terribly like you.

Because my imagination does not stretch either.

He was pumping a fair amount of adrenalin by now. This did not go well with the cocoa or hot chocolate. Or whatever was in the cocoa or hot chocolate.

In the interval, Lotte Weiss had placed her entire body weight on top of his flattened knees.

Women are delicate, gossamer creatures, Lotte or Lili Weiss more than most. Their weight on a flattened leg is enough to keep it immobile, just the same.

'Not bad,' she said. 'Not good but –' She lapsed into German, and opened out her penknife as she did so.

He was in no mood to concentrate on thoughts uttered in tongues.

Damn the bloody chocolate.

She tested the blade on a cushion tassel, then on his hair, and was satisfied. She wasn't being unduly sadistic. She hated him, that was all.

'It will be better,' she murmured. 'This way little Henk will be able to have a brother. We planned it, earlier this year, the General and I. He *is* Henk's father, you know.'

He did know. Or didn't know. He forgot. His cup was in no position to run over, either way.

She lifted the blade towards his body and addressed her task with her free hand.

'There's a man,' he said, 'right behind you.'

The knife handle struck his teeth, once, twice, drawing blood. His speech was irrelevant to her. It prompted her to realize that his scream might be excessive to a person with her sort of nerves.

She shouted at him and began to force the mutilated cushion down his throat.

He had only swallowed a mouthful or so when Lolly Lippiat loomed over her shoulder to hit her, once, with the edge of his hand.

'Sorry,' Lippiat said, almost to himself. 'I never was any good at talking to women.' He picked Lotte up under one arm and tossed her face down on to the bed, where she began to vomit. 'Good job I'm here, Paddy. The tearful young widow was just about to deprive British Intelligence of its dong with the luminous nose.'

'Get me, as they say, out of here.'

'Tight cords, blunt knife. Lucky she didn't let the great axe fall. It's got a bloody poor edge to it. You'd have recovered, no doubt, but think of the future Mrs Punch. Not to say the damage to this lovely piece of Montenegrin folkweave. I've seen a lot of these spoiled by meat stains.' Lippiat prised the cord from Matson's left wrist and the skin from his right. 'If anyone ever cuts your twacker off, Marcus Pomeroy's after-dinner conversation will haemorrhage to death.'

'Where the hell did you come from?'

'Been here half the night. Kipping in a corner, as we used to say.'

Popovic's notion of a hidy-hole was correct. Lippiat's sense of time wasn't. Matson touched the crease on his head: the hair was plastered over it, but the wound itself had filled with dried blood and was encouragingly flat.

'That was last evening, Paddy. You want to learn not to nod when old men are shooting round your ear.' Lippiat examined the damage, then pushed it away. 'Ta! But I've seen it before. Young fellow had a magnum on me. One of those guns that can't think round corners. He wasn't aiming to miss you. He was looking for an in-off. Me dead. You canonized.'

Enough awe and accusation. Matson's shirt was lying on the woodwork. He groped to retrieve it.

'Came down by car. Jeep actually. Japanese Jeep. Chukkered off the back of the mountain. Bad track, good headlights. A sight better than walking off the escarpment with all this frost about. Myself and a Serbian medic who's a mate of mine. Got him to look at your head, but you'd already gone.'

'I'll make the Irish jokes.'

Lotte stood up from the bed as groggily as Matson had

done. She saw Matson tucking his shirt into his trousers, recognized Lippiat, and sat down again.

'Shock,' Lippiat said. 'No relying on them when they get like this. Can't hug them, can't have them, can't hang them. I'll ask my pal to give her something in a moment. Still, she did the job for us.'

Matson's scalp was scabbed, so his brains had finished dripping. He was alert enough to barge towards the door, smart enough to stop when he came face to face with Lippiat's pistol.

'Sneaky of me, Paddy. Sneaky of me. But I couldn't bring my Lee Enfield into a lady's bedroom. Hardly suitable. Left it downstairs with the umbrellas.' Lippiat was holding an M52 automatic close to his body where it couldn't be grabbed at, pointing waist-high where only an imbecile would try to roll underneath it. 'Lovely guns the Slovaks make. Twice a magnum at half the price.'

'They jam. They all jam.'

'And you'll be the bloody muffin the jam spreads itself on. I've never known any gun jam on the first round, have you?' He indicated Lotte. 'Herr Weiss is spark out, thanks to her. Sleeping like a baby. We'd arranged she would drug him, you see. Her boy for safety. Himself for surgery. He told you the deal, perhaps. Seems she drugged you both. God knows what made her decide to cast you as spare prick at the beheading, old chap.'

'God knows.' Matson watched the door in horrible fascination. Lippiat's M52 wasn't to be contemplated. Bottleneck cartridge, designed like an anti-tank round. MV markedly higher than a standard magnum. He probably wouldn't feel it, simply cease to be in three thousandths of a second's impact shock; and he was too tired to meet any dead poets just now.

'She decided to spare her father-in-law the ultimate embarrassment, I suppose,' Lippiat mused. 'Bananas won't do, but one man's saveloy looks much like another's, especially once you've wrapped it in some lettuce.'

'You're a coarse bastard, Lolly.'

'Dealing with Germans thickens a man. Not that I blame them for being as they are. While Queen Victoria was banning fuck, Bismarck was inventing Europe. It must have cost a deal of bad language.'

Lolly could have expanded on this theme, given some encouragement. Even with that empty-eyed pistol in his hand.

The house wouldn't let him. Without warning, but with a giant judder of the shoulder-blades, it screamed. Matson felt it before he heard it, and he had to unknot his back before he could listen to it.

It didn't break things, though a glass fell somewhere. It stretched them. It was too big for Otok, too tall for the house, too wide for the island. It was heard all over Jezero, where it tingled unrecognizable as a whale's cry or the death of an amplified foetus. Only when you closed your mind could you know what it was. It was a man howling his guts out.

He became polyphonal. Lotte screamed too, but she couldn't match the pitch.

He ran out of breath, choked, couldn't start again. Lotte screamed by herself now. Lippiat turned her off with a sharp slap on the mouth. He drew blood, but spoke to her kindly in German. He spoke reassuringly of her child. To Matson he said, 'Everyone's father and everyone's lover. What would you expect the Southern Slavs to do to him – cripple him with a paternity suit?'

The doctor came in. He wore a woman's apron from the kitchen, and household rubber gloves. 'I didn't mean so much noise,' he said in acknowledgement of Matson's presence. To Lolly he spoke Serbian. To Matson, 'I've waited forty-five years to hear that bastard scream. Him or any of them. I meant him no pain. Men are oddly wired. In my clinic I do vasectomies. We use a lot of local anaesthetic, but every hundredth hurts.' He grimaced. 'And in his case, we weren't stripping strings, we were pulling the Reich up by the roots.'

'The Reich, anyway.'

'And Prinz Eugen. They died hard.'

Lolly put his gun away. 'Go to bed, Paddy. There's a good lad. Go and have a nice sleep. And if Herr Weiss's bloody nose gives you bad dreams, take another walk to that tower of his.'

398

Anka stood outside, her face bruised from yesterday, her frock freshly spattered. She was holding something in her hand.

Lippiat said, 'Get what you want?' Then he spoke in Serbian.

It was a bad time for sub-texts, but Matson caught one. He nodded to the doctor, pushed past Lippiat and walked out of the door. He didn't acknowledge Anka. He went over to Constanz's room.

Constanz slept. He woke her. She slept. He shook her shoulders. She smiled, and slept again. Good news. She wasn't overdosed with whatever potion Lili dispensed.

Lotte Weiss had dumped her in bed with her clothes on, boots and all. This left the room relatively tidy and the typewriter very prominent.

Constanz's own machine had gone down with the Yugo. This one was a nineteenth-century Italian model, made in Fiume at about the time Italo Svevo lived there – little Italian Fiume that was now bustling Yugoslav Rijeka. Its cradle was full of onion peels and garlic husks. Constanz had obviously uncovered it in the kitchen.

A piece of paper was stuffed unevenly round the roller. It read: *World Exclusive by Constanz Zanetti.* Then, in arrogant caps: YUGOSLAV PARTISANS HAVE A BALL (*Kocevje Gora gets the other one*).

The typeface was western, and horribly familiar. Someone had sat in Weiss's back kitchen composing verses of revenge on it, then posted a copy to the media two weeks ago. Anka and Jug Bogdan's Widow were the best candidates.

9

Popovic arrived about then, with a lot of his people. They were no respecters of bedrooms.

He didn't arrest Lippiat, only his gun. He didn't seem to notice the rest of him, nor be bothered by the presence of the doctor, nor the bloodstained Anka; but he impounded several guns. He had neither beaten them nor joined them, despite Matson's suspicions. Merely waited till they'd served their purpose, then made sure they could do no further harm.

Popovic stood by Constanz's typewriter and grinned. To Matson he said, 'Have you got anything for me yet?'

Matson handed him a small piece of manuscript. He'd found it as he'd blundered across the upper landing. Presumably Weiss had dropped it when the doctor and Anka had dragged him upstairs.

'I've not seen this handwriting before, my dear. You know what it says?'

'I can guess. I've seen the same handwriting on a card that was delivered with a pair of castrated rats. There were three conditions, I notice. Not one.'

'So now you have the whole picture?'

'I think so, Popo. But like the earthworm, it's a beast with both ends.'

'Crazy man. Get some rest.'

Popovic made sure they were alone, them presented him with the M52 he'd taken from Lippiat.

TWENTY-FIVE

1

He surfaced only slowly. The first shock was that he hadn't left Constanz's room. Her bed, her typewriter, the rug on her floor – he'd fallen face down into one or the other and let exhaustion and Lotte's drugged cocoa do the rest. When he woke, the Ehrenberg-Zanetti was bathing his head-wound, and with warmed water. He'd left it too long for stitching, and he shrank from the Serbian doctor anyway. He felt numb but frisky. Sick bodies are often good at sex. They've got nothing else to occupy them. His had. It had the helicopter.

While he'd been sleeping, Popovic had taken two platoons of soldiers up the mountain and rescued young Henk in great style from an unguarded cave. The helicopter was returning him briefly to the island before it took the sedated Obergruppenführer Weiss to Belgrade.

Matson didn't go downstairs to honour his former ally and foe. The sight of him from the bedroom window was enough. Sunken cheeks, clenched eyes. No blood in his earlobes now.

Constanz went. She was made of sterner stuff. Sterner than Matson guessed. He watched her hand the helicopter pilot an envelope and give him a series of animated instructions, each of them embellished by Popovic. She was filing copy.

Then she was back in bed with Matson, his ally and former foe. She was warmer than a corpse, anyway. No, that wasn't it. She talked more. He knew there was a difference.

'You know why I'm in bed with you, Matson?'

'Because you don't like me very much.'

She was better on the belly than a blunt penknife.

401

2

She changed the sheets for clean ones from Matson's room. Then, when she considered they had lived in them long enough, she changed them for her own. Time passed, and by sheets she measured time. She didn't find the gun, safe among dirty socks in his mountain boots.

'Tell me the truth,' she said at last. 'All of it. I mean about why you came here and attached yourself to Henk. Then tell me about that funky Mr Lippiat. I *like* Mr Lippiat.'

'You've certainly known him long enough,' he said. It was a bit soon for truth, but they would have to reach there sooner or later. He had a report to write.

He did not give her time to react. He said, 'Someone in London wanted to play Greenmantle.'

'How bloody London.'

'You're interrupting my flow.'

'You've got no flow. Your body's made of rock-salt and freckles.' She rearranged some freckles with a finger end, savagely.

'Lippiat was sent out to further someone's crack-brained scheme for the Balkans. To play Greenmantle, as I say. These people have to come up with a template from time to time, or they'll be shunted off and swopped for computers. Lolly probably saw it as the chance for another Balkan holiday. Whatever the scheme was, I expect he decided to let it go quietly wrong. He's fireproof, after all. Fireproof and way past retiring.'

Constanz was too much on the defensive to realize he was embroidering the story.

'The scheme probably included my being sent out to disown him. Or the schemers got cold feet. We'll never know, because Lolly certainly didn't. They never tell you more than a tenth of anything, to make it awkward for everyone else and to prove to themselves they're professionals.

'They had to tell me two tenths, because I'm doing them a favour. So they told me two tenths of a bloody big lie. Just like I'm telling you.'

'Why have a scheme at all?'

'For reasons that will soon become dangerously obvious to you.'

She was becoming uneasy again.

'What the schemers forgot was that professionals in the field have their sly ways too. They don't like route plans. Give them a car and they'll go by train. Buy them a boat ticket and they'll swim. Little things like that.'

Her eyes drooped, as if the subject was of no importance to her.

'Lolly knew there had to be a cut-off point. He deemed it prudent to have his own cut-off, a nice little explosion and fire. Something that would send complex signals in every direction he could think of – towards Rosental and Weiss, of course; but mostly towards certain bastards back home in London.'

Constanz snored lightly. He cured her by turning her over and slapping her backside.

'Your providing him with that lad's body was a bonus. I reckon he'd have used General Lenz if not, dead or alive, as he'd already intended. You did provide the meat, didn't you? Either to Popovic or to Lippiat direct? You were in on both men's thinking.'

3

'I'm not a detective. I don't have to win a conviction. I just have to know when to keep my back covered.' He kissed hers. 'You were never worried by the big set pieces of pseudo-danger. You knew they were coming. Rifle shots and angry pig-farmers surprised you, because they belonged to the chaos theorem and were no part of the scenario.'

With her eyes shut she said, 'There were about half a dozen attempts on Henk's life last year. This one was particularly inept. I was a visitor at Rosental on and off for the last two months. A boy tried to get in from a boat while I was there. The lads drowned him. They wanted to leave him in the *stausee*. They'd done it before. I said it wasn't sensible.'

'What did Lotte say?'

'She said it wasn't sensible. While she was having hysterics

403

we took him down to the cold store.'

'There you cut his guts out with the poultry shears –'

'These lads didn't need poultry shears. They used their knives.'

'God knows how they removed his head.'

'That was the really dreamy bit.'

'Then you – I say you only by association – suggested filling up the body cavity with some of the General's five-star brandy.'

'Korn, sweetheart. And some Austrian muck the dictionary has no words for. It was after that I made it to the master bedroom.'

'Lotte on her couch with hysterics and a sedative, Weiss excited at the ease with which you dealt with a bit of blood?'

'I like your lovemaking, Matson. You're nearly in the same class as Henk.'

'Flatterer.'

'Henk now, that is.'

He was glad the poor bastard couldn't hear that one. He ploughed ahead.

4

'Then Lippiat got to Lotte – or she had already been got at – with his castration wheeze. It sounds evil, but the Weiss monster *was* evil. She loved him, or loved his midnight visitations, but they'd been forced on her. He'd screwed up her marriage to his son by screwing her. He'd screwed her up by screwing everybody else as well.'

'Thanks, Matson.'

'Everyone who could move her bottom, that is. So why not agree to having him fixed? It's revenge. It's freedom. It also preserves the life of her child's father. Or she hopes it does.'

'And grandfather.'

'Ironically, no. Lolly is that. Or rather he's her husband's father, and that's a different matter. She's a classic case of paranoia, I'd say. She'll agree to anything that makes her mad life simpler. Especially after he's had you, yet another

404

house guest, inside his painting-the-town-red room.'

'That's a song.'

'You an older woman.'

'Two years older.'

'It shows. The knife that heals while it punishes, corrects as well as alters – such rubbish must have seemed attractive to her. Till she had to do it. Keep your child sedated and he'll come to no harm, she's told. Give the old fellow a sleeping draught and we'll have the best dong-doctor in Belgrade do the full frontal Abelards on him.'

'No woman would consent to that happening to her lover.'

'You did. You may plead your fine Jewish rage at the sod's history, Mrs Zanetti, but what you had done to him was a bit bloody close to the chest for a circumcision, wasn't it?'

'That's an ethnic obscenity.'

'You're the ethnic obscenity. You're not into the Jewish thing in depth – *if* you are Jewish. You simply assembled a case, then put your rage behind it. Journalists do it all the time, I know. But you must excuse me for finding it morally questionable.'

'La!'

'And extremely arrogant. That's where the list comes in.'

5

'Shit, Matson –'

'I wish you wouldn't, Constanz. It makes you a bit like Jonathan Swift's Celia.'

'What I'm trying to tell you is that the goddamn list doesn't exist.'

'I'm afraid it does.'

'It doesn't. I bloody well made it up.'

'Exactly.'

'So?'

'It exists therefore. I accused Popovic of you – oh, ages ago, back in Belgrade.'

'Celia, Matson!'

'That's better. He grew hot, said was I claiming the whole thing was no more than a newspaper story? I said most things

405

of any significance start that way.' He smiled, glad to be nearly finished with the personal bit. 'What happened was someone showed him or his office a poem they'd been sent, composed, as it happens, on this very typewriter.' He smiled even more; she hadn't guessed Anka was the author. 'You're not into poetry, darling, but you are a bloody good journalist. You knew the poem needed signatures, and with the right ones it would be a bombshell. Or at least a world story.'

Matson never expected to see Constanz put out by a little personal rudeness. She was. He pressed on happily, the way lovers will. 'I knew for certain that you were the author of the list the moment I got here and saw how the feminine names on it fitted life's petty domestic circumstances.'

'Detection by insult.'

'Until I met Anka, I thought you might have put yourself down for something modest, like Jug Bogdan's Widow. Then I realised Anka was she, in your fevered imaginings. So you had to be Kosovka, the Maid of Kosovo. I haven't read much Serbian folklore, but I reckon that's going a bit far, even for you. You being both a naughty girl and a foreigner.'

Constanz wasn't listening. Something outside was distracting her. She dressed, smiled vacantly and hurried downstairs.

6

Matson glanced from the window. Popovic's launch was approaching the raft at the edge of the lawn. He followed her through the door, then stopped. Someone was hurrying upwards.

Anka, her bruised eye making her as pert as a panda, was dragging Lolly by the wrist as if he were her teddy bear. She pulled him into her room, where she had been keeping him quite a lot of late. She wasn't hiding him from Popovic, that was for certain. It must be from somebody else.

A radio had begun to sing on the lawn. The radio that connected one of his signallers to Popovic's launch. Chant and stop, chant and stop, just like a cock bird at breakfast time. It was the command call-sign, and at some time before that the radio had transmitted and continued to transmit Popovic's pronunciation of a terrible word.

Matson went downstairs and sauntered outside. Not for the first time the launch itself had creamed up the lake at a speed the island couldn't quite match.

'Who's Pilkington?' Constanz asked.

'A beast with many heads.' He watched Mr Pilkington request Popo to slow down and give Otok a chance to catch up with him.

This Mr Pilkington was more important than the other ones. Even Anka walked across the lawn to greet this Mr Pilkington. Matson hoped that when she'd left Lolly in her bedroom she'd remembered to turn the key.

7

Otok was on the small side for Mr Pilkington and the boat, too, must have been a disappointment. That being said, Matson had never seen him so unsure of himself, and with such a need to talk his way in.

'I'm on holiday, as it happens. Catching a bit of leave.'

Matson didn't hoot. The boat was under-ballasted. With only two people aboard it was almost airborne, and he didn't want to blow it away. Mr Pilkington oscillated above it.

'Cross my heart and bless my soul in truth. I'm staying down the road in Athens, so I borrowed myself a car.'

Matson held out a steadying hand.

The visitor gazed downwards to pick his feet above the gunwale, flashing the famous bald patch he thought only God could see. It was bigger by at least two new pence. 'Fond boy,' he murmured. He allowed Matson to clasp him to his manly ribcage. 'Fond boy,' said Pomeroy again.

Being thrown into the lake took him by surprise. He let Anka help him from the water. 'I wish you hadn't done that, Paddy. I don't mind being dunked, but in a *bath*, my reluctant Kincora lad.' His suit dribbled on to the lawn. 'Lakes have fish in them, and sometimes mermaids and ladies with upraised arms that proffer swords. I'm sure they all suffer from terrible diseases.'

407

He stood in front of everyone on the lawn and wrung himself out. Marcus Pomeroy was exalted even by Popovic's standards of elevation. Anka was careful with his bag of spare clothes.

'If I'd fallen on one of those swords, it wouldn't have been so bad. I came to fall upon a sword, Patrick, I really did. Mine, of course. I owe you a –' He searched for words and began to shiver.

Constanz sat him in the sun with a flask of cognac. How did she know? 'Coffee?' she asked.

'I take it neat,' he confessed.

8

Matson faced him across the table. They had the lawn to themselves now.

'I am not here,' Pomeroy said. 'And if I am seen to be, then I am someone else.'

'I've a good mind to kick your teeth in, Marcus.'

'I'm too senior for that, and well you know it. However, I do owe you half an apology and a quarter of an explanation. And I can't speak a word of them unless you leave my pegs in place.'

'Handsome of you.'

'From me it's absolutely dashing.' He drank about a third of a pint of *vinjak* the way stallkeepers swill tea, then said, 'We don't want the Yugoslav bit giving, you see? If it goes it goes. You can't stop history. Most of history proves it. A chap like me can delay it for a season or two, just the same.' He drank more *vinjak*. 'Lippiat had this good idea –'

'What good idea?'

'Lippiat had this good idea, so I let him set forth. Then I got wind that certain of the ethnics at the Balkan desk wanted to stop him. So I sent you.'

'That's not what I was told.'

'Once he saw you, dear boy, telling him he'd been spotted doing things he hadn't done, he'd know the real ruse had been tumbled and he'd have to move fast.'

'So I wasn't told the truth?'

'You were given a message, and you delivered it. The Balkan wallahs also sent a man with a silver bullet. First it was for Lippiat. Then he was after you.'

'What have you done about this?'

'Sacked them.'

'On what grounds, dare I ask?'

'Inefficiency. They set out to kill you and they couldn't. I had them removed for it. Setting out to kill you was very bad form.'

Matson looked across the lake towards the shaded tree-line. 'Is he still out there? Silver Bullet, I mean.'

'In a box. Couple of good chaps at the Embassy down the road.'

'I've met them. One of them tried to kill me in Belgrade.'

'Obeying orders from the ethnics. Obedience being his bounden duty. A chap like yourself, you must see that.'

'What I see is he's lied to you, Marcus. There's no one out there, no Silver Bullet anyway. Not in a box, nor in the bracken.'

Pomeroy was dry now, and on another tack. 'We can't let the Balkans fall apart again. Not while I'm trying to give up smoking. It'd be like the Lebanon, nearer in.'

The bottle was empty, as so often when Pomeroy was near. He stood up to wave Popovic closer, then sat again to say, 'Judged purely and simply as a professional operation, I suppose you're jolly glad you were on leave.'

'In Italy,' Matson agreed. 'I still am. Are you "jolly glad"?'

'Colonel Popovic is. It's the story with everything. It's got revenge. It's got regeneration. It's got the ancient Kraut's bollocks – and *there's* justice for you. It's got the child's life. The old partisans got the one. The new police – and Popovic – got the other. Yugoslavia got it all. And as for yourself, well it's even got you some sex.'

'I'm growing to prefer love.'

'Bad for the brain. Buy a dog. Get a retriever from a good kennel.' He stood again, this time to find his bag and a change of clothes, then have Popovic return him to his car.

Popovic walked with Pomeroy back towards the launch. He interpreted Matson's nod, called in his signallers and embarked them as well.

409

Matson watched their progress towards the civilized end of the lake and out of sight. He ought to warn Pomeroy, but he couldn't spare the time.

He searched the nearer shoreline.

There was a movement opposite, among the trees. The rubber boat drifted out into the bay beyond the facing head-land. Two men were in it. At least two men.

Anka did not return to clear the table, and he sensed Lippiat had already gone from the house. Things would happen very quickly now. He had no time to wonder how the signal had been passed.

Matson turned and went casually inside and upstairs. Time to get his gun. Before someone was dead.

TWENTY-SIX

1

'The socks are even riper,' she said. Constanz looked at the climbing boots. '*They* stink.'

'Of mortality,' he agreed. He showed her the gun. He showed her by pointing it at her belt buckle. 'Close the door, darling. As furtively as you like.'

'Horse games?'

'Consequences.'

She closed the door very gently.

'Now count,' he ordered. Count in one of your voices of love. In words of love, if you like. Think of Henk and count to five thousand.'

'Shit, Matson.'

'It'll be easier if you count. Far less disturbing to my intellect.'

'If you are trying to grow one of those, Matson, you'd better keep it under glass. And water it well.' She counted.

The inflatable was nearly to the point beyond the tower. This time, with Popovic gone away, it had rigged an outboard. Matson lost it past the angle of the window.

'You can stop at a thousand. Time has speeded up.' He waved her towards the door. 'You go first.' He spoke with affection. 'It promises to be one of those occasions when I want my friends in front of me.'

'Why, for Christ's sake?'

'In case I have to shoot them.'

Once through the line of trees he had his first stroke of luck and his first setback.

The tower door was open; so this had to be the place. Unfortunately, a man stood there, obviously keeping watch. Matson recognised him as the one who'd helped the injured Anka along the path through the pines. In his belt, and now nearly in his fist, was a handgun. Noisy things, guns.

'Who the hell's that?' Constanz asked.

'"Matija Gubec",' he said. 'You can't know every guy on your list, not personally. And you won't be expecting the rest of what's going to happen, so get ready for a shock.' Speaking helped their approach look casual.

She hung back against his pistol. He held it away from her, flat across her shoulder blades. 'Smile at him, but don't speak unless he does. I don't want the others to hear us.'

Constanz was increasingly curious now.

Twenty feet away, and clothed in Constanz's smile, Matson heard the sound of iron on stone. No one else had detected their approach. Not yet.

'*Dobra dan*,' he grinned two steps later. 'Or do I mean *dobra vecchi*?' Still walking on.

The M52 came as a terrible surprise to the man, appearing from nowhere out of a woman's back. Matson put the safety catch on, smashed him in the guts, slid the safety off and pushed Constanz ahead of him through the door with it, on the way kicking Matija Gubec hard in his mythological ear.

'Sorry, Lolly. But I owe you a crease in the brain. And with a gun like this I hardly ever miss. Tell Anka not to do anything silly, will you? Because I really don't want to shoot her.'

Lolly inside the door, his face ghost-white. Anka's head peering up from a lamplit cleft in the rock, roughly in the middle of the dirt of the tower's floor. The other man from the boat somewhere down there, but unseen. Matson caught voices, then the stop of breath.

'Go round to the back of the hole, Lolly, with your arms up. Have Anka come out next, and move round beside you, two steps away, hands equally high. Then tell your friend to come out. If he's got a gun, he'd better drop it where he's standing.' He kept his eye on Lolly as Anka began her move. 'Explain to your pal down there that if he's brave he's got a chance. Because whatever trick he tries, you're going to die first. I can only work miracles on feast days.'

'Don't be so bloody filmic, Matson.' Constanz pushed Matija Gubec's pistol into his hand. 'Do you love me?'

'Brno CZ75. Another Czech wammer. Fifteen-shot magazine. One of the best. Take it and cover the gentleman in the pit.' If these were words of love, then good enough. 'Stand half a step ahead and to my right.'

'That's it, Paddy,' Lippiat said. 'Filmic.'

'Try the gun out,' Matson advised Constanz. 'Better shoot one into the hole down there.'

She shot one, producing a lot of muzzle blast in the confined space.

A man popped out of the hole like a jack-in-the-box, with his hands held high. It wasn't the doctor. It wasn't anyone Matson recognized.

'Double action,' she said. Or he thought she said. Things got very cloth-eared after that.

3

Matson had never taken Popovic's lot very seriously. Now he watched the reappearance of Smoke Ears, and his little driver, with gratitude. It had been a long walk from the tower, bringing four prisoners back with only a gun and a half to guard them.

Smoke Ears' friend with the nicotined face, and their gaggle of noisy signallers, were also here, barging in and out of Otok's big room and linking the strained atmosphere inside to the signal station they had re-established on the lawn. Otok's secrets were being passed on to Belgrade, with knobs on, some of them, knobs in abundance. Knobs of gold, knobs of silver, knobs fashioned from precious and semi-precious stones.

The two Amazons with sub-machine guns sat quietly behind Popovic. It was a bit late for Matson to learn their names, or to christen them 'Hair' and 'Trigger'; but their presence brought a deal of comfort.

There were a million, or a billion, or billions of pounds' worth of religious artefacts littered about the huge table like so much household junk waiting for the metal polish. No one was going to get murdered for it. No one else. Not now Authority was here. The killing was over.

Popovic emphasized the point. He had his people lay out leg irons for Anka and the three men, then ordered them not to be shackled. Not yet. *He* was running things now, not history.

He made way for Matson. 'Patrick, my dear?' He corrected himself. 'Captain Matson?'

'I've a story to tell,' Matson said. He felt apologetic that Popovic's men didn't speak English, and that not all of his women spoke it well enough. 'But I'm not going to tell it, because it will be a pack of bloody lies. And I've heard enough lies since coming to Yugoslavia.'

'No, not lies, Captain Matson.' Popovic was insistently formal. One of his women took notes. 'Layers of truth. We have to peel the onion, even though we know its centre is composed of tears.' He gazed happily at the table. There were no tears there. Not for Popovic.

'There ought to be a story. One nobody guessed at. And there is, but it goes bad early. It's about a woman digging a hole in her garden. Over there among her roses. I haven't seen it, but all kinds of night runners have come from that way, including one with a dish of rats.

'On my first evening here it was the only part of the island she was interested in accompanying us over, I suppose so we didn't stumble across her secret in the dark. And the people she was hiding there.'

Popovic mouthed an order. Two of his soldiers left the room, calling up others outside.

'She was digging her hole so she could be joined in a ritual by some friends and fellow sufferers – the locals hereabouts. A ritual to kill a monster, if he ever chose to return and haunt her. Perhaps she intended to spread him out on this table like the warrior he claimed to be. Just as she spread her baskets of dead rats. Perhaps he was simply to disappear. I haven't asked her.'

414

He looked at Anka. 'Her plan never changed. Nor her thirst for an appropriate death for him. It became engulfed in something else the moment she started to dig. Naturally, she chose the softest place, but her spade didn't strike any bones, any of the horrors she'd half expected. It turned up something like this.' He touched his hand to the table.

'Once she stumbled on Weiss's loot – perhaps only an item or two – revenge was no longer a local matter. She had the right connections, and her instinct was always to be responsible.

'She probably saw it as the answer to a prayer. She had fashioned her trap, and God had provided the bait for her. That sort of thing.'

Anka muttered something, then was silent again.

'Other minds took a larger view. SS Prinz Eugen raped the Balkans all the way from here to Istria, they argued. The loot had never been recovered. At last we have an indication that its commander must know where it is. Get the Obergruppenführer here in Jovanka's trap, and we'll dig out the rest of it. Dig it out of him if need be.'

Somebody knocked on the door. Popovic opened it and listened briefly. 'My people have found the pit,' he said. 'Quite the underground room, not to say palace,' he congratulated Anka. 'But full of absolutely nothing.'

'Anka went on digging,' Matson continued. 'She got dirty hands.'

4

'This was twenty years ago, perhaps longer. She picked her confidants, later to be her accomplices, very carefully from among her old friends. She hesitated most over telling the Englishman who was perhaps the oldest friend of all. He had been her lover; he was the father of her child. But he was, well, English.

'Her people made contact with him in Berne. They reported he retained his affection for Yugoslavia but that he was a case-hardened professional. Ex-SOE. She knew that. Ex-Military Intelligence – a natural step. Now a Foreign

Office full-timer, a non-specific diplomat, so presumably an officer in the British Secret Intelligence Service. End of story. The man bristled with danger.

'But they knew what his role in Yugoslavia now was. If Popovic could find it out, so could one of these partisans. They knew, so they persevered with him. They needed Lippiat's special brand of knowledge. He was running a Balkan network of repute. It would complement, and perhaps surpass, anything they could cobble together on their own account. If you are going to put pressure on a man like Weiss, you need a man who knows what pressure to apply. Besides, he was the alleged father of Weiss's alleged son. A factor like that could be the joker in a heavy interrogation.

'Then, one night, in a little restaurant in Berne, Anka's name was mentioned. Gerald Lippiat was in. Or they thought they had him in.'

5

'There were several forces at work. In Lippiat's case, there was divided loyalty. There was his loyalty to Anka, and his loyalty to the British Service, which anyway plays a bifocal role out here.

'There was also *Anno Domini*. Time began to pass. I daresay the plotters' first motive was nationalistic. Certainly, the cover plot filtered out by innocents like Constanz Ehrenberg-Zanetti – and misleadingly embellished by her – retained its nationalistic mainspring to the end.'

'I'll never forgive you "innocents", Matson.'

'We're forty years on. A young man's totems no longer seem so precious in old age, unless, of course, they *are* precious. In which case, why not convert them to money?'

'You're a bloody cynic, Matson.' Constanz again.

Popovic told her to shut up.

'A realist. You were the romancer who gave these plotters fancy names: Kotromanic, Banus Kulin, and the rest. Most of them started life as partisan leaders of at least the second rank. Most of the partisan leaders were communists. Weeping over icons was not going to be their most likely emotion. Some of them, doubtless, would weep over the plight of the country they'd bled for. Some came to weep over the state of their pockets.

'So they started to dirty their mitts. Or to get ready to dirty them. Just like Anka.

'This – strange though may sound – is in marked contrast to the behaviour of the British Foreign Office. While these old men were growing greedy, HMG kept at least one hand clean.'

'How little you know Marcus Pomeroy,' Lippiat snapped. 'He was going to hand back the icons, the paintings, the altar pieces and so on to central government. And do it incognito, true enough. But he wanted me to get the Mohammedan stuff out. Right out.'

Popovic said something to his note-taker, and she stopped writing. Popovic, too, was a diplomat.

'He intended to do something public with it in the Middle East. It doesn't belong in the Middle East, Paddy.'

'It doesn't belong in your greasy fist either, Gerald.'

'I'd have sold it back, believe me.' He wasn't speaking for Matson's benefit, but Anka's. 'I'm in need of a bit of pension, that's the shape of it. I've got wounds to bathe. We've all got those.'

'Yes,' said Matson. 'But whose blood were you going to bathe them in?'

6

'I'm not being moral about this,' he went on. 'After all, I am the man who could have stopped it. I should have killed Lippiat right at the beginning. I'd certainly have made it look a more convincing accident.'

'You'd have had a real corpse,' Lippiat scoffed.

'Yours? No, you're a zombie, Gerald. You ooze trouble. You've started to smell bad. You smelled bad then. Even with a stiff in your wardrobe, and another lashed under your dinghy.'

417

Popovic sighed. 'You weren't helped by being locked up by those Austrians, my dear.'

'Apologies accepted, Popo. Of course, you were in Willi and Albin's space-machine by the lake, feeding them my London background in return for them keeping me under their thumb. And, again of course, they let you sit in their interrogation cupboard in Graz while they sweated me.'

'How does even a Matson deduce that?'

'They pulled me in too quickly. They let me out too cheap. You weren't there the whole time – I know that. They ditched you before you heard about Gerald's second corpse. Probably because they realized you were twisting their tails for them.

'I rumbled that when you wasted time buying me lunch. Then you made a phone call, obviously to Willi or Albin, and found out about the second corpse. Hence your jest about the freshwater shrimps. You must have traded them something. I couldn't think what. Now I realize you must have told them Lippiat was alive but about to be locked up.

'My thinking processes were further hindered by those books of Lolly's that Constanz kept sending me. Confused again by the various ways you, Popo, as well as Lippiat – fine professionals both – made use of the women in Weiss's household.'

'I prepared the ground,' Popovic agreed. 'I needed them all, Lippiat included. Just as I needed you. A wise huntsman does not zig about, my dear. He leaves that sort of thing to his dogs.' He beamed at Matson. 'Even to his ferret.'

Lippiat was out of his chair and shouting at Popovic in Serbian. Somebody forced him to sit down.

'By my second morning in Yugoslavia, I knew Weiss was hiding gold,' Matson said. 'By the second afternoon, I knew where.'

'I should have greased you, Paddy. Greased you on the bloody lawn the moment bloody Pomeroy went,' Lippiat shouted.

'Shut up, Gerald.' Matson went over to him. 'If you play things close to your chest, we can work something out. I assure you we can.' He nodded towards the note-taker.

'Pomeroy won't want any of this.'

418

'My people will certainly ask to see something. And they'll be shown something. Colonel Popovic would doubtless feel he can cough them up a word or two on my behalf. So do yourself a favour and belt up.'

Popovic smiled and motioned his note-taker to leave. Anka didn't leave. Nor did Gubec and Lippiat's other companion. They had nowhere to go.

7

'You're a bad boy, Gerald Lippiat. Still, there's no need for the wickedness of an old war horse to go any further. We can tidy things up, you and I and Colonel Popovic. As at the end of every shindig.

'Providing, that is, I have Pomeroy's assurance that the geriatric Mr Lippiat is retired from the Service. Then I shall be entirely happy. You did tell London at the beginning, after all. Are you contented with that arrangement, Colonel Popovic?'

'He'll have to keep out of Yugoslavia.'

'The job isn't finished,' Lippiat said. 'Not a half, not a quarter finished.' He spoke as if there were still a deal to be struck. 'I've done my research. What we've got here is only a tenth of Weiss's loot. This stuff, on Otok, is like a dinar to a dollar to the rest of it.'

'The dinar is about to stabilize,' Popovic said.

'You shouldn't have let Anka carve the meat for you, Gerald. The doctor, at least, should have had a bit more sense. There she was, making extortionate passes over her rapist's belly with a surgical saw or tonsil spoon or some such. She frightened him so much that he blabbed something out. He blurted he'd buried the goods in his tower of skulls. Among her family's bones, and her neighbours' bones, and her comrades' bones. Naturally she took a hack at his dick. The image had been planted there in her mind long enough.

'Time ran out on you, Gerry. Just as it did in the mountains. Just as it did when Pomeroy arrived and you knew I knew you were skulking away from him.' Matson turned to face Popovic. 'Surely the Yugoslav state can do a deal of

419

some sort with Weiss while it's got him in hand? A million for a map reference, say – that sort of thing?'

'Weiss is dead, my dear.' Popovic went to the door and called outside. Called for guards. Called for people to carry away the loot. Called for his note-taker.

Having given everyone time to digest the news, he smiled apologetically and repeated it. 'Quite, quite dead. A hundred times over.'

8

He spoke to Matson. 'The pig farmers, you see.' He composed an appropriate face. 'Well, my dear, I was wrong. We all were. You were perhaps rightest before you fell under the spell of the thing.' He nodded to Constanz, as if to the senior spellbinder. 'He paid with his dick, and I told you the nation would appreciate the poetry of it. The little boy was spared. Ditto. None of it impressed the pig farmers. They're not into part-payment.

'Only two of them. A father and a son. Which means, in relation to the war, a son and a grandson. Two were enough. They heard the Obershitbag was going home.

'One of them blocked off Weiss's ambulance with a tractor and its trailer. The other one stuffed it with a clip from the family sub-machine gun.'

'The family –'

'A war relic, my dear. One of those throw-away stens you dropped us by the thousand. They're everywhere. Farmers single-shot them, and use them as humane killers.'

'Who's dead?'

'The Austrian ambulance driver, his paramedic, and – yes – the rest of them. I always said, and you always felt, that Herr Weiss would be a dangerous man to ride with for long. He lost his nuts and his luck deserted him.'

'The child?'

'All of them. Not at once. There was no traffic. The man with the sten had time to load another clip. And another.'

'How do you know there were only two?'

'They gave themselves up. Nobody loves them for it. But if

420

we try to hang them they'll become national heroes. If we try to punish them in any way.' His honesty allowed him to rub his nose gently between thumb and forefinger before saying, 'God knows why they went by road and not by aeroplane.'

'Where were they killed?'

'Between Livno and Knin. About an hour beyond the tunnel.'

'On the way to the extermination camp?'

'Yes. I told you Old Shitbag was greedy for death. This time death got greedy for him.'

There was a sound behind them, somebody sobbing, something.

'Did your helicopter take photographs, videotapes, anything, on the journey down?'

'Both.'

'Then you'll have a record of his stop on the plateau by the death camp. If you can pinpoint where he halted his car, I can show you the way to his loot in ten minutes.' He explained about the black sentinel of rock and the graticuled binoculars. 'If you can't, Popo, then it's going to cost you a couple of days and a few men with metal detectors. But you'll manage it.'

Popovic gazed at Lippiat, before murmuring, 'A dowser, my dear. It's blood money after all. I'll take a good dowser with a hazel twig.'

Lippiat wept. He was weeping for the child, certainly. The man without children had supposed the boy to be his grandson. There had scarcely been time for him to learn he wasn't, and no time at all for Anka and himself to adjust to the fact. So he wept. They both wept.

Matson couldn't take much of this. He looked through the window at the sharp blue sky, the lake that refused to mirror it. He saw fresh snow on the mountains. If Lippiat's world was ending, it was ending somewhere else and a fair way over the rim from here. He turned back to the room and saw two old people crying.

He walked over and touched Anka's shoulder. To Lippiat he said, 'Gerald, why don't I have Pomeroy come up from Athens? We can sort something out, as I said.'

Constanz found wine. It had a sour taste. It might be a

loving cup. It might be a poisoned chalice. Only time would tell.

Popovic was disposed to leave on his private high note of triumph.

Matson stopped him. 'Aren't you going to shift some of these people away?'

'I can't arrest this so-called Gubec, my dear. Thank God none of my people know who he really is. Nor this – shall we call him Banus Kulin or Primoz Trubar? Better they stay anonymous. The state has won back its gold, perhaps all of it, thanks to you.' His eye passed over Lippiat, as over the Invisible Man. He smiled at Anka, and his smile became a scowl. 'As for "Jug Bogdan's Widow", what do you take me for? And what shall I have on the charge sheet? Castrating a multiple rapist, her own abuser and husband's murderer, the nation's enemy, now conveniently gone before? I'd be the laughing stock, if the prosecutor let me bring it to trial. So would he.'

Popovic allowed himself to sound frustrated, but not to grow broody with it. 'I could never go up against these people, Patrick, as I truthfully told you. But I can rightfully deprive them of the gold that does not belong to them. *And* stop them beating the state to the next lot.' He looked at Lippiat this time, at him or through him. 'They *could* have some of their friends ambush me when I take it back to Belgrade. But I doubt they've got the means to deflect a couple of companies of motorized infantry, not nowdays. Once, perhaps, when Gerald was a boy.

'My young people don't think of these partisans as gods, or even heroes. They think of them as a bunch of old farts – an intellectual misfortune, but convenient for me. My youngsters will shoot.'

Teeth this time, instead of expression. 'These people are free to go, Captain Matson.'

'Which means free to stay.' Matson didn't want to be lumbered with Anka and her friends. He had just deprived them of millions of pounds and the sweeter part of their lives' ambitions. They posed a greater threat to him than Weiss and his entourage could ever have done.

'You're at liberty to leave the island too, my dear.'

'It may take some time to disengage.' He was thinking of Constanz. She would be in danger from them as well, if she could bring herself to see it. Or from some of them, one of them. It was going to be hard to persuade such a prime piece of curiosity to put skin before story.

As Popovic walked to the door, Matson tried one last whisper. 'Drop off a sentry or two. As discreet as you like, but let us have someone.'

'I gave you a gun, my dear. Continue to enjoy your exemptions.'

TWENTY-SEVEN

1

In bed, Constanz muttered, 'Why didn't you share any of this, Matson? I've lied to you maybe. I've never let you down. And that includes some very tight corners.'

'You were into too much. You were in it all. All the way round the edges. How was I to be sure you weren't in at the middle?'

His lovemaking was round the edges tonight. His ears were on other things.

At one point, he said, 'If you've got any sense, *any* sense, you'll get yourself out of Yugoslavia before the bureaucrats start looking over the files and tell Popovic to tidy things up.'

'Journalistic immunity.'

'Not here.' He swung his legs out of bed.

'Taking your pants off at last?'

'That's it.' He laced up his boots and left her.

2

The footfall had been light, but he'd listened for it. Other people in the house had good reason to be frightened of Popovic's bureaucrats and Matson assumed he was tracking one of the frightened ones.

He followed the night-walker across the lawn, then left along the water's edge.

Not the rubber boat. A fishing dory – he didn't know the local word for it. Matson glanced round for whoever had rowed it over.

He saw no one, but noticed the rubber boat had disap-

424

peared from its moorings. The landscape was full of activity tonight. Full of friends, too, if you were an old partisan.

The repaired planking in the bottom of the boat showed up first, then a rectangular package like a boxed work of art. Popovic hadn't quite got all of it. Torch beams rearrange the eye. Matson changed his grip on the lamp.

The figure in the blackness was the last thing it found. Head down, hands gloved, about to cast off.

Matson placed a careful foot on board.

Lippiat grinned at the torch. He grinned the way the wolf grins at the girl in the fairy story. He showed his teeth. They were his own – Matson was glad to establish at least one fact about the old trickster – and, like the wolf's, they were long. 'As I said earlier, I should have greased you when I had the chance.'

'Maybe you should, and maybe you tried. And maybe you missed. And maybe you stuck those bullets into my bed roll. And perhaps it was you who put rifle shots through my car. I didn't read you for it, but I've got no-one else. Now you've gone rotten on me. Rotten on us all. So who knows?'

Lippiat's smile was again harbouring something dangerous.

'You were in the nick, just, while a lorry shoved me off a cliff. But things like that don't get set up in a hurry. And they're beyond an embassy's means, unless their spooks are into a very big circle of thugs and runners. You have been into such a circle, and an insider in such a circle, for most of your life.'

'Bullshit, Paddy.'

'So now you're trying to collect your pension?'

'That's it, Paddy. My pension.'

'The way I'll do my report, and the way Pomeroy's bound to do his – *if* he ever soils his hand with anything so menial – well, that way your pension'll be safe, I promise you, Lolly. Absolutely promise you. I'll overlook a bullet or so I can't prove. But you'll have to play it straight with the loot. Pomeroy straight or Popovic straight. I don't care what you call straight, but straight.'

Lolly got his gun up at last, and fired it on the rise. *One* ... *two* ... *three* ... it went. Matson thought three; he hadn't brought an abacus.

425

Thought doesn't have much time at the muzzle end, but Matson also thought: Weiss's Luger. Old weapon, old war. New bloody Parabellums, like white-hot wasps.

The gun was in the lake by now. So was Lolly. Matson had been fearful of some such folly and kept his foot high on the gunwale, simply rocking Lolly and his dirty tricks right off the boat.

'Marcus is a bit of a twit, Lolly. In practical two-facedness, I mean. He thought you worked only to him, but you served the ethnics as well. You're a bloody ethnic yourself when it comes to the southern Slavs. And as for the ethnics trying to stop you, well, he was wrong about that.

'You were their Silver Bullet, Lolly. "Get Paddy," they said each time you checked in. "Get him before he jams the whole system in treacle".' He spoke quite a bit more, but only to the water.

There was no blood, no froth, no other mess to show that the brain on the trigger had taken over. Someone else's brain, Matson's trigger. He had been aiming for a gut shot under the notch of the ribs, and his trigger would never reckon to miss. Not with a gun like this. He couldn't scoff at Constanz again.

He went on watching the circle of ripples by torchlight. Lolly didn't surface, but Lippiat had tried these tricks before.

'Let me tell you what Pomeroy actually said,' Matson offered. He was thinking of a phone call at Mulhouse.

'He's not going to like the message,' Pomeroy said on the phone. 'He may get a bit out of hand, strum the old ukelele and wail. If he strops up rough, Paddy – I mean, I don't want it, especially when a chap's interrupting his holiday for me – but if he strops up rough, well, I am a bit like Henry the Second in such matters. Not to say Edward the Eighth.'

Matson sat down in the boat. He'd decided to leave. He still couldn't find any blood. Even without it, he couldn't bear to meet Anka's eye. And as for Constanz ...